The Book of Guilt

Also by Kym Lloyd

Erskine's Box

Kym Lloyd

The Book of Guilt

SCEPTRE

Copyright © 2004 by Kym Lloyd

First published in Great Britain in 2004 by Hodder and Stoughton
A division of Hodder Headline

The right of Kym Lloyd to be identified as the Author
of the Work has been asserted by her in accordance with the
Copyright, Designs and Patents Act 1988

A Sceptre Book

1 3 5 7 9 10 8 6 4 2

A CIP catalogue record for this title is available from the British Library

ISBN 0 340 82431 X

Typeset in Sabon MT by Palimpsest Book Production Limited,
Polmont, Stirlingshire

Printed and bound by
Mackays of Chatham Ltd, Chatham, Kent

Hodder Headline's policy is to use papers that are natural,
renewable and recyclable products and made from wood grown
in sustainable forests. The logging and manufacturing processes
are expected to conform to the environmental regulations
of the country of origin

Hodder and Stoughton Ltd
A division of Hodder Headline
338 Euston Road
London NW1 3BH

To Carol Cornish,
lady of myths, lighter of lamps

'The words, the words, the words – the truths, the myths, the lies.'

Dr Jabz R. Reemie

'Dou waye robin, the childe will weepe.'

From a medieval song, 'Miri It Is'

Before I begin, it has just occured to me – the Sins of Satan, would that not be the ultimate confession? Imagine, old Lucifer whispering into God's shell-like, unburdening his soul. What a tale that old devil could tell! What a relief for the Prince of Darkness! And what a weight for the Almighty One to receive, one that would surely send Him-on-High plummeting like a boulder out of those 'realms of light'.

I must admit to feeling 'sin-full' myself – have horns sprouted? – weighted as I am with their stories. Whose stories?

Yes, I had intended to begin: 'The five came to me, separately and on several occasions, to tell me their tales, innocent of each other's visits . . .' But first, let me establish that it is March 2004, in the year of the Lord, the day of the vernal equinox to be precise. Outside, spring's first sun shines upon a high street bustling with shoppers. The traffic is heavy and continuous. You may hear the drill of a road-worker, the wail of a fire engine, the megaphoned promises of a campaigning politician, the Hare Krishna drumbeat of orange-robed devotees weaving through the crowds – everyday sounds.

And how silent it is in here, now that I am alone, now they have left me.

But how strange that they should seek me out. As if I might have summoned them here. Or as if this might be some ancient sacred gathering ground. Or a place where damaged souls collect.

'They' I shall present cast-list-wise. Though no 'dramatis personae' they, but flesh and blood before me. In order of first appearance:

Gwynne Goode, younger daughter of
Phineas Goode, husband of
Marguerite (Maggie), then

Ms Allie Finlay, the mistress of Phineas, and lastly
Viviane, elder of the Goode daughters, the victim – the
  survivor.
(Although they were all victims in their own way – and all
  survived.)

Now, imagine the five as they appeared to me: Phineas, his
tall, lean frame, youthfully handsome for his fifty-two years,
despite the greying hair he sometimes wore in a small plait. Then
Marguerite, a big-boned woman, striking with her long dark
hair and piercing blue eyes. 'A feisty Amazonian', as her husband
once described her, and with her beads and flowing colourful
skirts appearing every inch the artist she is. Next, Ms Finlay, the
mistress, the 'glamorous academic' (for want of a better phrase),
that clear intelligence and, yes, cool detachment evident in her
spectacled brown eyes. As for the nineteen-year-old Gwynne, she
was as fair as fair, her blonde locks tumbling to her waist. A
dryad, a faery-child. You may have seen her kind in story books.
The deafness that struck her at an early age (four and a half
years old, I gather) gave her a depth, a sense that she hears
beneath the surface of things. Although even she did not hear
everything. Lastly, the raven-haired Viviane, the elder of the girls
by three years. Twenty-two when she came to me in January,
but I could see (already knew) the damaged child still hiding
within those stricken blue-grey eyes. How haunted she looked.
Though all five appeared stricken, as time went by, in each face
there was a leavening.

You would do well to imagine them in happier times. In their
Eden. The Goode family, in Castle Keep, their house high up
on Hart's Hill, a white-stoned square, solid construction rising
above the town, built, so I heard, in the nineteenth century. You
could imagine the house standing for ever, its surrounding
garden, encircled by a red beech hedge, like a planetary ring.
A world in itself, then – a stronghold. But with its own dark
tale to tell. It was Marguerite, I think, who told me what was

inscribed upon the plaque above the oak front door. '*Stet fortuna domus*' – 'May the Fortune of the House Last Long'. Ah, but not long. And no gentle irony in those words.

Now, picture the two daughters years ago, Gwynne – little Gwynnie – and Vivvy, five and eight years old, running carefree down the hillside, or roaming free in the forest below. See Phineas, contentedly nested among the tomes in his bookshop, the Reading Room, and Marguerite inside Castle Keep, painting with fierce obsession, to music turned loud to drown out the world, her flame-coloured skies.

See the Goode family, united, safe. And innocent? Yes, as much as they could ever be. It was a time that, in view of what came to pass within the walls of their stronghold, might be termed, with a little poetic licence – and to borrow a 'Reemie word' – 'prelapsarian'. A time before. Before those three terrible years from which the family emerged as strangers to each other, as disparate.

But what then happened after those three dark years?

I gather that Phineas left his family to set up home with Ms Finlay and Marguerite subsequently suffered a nervous break-down and was admitted to a psychiatric hospital, where she remained for almost four years, which left the sisters alone in Castle Keep, although they were both old enough to look after themselves. And each other? For by then their once deep, strong bond had been severed. But why? What really happened?

Suffice for me to say that by the time they appeared to me the family were reunited, but in a different way, all now vastly and permanently changed by what had begun in Castle Keep over thir-teen years ago. Did they come looking to be judged, exonerated, or forgiven? Or only to speak, to unburden themselves, as I must now, of what they all saw as their true guilt. But were they guilty?

If they were guilty of anything, might it have been of inno-cence? Even Reemie?

Ah, yes, Jabz R. Reemie. I heard six tales in all. Though Reemie's story shall be told posthumously, today being the first anniversary of his death. I did not mention to the other five that Reemie had come to see me a couple of months before he died. A year, then, before the five came to tell me their tales, about nine months before Phineas Goode received, last October, the package from Reemie containing the answer to the mystery of Castle Keep – and more.

My encounter with Reemie was brief, the nature of his illness hindering his ability to speak, and there was a reluctance to 'tell' perhaps. At first he was reserved, even curt, until he seemed to forget my presence and I began to feel I was eavesdropping on 'the very private voice of his heart'. Like the other five, I was mesmerised by that voice which, in prosaic terms might be described as soft, seductive. But a voice with deep and lasting resonance, one you might imagine speaking through the mists of time, the voice of the predator, perhaps, or the sorcerer, a voice that continued to sound long after the words had been spoken.

I have to say, simply, I felt sorry for him, was, even I, briefly beguiled. Even the lisp endeared itself.

I picture him now, here in the shadows, the heavy black caped coat, the wide-brimmed hat (minus the feather) shielding those bulging eyes, eyes that looked inward, were cast, I knew, upon the darkness of his soul as he spoke.

'I am going to die,' he said. 'Soon. In Lapland, in the Lemmenjoki valley, within the boundary of Inari's national park to be precise. Lemmenjoki, translating, according to my guide-book, as "river of love". *Love*, a lemon of a joke at which I shall afford myself a bitter-sweet smile (my last?).

'And so, my time is short. When the consultant gave me the diagnosis a few months ago, I remained calm. "Oral cancer, Dr Reemie. Of the mouth," he said. A particularly cruel twist of fate, wouldn't you say, for someone whose life's work has been language. I only half heard the prognosis: six months, maybe more, depending on my response to treatment, for I had already decided against intervention, was already planning the exact manner of my departure. I would be buried in the North, in the land of my mother's myths and legends, the land of the great Norse god Odin, hero of my childhood.

'After preliminary investigations, I realised my plans would surely be stymied by bureaucracy. Then I recalled a certain Herr Rottman, a German academic who had once visited the university, whose wife, I remembered, worked for the Scandinavian Tourist Board. I contacted Herr Rottman and within a matter of weeks I had managed to secure a plot at Inari and arrangements were finalised. It was a matter of a small bribe. I remembered Herr R. was, like me, a bibliophile. By way of a carrot, I proffered a gem, a clothbound edition – collector's gold – of a number of previously unknown essays: *The Myth Masters* by the brothers Jacob Ludwig and Wilhelm, that grim pair. Ach, even the puns are breathing their last.

'I have rented a small cottage near by. I am to be neither visited nor contacted. Once a week, at a pre-arranged time, I shall telephone Herr Rottman to tell him: "Reemie is here". If I do not telephone, Herr Rottman is to get in touch with a physician and the undertaker's. There is to be neither service nor ceremony. They will cut down my body from the tree. Then they will bury me. My solicitors, Guild, Guild and Sons (yes, I chose them purely for the name), have also been informed and, upon notification of my death, will issue instructions to Phineas Goode.

'Phineas, poor innocent. And what, I wonder, will he make of my bequest, of *The Book*, my "testament", as in "evidence", proof, of my sin, of my guilt, of my *innocence*.

'*Guilt gult gilt*. From Old English *gylt*. To be found in my pocket etymological dictionary, this *vade mecum* I happen to have here, "in my pocket" (a habit which will surely die with me!), to be found alongside *guild*, which is linked semantically with Old English *gyld*, as in "payment", and with Old Saxon *geld* meaning "sacrifice". And shall there be payment, shall there be sacrifice?

'Guilty. Guilty. Words. Just words. But what a world exists between the two, between being and feeling . . . And knowing? Ach, but I know now what I am.

5

'I leave tomorrow. In three days' time, I shall be on a coach, speeding along the Arctic Highway, swift as Sleipnir, the great Norse god Odin's eight-legged horse, racing to Lapland, my Materland. A fitting final resting place.

'And so, I shall finish, amidst the babble of Finnish. For the language is one of the most difficult in the world. Yet all translates to the same, is nothing more than words within words. Just words? But how they beguile and seduce, for as much as they clarify and reveal, they trick, deceive, are false promises, are where truth hides. How the words have both hounded and escaped me.

'But am I to rest in peace? Do I picture a sorry old man, *his soul eternally wandering the ice plains, his weak cries – "forgive me my sins" – snatched by these bitterest winds?* Do I?

'I might be burdened with the sins of mankind, I feel so weighted. And so cold. As if she is here with me, my mother, my Mutti, stroking my forehead the way she did, her icy fingers trailing a cold tear "from the tip of your nose, all the way down to Little Hans", she would say . . . *in whispers like feathers.* But how she could scream! Her bewildering anger thickening her accent, "Rob-err! Rob-err!", pronouncing my name as if I were the grossest mistake.

'Time is short. Ach, the pain. *And the dark already grows about me. And the flames shall burn eternal.* Soon will my silence come. For the cancer is growing by the hour, is rapidly eating up the words. But I shall save my last. Will she hear it, my lost daughter, my Ingebiorg? And will he, Phineas, hear it too when finally he reads my words? And will she, his raven-haired child? Will they all come to hear, *in articulo mortis,* in my final dying breath, what I needed to say?'

As if that voice had worked its way into my very soul, was speaking through me, was my own . . .

Had he said all he'd intended? Although he had finished speaking, he remained seated for some time, for what might have been for ever, until I stood and gestured – to show him the way out. He asked me then whether I knew of the Eastern-Finnish creation myth, and in a sure, chilling whisper – like that of the quietly confident opponent, perhaps – said . . . *And God stood at the top of a golden statue and when he looked down upon the calm mirror-like surface of the sea and saw his reflection, he ordered it to rise. And out of the waters it arose and this was the Devil . . . And God could never be other than Good, and the Wicked One could only be Evil.*

Then Reemie rose from the chair. And there we stood, face to face for what seemed an eternity, before Reemie tipped his hat and left. That was the last I saw of him.

It is only now, having heard the whole story, that I can give, let me say, a full confession. But before I begin, rightly or wrongly, I will introduce myself as 'the Confessor', meaning: the one who makes confession, or the one who listens. An aptly comprehensive moniker, you might come to agree. Then picture me within a small darkened place, let us say, something akin to one of those old wooden confessionals. Picture me, if you will, in the guise of an aged gentleman, wise in aspect, of the stamp of Phineas Goode's white-bearded, long-robed Abbot Lenten, perhaps.

I must admit that although I know the full version of each story, I have edited a little here and there, though I have been as truthful as I possibly could, to the voices, to their words.

But, as Reemie was only too aware, what power have the words – to lure and to beguile, to trick and to deceive. So, their words, then, listen—

A couple of months ago, around the middle of January, Gwynne Goode came to me. Of all five, it was Gwynne who seemed to find it easiest to talk. She asked me to turn to face her directly so she could read my lips, although I rarely spoke, mostly nodded my head now and then to show understanding, to encourage her to continue. I particularly remembered her voice, its mellifluous honey-like quality a stark contrast to the – for the most part – bleak monotone of her sister. Gwynne had an aura of light, a kind of shining. There was poetry in her sad words, and every now and then she'd fall silent, leaning forward, head tilted slightly, as though she were listening to my thoughts (which surely must set those with less innocent minds on their guard.)

Gwynne was a beautiful girl, a dryad, yes. And, as I have mentioned, had an awareness, was possessed of an insight, of which, I know, someone like Reemie would be wary. Just as I was briefly alarmed when she said I seemed strangely familiar.

Gwynne commented on my hands. They tell me you are at peace, she said, at rest there in your lap, open, relaxed, suggesting honesty, appearing to require nothing, she said. I notice hands, she said, and yours remind me of—

Then, briefly, she covered her face with her own, before beginning, 'Just a few months ago . . .'

All five would similarly say 'only months ago', their eyes widening in disbelief, as if months should have been years, as if they had emerged from a long-term ordeal, had long known the truth. And although it seemed terrible to think in such a way, said Gwynne, it was only because of what had happened to her sister Viviane a few months ago that after all these years the truth had finally come to light. (I did not mention, of course, that having read Reemie's book – oh, and seeing that newspaper headline – her father would have been enlightened anyway.) Though I was, as it were, 'on the edge of my seat', I waited for Gwynne to tell me – oh, would she? – what had happened to Viviane.

'I thought it was because of what he'd done,' she said, 'what *he'd* done. Someone she'd gone out with. One of those rough, nasty types. She wasn't exactly choosy when it came to men. Went out of her way to pick the worst. Men incapable of showing affection. Men she'd have a laugh with but who could never make her happy. Men who'd always hurt her. Because she seemed to like – needed – to be hurt. Punishing herself, I realise now. And I understand now why she seemed to want to punish me. When it was

8

just the two of us in Castle Keep, after Mumma and Pappa had gone. As if she were taking some kind of revenge. I'd get home from working at the deaf school all day and there'd be a crowd, Viviane and the bastards – the bastards, she called them – boozing, cans, bottles, plates of half-eaten food, the place a mess.'

Then Gwynne looked directly at me.

'Someone she knew,' she said, 'but it so often is, isn't it? Someone you know – that you think you know.'

And her expression now suddenly cleared, in what I must describe as 'a comprehension'. Too comprehending, perhaps, a look that made me physically recoil. I was about to ask Gwynne – as a 'by-the-by' – the reason for her coming to me, when she answered unprompted.

'The atmosphere in Castle Keep these past couple of months has been so strange, strained. The wrong kind of silence collecting thickly around us. We don't want to disturb it. Because it protects, insulates. We talk a little, day-to-day chit-chat. We keep going. We are grieving and we need to stay with our grief. And then we must move on. But how?

'The other day, with Pappa, in the garden. He was digging, preparing the ground, he said, to grow vegetables. He'd never so much as mown the lawn before. He was stabbing the fork into the earth with such force. I needed to talk, I said, about Viviane, the night she'd been out with that Ventman, about when I'd found her in the bathroom a few weeks later. Pappa stopped forking so hard, was gently turning the earth now. And I knew he was listening. But I couldn't say any more. Not to Pappa, not to Mumma, or Viviane. Like telling a story to someone who's already in the story. No one's innocent, you see. We're all in the story.'

I understood what Gwynne was trying to communicate, the need – shared by all five who came to me – to find 'an innocent ear'.

'He had a tattoo,' Gwynne continued, 'Ventman. A thin black snake curling around his throat. *Bastard, that bastard.* It was all Viviane would say. When she came home one night, at the beginning of last September. She'd started drinking in the afternoon. She should never have gone out. I'd sat up until two thirty in the morning. I was getting worried. When she eventually got in, she'd stood in the kitchen doorway, her face deathly pale. Her jeans were stained. Looked like wine. Her shirt was ripped at the front. She looked ragged, exhausted, like a hounded animal. She kept saying over and over, *the bastard, the bastard*. Who, Viviane? But she wouldn't tell me any more.

'I thought that was what had driven her to it. A few weeks later. The end of September. When I found her, in the bathroom, on the floor. The blood—'

There was a long pause before Gwynne spoke again. 'She was on the bathroom floor, just lying there. I thought of the unearthed remains of a Neolithic child. And as I gathered her limp body to hold her close to me, I imagined her bones falling from my fingers like spillikins. *Breathe, Viviane, please, don't go dying on me, Viviane.*

'Moments before, I was downstairs, in the kitchen. I'd looked up, felt it – quick-quick – as if heard, two notes, high, shrieks, a bow drawn quick-quick across tight-stretched string as the blade sliced her flesh. I ran up the stairs. Even before I opened the bathroom door, I could smell it. Fresh. Visceral. Her blood. Like a scream from a mouth split wide with anguish. Viviane's blood streaking the pure white porcelain of the bath, of the sink where she had held her wrists, *offered her wrists*, under the tap. I saw the handprints splayed over the white tiles. And in the mirror, a single bloody handprint covering, hiding, its reflection. She was on the floor, tucked into the small space between the sink and the bath. She was alive, barely. I saw the slow, slight rise and fall of her chest and, as I bound her hands with towels, glimpsed the exposed interior of her flesh, unexpectedly hued, pinks, cream, lilac – obscene. And I saw too the scars she usually kept hidden beneath her clothes, feathery flicks, like fossils in pebble, their terrible beauty, constellations of pain. Then the wider scars, like buttermilk ribbons, and one distinct fresh Y, as though cut by design. One by one I saw them, the way stars seem to appear at dusk, until you realise you are gazing at a whole night sky of brilliant points—

'I phoned for an ambulance, fetched blankets and, waiting for the ambulance to arrive, I lay beside her too-cold, too-still stiff body, a creature found too late in the forest. And I tucked the blankets around her body, just as I had tried to warm her years ago, those nights Vivvy used to creep into my bed. And when I saw the urine seeping from beneath her, trickling across the bathroom floor, suddenly she was ten years old and I was seven and I was putting my arms around my big sister Vivvy because she had wet the bed and I could feel her shame as she sobbed beside me. *Why did you wet the bed, Vivvy?*

'The paramedics found a pulse. But she'd lost so much blood . . . *so much blood.*

'They let me go with her in the ambulance. As it sped down Hart's Hill, along the village lanes, through the town to the hospital, its siren was the wailing of my heart, *don't die don't die don't die.*

'They gave her a transfusion. Later, when she was out of danger and sleeping, I sat with her for a couple of hours, next to her bed. She looked like a little girl again. That Struwwelpeter shock of black hair on the white pillow which had given her such a defiant, wild-child look when she was young. But her hand, pale, the long fingers inert, like a dead bird on the starched hospital sheet. A nurse told me to go home and get some rest, told me Viviane should be home the next day. Your sister's out of the woods now, she said. So I went back to Castle Keep, though I could not face going inside. The house seemed more than empty – besmirched. Couldn't even bring myself to open the front door, picturing Viviane's handprints, her hands climbing the bathroom wall, like the children's prints on the collage at the deaf school, only theirs were all colours of the rainbow. I went and sat in the garden, hoping the cold night air would clear my head. But all I could see was the blood, trying, in spite of my longing to forget, to recall its exact shade – carmine, or vermilion, or cherry, wine, crimson – naphthol crimson, Mumma's red, the special red she used in every painting.

'That cold end-of-September night, on the seat in the garden, I looked up to find the stars now covered by clouds. I was on a raft in an unnavigable dark. I realised how separate we'd all become. Pappa in the abbey, deep in some faraway countryside, Mumma miles away, Viviane in another . . . How emptied she'd looked, dead inside. Like the stuffing's gone from her, just skin and bones, the nurse said. Like a child. Like little-girl-Vivvy. Skin, bones. Spillikins. She'll need a bit of TLC, your sister, the nurse said. My sister. *My big sister Vivvy—*

'Me and Vivvy, playing spillikins with sticks we'd collect from the forest. We'd gather as many as we could then throw them into one big pile and take it in turns to remove them, one by one, without disturbing the others. You had to do it so carefully, you hardly dared breathe, didn't dare speak. *Didn't dare speak.* I remembered Vivvy, eight years old, near naked, flying, running down the steep side of the hill down to the forest. Clothes, strewn on the grass behind her, like shed skins. Her arms stretched out, wings of bone, unfeathered. Two of us running. Me, five years old, trying to catch up, thinking, Vivvy'll never stop in time, she's running so fast. And just when it seems she's going to crash slap-bang right into the forest fence, she comes to a dead halt. Then she turns. And her eyes are shining. And she reaches up, looks right up at the clear perfect sky. Vivvy, free once, laughing as she reached to the sky, her pale body, against the backdrop of dark green firs, like a sapling that has escaped the dark of the forest to find sky and sun and space and freedom. I hear it now, as I heard it, sitting on the Story Seat that night I'd left her in the hospital, her laughter, singing to herself as she played . . . *the north wind doth blow, and we shall have snow, and what will the robin do then, poor thing.* The lark song above us, that day, the wind-rush in my ears like the sea as I ran behind her. Hearing her voice calling . . . Like the sound of water, clear and fresh and flowing and sparkling, a spring-day-stream or stream-by-moonlight that ran from the day I was born right through the first five years of our shared childhood, through my mind even now, its laughter like water-over-pebbles or the play of light upon the surface of water . . . *Gwynnie . . . Gwyn-nie . . .* whispering to me at night when we should have been asleep when Vivvy was six and I was three, that in the early morning felt like first-sun-through-the-window . . . *Gwynnie . . . Gywnnie . . .* And her singing, oh, most of all I remember her made-up songs . . . *fish-ing fish-ing in a cardboard box for pots and pans and pretty maidens' locks . . . sliding down a moonbeam, spinning on a star, apples on the oak tree, snakes in a jar . . .* Vivvy's voice, Vivvy's voice like shining colours, like comfort, like the taste of tangy fruit lollipops in summer, of hot chocolate after swimming in the Easter holidays. Vivvy's voice was the shriek of delight tossing pancakes with Mumma, was her witchy cackling when I was the witch's helper making potions of vinegar and mustard and washing-up liquid, was the voice that told me the *Magic Carpet Stories* when we could fly to wherever-in-the-world-and-beyond . . . *where shall we go, Gwynnie? . . .* the voice that said . . . *Go hide, Gwynnie, don't cry, Gwynnie, I'll tell them it was me who broke the dish, it was my fault . . .* her voice was a jewel, of diamond-sapphire-amethyst, that I kept wrapped in tissue and velvet, in layers of memory, so precious and special, a silvery whispered thread, like the bond that linked us, that kept the two of us connected even when we were apart, though it seemed we had always been together from the moment I was born. Vivvy, my big sister, watching over my cradle, waiting for me to grow and join her play . . . *Come on, Gwynnie, hold my hands, Gwynnie . . . Stand up, walk, Gwynnie, run . . .* running down Hart's Hill escaping dragons that might eat us, the tingling of Vivvy's long lean fingers plaiting my hair, the lean sun-browned arm of my big sister curling around me, two halves of a whole. If the Vivvy-in-my-mind was a smell, was a taste, she'd be violets and chocolate and mint, if Vivvy was a shape, she'd be a star – twinkling, glittering, like her voice, like that special bond we used to have between us—

'I feel the suffering of the creatures: a rabbit ensnared in barbed wire, a bird pawed almost to death, a badger's white stripe blood-sticky and its hind leg crushed. At night, or just before dawn, going out to the fields behind Castle Keep, down Hart's Hill to the forest, tracking the creatures, mending, healing, relieving them of their misery. Those I cannot save remain in me as unlocatable wounds. My heart beats to the signals of their distress. I am attuned, my skin is litmus. I hear the silences, the spaces in between. As the spaces between words bring sense and meaning, I hear the sound. But the silence of my sister was a vacuum.

'Those last weeks before she'd tried to take her own life, I had sensed the escalation of her despair. Like clouds furnishing a storm sky. An orchestration of tragedy. But that night she'd been out with Ventman. I knew there was something terribly wrong.

'*That bastard. The bastard.*

'*Who, Viviane? Ventman, what did he do to you?*

'*The bastard. The fucking evil bastard.*

'I thought it was because of Ventman, what he'd done to her. I thought that was the reason she'd tried to kill herself.

'And then, last November, we found out why – Mumma and Pappa and me. Viviane told us. The day she came back, it was early morning, biting cold, a terrific gale that should have blown itself out in the night. I watched her coming down the path, bent, struggling. But she was pushing through a force far more powerful than the wind.'

And would Gwynne tell me what had caused her sister to attempt to take her own life? Reveal what was 'terribly wrong' with her sister? What that so-called 'Ventman' had done? But what a poignant image – the two little girls, at night, in Gwynnie's bed, one comforting t'other. Wet the bed – not a happy child, then? What had happened to . . . ? I waited.

But it was clear Gwynne would tell me no more. For the time being. Despite her wisdom and insight, though it was a good couple of months since she had discovered the source of her sister's troubles, Gwynne was still raw, still dealing with her own pain, the guilt of the knowledge that she, protector of suffering creatures, had not been able to protect her sister. And more painful for Gwynne, perhaps, the realisation that she had escaped that which her sister had been forced to endure.

Before she left, she turned. 'Her anger has gone,' she said, 'but I understand why Viviane was so angry with me all those years.' Then Gwynne raised her hand, as if to wave. But merely held it before her. 'His hand,' she said, 'in the mirror. That night. In the bathroom mirror . . . As if I did not want to know what I had seen.'

With that, Gwynne left. And who had come to speak next?

Swift on the heels of his daughter, Phineas Goode made his first appearance. He entered, his long arms raised slightly before him. He sank heavily on to the chair, like a man overcome by an unbearable weight, a weight from which, as his deeply troubled eyes indicated, he could not yet be released. And then, he began to speak – but oh, so quietly I feared I might not catch all he had to say.

'Maggie and I, were we not . . . ?'

What? Louder. Please.

'. . . not the parents we'd tried so hard to be? We'd always tried our best to—'

Then, 'Forgive me,' he said, 'but I feel just as I did with Abbot Lenten the day my vow of silence ended, that it is harder to end silence than endure it. But speak I must, for I have to face the truth. And though I can barely bring myself to even think of what happened to our daughter, I shall do my utmost to tell it as it was – I mean, before I knew.'

Phineas looked up and outward, his darkened eyes embracing the whole room, as though addressing his question not to me, but to all mankind.

'Was I guilty?'

(What of, I wondered, of what?)

'Of innocence?'

Then he sighed, leant back in his chair, holding each arm out awkwardly – like a bird with a broken wing – and unable, it seemed, to continue. (Little learnt so far, then – *nichts*, in fact.) Of course, I realised that part of his difficulty was having to speak now as if from that former time of innocence – to 'tell' with a voice untainted. For now 'knowing', Phineas Goode would have, I knew, the Devil's own job. For he had been changed by knowledge. The apple, having been picked from the tree, cannot be put back. (Oh, but worth a try, surely.)

Phineas then stretched out his arms slowly before him, regarding them with surprise, as if observing them for the first time.

'Not wings,' he said, 'do you see? Not wings but bone and sinew and muscle. Yet could these flesh-and-blood arms save her?' He shook his head. 'I tell you now, if I could only put these arms around that neck . . . I tell you, I could . . . would strangle the life out of . . .

'But what am I saying? He is dead. And his sorry sordid past is buried with him. But what about ours, the horror we are left with?'

('He'? Who he? Did I need to be told?)

Phineas broke off here for a while, broke down, overcome with anger, I think, with grief for his daughter. He cried silently, his body heaving and shuddering. When he had composed himself a little, I told him he did not have to continue, if it was so painful.

'But I must,' he said, 'unbearable this weight. These last couple of months, I have been haunted by questions – how could it ever have happened? How could we not have known? Perhaps that is why I am here now, to find answers. You know, life, the family, it all used to be so good, before this . . . this *thing* happened, and I was thinking just how good it used to be . . . On my way here today I decided to walk, such a beautiful morning. I stopped for a while, closed my eyes, turned my face to the sky, to the sun, receiving its power, its healing, its *goodness.* And I remembered one day, years ago, the sort of day that you feel could go on for ever.

'It was one of our parties. The middle of June. We were celebrating the summer solstice. We'd invited a crowd, people I'd got to know through the shop, Maggie's arty crowd, some of the locals from the village. The girls were quite young. Gwynne couldn't have been much more than three or four, but we'd allowed them to stay up as a treat. Such a long late afternoon, a typical balmy evening. As if the day was never going to end and the sun would stay high in that sky for ever. We were always having parties in those days. Maggie liked to do themes – you know, fancy dress, decorations, special food. For one Hallowe'en, it seemed the entire progeny of the village had descended. We'd sat up the night before, hollowing out swedes and pumpkins to make smiley-faced lanterns which Maggie placed in each window and on either side of the path. The whole place was aglow with orangey flickering candlelight, magical. For the solstice party, she'd hung green and yellow bunting throughout the downstairs rooms and around the garden. All the food was orange, yellow and green – trays laden with smoked salmon, dishes piled high with corn on the cob, with melons, pineapples and tangerines, with vividly striped vegetable terrines, golden rounds of quiche and lemon pie and cheesecake, deep bowls of potent fruit punch. Maggie was radiant. She wore a long robe of yellow silk, belted with a gold-tasselled tie, had replaced her silver jewellery with masses of thin gold tinkling bangles. I remember the sheen of her black hair. She had made the girls sunflower headdresses. I can see their faces now, smiling through large yellow petals.

'We'd had much to celebrate. Business was better than ever. I'd bought the tiny sandwich bar next door to the shop and the Reading Room now had its own café. Maggie had just won a commission to do some paintings for the new civic centre in town.

'Just before the girls went up to bed, someone proposed a toast: *To the Goodes – for life, love and laughter.* Then someone started singing – *you are my sunshine, my only sunshine.* Can you imagine, that gathering up on the hill, all of us singing, Viviane and Gwynne holding hands between Maggie and me, Maggie squeezing my hand, the brief pressure of her fingers enough to assure me this was no dream, but real. Real, real, real. The four of us, joined, connected, rooted.'

Phineas turned away, his expression relaxing, his face somehow enlightened, as though he were briefly encapsulated by the memory. Then, as if that long summer's day finally darkened, as if the memories of the joy and happiness that was once their Eden had grown silent and cold, though I sensed his reluctance to leave it, Phineas shook his head, looked down, closed his eyes, finding a way perhaps to enter that place of no music and no colour and no light and no joy – to begin his story.

'Where should I start? When my vow of silence ended? Because that was when I read the letter from Reemie, Jabz R. Reemie—'

(The letter, yes, yes, go on.)

But here, Phineas told me that he blamed himself. For what had happened to his daughter? For his daughter's suicide attempt? And then he told me. And to cut the story short: four years ago, in the final summer of the last millennium, Phineas told me, he had reached a crisis in his life. His relationship with Ms Finlay, for whom he had left his family, was over. About a year earlier, in April 1998, their daughter Orelia had died, and they were never able to recover. The damage to their relationship was irrevocable.

Phineas was crushed by guilt – for the troubles between him and Ms Finlay, for leaving Maggie and his daughters.

'I even blamed myself for Orelia's death,' he said. 'I was overwhelmed by guilt. But ever since I can remember, I have heard the words, whispered at first but sounding louder over the years, almost like the beat of another heart inside me, until all I could hear was a constant pronouncement – *guilty, guilty*. I was like Bunyan's pilgrim Christian, *driven out by a dreadful sound*. I began to question, not whether life was worth living, but whether I even deserved to live. Then, one night, unable to sleep, I was flicking through a book Allie had brought home from the university and I read about St Benedict's.

'What was the book? *Language and Silence*, if I remember, a study of deafness and communication. My attention was caught by a few pages describing an order of Cistercian monks who devoted their lives to prayer and silent contemplation, who had developed a sign language to communicate at mealtimes and so forth. The abbey, St Benedict's, founded by monks in the fourteenth century, was still in existence, and when I read that it offered extended "retreats" for those wishing to temporarily retire from everyday life, I felt the book had somehow found its way into my hands, like a hand itself, reaching out and offering another way. I decided immediately that this was what I must do. Indeed, it appeared the only way left to me. A temporary retreat, as I told Allie. Although we both knew our separation would be permanent.

'Within a matter of months, settling my business and financial affairs as best I could, I found myself deep in the countryside, on top of a hill, looking down at St Benedict's, which reminded me so much of Castle Keep. Although the abbey was an ancient, crumbling grey-stoned building, ensconced in the heart of the valley, while the white-walled stronghold was a landmark on top of Hart's Hill, both appeared protected, seemed to be offering protection. And the light, I shall never forget it, a radiance, emanating from the abbey, a golden light that would shimmer in the summertime, that later, even on the worst days, seemed still to radiate from the grey stone.

'And as I looked down at St Benedict's, I found myself yearning, wishing that our family could be reunited, thinking of the dream I had harboured since childhood of being husband and father, of having my own family, a dream I had realised but from which I was only to walk away.

'On arrival, my meeting with the abbot was brief. When I first set eyes on Abbot Lenten as he came shuffling round the corner, tall, the heavy folds of his brown habit gently swaying, the wooden rosary hanging from his belt, and his slightly slanting green eyes, I thought of Kimball O'Hara's first sighting of the lama in Kipling's *Kim* – the book having been a particular childhood favourite of mine. Yet from that first meeting and my first few observations during my retreat it became clear to me that the abbot had none of the lama's childlike naivety. For he was a wise man, had a gentle warmth, was a paternal presence watching over the community of monks.

'Abbot Lenten asked for details of my next of kin. My parents had died when I was a child, I said, but I had a family of my own who could be contacted if necessary. The abbot suggested that I should ask myself, though he seemed not to require an answer, what my purpose was at the abbey.

'To still the inner voice, I might have replied, to find peace, to find myself.

'My first insight came within hours of entering St Benedict's, when I awoke at dawn in my spartan cell the next morning. It was an insight prompted, I believe, by that hilltop view of the abbey and meeting Abbot Lenten, when the scene which had faded over the years came clearly into my mind. I picture it now, the summer air show, that intense forget-me-not blue of the sky, the breathtaking aerial display – daredevil stunts, the planes spinning, corkscrewing, looping-the-loop, the pleasure rides – *Roll Up! Roll Up! Fly With The Magic Bird! Ride of a Lifetime!* And I saw their plane, spinning, falling through the sky, like a swooping bird of prey, and I can see myself there too, my arms held out to catch them, to save what I could not save.

'Did I see it happen? Did I have the image of the Cessna falling through the sky with my mother and father inside imprinted on my mind? Was I there? Or was the scene described to me by some well-meaning guardian? One of those many "mothers" and "fathers" who mostly did their best to make me feel at home in a place that never could be home, part of a family that never would be mine.

'I survived, but my eyes were always searching beyond the clouds, drawn to, yet fearful of, the sky. I was Phineas the saviour who could not save, I was Phineas the survivor whose parents had died. I was Phineas the guilty. But it was at St Benedict's, over the three years of my vow, that the deafening voice in me was gradually swallowed up by the silence, until one day I listened. And I could hear nothing. And I found myself at last at peace.

'It took a month or so before I adjusted to the monks' way of life, as it did for those few others who had also chosen to retreat. We were like schoolboys at first, barely able to suppress our juvenile laughter over the dining table, mouthing at each other across the courtyard. Gradually we settled into the community, one entirely separate from the outside world. Yet, as I came to realise, separate also from each other, as if each one of us there within the thick stone walls surrounding the abbey and its grounds was just as much enclosed within our individual silence – and a silence that insulated, protected.

'I hear again now the swish of our robes, the soft tread of our sandals as we shuffled along the stone corridors, the percussion of daily ritual – the clatter of cutlery in the refectory – as if all sounds were muffled. Even the sign on the wall in my cell, *Let Silence Reign in This Place of Peace*, itself seemed to whisper. I remember the haunting plainsong of the monks at prayer in the chapel seeming far removed, as if reaching me from another world. And within that small microcosm, I came to learn and to hear so much.

'For three years I lived in my silence. I discovered intense pleasure working in the abbey gardens – the feel of the soil in my hands, its rich base smell, seeing the growth of what I had helped to plant and nurture – even the ache and sweat of physical labour was welcome. As if all my senses were awakened. I began to picture myself in the countryside, my feet planted firmly in the earth, working the land, as a farm labourer perhaps, at the helm of an ancient plough, whoa-ing to my horse. Or I might be a domestic gardener for some grand manor house. It was as if, up until then, I had never been in touch with my physical self, as if I had only then begun to properly live. And as I sensed my impending departure, my room appeared to contract back to the claustrophobic cell I'd had to adjust to when I first arrived. I felt like a hermit crab that has outgrown its borrowed shell. I even forgot to stoop as I walked through the door, and throughout those last weeks bore a permanent bruise on my forehead, as a sign of my separation. I was increasingly aware of a slow but steady awakening within, one that brought with it a peace such as I had never experienced, a letting go of all that was preventing me from engaging with life. I was beginning to feel my feet on solid ground.

'As Abbot Lenten said, my "transgressions" of those last few months at St Benedict's were clear indications I was ready to leave, to re-enter the world. I had found myself giving in to the temptation to communicate, to connect – a prayer uttered aloud, each syllable seeming to crack the night silence of the chapel, then the secret "conversations" with a fellow inmate from my window across the courtyard to his. This had begun with a brief wave from him one day when, without thinking, I waved back and was so surprised by his signed "hello" I could not help responding, my hands forming the language I had learnt years ago for Gwynne's sake, though I was a cack-handed student, unable to achieve the poetic beauty of Gwynne's talking hands. But it was a sign, like a mirror image, as though the stranger were my wakened self, beckoning me forward.

'And when I was sure my vow was coming to an end, I wrote the letters I had long been formulating in my mind, to Maggie at the psychiatric hospital, to Viviane and Gwynne, and one to Allie. I told them how sorry I was, that I had only ever wanted to do my best, as a husband, as a father. Though I dared to hope that someday I would see Maggie and my daughters again, that one day we might be reconciled in Castle Keep. But I never imagined just how devastated that reconciliation would find us.

'A couple of weeks before leaving St Benedict's, the Interlocutor brought a message from Abbot Lenten informing me that two letters had arrived. I knew I was not ready to read them, that they would remain in the abbot's safe-keeping until I was certain the time had come for my vow to end.

'I recall now the peculiar dream I'd had the night before my meeting with the abbot. I was standing on a vast glass disc. It appeared to be some kind of dial, a watch-face or compass, but without hands or arrow. A figure approached dressed in a black-hooded gown. It was moving slowly towards me. I was growing impatient, desperate to see what it had for me. The hooded figure came to the edge of the disc and held up a gold satin cushion which bore a scroll tied with gold ribbon. "I am the wise one," he said, "and I bring you the Story of Your Life." Then he unravelled the scroll, held it high. I saw that it was covered with minuscule writing, and as I leaned closer to read the words, I fell off the disc, down into what seemed a never-ending darkness.

'It was a warning perhaps, that I should not read the letters, but I took no heed. And part of me now wishes I had remained innocent of what I would, in time, come to know, while another part is thankful, glad – there is no word for it – that I learnt the truth, that she told me.

'She was a beautiful child, Viviane, beautiful in a different way to Gwynne. Self-contained. A dark-haired gypsy girl. Not difficult, never, not until . . .

'Just a child. Just an innocent child.

'The morning after I'd had the dream, I was in Abbot Lenten's study. I was eager to read the letters which I hoped were from the family, yet I was anxious as to the nature of their replies. I remember I could barely articulate a simple "good morning". I felt as a stroke victim must, having to relearn speech. My voice sounded alien, my words seeming to echo round the abbot's study, disturbing, challenging its cosy intimacy. The abbot appeared serene, regal, a brief intense ray of sunlight giving him an aura. I thought of the stained-glass God who gazed down from the chapel window. I felt momentarily in awe. But his "welcome, Phineas" was like a thick enveloping fleece, his voice rich, full, sweet: plum pudding laced with Jamaican rum, cognac, malt whisky, double cream, butter, soft buttery toast sprinkled with cinnamon. Yes, I could almost taste his words! My spartan existence soon to be over, I began to think of what I had missed. And I recalled then another similarly affecting voice.

'Abbot Lenten told me to be seated then lifted a heavy gold cloth covering a cabinet and took out a large envelope from one of the drawers, which he slid across the table, reminding me that reading the letters would officially mark the end of my vow. At first I could do little else but nod when he asked about my decision to leave and told me he understood my difficulty. "It is not that we forget the words, Phineas," he said, "but how we are to say them."

'Before I left his study he reached out, and I took his hand, keenly aware then of the warm, firm grip, and I realised that although we'd had little contact during my time at the abbey, I had always been very much aware of his presence. For to me, Abbot Lenten was like a father figure, ever present in the background, someone I could trust, one of those imaginary figures who had peopled my lonely childhood.

'The letters were not, as I'd hoped, from Maggie, or the girls. I recognised the handwriting on the small blue envelope. Allie. I did not want to read it. Knew I would find her name there: *Orelia*. As for the other letter, it looked official, from the bank, perhaps, I thought, or some matter of business concerning the

Reading Room. Since leaving the family, I had put someone else in charge of the day-to-day running of the shop.

'When I opened the envelope, I saw that the letter was from a firm of solicitors, Guild, Guild and Sons. My eyes picked out the word "death". I immediately feared that something awful had happened to Maggie or the girls. And then I read the name, Dr Jabz Reemie—

> Dr Jabz R. Reemie requested that you, Phineas Goode, should collect a package bequeathed to you by the deceased, Dr Jabz R. Reemie, from the offices of Guild, Guild and Sons, according to the instructions issued by the aforementioned, that the package should be received only by you, Phineas Goode, and no other person or persons, and for that reason formal proof of identification will be required.

'Reemie, dead? He had been such a friend, a mentor to me. I was deeply saddened to think he had gone.'

Reemie? I was all ears. But poor Phineas could say no more for the time being. I assured him he was welcome to come back, when he next felt the need. Just as he was leaving, he turned, and in the shadows of this darkened place, I saw his eyes, harrowed. How innocent I was, he said. Yet how guilty I felt.

But innocent *and* guilty – *en même temps*? Though I had little time to ponder, for here was Gwynne again. (And hadn't she brought something for me, something framed? But no, that was a later visit.)

'A key,' Gwynne said, before she had even taken her seat, 'what Ventman did – like a key to her silence. So many kinds of silence—

'The other day, a group of hearing children came to visit the deaf school. They were so excited as they gathered outside the door, straining to see in, and as soon as the door was opened, in they rushed, barely able to contain themselves, but only to stop dead in their tracks, arrested by the atmosphere of that noiseless room which held them in awe.

'I know that what I am without is something I have gained and it frees, protects. Every flicker of an eyelid, every blink, glance, every curl and twist of a lip holds a secret, is a cipher. The eyes of the deaf children will not let you go, are attuned to receive, from the signs of your hands, from the shape of your lips, words gleaned like pieces of treasure from a cache of silence—

'Last September, the day after I'd found Viviane bleeding in the bathroom, I was sitting in the observation room at St Eulalia's, trying to focus my thoughts on work, watching the children below, painting portraits of each other, the fierce concentration on their young faces. But my eyes were continually drawn away, looking out through the high window of the school hall, at the hospital in the town, brilliant white, its windows glinting gold in the autumn sun, like a multi-eyed fabulous beast. And Viviane in its belly, a small bone. And beyond, in the distance, up on Hart's Hill, Castle Keep, our stronghold, but like a centuries-old ruin now, a tide-washed shell, a sun-bleached skull.

'Then I saw one of the children waving, Nyssa, waving and pointing to her small suitcase in the corner, her face open and shining. Just like Viviane used to look. Same dark hair, grey-blue eyes. Like Vivvy . . . *laughing shining singing signing . . . Why don't you sign any more, Vivvy? Why won't you talk to me, Vivvy? . . . happy signing singing shining skull shell bone*—

'Bones, bleached, leached, like an unfed leech, on the doorstep, thin, in her black clothes. The day after she'd gone into hospital, when I'd got back home after school, Viviane was sitting outside the front door, head on her knees, arms dangling loose at her sides, cuffed with her bandages, like the cloth limbs of a doll. She told me she'd discharged herself from the hospital that morning, that she'd gone to the art gallery to look at her pictures. Gallery? Pictures? In the photography exhibition, she said. She was looking at the child, at Nyssa.

'It was clear from the start she did not welcome her presence in the house. But it was more than resentment. She saw in Nyssa what I could see. One morning, I looked out of the kitchen window and there they were, in the garden, Nyssa standing a little way behind Viviane. And on the grass behind Nyssa, her talking doll. The doll – Nyssa – Viviane. Like one of those time-line pictures showing the progression from child to adult, though Viviane was so far removed, there was nothing of the child left.

'"What's up with the kid?" she said as we went into the house.

'I told her Nyssa would be staying at Castle Keep for a while. Her mother was expecting a baby and there'd been one or two complications and she needed bed rest. Nyssa's father was working long hours and they had no family close by. She had grown fond of me, had told her mother she wanted to stay with me.

'"I did ask you, Viviane, whether you'd mind. And we'll be at school most of the time so we won't—"

'She was standing in the middle of the hall, her hands, her long-fingered hands, covering her face.

'"Fucking kid," she said, "Fuck the kid."

'I hated leaving Viviane when Nyssa and I went off to Eulalia's each morning. I worried about her not eating, about being alone, about that Ventman coming round, and just as I had done ever since Mumma went into hospital, I worried what she might do to herself, only now I feared far worse than cuts that would heal.

'Within a couple of days after Viviane came home from hospital, you could feel the tension. She hardly spoke to me and was sharp with Nyssa, who, reacting with the simple logic of a six-year-old, pretended that Viviane either did not exist or was a skulking ghost whose occasional appearances could be observed with nothing more than curiosity. One day, I found her on the landing, outside Viviane's bedroom. Your sister's making a real mess in there, she said, she's really naughty.

'I had seen the bathroom, the contents of the cupboard scattered on the floor. Viviane was in her bedroom, frantically going through all the drawers. I knew what she was looking for. I told Nyssa to come downstairs. I gave her biscuits and juice, a picnic to eat in the garden, I said.

'I was watching Nyssa skipping round the Lightning Tree. Just as I turned, there was Viviane, in the kitchen, plucking a knife from the block. Then she lunged at me, the blade of the knife at my face, and I stumbled sideways into her and the knife fell from her hand, spearing my foot.

'"You had no right," she screamed, vicious, spitting, "no fucking right to take my things. You shouldn't take things from other people."

'She sank into a chair. Like a rag doll. A puppet. As if the fragile structure of her bones had collapsed.

'"I'm sorry," she said, and she covered her face with her hands. "I'm sorry, Gwynne." And when she looked up, I could hardly bear it, that dead-eyed resignation. And she reached out her hand, her fingers half curled. "I never meant to hurt you, Gwynne."

'And she turned to me then and placed her hands across her chest, like spread wings, making the sign for *love*. "I'm sorry, Gwynne," she said again, one hand closing and rubbing small circles over her chest. *I'm sorry.*

'And in a moment, I felt all our years unfold behind me. Me and Vivvy – me and Vivvy – me and Vivvy. A row of hand-in-hand cut-out paper dolls. A tight fist unfurling into an open hand that beckoned. She was staring at the kitchen table, at the knots and stains, the signs and symbols of our childhood hieroglyphics.

'"I need to talk to you, Gwynne, tell you . . ."

'"What, tell me what, Viviane?"

'Then she looked up so I could see her lips, but her eyes were turned away from me.

'"Something," she said, "something about . . . years ago."

28

'Then Nyssa came running in, her face beaming – something to tell me, something to show me, lips moving, hands signing, a finger stabbing her chest, *I . . . I . . . I . . .* , her hand snapping closed in a grasping fist, *find . . . found . . . I found . . . Look what I found, Gwynne, in the garden. What, Nyssa? Show me.* Nyssa opened her hand to reveal the small pine cone in her palm. And I felt the screech of Viviane's chair across the floor, the thud as she overturned it before running out.

'*Never meant to hurt you, Gwynne . . . Shouldn't take things . . .*

'A couple of years ago, I was going away, with friends. It had taken me ages to get the money together. We'd all saved enough to stay in a hotel. One of those cheap mini-breaks. But I didn't go. Viviane stayed in most of that weekend, watching television, drinking. She'd been into town, had bought this black leather coat, zipped up from neck to hem, long, tight fitting. Like a snake. Looked expensive. My money. Stolen. Revenge. I understand why, now.

'She's been cutting for years. A dissatisfied seamstress cutting and stitching, retailoring a self that never fits. But it was some time after Pappa left when it took hold. I could sense it, her desperate need to cut, see afterwards, her eyes averted, head lowered, her veil of shame. Sometimes she'd lift it, briefly let you in.

'She was often careless about clearing up. Razor-edge lines of blood on the glass shelf in the bathroom and on the sink ledge, like haphazard arrows, useless indicators pointing every which way. Mumma and I always knocked in case she was in the bathroom cutting. Because for some reason she stopped locking the door, long before the cutting started. She used to lock herself in the bathroom. She was in there all day, once. At bedtime, Pappa had to break down the door. The lock was broken for days. Pappa wasn't much good at mending things.

'And then it got fixed. He came to the house one evening to look after me and Vivvy and he'd brought a shiny brass bolt and some screws. Reemie. He'd put the lock on the bathroom door. Kind man, Mumma said.

'One time I forgot to knock and I saw Vivvy doing it. She was sitting on the blue chair, bare legged, one leg up on the edge of the bath, scars like small runs in tights patterning her thigh. I caught her face twisted in pain as the blade slit her skin, saw the slight parting of her lips. *Oh, Vivvy, but doesn't that hurt you, Vivvy?* But I felt so intensely ashamed that I couldn't speak. I was looking at the line of beading blood, then the blood flooding her pale face when she saw me there.

'*Get out!* she yelled, the words falling from her lips in sharp-edged shapes.

'I could not forget it, the odd way she did it, flicking the blade with a light, almost carefree stroke, yet reluctantly, like a phobic forced to touch the source of their fear – or was it with curiosity, like a child touching something hot, not nice. As if it were not her leg, not herself she was hurting.

'I realised I had crossed a boundary. For not long after, she invited me to come and watch her. She was in her room, framing some photographs. She'd become quite accomplished by then, had won an under-twelves photographic competition. Black-and-white skyscapes scarred with aeroplane trails, wintry grey skies.

'"Can I help you, Vivvy?"

'"No, but you can stay and watch, if you like."

'I felt her tension, saw the quick creases at the corners of her eyes, her teeth biting her lips, her hands like two caged wild birds, fluttering, tapping, panicky. She started tearing up the cardboard mounts, and then she stopped, gathered together plasters, cotton wool, razors. She was standing in the doorway, her back to me. I knew she was waiting for me to follow.

'"Gwynnie," she said, "do you ever get all numb? Like every-thing outside your bones is nothing, like your skin's numb all over?"

'She didn't wait for an answer. I followed her into the bath-room. And I watched, fascinated, repulsed. My big sister Vivvy, blade between fingers, the baby one hooked as if she were doing something artful, a matter of etiquette. And I felt each stroke of the blade, felt the blade enter her skin, felt it with every nerve.

'The image is indelible. Viviane, hunched over herself, like a snake devouring its own tail, like an addict with their drug, protecting that which enslaves—

'Last October, Nyssa had come into my bed to sleep one night. Her doll wanted a cuddle, she said. *Angel's afraid of the dark, Gwynne.*

'Nyssa slept like a starfish, her limbs spread. Vivvy always tucked herself under the covers like a hibernating creature, curled into herself. I'd thought it was Viviane . . . *I thought it was Vivvy, waking me up in the middle of the night, tugging my arm . . . what's the matter, Vivvy? Why are you crying, Vivvy? . . .* It was Nyssa. I turned on the light to see her lips.

'"I want to go to wee-wee," she said, "but I can't because she's in there, your sister."

'I put on the landing light, showed Nyssa the bathroom in Mumma and Pappa's room and told her to go straight back to my bed.

'I pictured Viviane in the bath, her white body, the red water. But there was no blood, no water. Viviane was sitting in the bath, staring at the wall, hands clasped around her knees. She wouldn't look at me. She was wearing a long black T-shirt that did not quite cover the large fading bruise on her thigh. Bastard, she was saying, bastard. Her hand moved down to cover the bruise. I asked her whether it was Ventman, had Ventman done that to her? When I touched her shoulder, I felt the bone and I thought of the fox, feeling the bone of a fox once, as I'd removed the glass from its flesh.

'"He had a knife," she said. "I couldn't stop him, Gwynne. I didn't know how to make him stop."

'"You've got to tell someone, Viviane," I said, "you've got to

31

report this. I'll come with you to the police. Before he does it to someone else."

'"No, Gwynne," she said. "Because it's all over now."

'But it wasn't. Not for Viviane. Because for Viviane it had only really begun.

'And the look in her eyes then. Scared me.

'She used to scare me sometimes. Vivvy, years ago. I'd find her lying out on the hill. Like she'd just been flung. Like she'd never get up again. Eyes open, staring, not even blinking. Like she'd just died.

'Yes, Viviane was alive. It was Vivvy who had died. Once upon a time. My big sister Vivvy. You see, the real tragedy was not what had happened with Ventman, but once-upon-a-time-years ago. When, once upon a time, when she was eight years old, my big sister Vivvy seemed to acquire edges against life too soon, when she was all and only razor-sharp edges, when she lost her glittering, when her eight-year-old voice was so packed and pleated with secrets, so tight-closed-up, no one, no one could hear her.

'When Vivvy stopped being happy, I thought it was my fault, as if my loss had somehow become hers . . . *sorry I'm deaf, Vivvy . . . Where have you gone, Vivvy?* Where had she gone, my big sister Vivvy? That celebration of freedom. That shining face. Those arms reaching wide, high.'

Not the rape itself, then. But the result. As Gwynne said, a key, a catalyst – to what her sister had kept locked up all those years. But, as they who came had repeatedly asked themselves: what? and why? And – taking more than a little pre-emptive risk – who?

Not long after her daughter's visit in January, the mother, Mrs Goode, had come to me. Her passion was evident. The stronger of the husband and wife pair, I had first thought. Though all five had gained strength from their suffering.

Mrs Goode was tall, large – a dramatic woman is how best I can describe her. Handsome, engaging, a woman I might have . . . well, perhaps, in another life. I could call her Maggie, she said. (Not Mrs?) Oh, but Marguerite is a most beautiful and uncommon name, I said. And her voice was suddenly tender, wistful, as she told me she had been named after her mother's favourite artist. Marguerite frequently referred to certain paintings in order to communicate what she needed to say. She held herself a little stiffly at first, with that kind of determined dignity acquired by those who have suffered and survived, the pride of the Indian warrior, yes, and with that long-haired, beaded Indian warrior's androgyny. Yet she was volatile, by turns subdued then aflame, often speaking 'at me', as though needing to vent her rage. I thought of the fiercely protective instinct of the lioness whose offspring face danger, could imagine the scene if she'd had a chance to turn predator into prey.

Her long-fingered artist's hands were mostly animated throughout, as though words were not adequate. I could imagine them flying at the canvas, like those of a sorcerer or shaman, as she created her visions of red skies, those sunsets, she told me, that had disturbed her since childhood but which during those traumatic years at Castle Keep had filled her with fear. And for Marguerite, it seemed, it was necessary to reach right back into her distant past to fully come to terms with what had happened to her daughter, Viviane.

'Pentimento,' she said, 'when traces of original marks reappear in an oil painting over the years. There's the famous double hat brim in Rembrandt's *Flora*. And Goya's lady with a secret, *Dona Isabel de Porcel*, he'd painted over a portrait of a man in uniform. Is that what I mean to say – truth will out? It was Ruskin, I think, John Ruskin, who wrote about *the innocence of the eye*, that an artist must attempt always to see, as if for the first time, the real picture. Am I only now beginning to see *traces of the original*, those spaces between our clouds . . . what happened in Castle Keep over thirteen years ago?

'You know, it's like being back in hospital, sitting here talking to you now, just like I did with Max, with Dr Kenning, my therapist at St Bernard's. It's like confession in some ways, isn't it, therapy. Something to do with forgiveness, with unburdening. You're relieved of the weight – no, the weight is still there, but you find a way, perhaps, to bear it.

'What was it Phineas wrote in his letter? *Hoping for a reconciliation* . . . That's what it's called, isn't it, when penitents confess their sins, when they obtain forgiveness through absolution, the state of reconciliation. But there is one sinner who will never be forgiven.

'I saw her. Last night. Put my arms around her. She was in the bathroom. Viviane. Cleaning her teeth. Hunched over the sink. She was in her nightie, one of those washed-out baggy T-shirts she wears to bed, that drown her. I was looking at her thin legs, her narrow bony ankles, and suddenly fifteen years were wiped away and she was my little girl again, getting ready for bed, when I'd go up to check that the girls had done their teeth and give them a hug and a kiss goodnight. Those dressing gowns. It could get so cold in Castle Keep. The old boiler was forever breaking down. One winter, I'd bought them quilted dressing gowns. Just like one I'd had as a child. Lilac for Gwynne and blue, twilight blue, for Viviane. Silky, pouchy soft. Like the skin of soft fruit, of berries, raspberries, like a baby's skin. And I loved hugging them in their dressing gowns. My two cosy bundles. That I kept them warm and cosy warmed me. And I loved the way they'd reach and put their arms around me, squeeze . . . *love you, Mum . . . love you, Mumma*. Then, one night, Viviane pulled away. And then she stopped hugging me. I told myself it was probably just her age, you know, the way girls can get self-conscious about showing affection.'

34

Marguerite hung her head then, her long black hair falling over her face – like a veiled penitent, I might have said, if between the words I had not heard the voice of a mother aching with every cell of her being for her child. And I let her remain in her private space until, after a long silence, she looked up, brushed the hair from her face and told me she would read the letter Phineas had sent a few months before leaving St Benedict's.

'Because I'm finding this hard,' she said, 'and maybe it's easier to begin with someone else's words.'

She then told me she had received the letter last summer, in August, but it was a couple of months before she could face reading it.

'Poor man,' she said. 'He had no idea, you see, when he wrote the letter. None of us knew, until Viviane came back to Castle Keep last November, when she told us.

August, 2003

Dear Maggie,

Firstly, I hope this finds you well and that you are making good progress with Dr Kenning.

You will recall, I hope, when I wrote to you over three years ago informing you of my decision to go on retreat. I did not expect you to understand. I barely understood it myself. But just before writing that letter, when I visited you at the hospital, you made it clear you did not want to see me again, and I did not, in truth, expect otherwise. But I wanted to let you know of my decision, in the event, the faint hope, that you might have a change of heart. What I am really saying is, I wanted to let you know of my whereabouts, in case you ever changed your mind. But, sadly, you did not.

Can I explain even now why I took a vow of silence? You knew how I was, Maggie, all that reading, studying – religion, philosophy, psychology, self-help – endlessly searching for anything that might help me make sense of my life. Was that one of the reasons I opened the bookshop, so that I would have

35

a constant supply of what I believed, in my innocence, would provide the key to myself? But I realised I had exhausted my outward searching, that I had blinkered myself with the words and thoughts of others, instead of listening to my own voice. Does it seem too entirely obvious to say that only in silence there is peace? But it now makes absolute sense. I have to tell you, Maggie, while here at the abbey, I have experienced a kind of revelation, an epiphany, if you like. I came down to earth with a bump, you might say, and I would dearly love the chance to tell you about it someday. Perhaps as an artist, you might think of it as looking at a familiar object as if for the first time and drawing it, not as others have drawn it, or the way you think it should be drawn, but simply as you see it. Are you painting now? I wonder. I know that after the Mother paintings you seemed to have lost all heart. We are allowed no pictures here, nothing but bare walls. But in my mind they are adorned with those wonderfully vivid sunsets of yours. Remember when we first met, when I persuaded you to contribute some paintings to the exhibition I organised at the Reading Room? Your paintings were the first to be sold. I thought then, a woman who could paint such skies, such passion, such drama – I was determined, knew I could not, would not let you go.

Maggie, I know I have hurt you. I know too that I have hurt our daughters. And I have often wondered, is that what led me to the retreat – in order to punish myself, to deny myself the freedom of normal life? Because of what I did to you and to Viviane and Gwynne, to others, I did not feel worthy of life.

How did it all go so terribly wrong? I think of us, in Castle Keep. The Goode family. Together. Like a strong tight fist. And then the fist began to open, each finger separating out, away – us, growing apart, a hand that lost its grip. I explain it badly, I know, but that is how it felt to me.

Castle Keep, our stronghold, a keep to keep us, our castle-in-the-clouds, standing high on the hill, immutable, all those years, a shell waiting to be filled. And we did, Maggie, didn't we, the four of us, we were its flesh, muscles, organs, blood-flow. We were its life. From the moment it was ours, we imagined our children running about the rooms. Hordes of children, we said. (We had such intentions, didn't we?) And we were like children ourselves, shrieking, yodelling, as we ran down the hill. Rolling down Hart's Hill, do you remember? Arms and legs entwined as we rolled as one, turning over and over, the blue of your eyes spinning a continuous thread that bound me to you, and at the bottom laughing until we ached, grass in our hair, our clothes. What scarecrows we looked. But we didn't care! They must have thought we were crazy down in the village. Up in Castle Keep, on top of the world, always happy. And even on those thick-misted days, when the clouds hung low enough to blank out the world around us, you would wander contentedly about the garden with – yes – with the insouciance of a child . . .

'Phineas was so proud of Castle Keep, had a love of our home that was almost reverential, as if he couldn't quite believe it belonged to him, to us, smoothing his hand along a wall, along the length of a sideboard, touching things, you know, like a nervous host before the guests arrive, adjusting the tilt of a lampshade, setting cushions in place, loving, feminine gestures, somehow intimate.

'The house was in good repair when we moved in. Which was just as well. Phineas has never been a DIY man. But he'd needed more bookshelves and was determined to make them himself. Took him weeks. We thought someone had broken in one night. Woke up to crashing and banging downstairs. Sounded like the place was being ransacked. Phineas crept downstairs, I followed. It was like a scene from some slapstick, Phineas in his pyjamas, sink plunger in one hand, lace table-cloth in the other. And the look on his face of utter dismay! Of course, his precious shelves had collapsed. We opened a bottle of wine, laughed over his choice of weapons . . .

. . . We were happy there, for a time, weren't we, Maggie? Perhaps so tightly bound together there was nothing else for us but to come apart. Was our life enough for you? For you know I have always been a private person. My family was enough for me. It was all I had ever wanted. Here, at the abbey, I have been content in my own company. Until now, that is, when I have to fight the urge to communicate, with a smile, a wave. I wish I could reach out to you. You, Maggie, were so alive, larger than life, so full of passion. Just like your paintings. And I saw you give that passion to your daughters, the hours you spent making things with them, cutting and sticking and painting, the puppets, the kites, the masks – the 'green sprites', Maggie, remember, they were green for a week . . .

'Cobalt green. Yes, I remember. We were always making things, painting. When I was a child, I wasn't allowed to paint. I wanted Viviane and Gwynne to have the freedom, the kind of child-hood I never . . . When the weather was fine, I used to set out a couple of trestle tables and chairs in the garden for the girls, put out pots of poster paint, thick brushes, rolls of old lining paper weighted with stones at either end. I'd get them started then go and work in the studio, keeping an eye on them through the French windows. One time, I looked away from the canvas to find the girls had stripped to their knickers. Painted them-selves green from top to toe. Like sprites, they were, dancing about the garden. Then Phineas arrived back from the shop and they ran to him for a hug – he was covered. So I joined in, painted my face. What we must have looked like! The four of us, whooping around the back garden. Like the ritual dance of some tribal family. Happy times that I remember clearly now, our good times. Those holidays . . . You know, Phineas had this ancient tent from somewhere, covered with patches. We'd pack up a trailer on the back of Beelzebub, the girls in the sidecar, me riding pillion. One holiday, the heavens emptied. The roads were flooded. I made the girls capes out of black bin liners. The tent leaked. It was like Noah's ark. Every evening, we'd do a sun dance, and every morning wake to grey skies. But happy as pigs in muck, as my father used to say.

'Scenes, snapshots, paintings that, during those long dark years with Viviane, slipped one by one from the walls of memory until, by the time Phineas had left, when I went into hospital, they had all been forgotten, lost to me . . .

. . . *It seemed as if our troubles had killed the passion in you, Maggie. Our problems with Viviane over those three years – that awful period she – we – went through. Nine, nine years old, was she? Those strange things she did. That time she had the rope, by the Lightning Tree. Sometimes, it seemed as if she was intent on destroying our family. I am ashamed to admit that at one point I thought of her as our scapegoat, our black sheep. Though you must know, I always loved her. We did all we could, didn't we? The doctors, and when we took her to the child counsellor. I should have tried harder, should have found some way to help her. Like a wild child, you said. But then, when it seemed it was over, when she seemed 'back to her old self', that whatever demons had possessed her had fled – like the calm after the storm. But too calm, wasn't she? Too locked into herself. And what could we do? It was as if she did not want to be helped, that last year, before I left.*

But this letter is not intended to be an apologia for being a bad father.

What I have come to realise is that I must begin to forgive. I know I have never spoken to you much about my childhood. For whatever reasons, neither of us shared much of our past. You knew only that my parents died in a plane crash when I was very young. But I feel in many ways, that was where my life stopped. As if, since then, I have been held in suspension. As if my life has never really begun. And I want to begin, Maggie.

Which brings me to you, and the girls. You and me and Gwynne and Viviane. How apart from each other we are now.

Yet you have never left my heart. This is hard for me. I have written this letter over so many times and I expect you will rip it up anyway. I am almost too ashamed to ask. That I might dare to think you would ever wish to see me again. I know we cannot ever be the family we once were. But could we ever reconnect? Dare I think that we might one day be reconciled? At the age of fifty-two, I feel as if I am starting my life over again. But this is not to suggest we might. But could we ever be happy again?

You were a good mother, Maggie, a good wife.

I do not know precisely when I shall be leaving St Benedict's. In a couple of months, I should think. I should rather like to see out the summer here, enjoy the fruits of my labours in the gardens. Yes, your impractical husband has green fingers, it seems! But I do hope I have a chance someday to tell you more about such things. Abbot Lenten will keep my room free for a time, should I decide to return, though I am quite sure I shall not. I shall not have a fixed address for a while, though I shall let you know of my whereabouts – that is, should you ever wish to contact me.

You will always have a place in my heart.

Yours

Phineas

PS. I have had great difficulty with this letter. It would not have been an easy one to write anyway. But my communication skills are rusty. And it seems to me now not to make sense, not say what I want it to say.'

After she had read the letter, Maggie dried her eyes. And when she looked up, they shone, with such fierce clarity, with such a supernatural blue, it 'fair took my breath away'.

'Happy,' she said, 'once, we were so . . . And could we ever be happy again?

'At the time I received the letter from Phineas, I was beginning to believe we could. By the time I came to read those words, *a good wife, a good mother,* I was almost ready to leave the hospital, had come to understand what lay at the heart of my guilty feelings, was at last out of my clouds, could finally accept those words as truth. But then I began to question – if it had once been so good, if I had been a good enough mother, then why, why had it all gone so terribly wrong? Why did our family fall apart? Why had Viviane become such a . . . no, not a monster . . . such trouble, such a troubled child? Those crazy things she did . . . frightened us. Then, as Phineas said, that last year, too calm, silent – silenced. Until that day she came back and we found out why.

'I'd left St Bernard's and had returned home. About a week or so later, early morning . . . I hadn't slept that night. The wind was fierce, howling round the walls of Castle Keep. Felt so entirely at its mercy up on that hill. I was in the kitchen, making tea. Gwynne came in. Viviane's back, she said. Will never forget – opening the door – seeing her there . . . want to hold – stop it there now – freeze-frame that scene – a wave on the cusp, before her words came breaking down upon us, before we knew.

'I think I realise why I've come here. Because though I know now about my daughter, about Viviane, I keep asking myself, still cannot understand – how could I have been so . . . Oh, but how would you understand? You, sitting there so trouble free. How could you ever know what it's like to be so . . . so . . . ?'

(So . . . what? my dear Mrs Goode, I thought. So blind? So happy? Is that what you had meant? Then, no, no, I do not. Ah, but had the word been 'tricked', say, or even 'violated', then, yes, oh yes, I do. And the questions keep changing, I thought. Not 'why?', but 'how?'. Oh, good-Maggie-Goode, I thought. Because it was the 'how' that I was waiting to hear.)

Then Maggie fell silent. Though, just as Phineas had done before her, she turned before leaving, looked at me – those eyes, that blue!

'Please,' she said, 'I apologise for what I said. It is wrong of me to assume you are without troubles. It is good you are here, willing to listen, waiting only to receive. You know, you have the face, the look of a very wise and good and kind man. By the way,' she said, 'pentimento, when traces of an earlier painting show through. It's from the Italian *pentirsi*. It means "to repent".'

Then, as if to herself, she said, 'Repent – could such a devil ever repent enough?'

But, before I could answer, she went out. Before I could tell her – oh, that 'wise', that 'good', that 'kind' – how very pleasing it was to my ears.

Next in line, if I remember rightly, was, yes, Ms Allie Finlay, the one-time mistress of Phineas.

'It is as if you were expecting me,' she said. (Which I was, though naturally I could not say.)

She told me I reminded her of a priest she had met while visiting her daughter's grave last October. Ms Finlay was a petite woman, blonde, quietly beautiful, her dark brown eyes hiding behind gold-rimmed glasses, her hair rolled and pinned in what I believe is called a 'French plait', which ran like a seam down the back of her head. Allie Finlay appeared the very opposite of Marguerite Goode. And with due respect to Phineas (and indeed to his wife, who doubtless turns many an eye), I could understand the attraction. For, like Mrs Goode, Ms Finlay was a strong-minded, complex woman. Although not 'one of the family', she has her place in the story, had a need to speak of her guilt – about her relationship with her sister, the death of her daughter, Orelia, about, in her words, 'luring Phineas away from his family', at a time when they, when Viviane, needed him most, she said. Ms Finlay told me she had not been in contact with the Goodes for several years, until towards the end of last October, when she had unexpect-edly met Gwynne at the abbey.

'She was desperately worried about her sister and went back home. And I heard nothing more, until a month or so later, when I received a letter from Gwynne relating what Viviane had told the family. Viviane had wanted me to know, Gwynne wrote. Because I was there, regularly visiting Castle Keep throughout those three years it was happening. And I can't help thinking now, if only Phineas and I had not met. He would have been there. For the girls. Looking after Viviane, instead of being with me.

'I've often wondered why I ever got involved with Phineas in the first place – with a married man, I mean. One of my rules. Especially one with a family, with young children. There was enough guilt in me already. We both knew it was wrong. The pains Phineas took to keep us secret. Like that old diary he used to arrange our meetings. Almost as if he were trying to conceal it – us – even from himself, I came to think. He wasn't wearing a wedding ring. Although the first time we met, he did not hide the fact. But I could tell he wasn't single, even before I found out he had a wife and two young daughters.

'How did we meet? It was at St Bartolphs's, at the univer-sity. Some departmental party. He was looking for a tutor to work with his daughter, with Gwynne.

'The attraction was instant. I sensed in some way that Phineas was vulnerable. Not that I wanted to mother him, you under-stand. What, then? Phineas seemed so open to everything, so eager to learn, but in his own quiet way. Sometimes you meet people and straight away, however unlike you they are, you sense a connection, that you have shared similar experiences in the past, that you each carry the same hopes and burdens in your heart. We were meant to meet. Well, that's what Phineas and I told ourselves – fate, beyond our power – to assuage our guilt. When did it begin? A few months after I'd started going to the house. Phineas came to my office at St Bartolph's. He'd been working in the library, wondered if I'd like to join him for a drink.

'I really had little to do with Viviane. I was aware the two sisters were very close. I did my best to include her. But the work I was doing with Gwynne, though mainly in the holidays and some weekends, was intensive, one to one, you understand. Viviane resented me, that's how it appeared at the time, interrupting us, drawing attention to herself. She made me feel like an intruder, which was what I became, of course, as my relationship with Phineas deepened. Because I had taken her sister away from her. Because she suspected, knew, about me and her father. I was so sure she would tell. But that last year, before we went, before Phineas moved in with me, I couldn't tell what she was feeling. She appeared so removed from everyone, and as though she had given up the fight, as though she had renounced all feeling.

'Anger, fear, shame, love, hope – all had been pushed down deep, out of reach.

'Last October, just months ago, as I closed the door on the flat where Phineas and I had lived, where our daughter had died, I believed it was a new way forward, a recognition that I had to change, was changing, a recovery, not as a result of coming to terms with the loss of my child, but of myself. Then, when I found out about Viviane . . . I feel partly responsible. I should have known.

'Love, feelings – dangerous, aren't they?'

At this point, Ms Finlay stood up to leave.

'But I will come back,' she said, 'because I need to talk. And I cannot. Not to the family, especially not now. I've realised I have spent most of my life not telling the truth. That is why I come here. And though I'm not used to talking like this, to opening up my heart, I will return.'

And she left, clutching the file of papers, the manuscript, she told me, of a book she was working on, that she always brought with her, that she held like a shield but which over the course of her visits seemed to matter less, so that often papers would flutter to the floor unnoticed, like the wisps of hair from that once neat roll, as gradually her seam came undone, as if, for Allie Finlay, in telling her truth, she found her 'self'.

So, Ms Finlay returned to tell me her story, starting the previous autumn, the day she left the flat she had shared with Phineas.

Just as they all were to return in due course. Though the burden of guilt each bore related to the past, even the distant past, all five chose to begin their tales around the same time, as September gave way to October, as summer darkened to autumn. For Gwynne, it was Viviane's suicide attempt. For Mrs . . . for Marguerite, it was reading the letter from Phineas. For Phineas, it was ending his vow of silence and leaving St Benedict's. It seemed as though the memories Viviane had begun to recover after the rape by a man she called Ventman had touched them all, like an alignment of planets, a bringing together of loose threads, thus completing a picture that could only be made sense of as a whole. A picture I see now, entire. All ends neatly tied.

Six individual voices, yet at times all coloured by a similar dark tone, at times, then, as though all had spoken with one voice. Six stories but only one truth. Viviane's. The victim. The survivor. But I have said nothing yet of her visit to me.

Perhaps Viviane was the only one who appeared to have reached a kind of acceptance, enlightenment. She looked to me, at first like an adolescent, or rather an anorexic, all clutched up in herself and with, as Gwynne once described, 'an animal's powerlessness and lack of speech'. Indeed, during that first visit Viviane had sat looking down the whole time without saying a word.

But for now, a few last words from me, though they are not mine. Something Phineas once wrote to Allie Finlay:

Psalm 32, verses 1–5: Blessed is he whose transgression is forgiven, whose sin is covered . . . when I kept silence, my bones waxed old through my roaring all the day long. For day and night thy hand was heavy upon me . . . I acknowledged my sin unto thee, and mine iniquity have I not hid.

And I shall give you a drawing Viviane left behind that first time. Somehow I knew she wanted me to have it. For I, perhaps more than anyone, understood its awful significance. Then . . . no, I shan't. For the drawing has, for the time being at least, been incon(or 'con'?)veniently mislaid. Shame.

But what I can give you is the verse, copied in fine gold lettering and framed, which Gwynne (her turn now) brought with her. And would not take away with her when she left. Indeed, she seemed eager to be rid of it, as though it were some kind of bad-luck charm. Easier perhaps to blame a curse, to believe in such magic. For what had taken place in Castle Keep fifteen years ago must have been almost impossible to come to terms with, must surely have seemed 'not of this world'.

I noticed that the glass was cracked. (Why? Accident, temper – fear?) Like a photograph hit by someone betrayed by a loved one. (Or the beak of a bird flying at a window pane, perhaps.) It had been thrown, Gwynne said, by her sister. The crack, Gwynne said, was in the shape of the symbol her sister had carved into the Lightning Tree in the garden of Castle Keep when she was a girl, the one Viviane had, only months ago, painted on the walls of her bedroom, that she had, around the same time, cut into her arm.

The verse, then:

THE TALE OF MIRI-ANNE DUPREE

Since 1883, two tales have been whispered of the family Dupree
of the mad dark-haired daughter locked up out of sight
who one winter's morn was found hanging from the garden tree.
Blood-curdling screams, cries for mercy were heard in the night.
But all four, it seemed, must have put up some almighty fight

for down in the dungeon ma, pa, sister were found slain all three
and what really happened in Castle Keep never came to light.
Oh mad sad bad Miri-Anne Dupree, pray, were you innocent or guilty?

Was it because she threatened to tell her dark story
of how they beat her and starved her and in chains bound her tight,
that they let her swing merely to save the name of the goode family?
But a little red-breasted bird on a branch of that black tree did alight
told the sinners how he had witnessed the deed with his eye bright.
So the wicked cowards in haste to the dungeon did flee
and there they did perish for the door had stuck tight.
Oh bad mad sad Miri-Anne Dupree, pray, were you innocent or guilty?

Or was it because poor Miri-Anne could take no more that she
lured her cruel kin down to the dungeon purely to spite,
then filled with remorse at her deed, tried to set them free
but in her haste lost the dungeon key and overcome by her plight,
to the garden she ran, put the noose around her own neck pure and white.
Poor sad Miri-Anne swung alone to her death. But one who did see
was the little red-breasted bird who with the key, promptly took flight.
Oh sad oh bad mad Miri-Anne Dupree, pray, were you innocent, or
    were you guilty?

Two songs sung but who killed who that terrible night?
Whom from whom had endeavoured to flee?
Who was wrong and who was right?
Oh sad sad sad Miri-Anne Dupree, were you innocent and were you guilty?

47

Gwynne

'Pappa found the verse in a book on local history. He had it framed and hung it in the hall at Castle Keep.

'As if the dark tale of Miri-Anne had cast a shadow over us all.

'But Castle Keep wasn't dark. Once upon a time, Castle Keep sang with colour – yellows, oranges, lilacs, pink and green – light magenta, prism violet, ce-ru-le-an blue hue, as Mumma would say. Sometimes, after Vivvy and I had been out playing all day, down in the forest, out on the hill, we'd come home to find Mumma up a ladder, painting the last wall of a pink room turned into the gold of brilliant yellow cadmium. One day, Mumma came home with a red carpet from some country house auction – like an arterial network running through Castle Keep, linking each room.

'It was never dark, but a wondrous magical house where, stepping over the threshold, you felt you'd entered another world, a story-book house with turrets and winding staircases up to attic rooms, and corridors, corners and closets to make worlds in, places to escape to, places to hide. Like the cellar under the hall.

'Pappa used to tell us not to walk over the mosaic mandala in case we damaged the tiles. Mumma copied the design, a gold key at the centre of a pentacle from which grew long, thin willow-like leaves, each tipped with a pine cone. She painted it and mounted it on the wall. At night, the lights dimmed, the real mandala appears like an image reflected in water. It was only when Pappa unearthed the original plans of Castle Keep years after buying the house that they discovered there was an underground room. The mosaic circle was a trapdoor. It was Vivvy who eventually found how it worked, that you had to press on the sides of two of the black tiles on either side of the

48

radius so they lifted and could be removed, then the disc could be lifted out to reveal a ladder which led down into a small dungeon, an oubliette—

'Me and Vivvy, once upon a time, in our castle, taking turns at playing the king and queen, wearing crowns Mumma made from silver foil stuck with sweet-wrapper jewels, our robes cut from Mumma's old evening dresses, anointing Pappa – *lunch is served, your royal highnesses.* Pappa on bended knee before us, with an umbrella sceptre – *Arise, Prince Phineas.* Or we were the heads of the king's army, protecting our fortress from the enemy hiding in the forest below, and we'd cut out chains of paper soldiers, an army of hundreds we'd rank at the doors and windows like the hundreds of flickering nightlights Mumma used to set out all over the house at Christmas. And when the children from the village came to play, we'd make kites with Mumma from newspaper and garden canes and Pappa would take us all out on to the hill and the sky would be filled with vivid coloured diamonds. Like growing up in paradise. As if that house could only have belonged to us, as if it was meant for us—

'There's a print in Mumma's studio. It must have reminded her of us – two girls, one fair, and one dark, on the landing at the top of a wide stairway, their white dresses in tatters. The fair-haired girl is leaning against a door frame, the dark girl, her hair floating upwards defying gravity, is looking at a giant sunflower on the carpet before her, its twisted, broken stems, like hands, reaching for her. Three numbered doors are closed, but the fourth is ajar and light is shining from the room within. I realised Mumma had copied the green of the walls in the painting, its dark blood-red carpet. The painting has a quality of menace, of horror even. Like a nightmare. The two girls, the half-open door, the light inside, something in the room – luring you in. Like some kind of terrible prediction—

49

'Just a painting. Like "The Tale of Miri-Anne Dupree" was just a story. "Just a story, folklore," Pappa said. We used to act it out, Pappa reading the verses, the four of us wailing and flailing like characters in some Victorian melodrama. We were young then, me and Vivvy. It was fun, a game, just make-believe, *pretending to be the sisters Dupree*. But Vivvy said she didn't want to be Miri-Anne any more. *It's like she's still here, Gwynnie, mad Miri-Anne. Like a ghost . . . A story, Vivvy, just made up.*

'But I think it really scared her. Vivvy, in the hall at Castle Keep, looking up at the ballad on the wall, lips mouthing the words . . . *Was it because she threatened to tell? . . . poor Miri-Anne swung alone to her death.* Vivvy, her face death pale, her eyes . . . haunted. Like those words had got right into her. *Just a story, Vivvy.* Like the spirit of mad Miri-Anne got inside her. *Is that why you've gone all strange, Vivvy, why you don't seem like Vivvy any more?*

'You know, she used to hide down in the oubliette . . . *where ma, pa, sister were slain all three.* What was she hiding from? I remember the last time she hid down there. I remember the stain on her jeans when she came back up through the trapdoor. The bloodstain. Like a red full stop. Her periods had started. That was the end. When it was all over.

'*Why did you never tell me, Viviane?*

'*Better not to, Gwynne. Like a story, just a story in my head that telling would make real. Because when you were a little girl, Gwynne, what you didn't know could not hurt you. Protected me. Since that day by the weir. When sound went.* She was there for me—

'That day, years, over fifteen years ago, when we had the picnic by the weir, when sound went, I remember Vivvy's face, a quickening, as if she had felt it too. That end-of-the-world silence, when the world stopped turning and the moon slipped over the sun and all the birds turned to stone and all the seas to ice, that split-second snow-bright-white hiatus, when sound went, that moment, edge, between the sounds from the outside – the birds and the wind and the rustling leaves and the drone of the planes – and the sounds I now feel—

'If you put your ear to the ground so the smell of the grass and the earth is a taste, you can hear the turning of the world, all the sounds collected on its surface. Sounds as words. Words as sound. The crack and buzz of the stars. Bird calls are patterns in the sky, are silver threads, points of light. Flocks of birds, a constellation of stars, a tapestry that glitters. And rainfall tattooing my skin. Sound bruising, sound caressing. Soft, like feather-fall on the inner surface of my skin. The xylophone of Mumma's trays of paint tubes. Animal pain is blades. *Hiss babble jangle purr thwack squeak ping crunch sizzle swish*. I do not hear, I feel. Ever since that day we had a picnic by the weir.

'I was four and a half years old and Vivvy was nearly eight so she'd say but she wasn't. We were having such fun. We were laughing. And I see now, the memory recoloured, enhanced, made more vivid because of what was taken. Blue sky, green grass, lemony light – and me and Vivvy playing by the water, Mumma and Pappa farther up the bank. Mumma had earrings of orange and yellow beads, like bundles of strange fruit that clicked when she moved her head. Mumma was chatting to Pappa about her paintings. There was a smudge of paint on her cheek. Cadmium. Like a tribal mark. An Indian squaw. She was wearing a yellow and green and turquoise dress. Pappa was stretched out beside her, looking up at the sky. Mumma had tied one of her scarves around his head, had placed a string of coloured glass beads around his neck. Vivvy and I were throwing stones into the water, seeing who could make the biggest splash.

'I remember the shape of the water. A solid curve, it seemed, as it flowed over the step of the weir before breaking into a ruffle of foam. I was thinking how one thing could suddenly appear so very different. Each stone we threw entered the curve, disappearing as the water closed over it.

'Behind us, Mumma laughing. What were the sounds that day? The water, the breeze, the words, the "plop" of the stones falling into the water and far-away engines, a tractor, and birds and Mumma's laughing. Hard to think of them as sounds. For they have shape and colour and substance now, have touched, have entered me. Mumma's laughing . . . *laugh, Mumma, do your laughing* . . . we loved to hear that laugh, a beautiful drawn-out laugh, like rapid rising-falling piano scales, the celebration peal of church bells, like a dividing line, that day by the weir when sound went, between hearing and not hearing, half heard, half unheard, a piper abruptly running out of air. Then, that hold-your-breath silence. The cusp. Breathless. The second before the newborn takes its first breath. The second before the first thunder roll and then that *stop*. When something made me turn away from the water to look at Mumma. Her mouth was wide open, her head thrown back. And I ran to her and put my hands around her face, my ear to her mouth. And though I felt her words, I could not hear them. And I looked at Vivvy. As if she knew—

'Vivvy would always protect me, chasing off the boys when they called me names . . . *Cloth Ears, Dung Lugs, Ear Muffs*. She winded one so badly once he had to be carried home. They kept their distance after that. She'd taught herself to sign as quickly as I'd learnt. But we had our own private language. Hands open, palms up, like a book, meant *Pappa*; *Mumma* was a hand curled into a rabbit's head, the way she held her paintbrush; a pirouette, arms raised, meant *Let's play outside*; a hug meant *I'm sorry*. And three fingers – *Help, I need you.*

'For a time, my deafness made us even closer, practically inseparable. Between our two worlds of hearing and silence, we'd created a new special place, which only we could inhabit. And when Vivvy was eight years old – nearly nine, so she'd say,

52

but she wasn't – her hands stopped signing. And Vivvy didn't seem to want to be with me any more. And I didn't know why. And the silence between us then was worse than the first silence that day by the weir. Cold and hard and Vivvy was lost in it —

'Then Vivvy is nine and a half and I am six and a half. And that's when Vivvy starts to go mad. Just like mad Miri-Anne. Like she's not my big sister any more. Like a knife's cut through that glittering thread that's always been between us.

'In the back garden of Castle Keep are two trees. The vast healthy oak at the far end we called the Goodes' Oak, where Pappa fixed a home-made swing for us years ago. Swing high enough out over the beech hedge, the hill falling away below, and you can almost believe you are flying. And the Lightning Tree, dead centre, an oak struck in some storm long before Pappa bought the house. In a certain light, it appears like some maimed creature, suggests a quiet desperation, its limbs blackened and twisted, forever caught in the agony of the lightning strike. Once, only once, long ago, one spring, the few small twigs growing from a branch sprouted green shoots. I picture the tree and I see Vivvy, that day, the camera hanging heavy around the fragile stem of her neck.

'Pappa had bought a second-hand camera for her tenth birthday. She wore it continuously. Like a third eye staring from her chest. She even took it to bed sometimes, as if it protected her. Pappa had bought her plenty of film too but she wasn't interested in taking photographs, not for a long time. She'd use the camera like a pair of binoculars, like she was spying on us. She'd started doing bad things. A different Vivvy now. Bad, bad Vivvy.

'That day, when it had already begun – all those bad things she did – I was in the garden, on the swing, and then I see Vivvy coming from the house, walking towards the Lightning Tree, and she gets a bit closer and I can see she's got the camera but there's something else around her neck, coiled, like a thick brown snake. I keep swinging, watching Vivvy, wondering what she's up to because she's got this really strange look on her face, all tight, like someone's just told her off and she's trying not to cry. Then she starts going round in circles, round the Lightning Tree, going round and round, like she's in a dream or something.

'"You'll get all dizzy, Vivvy, doing that, you'll make yourself sick."

'But she takes no notice when I call out, just keeps walking, staring down at the ground like she's lost something, like she's following an invisible circle, like she has to keep on the line *because if you step off the line the Devil will get you.* I want to do it too and I jump off the swing and run towards her but as I get near I start to feel prickly all over, like a warning that I mustn't get too close, like Vivvy's a dangerous animal or something. I look over at the house, see Mumma in her studio, and I feel it, that pulsing through my whole body, throbbing right through me, the music she plays so loud when she's deep in her work until the whole house seems to shudder, though Pappa never notices, but Vivvy does and sometimes she marches right into Mumma's studio even when she's in there painting and *not to be disturbed, girls, please* and she unplugs the machine, and then they start screaming at each other, I see them, like some mad dumb show, and it frightens me the way they go at each other.

'But this time, Vivvy doesn't seem to hear Mumma's music and I can feel the air getting hot and buzzy like electricity and I want to run off down to the forest, to escape now.

'Vivvy's like a robot, going round and round, and one end of the rope slithers down her chest and the coils around her neck tighten.

'I call out to her again, "What are you doing that for, Vivvy?"

'But she won't look at me, just keeps walking. Like one of

those poor donkeys turning a mill wheel. Only she's got this stone-hard look on her face. *You know nothing, nothing, get it? You're just a stupid seven-year-old kid!*

'Then I see the knife in her hand. Sticking from her hand like a silver finger. Then she stops walking, uncoils the rope and throws it up over the longest branch of the Lightning Tree until it catches and drops over. Then she fetches a box from the shed.

'"Vivvy, can I play too?"

'"It's not a game, stupid kid," she says. And then she stands on the box and knots the rope and pulls on it with her whole weight. And then she cuts something, some sign, into the bark of the tree with the knife. She's still got the knife in her hand as she stands on the box she's put under the rope.

'I'm really scared now, and when I look back at the house, I see Mumma and she's staring out through her studio window, holding her paintbrush high, like a spear. I can see Pappa looking too, from another window. It's as if we're all playing musical statues and the music's switched off, but Mumma's music's still sounding out, still thudding through me as we all watch Vivvy slip the loop of the rope around her neck. And Pappa comes running across the garden, on tiptoe, bent forward, like he really wants to get to her faster than he can run. But he's holding back at the same time. Because he knows, as we all know, what she's going to do . . . *swing from the tree like Miri-Anne Dupree . . .*

'But nothing happened. Vivvy didn't jump. Pappa grabbed hold of her legs and took the rope over her head and lifted her off the box. And Vivvy was straight and stiff, her face frozen. Like a shop-window mannequin. Like a corpse. *Why, Vivvy? Just a story, Vivvy.*

'And that was the end. Of all we'd had between us. *Don't you want to play with me, Vivvy, down in the forest, out on the hill? Aren't we friends any more?* Like I had the plague, was a leper, had grown two heads. Like I didn't know my Vivvy any more. Like she didn't want to be my sister. Like maybe the ghost of mad Miri-Anne really had got inside her after all.

'She wouldn't speak, hiding in her room, like no one else existed, not even herself. Blue sky gone black. Sun's burned out. Birds don't sing any more. Like someone had taken her away and she was only pretending to be.

'Eight years old and nine years old and ten . . . Three years. Three Vivvys. Mad bad sad Vivvy Goode.

'The end of last September, when she came out of hospital, Viviane asked me, "Do you remember, Gwynne, do you remember – the stories?"'

Viviane

'Sorry. When I came last time. Nothing I could say. Yet every-thing. They know. Now they do. Now I've told them. Phineas and Maggie and Gwynne. But not like it really was.

'In the art gallery. Last September. Just got out of the hospital. Cut my wrists. Because of Ventman. What he did. I remembered. Oh, sweet Jesus. Bastard. The bastard. Going down the steps into the art gallery, into the basement, felt like a submersion. Entering a burial mound. Had I died? Dead. Was I? Would've been nice. This is hell, then, I thought. In the exhi-bition of photography. Sitting there, black-and-whites mounted on the wall before me, looking at people looking at my pictures, leaning back or going right up close so their noses almost touched the glass. Like they could see. What? What could I see? Catalogue said:

A series of thirteen black-and-white photographs

BY VIVIANE GOODE

The surface of each photograph seems reduced to less than surface, to a filmy layer of single cells. Yet a photograph is the surface of what was, is an edge of memory . . .

NUMBER ONE: Could be an easel, a window, a bar across an opening (not a way out?), a stick-thin figure holding out a cloak. Look closer, see it is paper, thick textured, and a line (or stick?) divides the paper in half, is resting along the centre line between two pages. Close up, read PAGE ONE in the bottom right-hand corner.

NUMBER TWO: A wintered tree, a scrap of paper attached to a branch, like a leaf, the last leaf about to fall from its branches. Title: THE END.

NUMBER SIX: What is peculiar about this knife? The blade is reversed, the tip of the blade is spearing the handle.

NUMBER SEVEN: A book, the pages lifted as if by a current of air, or invisible fingers.

NUMBER TEN: What is it? A horn, a cloven hoof, a fingernail, a nib?

'Could have been in church, not hell. There was an air of reverence. A congregation of spectators wandering, looking, some in solitary silence, some in whispering couples or groups. As they passed by, I was eclipsed. I was aware of their edges, neat black "aesthetically pleasing" photograph frames, their edges complemented, defined, just the correct thickness. But my edge was millimetre thick. Thin, I knew. Was all I knew. I had cultured the space between my edge and other people's. Grown it like a mould. It was impermeable, allowed nothing in or over or through or under or inside. The edges of other people are rich. Inside me was unknowable, bad, was nothing. Waking that morning in the hospital, my wrists on fire, my wounds stigmata. I crucified myself. Didn't want to open my eyes. Sickening yellowed light creeping in through the window. September sun. Exhausted, like me. I was used up. They wanted to keep me in another day, the doctor said, for observation. Didn't want to be watched. The doctor asked about the scars. Almost told him, *My hieroglyphs, Doctor, my secrets, where I hide myself. Why don't you sew me up, Doctor? My eyes my nose my mouth my . . . Why don't you sew up every orifice?* I was a house of cards, uninhabitable, my pain pressed to my edges, compressed card thin so I could not read it, nor could anyone. But somewhere in me was a coiled snake, a film that had already begun to unreel. And I didn't want to watch. Sitting in the gallery so long I was an exhibit. Little boy prodded my cheek. *Mammy, is she real?* No, kiddo, unreal, and don't touch! The sculpture at the other end of the room was two cubes of stacked rubbish, food packets, cartons, crushed cans, magazines, books, broken toys, the faces of dismembered plastic dolls staring blank *like long-imprisoned children*. Each cube was set upon four lorry wheels. They'd called it *DUMP TRUCKS STRUCK DUMB*. Dumb or what? Better if the dolls' mouths were taped over, silenced, like in the story . . . what story? *The Child and the Severed Tongue*. The tongue was cut out and pickled in a jar kept on a high shelf. Why was her tongue cut out? To stop her talking? Or because she's already talked too much. Who cut it out? Silence is meaningful. Who is to be silenced, the innocent or the guilty? If I was an exhibit, I was thinking, then my title would be:

ART SUFFERING
OR
THOU ART SUFFERING
OR
RETURN OF THE SUICIDE
OR
LIFE GOES ON, INEXORABLY

Or all of those. There should have been a sign above my head: DO NOT DISTURB THIS INTRICATE CONSTRUCTION, in other words DON'T TOUCH! Hate to be touched. Light to a vampire. Oh sweet Jesus, Gwynne, please hold me. But I didn't want to go back. Not back to Castle Keep. How to face Gwynne when already I saw her lips shaping *why?* Had to do it, Gwynne, end it. Since weeks ago, ever since that night with Ventman. Should have let that bastard finish me off. He'd taken me to a pub then a club then back to his place. Stale piss and sweat and the bastard coming inside me, over me, in my mouth. Lying on that piss-stinking mattress, like I was there with Ventman and not there, like it was Ventman and not Ventman at the same time, like staring at my photographs so long I couldn't see them any more. With that bastard Ventman, him lifting my legs high as he pulled off my jeans, like I was *light as a feather*, and then he threatened he'd cut me with the knife if I didn't do it but he wouldn't have cut me I knew because it was a bread knife, a cheap knife with a thin steel bendy blade, and I'd laughed in his face when he'd showed me, laughed at him trying to fuck me and holding this knife at the same time and I wasn't afraid and even if he'd stuck the blade in I knew it wouldn't have hurt. Cut the cackling, bitch, he said. When he rammed his fist in my thigh – then it hurt. Went on for ever, Ventman humping and humping and grunting like a pig. And then I heard me. The voice of another me in my head . . . *hurting, you're hurting me, bastard*. And then I started to feel. And then it really hurt. Like I was squeezing my foot into a tiny shoe. Like I was trying to swallow a lump of something hard. Like there's a big sticky sweet stuck in my throat and I swallow and swallow and swallow but it won't go down. Ventman was hurting me down there because I was so dry, because I'd give him nothing, because I never gave the bastards anything of me. I'd want to bite off their cocks sometimes, twist up their balls like pulling fruit from a tree, but I let them hurt me instead. Hit me, hit me hard, I'd tell them. But Ventman went too far. They're frightened, you know, when they're doing it, when they're hurting you. It's in their eyes, spiky, flickering. Like fear is inside you. Like they're really wanting to hurt themselves. He had it too, that look, the look that says *I know this is painful but I am hurting just as much as you* . . . Gave them nothing. Gave it all away. Long ago. And then I heard it, *tap-tap-tap*. On the window. And I looked over at the window of Ventman's bedroom but there wasn't anyone there. Just inside my head. The way Gwynne hears things. *Tap-tap-tap*. But, sweet Jesus, I knew that sound. And it was all coming out, the inside of me trickling out into the gallery. I was there, in the gallery, losing my edges. My skin was rice paper, communion wafer, less than a seed purse of honesty, wing of moth, that part of photographic paper changed by light, because to have patterned it the light must have entered it, must have, at particle level, gone through, like a spectre passes through a wall. Staring at the photographs, seeing and feeling that bastard fucking me. In my mouth, briny. Cockles and mussels. The fishmonger's, seaside holiday, tinned sardines, fish and chips. Learning to swim and going under and gulping down sea water, salty, gagging, choking. I was on Ventman's bed, Ventman whispering in my ear, he knew I'd be a real tight fuck, real sweet fuck. I was with Ventman but not Ventman. Then we rolled on to the floor. No carpet just lino. And cold cold cold cold. And the bread knife right in my face but I wasn't seeing the blade but the gold-tipped end of . . . of what? Oh, sweet . . . And my skin tingling all over like it is now just telling you. On the cold floor. It was a bread knife. It was that bastard Ventman. But what could I see? In the art gallery looking at my photographs, what was I seeing? Inside the black frames – knife, book, bird, feather. And then I found myself down on the marble floor of the gallery – icy cold floor. And strange faces peering down at me, blank faces, no eyes, no nose, no mouth. Except I could see that bastard Ventman's face but the face was melting. And I saw the flames. Hell. Hell. And I felt again the cold floor. Like ice, ice.'

Then Viviane shook her head. Looked at me.

'I can't,' she said, 'I don't think I can.'

Was that to be the last of Viviane Goode? Would she come back? Tell all?

I do hope not.

The way she had looked at me – as if right through me. Something I said?

Phineas

'*My young innocent*, that's what he called me. And how I was.

'The last time I saw him, when I asked a certain favour – *in all my innocence*. Yes. His face, his eyes, a look that now, now, I understand – that momentary blanching fear. How swiftly he left. How desperate he must have been to get away.

'He'd appeared uncomfortable throughout what was to be the last occasion we'd meet. I felt I had let him down, you see, my "dear friend and mentor", that what I sensed, what I read in his eyes, was deep disapproval. Because I had left my wife and daughters. Because I had left them to set up home with another woman. A feeling only confirmed later when I came to read what had happened to his own family. I thought that was why, since I'd left Castle Keep, despite several attempts to get in touch with him, he remained elusive. Then I heard he had undertaken a variety of research positions in Europe. I was never able to pin him down, not until a little over four years ago, just before I entered St Benedict's.

'I had a particular reason to speak with him which I hoped would be enough to convince him, both that I still cared for my family, that leaving was entirely to do with a realisation of my failure as a husband and father, and that I still deeply valued our friendship. Although I was in extremely low spirits, I had planned to make the occasion a special one, to treat Reemie to an extravagant lunch near the university at a newly opened restaurant called The Herring Boat. He kept rearranging the date, finally insisting we met at the university coffee room. Surely I knew by now, he said, that he could not abide fish in general and herring in particular. Ever since he was a boy, he told me, when his mother had taken him on a Norwegian cruise and the menu had consisted solely of herring.

'"Pickled herring, smoked herring, marinated, baked –

nedlagsild nedlagsild sild sild sild! The trawling nets were alive, dear Phineas, with the Gottforsaken fish flapping and writhing like a thousand severed tongues!"

'I remember I had laughed at his impassioned outburst, the way he flapped his small, delicate hands. Not because it amused me, but through a feeling of awkwardness on my part. I was embarrassed, taken aback at his sudden anger. Just as Reemie himself, dabbing the spittle from his lips with a handkerchief, seemed shaken by the power of his emotion, his fury.

'And it was then that I became aware of a darkness in him I had never witnessed before, a mood that was to hang over our last meeting, like a cloud over the promised sunshine. He was not the benign, sometimes jovial, grandfather figure I had come to know. Indeed, he appeared wary of me, had not taken the hand I held out to him in greeting, but slipped his own hands deep into his coat pockets. And there was something about his eyes, I thought, that startling protrusion now less pronounced, as if the eyeballs were receding into their sockets, the eyelids beginning to fold like loose hoods. He appeared desperately weary, his face bloodless. Yet he also seemed on edge, those thick lips of his parting, closing, parting, as if he were continually just about to speak. I thought of a suspect, resisting, but only just, the inter-rogator's demands for confession. And looking back now, I see there was something resolute, conclusive about the way he left me that day – his abrupt cold manner. Although I have always been sensitive about people leaving. As Allie once told me, in a rare bitter moment, when I informed her I was going to St Benedict's, that I would not be coming back, *You hate people leaving, Phineas, so you make sure it's always you who leaves first.*

'He asked if I was well, the question addressed not to me but as if to the room in general.

'"Well, Reemie? I wouldn't exactly say—"

'"Yes," he said. *Yeth.* The lisp, usually reduced to a controlled sibilance, becoming pronounced whenever he was agitated. "Yes, I can imagine."

'A hand then emerged from his pocket to flick invisible crumbs from the table, the black onyx ring he wore on the baby finger clicking impatiently against the Formica surface. His hands, almost child-small, seemed like a congenital deformity, and out of proportion with the rest of his bulk, which was emphasised anyway by that heavy caped coat – black, with the most wonderful crimson silk lining, which he rarely removed, as if it were an extra skin, a hide. I noticed how his hands always looked pearly clean, just washed.

'"Yes," he continued, "I heard about the child. Unfortunate."

'*Unfortunate*. Was it his choice of word or the way he said it that sparked a flash of anger inside me? Unfortunate. As if I had lost a key, a book, a *thing* I would not miss, could easily replace. I did not even try to blunt the edge to my voice.

'"Jabz," – I rarely used his first name, but I wanted him to hear me, to understand. "Jabz, almost seven years ago I left my family and went to live with Allie Finlay. You must have known about us, seen us together around the university and when you came to Castle Keep while Allie was there working with Gwynne. A couple of years later, Orelia, our daughter, was born. And it was wonderful for a time – me and Allie and our beautiful child. Three years of joy. And some regret, yes . . . And then Orelia died. It was a horrific, a tragic accident. Then, almost a year after her death, I learnt that Maggie, the wife I had abandoned, was in a psychiatric hospital miles away having suffered a breakdown. Nothing to do with fortune – or lack of it."

'He was still looking away, the hand now at rest on the table, the onyx stone an eye, small, but glaring.

'"From your precis of your misfort – of past events, it sounds to me, Phineas, as if you blame yourself. My interpretation is correct? Your child dies. Because you left your family. Because you did something wrong."

'*Because I did something wrong?* Tell me, did the man have no conscience? Oh, it is crystal clear as I am telling you this now, the fear that glanced out behind the cover, the ever so nonchalant way he said,

'"You are not in contact, then, with your family?"

'I had seen Gwynne, I told him, occasionally over the years, had visited Maggie at the hospital a few times until I sensed my visits were probably interfering with her recovery. But I had not been in contact with Viviane for over five years, I said.

'And I realise now it was at that moment that the guard dropped. But what I asked him next . . . I can hardly bring myself to tell you. I told him I was going away, on retreat.

'"I'd like to ask of you a favour, Reemie," I said. "It is likely Maggie will be in hospital for some considerable while. Naturally, I am concerned about the girls. Although Viviane's nearly eighteen now, and Gwynne's mature for her years, I don't like to think of them entirely alone. I'm aware you've not been in touch with the family since I left, Reemie, but it would give me great peace of mind if you were to keep a weather eye on Castle Keep."

'Impossible, he said. He was going away. Travel. Research. He was curt, dismissive. I recall how hurt I felt at the time.

'"So sorry, Phineas. But I cannot help you." And he tipped his hat and left.

'What was different about his hat? I remember asking myself. I couldn't think what it was then. But now I know.

'I watched him depart, picture him now, in that coat of his which almost reached the ground, making it appear as if he did not walk but glided. Yes, how swiftly he went. Out of our lives. Escaped . . . *his feet barely touching the ground.*

'When I found out he'd died, I was truly sorry. I had hoped we would meet again. After my retreat at the abbey. When I'd sorted myself out. Resume our relationship – our *friendship*. Rekindle the flames. Now I think may he burn in hell.

'And had I "got myself together", as they say? I believed so.

'The day I left St Benedict's, the beginning of last October, wiser, equipped with my new-found self-knowledge, was the beginning of the "new me", I thought. I stood upon the hill, my rucksack packed with my few belongings, surveying my path forward. I felt a true journeyman and one now sure of his destination. I felt so alive as I filled my lungs with the fresh autumn air. I walked through the grounds, away from the abbey. I was a carefree child kicking up the mounds of dried and yellowing leaves, like flakes, or scales of an old skin sloughed to reveal the new. How suddenly autumn had come, had gripped October in its jaws. Yet I felt a sense of rebirth. In my mind's eye, already, the greening buds. My skin tightened in the wind. I was a metamorphosed creature drying, ready for life. Behind me, St Benedict's, its yellowed stone exterior curiously insubstantial now, was a cocoon from which I had emerged.

'There was no ceremony when I left. The Interlocutor simply knocked on the door of my cell, indicated I was to follow him as he led me to the main entrance. He pushed open the heavy door and as I put my foot over the threshold it was as if I had never stepped outside for the whole three years I had been at the abbey. Such an overwhelming sense of release. I heard the world outside, felt it, smelled it – that fresh early October air. I looked back, wanting to say goodbye to Abbot Lenten, but he was in the shadows at the far end of the hall, watching. He made a sign of farewell, or blessing, then he bowed his head, just once, before stepping back. As if allowing me to slip free. Of the word that had weighted me all my life – *guilty*. I was free. *Not guilty . . . not guilty*.

'And I will tell you now when I first heard those words sounding within, which, as I thought, marked the beginning of a sense of inner peace, of freedom from the voice of judgement.

'It was a couple of months before I left St Benedict's. The height of summer. I was working in the gardens, tying the creepers that grew over the abbey's boundary wall. From the top of the ladder, I had a clear view of the surrounding hills. I became aware of a distant drone, looked up to see, in the distance, what appeared at first to be a bird of prey, only to realise it was a small plane operated by remote control. I watched it for a while as it danced above in the near-cloudless sky. In the warmth of the breeze, beneath the sun, amidst those green hills, I was, yes, content. Suddenly the drone changed to a high-pitched wail as the plane swooped, circled, then fell silent as it began to dive and then drop, simply drop through the sky, just as I, straining to see it disappear into the gorse, lost my balance, toppled and fell from the ladder.

'I lay shaken, though laughed out loud at my mishap. And I became increasingly aware then of the ground – solid beneath me, as if somehow my spine was taking strength from it. And I did not want to move, conscious now, of a stillness within, for that which had filled me for so long had left a space, a place into which I had fallen. As if, like Alice, I had fallen through the looking glass into myself, slipping not into but out of a dream. When eventually I got to my feet, I stood firm, and with a new clarity. I kicked off my sandals and walked about, flexing my uncurled toes, aware of the grass, the soil on my bare soles. I had, I realised, been inhabiting a fantasy from which I had fallen and was now free. And though there were other burdens I could not set down – one, I had left my family; two, the loss of my daughter, for at the time I still blamed myself for not locking the balcony door – I had at last been released from the burden of what I had always believed was my "original sin".

'Free, yes, free, I thought, the day I left St Benedict's, a spring in my step as I walked up the hill. At the top, I turned, looked down at the abbey for the last time, said a few words of gratitude. I was released from a prison of my own making. As I descended the hill, I pictured the abbey disappearing behind its crown, an old sun going down below the horizon, began to focus on what was before me, the crisp outlines of trees, hedgerows, cattle, a distant farmhouse, a tractor turning over dark earth. As I reached the road, I could see workmen in the distance, laying a gleaming vein of fresh tar, like a path of onyx, and I thought of the lama's search for the River of the Arrow in Kipling's *Kim*, the river that cleansed those who bathed in it of sin. I wondered whether I was the first to walk the new path. I could smell the tar, oily, sharp, like petrol, or nail polish remover. I suddenly thought of Maggie's hands, how sometimes she used to paint her nails, each one a different colour. I imagined her hands, the rainbowed fingers reaching to me. Would she? And would I reach out to her too?

'I remember an old woman joined me at the bus stop, her sudden appearance, as if from nowhere, invoking a brief yet disturbing sense of unreality. She had the clearest blue eyes, like Maggie's, in contrast to her weathered face, as if they had just been painted in. A silvered grey plait wound round and round her small head, like a sleeping snake. She was dressed in a shawl and long skirts, looked as if she might have stepped from a fairy tale, the godmother in disguise, reminding me of old Nan Lovatt from the village below Castle Keep. The old woman carried a basket that bore a straw nest of eggs. She asked if I'd come from the abbey. Was I going far? To the city, I said. Quickly warmed by this first connection with the real world, I asked if I could buy some eggs. She picked out six: three white, three speckled brown, a few with downy feathers sticking to their shells, and hidden beneath these a small powder-blue egg she quickly covered with straw. She fished a small folded brown bag – like those provided for airsickness – from her skirts and carefully placed the eggs inside. As I walked away, I heard her call softly, *You might do well to pick some rowan.* But when I turned to ask why, the old woman was no longer to be seen.

'I guarded my bag closely on the bus. You'd have thought I had never seen eggs before! I took it as a good omen – birth, rebirth, new life. And I looked out as the scenery gradually changed from countryside to village to town. The journey seemed to take for ever, the old bus groaning throughout its tortuous route. I was growing impatient. And then Abbot Lenten's words came to me. *In our rush to find the grail, Phineas, we are in danger of knocking over the very cup containing that which we seek*. I had missed so much, I realised, lost too much, had skimmed the surface of life too long.

'And here was life, I thought as I got off the bus and stepped into the noise, the throng, almost too much of it. I was momentarily disoriented. Where was I going? What was I to do? I had an urge to flee, to run straight back to the abbey. But my path was forward. I was tired, cold, ravenous. Checking the address of the hostel, "Paradise Close" of all things, I realised it was right at the other side of the city, that before I could satisfy basic physical needs I would first have to face the complications of Tube trains and buses, battle through crowds and rush-hour traffic. It had slipped my mind completely, my intention of going straight to the solicitors', to collect whatever it was Reemie had bequeathed. As I set off to make my way to the hostel, I found myself wishing I was on another road, one that would lead directly to Castle Keep. I suddenly longed for home, for the familiar, was not looking forward to the strangeness and anonymity of a hostel. Though, as it turned out, I was not to remain at Paradise Close for very long.

'It was a confession. But without admission. A story full of stories. A tale that did not tell. A way with words. He always had. Reemie.'

Gwynne

'The stories. On the Story Seat. Yes, I remember.

'Mumma found the old garden seat years ago, among the bushes at the bottom of Hart's Hill. Tied it with ropes and dragged it up the hill, her and Pappa, this huge iron seat big as a bed. Took them all morning. Me and Vivvy cheering them on from the top. Mumma rubbed it down and painted it crimson and gold, revealing its giant paws, the scrolls and markings on its body. She transformed it into a mythical beast and we rode its back. It was a dragon, a chariot, a Spanish galleon, a star ship, a Viking longboat. Then it became the Story Seat. And we used to sit out there, me and Vivvy, cosy, our arms around each other, while Pappa read us stories, his "old favourites", he said. *The Water Babies*, *Swallows and Amazons*, *Alice in Wonderland*, *The Little Prince*. Sometimes at night we'd sit outside and look up at the sky to search for the Little Prince's star. And Vivvy always said she'd found it.

'Last October, since Viviane had come back from the hospital, I wasn't sleeping. One night, I'd got up to make a cup of tea. Before I'd turned on the kitchen light, I saw her, in the back garden. I couldn't work out what she was doing at first. Then I could see. The Story Seat. She was pushing it, rolling it over, heaving its cast-iron frame over and over, like she was battling with it. She got it halfway across the garden, almost to the Lightning Tree. Then she dropped to her knees, exhausted, leaning against the seat which was on its back now, its legs in the air, like a slain beast. When I went out to her, she covered her face with her hands. Did I remember, she said, when we were young, sitting out there, on the Story Seat?

'Oh, yes, Vivvy, I remember, sitting together. Because it was the only time we ever were together then. Like you were in a different world. And not even a magic carpet could reach you, Vivvy. We used to sit on the seat and listen to the stories, sucking sticky toffees. Three of us on the Story Seat. Me on one side. And you, Vivvy, on the other.'

Marguerite

'On my way here today, I saw a little girl, dark haired, peering through the window of a house as I walked by. And I thought of one time during those awful years, when, on my way out to teach my art class one evening, I'd turned to see Viviane staring through the window. Her face close to the glass, as if it contained her.

'Snapshots of early joy in my mind. Viviane, running from the house, waving me off to the shops, or waving Phineas home after work. Gwynne and Viviane running out on the hill, two birds in flight against the wide blue of the sky, against the peach and the salmon, the magenta, the scarlet and the crimson of a sunset.

'And I remembered that Viviane had not waved the day I left, when I walked away from Castle Keep over four years ago.

'I had only intended to be away overnight. Viviane was seventeen – nearly eighteen – and Gwynne not yet fifteen but more than capable of looking after herself and her sister, and there was someone in the village – a kind old lady, Nan Lovatt – they could go to if they needed. Gwynne said she understood. Viviane told me she couldn't care whether I went or not. I was going to see my father. He'd gone back North to live by then. We weren't in regular contact, had lost touch. By that time, because of all the troubles at home, we were practically estranged.

'Since Phineas had left, for five or six years I'd been fighting depression, trying to keep strong for the girls. But there was something on my mind. Those last few months before I left, in my increasing dark, a spark, the last flicker of a dying star, a glimpse of a childhood memory, something I needed to understand, to see clearly. And I was sure my father could tell me. I had to see my father.

'I was in no fit state to travel. Halfway through the journey, I got off the coach, booked into a bed and breakfast. I could barely walk, shuffling along like a bent old woman, as though physically weighted by guilt, about Viviane, about Phineas. What kind of a mother had I been? What kind of a wife? And the rows and the silences, the hell we'd been through. The next morning, as I was leaving the bed and breakfast, I collapsed, and that's how I ended up at St Bernard's.

'They had to put me in a padded cell the first night. The most spectacular breakdown, apparently. Told me I'd kicked the nurses, was cursing, screaming, *May the wrath of God descend upon you sinners! . . . Thou shalt bend and buckle beneath the weight of thy sins . . .* Fists in the air. Just like my father up on his soapbox, preaching to the shoppers on a Saturday.

'But I loved being in that cell. White, soft. Like a cloud. Like a womb I could have stayed inside. When they opened the door the next morning, the walls of the corridor outside were bearing down on me. I couldn't look up, wouldn't look out, kept my head down, terrified of every door, any opening to the world outside, of the windows through which the sky pressed in, threatening to crush me.

'*How are you feeling, Mrs Goode? You don't go outside. You turn from the windows. What are you so afraid of? Tell me, how do you feel, Mrs Goode?*'
'Guilty, Doctor. Guilty. Guilty. Guilty.'

'Apart from those sessions with Max in his office when I sat in silence, the first few weeks at St Bernard's I stayed in my room, curtains drawn. I didn't go outside the building once. I didn't go outside for some time. Phineas must have told them I was an artist. They'd given me pencils, a pad and a box of paints. Sixteen coloured squares. Like the one I kept at my teacher's house when I was a girl, with a picture of a girl painting her own picture on the lid. Only the hospital paintbox had a label – *Property of St Bernard's Psychiatric Unit*. I didn't touch the brush. I dug out the small squares of paint and stacked them in towers which I'd topple then restack. I stared at that white sheet of drawing paper until it sucked me in, seeing only the faces of my daughters, Gwynne and Viviane, watching through the window as I left. Two pale ovals, their features indistinct. Like the girls in the painting, the girls on the pier. My daughters, left, in the shadow of my leaving.

'I'd bought the print just after I'd met Phineas. *Girls Running*, by Philip Wilson Steer. I was envious of the subtle quality of the light, so entirely different from my bold colours. In the foreground are the two girls – their faces appear unpainted, blank. They're dressed in red-sashed Victorian summer dresses. They're running towards you, away from their mother, who is standing at the rail of the pier in the background. The mother's looking out to sea, oblivious, it seems, to her two daughters on either side of her. All three are turned away from each other, so the figures appear quite separate. The mother's tight-fitting black jacket emphasises her turned back. The other two girls appear to be running towards the sun, away from the mother and her daughters. As if the running girls are their spirits slipped free. Yet their long evening shadows stretch right out behind them to meet, to touch, the three figures in the background. And there are shadows lurking at the bottom edge of the painting, that, physically, could not be possible, but which appear to echo the tall mother and her girls, as if even the free spirits of the running girls cannot escape the shadow of the mother.

'Just as I could not escape the shadow of my own. Only hers was red. The red of her paint. Of her blood. Of those sunsets I feared. What was I so afraid of?

'"The red skies, Dr Kenning," I said, when I finally found my voice and I began to talk a little about the family, about Viviane, about Castle Keep.

'"The red skies, Dr Kenning," I said.

'I picture him now, Max, sitting in that red leather chair, like a huge enveloping heart. I was fond of Max. The Laughing Cavalier, I called him. That round-cheeked smile, the moustache,

74

the goatee beard. I loved the way he spoke, softly, in a measured, sometimes hesitant way, like when you have to wake
someone from sleep. And the way he pronounced my name –
Markeet – delicately. I couldn't place his accent – Belgian
perhaps, I never did ask. He had a funny turn of phrase. *For
someone obsessed with red, Markeet, today you appear the
most awful blue . . . Too bad I forgot my matador's silk, you're
a vereetable bull today, I fear . . .* And that wicked black humour
of his. When I was eventually able to tell him about my mother,
how she had died giving birth to me, *A natural born killer,
then, Markeet.*

'"But tell me, Markeet, given your overwhelming fear of
sunsets, however did you survive in such a house, on that high
hill, you tell me, such views, all that sky! A *leetle* masochistic,
wouldn't you say?"

'And I remembered then, it was winter the day Phineas took
me to see Castle Keep for the first time. There was a late afternoon fog, a thick blanket that had rapidly descended on our
way to see the house. Phineas was like an excited child, jigging
about, flapping his arms, telling me some story he'd read as a
child. *Out of this world, Maggie, you'll adore it, I know*. Like
something from a fairy tale, he said.

'That's what had attracted me to him the first time we met.
The child in him.

'I was sitting by a river, sketching, I think – yes. I thought it
was leaves, rain, birds, looked up from my drawing to find paper
aeroplanes falling around me, each one perfectly formed. He,
Phineas, was standing on a bridge a little distance away, deep
in concentration, carefully folding squares of paper. I'd watched
him for a while, then, on impulse, gathered up the planes and
went to return them. I think the bushes must have hidden me
from view. He looked surprised, shocked even, to see me. He
was wearing sandals, no socks. I noticed his feet. He had the
strangest feet, almost clawed, the toes curling inwards, like he
was gripping with each step.

'You know, I've noticed, he doesn't do that any more. Though we all tread carefully, he wants to walk firm. And he will.

'We stood together on the bridge, flying the paper planes, seeing whose flew farthest. As we cheered them on, I think he forgot we were virtual strangers and he reached for my hand. Whenever we made love, Phineas would hold my hand. Just passing by, he'd briefly clasp my wrist, touch my arm, place his palm on my face. But in the way of a child seeking reassurance. And he does that now, reaches out in passing. But in support. Just as I reach out to him.

'He was like a boy that day he took me to see Castle Keep, made it an adventure, stopping some distance from the town to blindfold me. The house could be seen from miles away, he said, he wanted to keep it a surprise until the last minute. From the angle of the car – he hadn't got that damn motorbike yet – I realised we were going up a steep hill. Then he led me down the path, only removing the blindfold when we reached the front door – that tall front door of oak and iron. A castle door. And I stepped back, looked up, at the white walls, the castellated roofline, the four corner towers. Then Phineas placed the key in my palm, the handle, a primitive heart shape, inverted, its point touching my wrist, the unusually complex and beautiful code of its five teeth reaching the tip of my middle finger. The original key, Phineas said, just like the one at the centre of the mandala in the hall.

'Opening the door, I found myself entering a vast oak-panelled hallway, each wall hung with a faded arras depicting battle scenes, knights on horseback, scenes from the Arthurian legends, Phineas said. I followed one of the passageways leading from the hall to find myself in another high-ceilinged room with a large fireplace and a roasting spit and a small minstrel gallery overlooking a long dark wood dining table. Phineas was eager to show me another room at the back of the house. My studio, I realised, with two large skylights and sliding doors leading out on to the back garden. I was already picturing my easel in the corner, the table covered with pots of paint and brushes. I walked out into the garden, past the two trees, looked out over the beech hedge at the thick mist below, then up at the low clouds hanging heavy above.

'I see it in my mind now, the house, as if viewed from afar, high on Hart's Hill, barely distinguishable on certain days amidst the mists and clouds. I'm thinking now of the Turner, *Bellinzona from the Road to Locarno*, the buildings on top of the hill in the distance, lost in the haze of amber and grey sky. And I picture Castle Keep clear in my mind, and the view extending out below. Like that painting by Schinkel of a church on a hill, the city and river below, its remarkable clarity – the light is astounding, that arcing rainbow, then those dark rain-laden clouds.

'I adored the house. Before we'd finished unpacking, I'd managed to get hold of these huge rolls of muslin. For curtains, I said. We wouldn't need curtains, Phineas said – who on earth could see in apart from the birds and low-flying aircraft? He leant to kiss me, then, and I pulled away. Grabbing an end of one of the rolls, I ran through the house from room to room, along the corridors, up the stairs, entwining the cloth around chairs, door handles, the banisters, the muslin trailing out behind me like a milky river. I hadn't realised Phineas had joined in, had run with his own roll of cloth. We left it like that for days. Other-worldly. The entire house swathed in muslin.

'That first visit to Castle Keep, I had not realised how high we were and the extent of that view. Not until the house was legally ours, a few weeks later, when I was sitting beside Phineas in the van full of our furniture. The drive up Hart's Hill, "the ascension", as Phineas said, went on for ever. That evening, we'd drunk champagne, and, just as I had done with my father on Mount Repentance, we watched the sunset. Like we're in heaven, Phineas said, *like we're on top of the world*. The sky was beautiful, breathtaking. But I still half shielded my eyes, had always felt uneasy, always turning away. But it wasn't until later, until those hellish years, that my childhood fear returned.

'When I was very young, before I knew the facts of my mother's death, when all I knew was simply that she was not there, my father used to swing me up on his shoulders, carry me, *like St Christopher, lass*, as he walked through the village and up the steep hill he called Mount Repentance, because, he said, by the time you got to the top you felt you'd paid for the sins of every living soul. We'd go right to the very top, to what he called "the crown of thorns", and sit on a grassy mound amidst the bramble bushes, me beside him, sharing a bag of toffees and a bottle of lemonade as we looked down at the town below, *like we're in God's heaven, lass.*

'When I was a little older, we'd go up the hill to deliver the sermons he'd print on the old printing press, Old Balthazar. It stood in a corner of the kitchen all week, like some great beast asleep in its lair, until Friday, when Father cleaned and oiled it and the beast woke up, clanking and clunking, breathing out my father's sermons on hellfire and damnation. *Hold thy burden high, you sinners, stare thy burden in the face, know it, sinners.*

'Every Saturday afternoon, I'd go with him into town, Father carrying his soapbox and placards, me with my school satchel bursting with the pamphlets. Father would set up his pitch on the pavement, stand up on his soapbox, me at his side holding the placards, wishing I could be somewhere else, while he pronounced in his loudspeaker voice, *Be not cowards, bear the weight of thy sins! Thou shalt not run from the wrath of thy God! The serpent beguiled you and you did eat!* The people passing by mostly ignored him. But there were always one or two who stood briefly to listen, through curiosity, I think, the women shaking their heads, tutting, looking at me, it began to seem, with pity.

'*Your father was a preacher, then, Markeet?*

'It was grief, as my father was later to explain, a way of dealing with my mother's death, which both contained and revealed his rage, against the very God about whom he preached. But, as I told Dr Kenning, such was the power of his voice, of those words, that as a child I came to believe that the sinner, the only sinner, was me.

'On Saturday evenings, my father would fill up my old pram with the pamphlets to distribute around the neighbourhood and sometimes I'd go with him, my father pushing the pram while I ran from house to house delivering sermons for the Sunday. The road up Mount Repentance we kept until the very last, when the pram was lightest. I loved helping him. I'd get extra pocket money and sometimes we'd stop for chips and eat them on the "crown". And I don't know how – the way he used to chew over those chips, perhaps, deep in his thoughts – but I knew he was thinking about my mother. Before I got too big, he'd let me climb into the pram and run me fast back down, while I'd beg for him to stop, screaming with the thrill.

'But one day, I stopped wanting to go up Mount Repentance. Because of the skies, suddenly terrified of those red skies.

'*Your agoraphobia stems not from your fear of the outside, Markeet, but of that which is within yourself.*

'Over those years of therapy with Max, I came to understand the fear I had experienced as a child, that I had buried deep inside, that was to rise up again all those years later when the problems with Viviane began, a fear that would send me running back into the safety of Castle Keep, until, by the time Phineas had left us, days went by when I'd never leave the house. *Don't look at the sky, Maggie. Keep your head down, Maggie. Like the guilty, Maggie. Like a sinner who knows they have sinned, Maggie Goode.* Could see it in his eyes, in my father's eyes. In Viviane's eyes.

'The day they came to see me, some time during those first weeks at the hospital, Phineas and Gwynne and Viviane, I couldn't get my words out. And Gwynne was looking so worried, straining to make sense of what I was trying to say. Phineas was staring down at his hands. And Viviane was sitting with her legs crossed, arms folded, looking at me. And I thought of a painting, then, Ford Madox Brown's *Le Mauvais Sujet*. Do you know it? A painting of a young girl. She's sitting at her desk, holding a quill pen, the tips of her fingers covering the nib. In the other hand, she's holding an apple to her mouth. She's staring back at you, her expression complex – nonchalant, and yet defiant. There's a thin black ribbon tied around her neck, almost inviting you to undo it, or pull it tighter. Like a delicate noose. It's almost as if the girl is caught. And she's wearing an earring. A red bead. A drop of blood. That black-haired, black-eyed girl was the image of Viviane as a child. That wild mass of black hair. Unruly. Almost the image. Only Viviane's eyes are blue-grey, have never seemed to know their true colour. But the way she'd look at me sometimes, as if from some inner darkness, you could almost believe they were black.

'The way she'd look at me. The way I'd see my father looking at me sometimes. In his eyes, in her eyes, seeing only what I thought they held.

'There's a painting that hangs in my mind. I might have called it *Accusation* – a memory.

'The scene is the back garden at Castle Keep. Gwynne is about six or seven years old. She is over by the Goodes' Oak, on her rope swing, and the swing's right over the beech hedge, the rope stretched to its farthest reach and about to fall back. Her chest is pushed forward, her legs tucked and splayed under the seat, her hair a white-blonde spray. The sun's shining, I think – yes. And where is Phineas? At the Reading Room, I expect. I am in the studio, working. I'm looking up, brush poised midair, looking out of the window. At the red. That's what I see first. Blood red. Crimson. All over her body. She, Viviane, is naked except for her knickers. She is leaning back against the black trunk of the Lightning Tree, head right back. Are her eyes closed? I'm not sure but she's got her arms stretched out to the sides, like she's being crucified. And she's bleeding, from her hands, her head, her feet. Like a crucifixion. Then the painting comes to life as I throw down my brush and run outside, right to where she is. I thought, Christ, I thought it was blood. But

I can see now what it is as I get up close, realise what she's smeared over her body. Crimson. Mine. She had taken it, stolen it. One small tube of paint. But all I had left of my mother. Like a dagger stuck in my heart. As if she had tried her hardest to hurt me. And when I looked at her, when I saw then that look in Viviane's eyes . . . It was a cry for help. I didn't know how to help her. I tried. I didn't know what to do. And the way she was looking at me, the way I saw my father looking down at me when I was a little girl. His eyes, like mouths, they seemed to the little-girl-me, pronouncing silent judgement.

'Yes, there was evil in Castle Keep. The serpent beguiled us all.'

Forgive my intrusion but I have to say my heart went out to the woman – to the mother. Maggie had left, somehow changed by having spoken. And I sensed that in a small way it had done her good. Though she told me she had intended to say so much more.

And what else? Oh yes, she had returned the next day, had brought a picture Viviane had drawn as a child. Of Castle Keep, Maggie said, handing it to me. I saw the elongated hill, the path like a zip, or seam, or scar. I saw the house with its eye-like windows. And I knew what it was she could not say – that it looked more like a swaddled child, a tightly wrapped child.

Gwynne

'Last October, on the Story Seat with Nyssa, the two of us wrapped up in coats, needing to be in the fresh autumn air, Viviane was inside, watching from the kitchen window, her bandaged arms raised – the way she used to watch me and Allie.

'I know what Viviane saw when she looked at Nyssa.

'Sitting with Nyssa, beating out the rhythm on a tambourine, Nyssa studying my lips, repeating the words of the rhyme, learning their shapes,

> *who killed – Cock Ro – bin?*
> *I – said the spar – row*
> *with – my – bow and ar – row,*

just as I used to with Allie. Pappa had told me about Miss Finlay, who worked at the university, who knew all there was to know about deaf people. She was an expert-in-the-field, Pappa said.

'Me and Allie, in the garden, in the sunshine. Vivvy inside, her face in the window, white iris in the glass. Staring at us, her arms raised, palms pressed against the window pane, like a prisoner aching for release. *Who saw him – die? I – said the fly – with my little eye – I saw him – die.*

'Vivvy, sitting on the Story Seat the way she liked to, perched on the back, but kicking her heels then, hard, hard into the wood. *Come and sit with us, Vivvy.* Allie didn't want Vivvy to feel left out. But Vivvy hated Allie. Because she'd come between us, between Vivvy and me. So Vivvy thinks. *Vivvy's jealous because I've got Allie. Vivvy hates Allie and now she hates me.* That's what I'm thinking, one day when Allie's reading me a story and I can see Vivvy standing behind the Lightning Tree, her arms behind her, around the trunk, like she's chained to it. And there's something in her hand, something glinting in the sun. Like a small silver fish. *Come and sit with me and Gwynne, Vivvy.* And Allie carries on reading the story, telling me to repeat words, taking my hands and placing them on my throat so I can feel my voice. And I can see Vivvy's fingers moving. And I can see it's not a fish but a blade and I'm thinking, that's what my big sister's like now, that's just how she is, all thin and sharp, like a blade. But not shiny, not shining. Then Vivvy comes round the trunk of the tree so I can see all of her now, and she leans back against the trunk with her head back, and she looks like one of those ladies at the front of an old ship, like in one of Pappa's sea-adventure stories – *a figurehead at the mercy of the waves, impotent.* And Vivvy's coming over to us now, slowly, like she's frightened, like she's mad at us and her lips are tight shut, her fingers tight around the knife. Then she stands behind us. Then she starts stabbing the seat with the knife. And Allie gets cross. I think Allie's a bit afraid, like me. *Give me the knife, Vivvy.* But Vivvy won't. She just carries on, stabbing the point of the blade into the Story Seat. Like it's something . . . like it's someone she's killed, like she's really making sure they're dead. *And they're never never ever going to come back to life—*

'Reading a story to Nyssa one evening before bed.

'"It's my turn now," Nyssa said.

'She'd shut the book on my lap, her small hands clapping the covers together, with the delightful nose-in-the air authority of little girls pretending to be mother or teacher. Viviane was sitting by the fire, on the floor. Nyssa began to sign the words. I told her she must speak, so Viviane could listen too. But Nyssa didn't want to tell Viviane a story.

'"Bad people don't deserve stories."

'"Viviane's not bad, Nyssa. She's just not feeling very well right now. Please, Nyssa."

'"OK, but only because *you* want me to."

'Nyssa moved to sit on the arm of the settee, swinging her legs over the edge, facing me, but looking at Viviane.

'"Once upon a time, there was a really bad girl. She was so naughty that no one ever wanted to speak to her and she was all alone and had no one to play with and she had no mummy and daddy and no brothers and sisters and she'd done this terrible thing and she knew she was going to die because there was this really bad man who said he'd get the biggest axe in the world and because she'd done this terrible thing, he'd chop off her head—"

'And Nyssa stopped, still looking at Viviane. And then I looked too. Her head was thrown right back, her eyes tight shut, her mouth open, her face contorting. And I knew there was no sound, that the pain she was silently screaming must surely have been too deep for words—

'I knew what Viviane saw when she looked at Nyssa. Nyssa was an angel, had brought life back to Castle Keep. I'd close my eyes when Nyssa came running, imagine it was Vivvy I was scooping up into my arms. When Nyssa took my hand, it located the memory of Vivvy's hand in mine. Sitting together on the Story Seat, my arm around her, aware of soft flesh, the small bones, remembering the feel of Vivvy's bones when she slipped into my bed at night and her hands, like shells, covering her eyes even in sleep.

'Out on Hart's Hill, with Nyssa, collecting feathers to make wings for Pappa. Nyssa and I, collecting acorns that had fallen from the oak, to make figures with matchstick arms and legs. Just like me and Vivvy used to. We walked around the edge of the forest, Nyssa and I, crunching beech-nut husks underfoot. *Why don't you come to the forest any more, Vivvy?*

'When Viviane looked at Nyssa she could see the ghost of her little-girl self. Untouched, innocent. Nyssa, an angel. At times, less the flesh-and-blood child than the memory of how Vivvy used to be. Before—'

Allie

'*Blessed is he whose transgression is forgiven, whose sin is covered* . . . What evil has been uncovered. A snake of a man. My skin crawls. Almost as if I feel his presence, as if he's here, right here in this room, somewhere in the shadows.

'Before Phineas went away to the abbey, he left a card on my desk at the university, an art-gallery postcard of Antonello da Messina's *St Jerome in His Study*. At first, I didn't understand the significance of the painting. I was more struck by what he'd written on the back, by the words from the psalm . . . *whose sin is covered*. To cover – "to protect" but also "to conceal".

'By concealing, she was protecting herself, wasn't she? Viviane. And I can understand that. Although what I had to conceal was a far lesser evil, was my own small sin, that I kept in a little black velvet purse, my own secret guilt. Wrong of me, perhaps, to say that I think I understand Viviane's silence. But that is how I have always been – covered, protecting myself, concealing . . . I'm sorry. This is hard. Telling you. Ironic, isn't it? That I have spent my working life teaching others to communicate, and now I am struggling to . . .

'I really believed she hated me. Because of me and Gwynne, yes. And because of me and Phineas. She caught us once, "locked in a passionate embrace", as they say. Me and Phineas, in Castle Keep, at the bottom of the stairs. Our paths through the house so consciously kept separate, suddenly crossing – we held each other, kissed, I rested my head against his shoulder. And then I glanced up, to see her, Viviane, on the landing above, looking down, her face telling me nothing, giving nothing away, no anger, no hurt, deadpan, dead. Then she turned away, went into her room. Phineas hadn't seen her. He was looking the other way. And I didn't tell him. *I couldn't*. Because I knew she would.

85

'She had every reason to hate me. Every reason to act the way she did.

'I feel ashamed to admit it now. But I knew there was something wrong, something else wrong in Castle Keep – with the daughter of my lover, yes. Did I play it down? Did I try to reassure him that she'd grow out of it? Did I not voice long enough or often enough my concern? Because I feared – such a selfish fear – that he would not leave them?

'I have been silent for too long. And I cannot help thinking, for the whole of my life I have been paying some kind of penance for that small sin. Not for the deed itself, but not admitting it. I know I cannot be silent any more. And that is why I must speak now.

'Last October, selling the flat, taking a sabbatical – it was intended to be an end, a beginning. But not the one I had imagined. New surroundings, a book to write, another lover, perhaps.

'That day, last October, leaving the flat where Phineas and I had lived, where our daughter Orelia had died, my fear, unfounded of course, was that, closing the door behind me for the last time, I would be closing it on the memory of my child. And I felt there could never be another. I had no idea then, that my child would live even stronger in my mind, that she would give me hope and I would let myself love again.

'No closing of doors, can you understand, but opening myself up.

'That last day, I sat amidst order and conclusion. Packed, ready to go. But always, always, that feeling of incompletion, of being left. Is it the same for every twin? That memory of the first separation, between the womb and the world. Whichever twin is born first, both experience the shock of being apart for the first time. Is it worse to be alone in the unknown, or to be left in the womb? The previous night, I had dreamt that the whole of my right side was a bleeding wound. As if I had been torn from her, or she from me. But whether from Orelia or my sister, Jo, the dream did not tell me.

'Something I wrote in my book, *Acceptance does not come down swift like a guillotine blade*. It's what I had planned for my sabbatical. To write a book. *The Gilded Angel: A Parent's Guide to Bereavement*. How could God, how could any god, let such a thing happen? How does losing a child affect belief? Do you look to or away from your god? What part does guilt play in all this? There must be someone to blame. How easy to transfer feelings of guilt. If not God's fault then it must be my own. To survive a child runs counter to the rules, to the natural laws of life, indeed, seems to threaten your own existence. It is life reversing itself. For every child's death, is there reborn an existentialist? The refusal to accept. Acceptance does not come down swift like a guillotine blade. The meaning of everything is called into question, is measured against your loss. Guilt builds layer by layer, until you shine with it. No. Guilt dulls, hardens, keeps you trapped. Sometimes, is easier to live in guilt, to hide. Guilt is a mantle . . .

'Although I had intended it to be a parent's guide to bereavement the book turned into something else, was, in a way, a confession. Of something that had haunted me since I was a little girl.

'Someone asked me not long after Orelia died how I could go on living there after what had happened. *But acceptance does not come down swift like a guillotine blade.* You replay it over and over. Like some real-life disaster shown on television. Until what you cannot accept as truth is slowly, painfully, absorbed as fact. I kept thinking, hoping, I'd wake up one morning and find her in the living room, playing amidst a nest of toys. And for months after, I'd hear her laughing, calling for me. I'd see her, running from room to room, my eternal three-year-old. Yet, somewhere in me, she incubates, is growing into the young woman I will never see.

'She was a Phineas in miniature, would have grown lean and tall like her father. And like her father, reaching for endless summits, climbing out of her cot, scaling the pantry shelves when she could barely walk, always one of the first children to get to the top of the climbing frame. I'd look in cupboards, under the beds, behind doors. I had to leave the flat. I had to go where I knew I would not find her.

'We used to sit, Phineas and I, with our chairs facing away from the balcony. Even when Phineas boarded up the glass so we couldn't see through the door. Just a few months after Orelia's death, Phineas stood there, his back turned on an exit through which we both would willingly have hurled ourselves if it would have brought her back.

'I have something to tell you, Allie, he said. I knew. I knew we could not go on. Not with each other. Could not have endured any longer that continuous avoidance, eyes closed from each other, from that view we could no longer bear because that view stretching out over the park and the town had become two-dimensional, like scenery from a film set. And there was no view stretching out to the horizon, but only a sheer drop, down. And I realised, until I was able to look, until I could step right out on to that balcony, I would never get beyond her death, that I would be forever teetering at its edge. So I edged closer and closer and one day I opened the door. That warm wave of summer air, as if she had briefly returned . . . a fleeting sense of her. I never thought I'd be able to have a child again. I thought I did not deserve to.

'Before leaving the flat, I'd placed a vase on the balcony with a red rose. I closed my eyes, tried to think of a prayer, but nothing seemed adequate. When I opened my eyes, I saw a flock of migrating birds forming and reforming and settling into a beautifully unified pattern. And I knew that was my prayer. And when I closed the front door, I realised my fear of leaving was not only because that was the place where Orelia had died, but because it was where she had lived, where she had brought me alive.

'When she was born, as I reached to hold her for the first time, I felt a skin slip from me. She looked right into me. I saw

88

myself in her eyes. As if she could see the child inside, the child hiding a secret. She knew and did not judge me. She looked at me the way I could never look at myself. Phineas could never understand why I hated mirrors. Even teaching the deaf children, using mirrors to learn to lip-read, I could never look in my own eyes. There was a mirror Phineas had brought with him when he moved in. The only one in the flat. I left it. Like a round protruding eye. A family portrait from which the faces have slipped.

'As I walked away, I looked back, saw the red rose up on the balcony, like a drop of blood, a sign of life.

'A sign of life? It was, perhaps. Weeks ago, at the abbey, at St Benedict's, where I had gone to see Phineas, I was looking after the child, Nyssa. Gwynne had asked if I'd look after her while she returned home, back to Viviane. Holding the child, those few hours with her, gave me hope. Almost as if Orelia's spirit had returned to me.

'Yes, now I have hope. But do they, the Goode family?

'I saw him, you know. I mean, I thought I did. The day I left the flat, before going to visit my sister, Jocasta – Jo – for a few days, I stopped by at the university to tie up loose ends, clear my desk. Standing in my office, I felt us, Phineas and I – the memory of us making love on the floor seemed to assume solid shape. It was where Orelia was conceived.

'A couple of weeks after Phineas left, it came to me, the Messina, what it meant. I must admit I am not much of an art expert. I remember, we were in a café, Phineas and I. There was a mural. Our table was right next to it, a chocolate-boxy Norwegian fjord scene. I kept touching it. Phineas thought it was the painting I liked. He shook his head in disbelief. For someone with such a fine mind as yours, Allie . . . he said. I told him it wasn't the painting, but the surface, the feel of the paint.

'I have always been drawn to surfaces, the need to touch. Because I am only too aware of my own perhaps. Because sometimes it seems that is all I am?

'I remember looking at the card, the Messina, smoothing my fingers over the glossy print. The stone of the portal that surrounds St Jerome appeared more like wood, polished walnut, bone. *St Jerome in His Study*. He's sitting at a desk, inside a palace or church, reading a book, the desk forming a kind of wooden booth around him – a carrel, I think it's called. In his red cardinal robes, he looks like a heart, is the heart of the painting. Inside, interior, enclosed. Yet, through the windows, you see birds soaring, a detailed landscape, become aware of the outside.

'The first time I saw the painting, I was at Castle Keep. Phineas was studying at the kitchen table. I'd been doing some lip-reading work with Gwynne. I had come in to make drinks. Phineas had a book open at the table. He asked me about the two birds in the foreground of the picture. Symbols, he said, but of what? I leant over to take a look, placed my hand on his shoulder and he covered it with his own.

'Truth, she said, the peacock symbolises immortality and the partridge represents truth. Maggie. She was staring hard at us, framed in the kitchen doorway, her face bright, smarting with sudden awareness, with painful discovery. Phineas had slammed shut the book. As though to hide us. And though neither of us spoke of it, though it was still early days for us, though a hand on a shoulder could be quite innocent, there was, I think, in and from that moment onwards, a sense of loss, a presage, when we both silently acknowledged our truth as wrong, as evil, even.

'Emptying my desk the day I left for my sabbatical, it was like opening a box of secrets. I found the manuscript of my book, *Beyond Hearing*. The unedited version I had written for Jo, that she had never read. Then the old diary Phineas used to arrange our meetings, out of date even at the time he used it. What was it Phineas said? *The frisson of the subterfuge*. But his nervous laugh gave him away. He would slip into my office while I was out, note in the diary the date of our next meeting, the correct month, then NBP, then an arrow, then the hour.

Note Bene, Phineas, 8.30 The arrow meant eight thirty the next day. It made it more acceptable perhaps. A false date, as if it wasn't really happening, was fantasy.

'In the bottom drawer, tucked right at the back, the small black velvet purse. Could feel through the velvet, tiny, fragile, like the bone of a small creature. The pea in my princess bed. I took it to give to her, to give back to her. Such a little thing. Yet it had shaped the entire course of my life.

'Just at that moment, I happened to look out of my office window. Someone caught my eye. The black coat, the hat, that smooth gliding walk. Like some stuffed toy, a funny old cuddly animal, I always thought. But he'd left the university some three or four years previously. His ghost, perhaps. Dr Reemie. Come back to haunt us.

'I will come back, to talk. You know, I've worn glasses since I was a little girl. They told me I didn't need to after the first few years. I'm going to leave them here. You may do as you choose with them.

'You know, she didn't tell. Viviane. About me and Phineas. She never said a word.'

Gwynne

'When she came home, when she told us. Can't imagine what that must have been like for her. She was standing in the doorway, the bitter wind rushing in, chilling the house. Pappa put his arm around her, urged her gently to come inside. As she handed her bag to me, I saw the protection symbol drawn on her palms.

'Last October, after her suicide attempt, she looked like death. Didn't wash, didn't change her clothes. The bandages around her wrists – grubby, stained. Sleeping through the days, exhausted. She was fighting it, what was inside, fighting – to keep it in, to let it out.

'"What's wrong, Viviane? Tell me."

'*What's wrong with Vivvy?* Not very well, Mumma and Pappa said. But I saw their lips when they sat talking after supper . . . *seriously ill.* Vivvy's uneaten food in the warming oven, her place at the kitchen table, laid – as if in memory of someone deceased. Sometimes Pappa got all worked up – *if she refuses to eat, if she carries on starving herself, she'll die.* On the phone to the doctor – what's Pappa saying? – *something new-ra-logical.* Is that what's making you so strange, Vivvy, so silent? Ten and a half. Too young to die.

'*Is someone bullying you at school, Viviane?* Mumma said.

'*No one,* Vivvy said.

'*Is someone hurting you, Viviane?*

'*No one. Nothing. Leave me alone. Or I'll make something up,* she said, *just to shut you up. So you'll never know now,* she said, *if I'm telling the truth.*

'In my nurse's uniform that Mumma made, with the red nail-varnish cross on my handkerchief cap and two red ribbons sewn crossways on an old white sheet for my apron. Orange-juice medicine. Jelly-jube pills. Where's it hurt, Vivvy? Where's the pain? Wouldn't tell me. Couldn't tell me.

'She looked empty sometimes. Skin. Nothing inside. Other times, tight with it. That secret, pleated inside, folded over and over and over, the worst secret in the world.

'Opened it up. Last October. And the pain came all over again.

'I went up to her room. She was lying on the floor. Naked, fetal. Fish on a seabed. On her thigh, a fresh red slash. And sprayed over the walls, in thick black, like a forest of Lightning Trees. Like this . . .'

Phineas

'That which has been can never be again. Can we recover all we once had? Will we? I once read the account of a plane-crash survivor, about how, only days after the terrible event, he had tried desperately to recall the exact sense of peace, the exact beauty of the cloudscape, before the plane fell. Memory is redrawn by that which follows. However certain we think we are of how things were, how it really was is ultimately lost to us. Will we recover, me and Maggie and Gwynne? And Viviane?

'As I said, my stay at the inappropriately named Paradise Close was more temporary than I had envisaged, no more than three days, thanks to Nathan.

'The hostel was as I'd imagined, somewhat shabby, impersonal, made me think of an outpatients' waiting room. Straight away, I began to miss the abbey. Each hour seemed endless. I washed, slept, ate little, having suddenly lost my appetite. I lay on my bed longing for a garden to sit in. People came and went, vacant-looking youths, a few drunks, down-and-outs. I considered booking into a hotel. On the second night, I got up, mooched about the corridors in my pyjamas, barely nodding at one or two other restless souls staring out the window, smoking away the hours.

'Then I met a young lad, Nathan. I'd seen him in the kitchens the previous evening. He was locking up for the night. He said he'd noticed I had not gone to the canteen that day.

'"It's not exactly five-star, mate, I know, but I do my best with what they give us to cook. Look as if you could do with a good dinner in you." He held out his hand. "Nathan Hobbs – at your service. You sit yourself right there in the telly room, mate, and I'll nip round to the all-night mini-market. Cook us up a feast."

'An engaging character, I thought, as I waited for him to return. Out of his chef's uniform, evidently a character, an

94

individual – black drainpipe jeans, short moss-green jacket over a mustard-yellow long shirt, its cuffs and tails sticking from beneath the sleeves and bottom of the jacket. How precise I sound! But I was taking in every detail, aware that I had been looking as if from on high for too long, and not with an eagle's eye, for mine had been an aerial view, one that had missed the finer details. Oh, and what I had missed.

'A feast indeed it was. Nathan seemed to appreciate my need to satisfy both belly and taste buds, waiting until I had finished the plate of garlicky pasta and fish in white wine sauce before asking my name.

'"Fin-ee-ass! What sort of funny-arse name is that!" And he laughed, an unexpected deep "ho-ho" that seemed to surprise even himself, which threw him back against the chair, though a laugh that came easily, that would frequently punctuate our future conversations.

'When I told him about my time at St Benedict's, about my vow of silence, he pursed his lips as if to suppress a smile, his long thin eyebrows rising, like the opening halves of a bridge, almost meeting in an apex above his nose, as if in wonder. Yes, the lad had an immediately likeable way about him. He looked like he'd come from another time, another world even. A character out of Dickens, a cocky street urchin, peaked cap at an angle, thick hair sticking out all ways as if crudely chopped. His features were all points and slants – eyes, ears, brows, nose, the corners of his mouth permanently upturned, his lips stretching occasionally into an endearing pursed grin which gave him a mischievous mock-reproving "puckish" sort of look.

'When I said I didn't think I would ever get to sleep, he suggested a game of ping-pong. I can't help laughing now. Me, in my pyjamas, playing ping-pong at two o'clock in the morning. But I was enjoying myself, especially when it came back to me, the time when I was a boy, at the orphanage. Mr Williams, Wills the Whiff, we called him, the night-duty man, used to let us boys who couldn't sleep play darts and table tennis in the common room. He'd set up this flash-lamp, "like in the war, boys, so the enemy won't spot us". I was fond of old Wills. He always wore these clod-hopping walking boots, thick grubby socks. He stank of feet. Sometimes he told bedtime stories, always about the war, like the time he'd gone to the latrines in the night and stepped on what he thought was a football but turned out to be a decapitated rotting head. We reckoned that accounted for the boots. We didn't believe half of what he told us. I remembered too playing table tennis with Bobby Summers, a younger lad than me but he seemed older, looked out for me. It was people like Bobby and Mr Williams who brought warmth and comfort, who made up some of what I lacked during childhood, who gave me faith in human nature.

'But the effects of the meal and Nathan's company soon evaporated. The following day, my spirits sank low enough for me to decide to leave the hostel, and on the third morning I checked out of Paradise Close, regretting as I walked down the street that I had not said goodbye to Nathan. And then I heard him calling out and turned to see him running towards me.

'"You're not leaving us, Funny-Arse? Don't like the grub? Something I said?"

'I assured him it was only his presence that had made my brief stay bearable. But I knew the hostel was not the place for me. I'd find a hotel, a bed and breakfast. I wished him the best and went on my way. Seconds later, he was running after me again, told me if I wanted I could stay at his place. I thanked him but declined. Then he said I could pay him a bit of rent if it would make me feel better.

'"And we get on all right, you and me, mate, don't we? Had a laugh last night, at the old ping-pong. What do you say, mate?"

'I had no other plans, knew a hotel would offer me little more than the hostel. And yes, we did seem to get on well. I felt we connected in some way. And I think that was what I most needed then. And although it seems odd to me even now, perhaps even a little risky, I found myself accepting Nathan's offer of bed and board, what quickly became not just a stepping stone to everyday life but, though short, a friendship for which I shall ever remain grateful.

'I found a coffee shop where I spent a couple of hours reading the newspapers until Nathan's shift at the hostel was over, when he took me back to his flat, insisting on carrying my rucksack. "You look worn out, mate. Not slept a wink, I expect. What have you got in this thing anyhow, bricks?"

'As we walked to his flat, he gave me a potted biography. He was nineteen, worked part-time at the hostel. The rest of the time he helped out on his mate's stall down the market. He liked to cook, told me he and another of his mates were going to go into the catering business. And he liked making things, he said – models, painting, and so on.

'We reached the estate where he lived in the middle block of three blocks of flats. His flat was on the sixth floor. I insisted on taking the stairs.

'Since Orelia's death, I have had an inexplicable fear of lifts. Is it the descent, that free-falling? Is it that I fear the cage will slip from its bonds and come hurtling, crashing to the ground? I remember trudging those interminable stone steps up to Allie's flat which I now shared, aware of my heavy steps sounding, echoing, like a daily funeral march, then hearing too the lighter steps of a child. Like lilting music playing counter to my dirge. As if she were alongside me, a child beside her father, her hand in mine.

'Seeing I was so tired, he said, he'd keep the guided tour brief. He told me I could have his parents' room. They were both away, working. As he quickly showed me around, I saw the numerous souvenirs, shell ornaments, carved wooden figures, ashtrays printed with pictures of exotic locations, and so on, while the walls of Nathan's bedroom were papered with postcards from the Seychelles, the Bahamas, Florida, Greece, all from his ma, he said. On a shelf of a display cabinet, a statue caught my eye, the strong, muscle-packed physique of

Hercules which had been dressed in a pair of tiny boxer shorts, apparently at the request of Nathan's "pa". On another shelf, a small candle, gathering dust, in the form of a winged figure that had to be, yes, Icarus. The souvenirs and trinkets gave the place a transient quality. It appeared a place of departure and arrival, of impermanence. Yet I felt very much at home.

'Nathan told me his mother was a cabaret singer on a cruise liner. She was saving to buy a villa abroad. It was her dream, he said, like on the bedroom wall. Then he showed me the mural in his parents' bedroom. A tropical island scene with palm trees, beach, sea. And a rising – or setting – sun. Flamingo pink. Quite unlike Maggie's vivid crimson sunsets. Yes, it was a sunset, I decided, for there was a sense of closing in, a suggestion of coming darkness.

'I slept for a while, waking to find Nathan in the kitchen, making an omelette with the eggs I'd realised were still in my rucksack, that I'd hoped were still fresh enough. The omelette was delicious. "Cheese, mushrooms, onions, peppers – the works." Nathan wore a red apron, the words REAL FOOD printed across the chest. It hung from his neck, the middle ties undone. So as not to damage his credibility perhaps. But beneath the bravado, I sensed a liking for domestic routine, a need perhaps, which then, more than ever, I had myself. Nathan rather enjoyed having someone to look after, I think, cooking delicious meals, bringing me cups of tea in the mornings, cocoa at night. If he was working the early shift, I'd wake to find breakfast keeping warm in the oven and I'd tuck into a plate of grilled bacon and mushrooms, or sausage and tomatoes, or porridge laced with syrup. A proper mother hen. It was like a convalescence, or rather a preparation. I was gathering strength emotionally and mentally for my return to a world I had lost touch with during my years at St Benedict's, perhaps long before I entered the abbey, I now think.

'But I insisted I should earn my keep – "work my passage" – while at Nathan's, and my tasks were duly assigned. I washed up after dinner, bought milk and bread every day and did the laundry.

Otherwise, I occupied myself walking, thinking, practising medi- tation as I had learned at the abbey and going to the local library, preferring its hushed atmosphere to the busy streets. It was while sitting in the library one evening, thinking back to those long evenings of study in the library at the university, working on essays Reemie had set me, that I remembered. I had settled so comfort- ably into Nathan's flat, I had forgotten all about my visit to Reemie's solicitors. I would go first thing the next day. I checked the address in the letter from Guild, Guild and Sons. Nathan would surely point me in the right direction. There, in my rucksack, still unread, the letter from Allie, which made my heart sink a little. Because I knew she would have written about Orelia. And I also knew that if I was to move on, I would have to face whatever she had to say, to clear up loose ends, I suppose.

'I remember looking at the neat, precise handwriting, its clarity, wondered whether she herself had achieved clarity, or was she still as I was, living in the shadow of our daughter's death?

'In her letter, she wrote of learning to forgive, wondered whether I blamed her – "the scarlet woman", as she referred to herself, *tempting you away from your family, Phineas.*

'No, I did not blame Allie. It was . . . she was . . . I am ashamed even to think . . . our relationship – it was a way of escaping, but I don't mean it could have been anyone. I was attracted to her. The first time I met her. She intrigued me. That first time, when I saw her in her office at St Bartolph's. I'd gone to the university to discuss how she might be able to help Gwynne. It was Reemie, in fact, who'd set up the appointment, who'd urged me to get in touch with Allie. She was sitting at her desk, pen in hand, surrounded by book-lined walls. It struck me how "in place", how rooted she appeared. And I envied that. I'd meet her there, after work, after the last of her day's tutorials, lingering in the corridor until the students had left.

'We used to make love there, on the floor of her office. Afterwards, always, she'd go to sit at her desk . . . *as if you're going to write up a report on my performance, Allie.* Though I liked this habit of hers, and the way she'd put on her glasses straight after, automatically reach for her pen.

'"And what would you say, Allie? How many marks out of ten?"

'"That you're a . . . gentle lover, Phineas."

'I worried then whether I had disappointed her, had heard in that brief hesitation possible criticism, the word found just a little too late.

'"Gentle and generous and respectful, Phineas," she said. "Eleven out of ten. And counting."

'Once she told me I freed her. And I felt that freedom, felt the most intimate place in her body quiver and shudder, heard the gasp of disbelief, of joy, when, the two of us still joined, she told me she had never experienced that pleasure in the act of love before.

'We thought we had found what each other needed, you see. Maybe Allie did. But I was fooling myself.

'As Viviane's behaviour worsened, the more fractured family life became at Castle Keep, the more I retreated into my relationship with Allie. It was a story I lived within, its pages offering me a painless, pleasure-filled world, a secret place. And I told myself she was my freedom too. But I realise now it was, in fact, the opposite. Allie was my refuge, a hiding place. Maybe Allie sensed that. After Orelia's death, almost six years after I'd left Maggie and the girls, when instead of making love at night Allie and I spent those hours raking over all that was left of us, she told me, *I have never felt I had all of you, Phineas. Not that you are holding back, but part of you has always been elsewhere.* And I remember how her deep sigh made it seem a long-held confession, that it was a relief to tell me.

'I used to wonder whether Reemie knew what was going on between us. Did I have the feeling – or is it only what I know now? – that his silence concerning Allie and I was one of approval, almost as if he sanctioned it?

'But it was wrong, so wrong. In her letter, Allie described

too, just as I'd felt, how Orelia's death seemed a punishment, *because it was wrong, Phineas, what we did, leaving two girls without a father*. Then, *How many times have I said it, Phineas, what happened to Orelia, you are not the guilty one.*

'There were one or two things Allie mentioned in her letter that struck a chord, though I did not give much thought to them at the time. *Silence is my guilt, Phineas*, she wrote. I never did find out what she meant. Something to do with her sister, Jo, if I recall. But I remember now, it was what she had said the day of Orelia's funeral. Allie was looking down at the small white coffin. They were covering it with earth. Dark, near-black earth. I thought of the last time I'd seen Orelia, playing in the kitchen, making music with pans and a wooden spoon. I had not been able to look at her in the coffin. She was perfect, Allie said. The only wound from the fall, you see, was at the back of her head, hidden beneath her hair. Allie was staring down, then she whispered, *Silence is my guilt*. Then, something she added at the end of her letter, *It haunts me, there was something dark, unhealthy, in Castle Keep.*

'I left the library and, walking back to Nathan's, I began to wish I had not opened the letter, the chill of the past getting into my bones. That cold October night, my shadow, darkened in the light of the moon, seemed just then more substantial than my flesh-and-blood self. Perhaps this was what Abbot Lenten had meant when he spoke of a test. *After leaving us, Phineas, you may experience a period of questioning, a test of your new-found faith in yourself.* I knew I had to continue on the path that had led me away from St Benedict's. I scrunched up Allie's letter and threw it in a waste bin. My carefully aimed throw was deliberately symbolic – instinct told me she would not be expecting a reply.

'That night I had another curious dream. I was standing on top of a white tower. I was wearing a small gold crown. It was dark and windy. I was cold, felt terribly alone, bereft even. I could hear music in the distance, but coming closer. Then I saw a band of people. Like a snake, sinuous, coming over the hill. It grew light and in the dream I knew these were the People of the Dawn. When they reached the tower, I saw they were all standing on a long ship and at the helm was the Bearer of News. As the sun rose in the sky, the people began to clap, a slow, incessant clapping. Then a figure standing tall above the rest of the crowd floated up towards me. He bore a gold silk cushion upon which was a scroll tied with a gold ribbon. As he reached the top of the tower, his fair hair turned dark and his colourfully embroidered coat turned black. He handed me the scroll, upon which was written "The Story of Your Life", and then he put his mouth close to my ear, whispered, *Read, Phineas, read*.

'In my eagerness to see what it was Reemie had left for me, I arrived at the solicitors the next morning before they had opened. I waited on a park bench in the public garden opposite the office. The garden was encircled by a ring of beech trees, reminding me of the beech hedge surrounding Castle Keep, of the old red gold of Maggie's wedding ring.

'I still found it hard to take in that Reemie was dead. I was aware he was approaching seventy, was not a particularly sprightly septuagenarian. Yet he'd had a kind of timeless aura, as if he had always been just as he was and would ever remain that way.

'I sat for a while, observing a quality of the autumn sun I had always taken for granted. I was an alien from a sunless planet. I was looking at the beech trees, the leaves appearing in the sunlight, not brassy, but as if each had been dipped in liquid gold. And I could hear – what? *Bok-bok-bok*. Like strange bird call.

'And I remembered Reemie and I, walking through the grounds of the university, when suddenly Reemie stopped beside a pair of beech trees, then called softly, *Bok bok bok*.

'"Be-oh-see, Phineas," he said. "The Anglo-Saxon for beech was *boc*, which, etymologically speaking, became 'book'. Interesting, you must agree, Phineas, for *Buche* is the modern German for beech and *buch* is book, while the Swedish equivalent of both book and beech is *bok*."

'And was I aware, he continued, that the first book was formed from thin slices of beech wood, thus the beech is strongly associated with ancient wisdom and knowledge.

'"Wisdom and knowledge given to us, Phineas, by the gods, who also gave us ways to preserve that knowledge – stone, animal hide, a slice of beech wood, ink upon a page. Odin, father of the great Norse gods, Odin and the runes," he said, his voice trailing into silence. And he began to speak then of his childhood. A rare occurrence, for despite Reemie's passion for tracing words back to their origin, when it came to his own he was more than evasive, was a closed book. So it surprised me when he spoke openly and with great fondness of his mother, how she would take him to sit beside a beech tree near their home and tell him the stories of Odin and the Norse myths.

'He had a particular, even eccentric, way of expressing himself, often lingering over, repeating, words and phrases, as if language was an end in itself, the words dissociated from their meaning. And at the risk of expressing myself badly, words that masked, that cloaked the real man. And how they did. And how he hid.

'But on that occasion, I recall it clearly, he suddenly became wistful, unguarded. Both mask and cloak slipped, this time his words suggesting pure feeling. *Shafts of sunlight, Phineas, like spotlights, raying through the branches upon us, my mother and I curled together on the grass, embracing beneath the green canopy of beech leaves, like actors playing a love scene on the otherwise empty stage of our world, our own world, as though we were the only two people in existence.*

'Do you understand? Can you?

'How cold it suddenly is in here. A shiver runs through me, recalling his voice, its alluring rhythm, its tones – like the dangerous magic of the Pied Piper's tune. And his eyes when he listened . . . *as if he knew what magic slept in his quiet pipe.*

'How eager I was to discover what Reemie had left me – but what a discovery it was to be.'

Marguerite

'This book? *The Book of Madonnas.* A present from Phineas when Viviane was born. See the cover – yellow orange azo. Rich, golden. Colour of the sun, of life. Egg-yolk yellow. Then that shock as you open the cover, the stark zinc white of the flyleaf. See the inscription Phineas wrote: *To the Goode Mother.* Last November, when Phineas brought me home from hospital, when he told me about Reemie's book, when he told me about Viviane, it was as if all the blood had suddenly drained from me, all sense and memory suddenly removed, a page wiped clean of words.

'I keep looking at the paintings of the madonnas, just as I did those first few months at St Bernard's. *What is that book you clutch like a breastplate, Markeet?* Mothers, Dr Kenning, I said, Mary, Nurturer of Humanity, of Goodness. All I could not be, Dr Kenning, I said. And I kept the book with me. Just like Gilda and her pushchair. That old pushchair never left her sight. Like a part of her, an extra limb, a crutch.

'I loved Gilda. She looked after me, let me sit with her in her room. *Staring at that sheet of paper all day like it's the telly, Maggie Goode, that's not going to get you well.*

'Gilda looked like a pantomime dame. Golden hair, like candyfloss, spun into small bouffant rolls, like a Marie-Antoinette wig. A plump yet dainty dame, a puff-gowned, tiny-toed fairy godmother. *You'll go mad, Maggie Goode, in your room all day on your own.* She had the face of the artist Drouais's Madame de Pompadour, gentle, benevolent, yet, like the Drouais, one that contained suffering. And I saw on Gilda's face the mask of particular tragedy, the vacancy where once had been a candlelit shrine within those women who cannot have yet long for children, which grows cold as the candle burns away, remaining forever an empty space.

'I kept to myself at the hospital, talked to no one except Max. One day, Gilda came to my room, took my hand. *You come and keep me company, Maggie Goode, you come and sit with me*. I feel it now, her plump hand holding mine, soft, strong.

'In Gilda's room, I could almost forget the hospital around us. It was another world in there. Homely. Antimacassars crocheted in gold silk, potted plants, ornaments, pictures. She might have lived there all her life. From the walls, urchin boys looked back with hopeful faces, others were pool eyed, tearful. And lined up on the sideboard, ageing the son who lived only in Gilda's mind, a pair of brown crêpe-soled boy's sandals, then a framed though unnamed cycling proficiency certificate, and a photograph of a young man in cap and gown, brash and beaming and bearing a graduation scroll, like all the other prints on shop shelves sold along with the frames.

'Gilda liked to chat, about the doctors, the meals, what she'd watched on the television. Or she'd sit quietly, occasionally humming along to the radio while she knitted for the hospital bazaar, scarves and balaclavas in bottle green and brown. *Good boys' colours, Maggie Goode*. And sometimes she'd sigh, smoothing her knitting, and in her sigh and the slow smoothing of her hand I sensed both yearning and acceptance. I thought of a painting, by Norman Blamey. Of a mother and son. The perspective is strange. Her son appears to be standing beside her, but he's actually behind the mother. As if the pair exist on separate planes. She's looking away, as though waiting for him, as though he's lost to her, or a memory, a ghost she's summoned from the past.

'I showed Gilda *The Book of Madonnas*, pointed out the sad faces of the mothers.

'"Can't you see, Gilda, their downcast, heavy-lidded eyes. Like coins placed on the eyelids of the dead. Can't you see, Gilda, the lowered heads, as if those golden aureoles are weighted. See, Gilda, how their eyes are turned away from the child in their arms. Such a strange absence of love, that inward pensive gaze, as if they know their child has suffering to come. See the limpid eyes of Murillo's Mater Dolorosa. Though the fingers of both mother and child bury into each other's flesh like roots, they both gaze outward, away. So much sorrow in these pages, Gilda."

"'Sorrow, sadness, Maggie Goode? But I see adoration, the love of a mother for her child."

'Listening to the rhythmic clicking of Gilda's needles, following the intricate dance of her fingers, I imagined her filling the spaces of my childhood memories.

'While I was at school, I used to picture her, my mother, at home, doing the things that mothers do, each scene a perfect tableau, like an advert in a magazine. At the kitchen sink, the large bow of her ruffled floral apron tied at the back of her waist like a smile, her hair waved and shiny, the dishes glinting in the sunshine as she rinses the suds. My mother at the cooker, stirring a pot of home-made soup, checking the casserole and fruit pie in the oven. I could hear her laughing, singing along to the radio, calling me in for tea. I could smell her, a lemony-vanilla scent, like expensive cakes. She had perfect skin. Peachy. And the prettiest hands, hands that smoothed the freshly laundered bed-linen, that sewed name tags on to my school uniform and smoothed the hair from my eyes, that held a paintbrush as she painted me playing, sleeping, reading, portraits she painted as obsessively as I would, years later, try to recreate hers.

'I tore a page from a library book one day, scared they'd find out when I returned the book. A mother and baby book with photographs of mothers nursing their babies. I was fascinated by their faces as they gazed down at their newborn. But the page I kept returning to was the one with the illustration of the baby in the womb. So neat, compact, perfectly fitting its space. I kept the page under my pillow, looked at it every night before I went to sleep, the image imprinted in my mind, imagining what it felt like, inside her, safe, picturing the cord that joined us, hearing her heartbeat.

'At first, I explained her absence. My mother was not there because she was somewhere else. I conjured about me reorder and change, sought proof of her existence in the smallest things, a trail of crumbs, a crushed cushion, a rumpled newspaper, a mug of tea dregs. All these were signs of her. And she existed in my "elsewhere" for some years, until absence, like belief in fairies and Father Christmas, gradually translated into loss, when it was no longer "the room she had just left" but "the room where she should be". Yet I sought her still, in the faces of fairy-tale good queens, of those women who stopped to hear my father preaching from his soapbox, in the faces of my teachers, of Miss Connova, who let me paint in her house after school. And at the hospital, in Gilda's face.

'I have often imagined my mother in the agony of childbirth, often wondered whether, in that moment between living and dying, on the cusp of life, she loved me, before she slipped away as I slipped into life?

'I swam from her through an ocean of blood. That much blood. The doctors and midwife up to their knees in blood, up to their waists, necks, drowning in my mother's blood. Those pristine white coats, like slaughterhouse aprons. Did they put me to her breast? Did I feel her skin grow cold? In my mind, a picture. Me, a newborn, birth-blue, the cord still uncut. Her blood covering me, like the red of the robes of Mary, the red of the coverlets of the infant Christs in my book of madonnas.

'Yellow orange azo – the colour I painted the kitchen at Castle Keep. Like the yolk, Phineas said, when it was finished, within Castle Keep's white shell. Oh, Phineas, I said, you should have been a poet. And I'd laughed but only because I loved the romantic in him. Are you laughing at me, wife, he said, and he chased me round the kitchen clucking like a hen: *Eggs, eggs, Maggie Goode, won't you lay me some eggs!*

'Around that time, Viviane was conceived. They were big

babies, the two of them, Viviane and Gwynne. I grew huge each time. Full as an egg.

'The night before my waters broke, before Viviane was born, I dreamt of a row of premature babies, like a grotesque chorus line, linked hand in hand like a chain of paper dolls. They were twitching slowly, weakly, as though losing the will to live. I looked behind me to see a line of fetuses stretching out. And then I looked down to see the line still slipping from me, fetus after fetus, one by one, hands held. I tried to reel them in, tried to find one alive and healthy. I could hear this desperate wailing. But no matter how many I reeled in, I could not find the living child I was convinced was attached to the end.

'I gave birth to her in silence. You could have heard a pin drop, the nurse said. A beautiful child. Thick, shiny black hair, already so long when she was born the nurse had to cut the fringe from her eyes. She had a line of dark lanugo running down her spine. She looked almost animal, feral. The wild child in embryo. I cried my heart out. *Because we're alive, Phineas, we're both alive.* We'll name her Viviane, then, he said, for "life".

'I held her so carefully, holding my breath as I lowered her into her cot, laying her gently on the brushed-cotton sheet, soft as her skin. Before she was born, I was so scared, that I'd drop her, that I'd not be able to feed her, that we would not bond. You know, Phineas had got hold of this book, *Secrets of Good Enough Parenting,* or something. But we'd had enough, Phineas and I, of all those secrets no book could ever tell you, that somehow I knew the minute she was born, when they put her in my arms. From her fragility, I gained strength. And when I put her to my breast, it seemed not that she was drawing strength from me, but that I received strength from her, even as she fell asleep in my arms. I made sketches of her sleeping, filled pads of drawing paper. Couldn't believe she was real, trying to express my love.

'*Love and adoration* . . . Now, when I look through the pages of my book, I see the love of a mother for her child. Looking at the Botticelli, at the deep gilding gaze of the Christ, a kind of forgiving in those eyes. The way Gwynne would look at me sometimes when I'd feel she was seeing right through to my heart. Even before she lost her hearing, you could sense something, something extra in her. She might have been found under a gooseberry bush, Phineas would say. So breathtakingly fair. Viviane and I so dark. Her hair was a white wave's crest falling down her back.

'A cherub. You know, people used to stop me in the street. You could almost eat her, they'd say. I remember once, we were walking in the park. I had stopped to buy Viviane an ice cream. An elderly gentleman was looking into her pram, right up close. He touched Gwynne's cheek with a small pale finger. A strange-looking man. All wrapped up on a fresh spring day in hat, scarf, thick coat. What a delightful child, my dear, he said, truly an angel. When he turned from the pram to face me, I saw the milky-white pupils of his eyes, noticed then the white stick.

'Love and memories, Gilda once said, that's what children give you. Picnics by the weir. Watching from my studio while they played with their toys on the lawn. Me and Phineas walking through the forest, a girl on each back. Such good times. Making birthday cakes. Playing Statues, Dusty Windows, Pass the Parcel, running down Hart's Hill with the children from the village. But Gwynne and Viviane seemed happiest in each other's company.

'Scenes that had faded, that would not reappear, that, as I sat beside Gilda in the hospital, were clouding with later, darker memories.

'I shook her once. Shook her hard. Hard. Hard. Hard. The way you should not shake babies. *Talk to me, Viviane. At least you've got a mother you can* . . . It was the day she'd gone to the Reading Room, when she'd stood naked in front of her father. Phineas and I sat holding each other that evening. Held each other close. *What is wrong with our little girl?*

'Naked. Desperate. Such a primal act. A cry, like Munch, *The Scream*, her last.'

Gwynne

'Unlocked. Open. The door of her Dark Room. A sign, a clue. But of what?

'She left, Viviane, one night last October, just over a week after she'd come out of the hospital. I knew she'd gone, felt it. I was waiting, knew she was already leaving when she had come to St Eulalia's a couple of days before. I searched for her everywhere. The pub where she met friends, where she went to "pull the bastards", the photographer's studio where she sometimes helped out, but they all told me they hadn't seen her for weeks. I stood on Hart's Hill, calling her name over and over, knowing I wouldn't hear, that she probably would not answer anyway.

'I'd forgotten about the Dark Room. The door was open. She'd always kept it locked. Her space, her place. But when I went in, the room was empty. Her absence was palpable, and I thought of the shelter in the forest where I had once nursed a fox, how it appeared to acquire dimension after the fox had died.

'I sat in her room, the half-open window breathing the chill autumn air. Like a mouth she'd slipped into. The curtains like white-shrouded struggling souls. In the wardrobe, her black clothes hanging like a row of shed selves. I thought of the fox skin I had found once on Hart's Hill, the innards devoured, the skin perfect, intact.

'Where had Viviane gone? The forest of black symbols on the walls enclosed me – Y Y Y. In each black fork, in the wintered trees of her photographs, I saw her reaching arms. Each branch antlered with reaching fingers. Viviane's white-bone hands signing. *Help me, Gwynne, please, help me.* Seeing her hands, making the sign, behind the children's hands at the deaf school. Then again, at the door, just before she went. The sign, our own private sign. Three fingers. *Help, I need you.*

'A couple of days before, she had come to St Eulalia's. One of the teachers told me my sister was at the door. I looked up to see her face behind the glass.

'She used to wait for me sometimes, stopping by the school on her way home from work at the photographer's studio. That faint chemical smell about her, that seemed to surround, enclose her. The two of us walking in silence back home, Viviane always hanging back a little, a shadow behind me, walking up the winding track of Hart's Hill, slowing as we neared Castle Keep. Once, she pulled me back. *Gwynne, do you remember . . . ?* But whatever it was, she did not tell.

'We were in the middle of a signing lesson when Viviane had appeared at the door of the deaf school. The children's hands were like a swarm of butterflies as they copied mine – *happy, sad, I am angry, I am tired, cross, afraid. I am deaf, can you help me, please?*

'She was sitting at the back of the room where I had told her to wait until the break. Her hands lifeless in her lap. Birds shot from the sky. *I am angry. I am sorry. Can you help me?* And I looked up to see her slowly bringing her hands together, making the sign, closed hand resting on the palm of the other, thumb raised. *Me, me, help.* And her lips mouthing, *Help me, Gwynne.* Then she shook her head, her hands falling limp.

'Later, during the break, we'd sat in the observation room, looking down at the children playing. I was watching one little girl carefully setting out coloured counters in a pattern. I asked Viviane why she'd come. But she said nothing, looked away, out, through the high window.

'"You can see it," she said, "the house, Castle Keep, you can see it from here."

'I don't know why I told her then. Looking at the little girl's pattern, seeing Viviane's face, that hopelessness, the words, *Help me, Gwynne.* But I told her what I had done once long ago, after Pappa left, when Mumma took some pills, how I thought I was helping her. On my conscience, waiting to be told—

'After Pappa left, it seemed as if Mumma was grieving herself away. Viviane didn't seem to care. She was out of anyone's control by then, staying out all hours, coming home blind drunk, falling over in the kitchen. Once Mumma grabbed her, pulling off the plaster on Viviane's arm. *Don't you touch me, you fucking bitch of a mother!* Mumma slapped her face so hard you could see the shape of her palm on Viviane's cheek. I knew she'd hated herself for hitting Viviane. She was trying to help her. But I don't think she knew even how to help herself. Most days she sat hunched by the fire, until the flames had died and the coals went black, until her skin was as cold as a dead creature when I touched her, like the muntjac deer trapped in the fence I could not stir. *Help me, Gwynnie.* I thought I was helping Mumma, giving her the pills to make her better. I was nine years old. I never told Vivvy it was me who'd given her all those pills.

'Mumma had looked so poorly. Her hair all matted, eyes sunken. *Mumma, can I brush your hair?* But she would never answer me, just sat there, staring at the black coals.

'One day, she asked me for her tablets and I fetched them from the bathroom cupboard, the ones she took when she couldn't sleep. I fetched her a glass of water too. Mumma took a couple of the pills, sipped some water. The tablets looked pretty. I emptied the bottle and set them out in a pattern on the table. Red white red white. Like the pegboard pictures we made at school. And Mumma reached out her hand. *Mumma?* And the look on her face frightened me then. *Help me, Gwynne, help Mumma.* So I passed her the tablets. *Take the tablets, Mumma, they'll make you feel better.* I just wanted to make her well again. One after another, one by one, until the pattern had disappeared. After a little while, her eyes looked funny, her face went grey. *Mumma? Mumma?* She lay on the floor and I lay beside her, smoothing her face. It felt cold, clammy. And she seemed to be barely breathing. And I asked Vivvy to call the doctor. And then the ambulance came—

'Sitting with Viviane, in the observation room at the deaf school, I told her.

'"I kept giving her the pills, Viviane. I thought I was making her better."

'"You were just a kid, Gwynne. Maggie was too sick to know what she was doing. It wasn't your fault."

'Then she turned away. But I could see she was blinking back the tears. And then she looked hard at me.

'"Does it change anything, Gwynne," she said, "now that you've told me? Does it make a difference, to tell? Something you've kept inside all these years," she said, "does it change what you did, what you thought you'd done? Do you feel less—"

'Then she shook her head, looked away again.

'I told her I had to leave her because break-time was over and I had to get back to teaching. I told her to wait for me. She followed me, grabbed my arm.

'"Gwynne, the stories. You remember," she said, "you must remember." Then, lowering her eyes, "To frighten us, Gwynne. But you didn't hear," she said, "he didn't tell you."

'Frighten us? I reached out, but she ran across the hall, through the groups of children. Just as she disappeared through the door, she turned, raised her hand. Three fingers.

'That morning, when I realised Viviane had gone, I sat on the oak-tree swing. Swung back and forth, leaning right back. Like when I was a little girl, seeing the world upside down, seeing upside down, behind me, the Lightning Tree, Castle Keep, and, in between, the Story Seat. *The stories, Gwynne, remember – to frighten us.* And it started to come back to me. All those stories about the silenced children. Mustn't speak. Mustn't tell. *Muthn't—*

'Three of us. On the Story Seat. Me and Vivvy, and Dr Reemie – Professor Reemie from the university. A very clever man, Pappa said. And I liked Dr Reemie. At first I did. Funny little hands. Like a child's almost. And a black ring on one finger. An eye.

A blind eye. He used to bring us toffees in greased white paper bags. Sometimes, when you put your finger in, he'd close his own fingers round the bag and catch your hand and pinch it. It made me laugh. But sometimes, sometimes he wouldn't let my fingers go.

'Mumma used to buy him cakes. Cream cakes. Seeing his fat wet tongue licking his fat wet lips. Thick lips. Big bulging eyes. I used to imagine what his voice sounded like. Soft, I thought, and hissy. Speaking slowly, as if he tasted every word, savoured it. But I couldn't always follow the stories. And sometimes, he'd turn his head away, turn towards Viviane so I couldn't see his lips, put his mouth right up close to her ear, so I couldn't see the words. *You didn't hear, Gwynne, he didn't tell you everything.* One evening, I was sitting on the oak-tree swing, swinging back and forth. Dr Reemie had told me to go out and play. They were sitting on the Story Seat. Him and Viviane. He liked Vivvy more than me, I knew. He was telling her a story. So I turned my back on them, looked up at the sky. I didn't care. And I leant right back, following the sky, right back, until I was looking at them upside down, at his feet, at those funny pointed boots. Dainty little feet. Not like Pappa's. Saw them walking over the garden towards me. *Sleepy-time, Gwynnie, time for bed now. Thleepy-time.* But I didn't want to go to bed. I don't want to go to bed yet, Professor Reemie, I said. But something in his eyes told me I had no choice. And I said goodnight, to Vivvy. And she wouldn't look at me. Her face empty, a mask. Arms limp at her sides. Hands limp. Helpless.

'After Viviane had left, every evening after work, walking up Hart's Hill to Castle Keep with Nyssa, praying Viviane would be there, knowing I'd still find only her empty room. The nights were closing in early, too quickly. I had never known it so cold. I worried she was cold. Somewhere, cold.

'One night, I saw the clearest moon, caught in the branches

of the Lightning Tree. White moon. Moon-stone. White hand. Black stone. What? What was I remembering?

'A week after she left, I had a dream. She, Vivvy, was in some dark place. Down in the ground. I knew she was close by. But I did not know where. I knew I had to find her. I was running through tunnels, calling to her. *It's OK, Vivvy, I'll find you.* I felt her cries travelling up through the soles of my feet, up through my body, until every cell was filled with her crying. And it was pulling me towards her. And I stopped, my whole body vibrating with her cries. And I knew she was below me, right beneath me. And I began to dig until my fingers were raw and bleeding, digging and digging. But as the earth was piling up around me, as I dug deeper into the ground, her cries sounded farther and farther away. And I couldn't get to her, just couldn't reach her.

'In the morning, just before dawn, I got up, fetched a torch. She used to hide from us, down there, years ago, in the oubliette. I pressed the black tiles of the mandala as she once showed me, lifted the heavy disc, dreading what I might find. I thought of mad Miri-Anne, leaving her family to perish. I would not let Viviane perish. I shone the torch down into the small chamber, steeling myself for the scene I had imagined, her skeletal form, curled in a corner, just as I had found her in the bathroom weeks ago. The chamber was empty. Then I noticed something on a small ledge jutting from the stone wall. I climbed halfway down the ladder, reached.

'A feather. A small feather.

'Later that day, it dared to come in, into the kitchen, stayed for a few minutes on the back of the chair before flying to the door, hopping over the threshold, in no hurry. I had turned from the cooker, saw it, perched on a chair, its black beady eyes on me. It had been coming closer, homing in.

'The first time I had noticed it, it had been on the beech hedge, days before, when I had gone out early one morning, having lain awake most of the night worrying where Viviane had gone. I walked across the back garden, breathing the cold crisp air, trying to clear my mind. I was looking down the hill at the town below, wondering whether she was there, somewhere. I had the feeling, like in the dream, that she was not far away. And I saw it, just feet from me, then it flew off into a tree.

'The next time, a day or so later, it was on the seat of the swing. Then I saw it perched on the Lightning Tree, on the back of the Story Seat where Vivvy used to sit, on a shelf in the outhouse. Getting nearer. Waiting for its chance. I remembered the magpie that had scattered its pied feathers over the kitchen in its panic. One for sorrow, Mumma said. *A bird in the house, ill luck will out*. It took hours for Pappa to catch it. Finally he managed to fold it into a tea towel and set it free outside.

'But the robin, brazen, remained, fixing me with its eyes, its red breast puffed proud, its claws curled tight around the wood of the chair, claiming its territory.

'One day I was sitting in Viviane's room, sensing her presence fading over the two weeks since she had left. I had searched through the drawers of her desk, invading places I knew I should not see. Finding only scraps of paper, pens, boxes of unused film, the loose coil of a film pulled from its cartridge. But there was nothing to tell me where she had gone. On the desk, the small white card the gentleman gave me in the gallery earlier that day.

'A few days after Viviane had left, me and Nyssa were walking through town on our way to visit her mother. We passed by the art gallery. The exhibition. Her photographs. I was so sure. Because that's where she'd gone when she'd left the hospital. Why hadn't I thought of it before? The art gallery. Had to be there.

'I ran inside. But – no Viviane. Only her photographs mounted across the length of the wall. They were like nothing Viviane had done before. I realised one was the view across the back garden of Castle Keep. Grainy, as if veiled, mystical, a depth that drew you in, a fragility. But in place of the Lightning Tree, a fir tree, its branches frosted, delicate, feathery, and on its uppermost branches a tiny bird. Another was of five black twisted branches arranged in the fork symbol she'd painted on her bedroom walls. The fork, at the centre of a jagged barbed circle, like a crown of thorns – three drops, like tears, falling from it, like black blood. The symbol, from a distance away, appeared like a trapped reaching figure.

'I was looking at her photographs when someone tapped my shoulder. I turned. The face was weather-beaten, the sharp blue eyes accentuated by lined leathery skin. Silvery-grey hair flowed beneath a battered cowboy hat to his shoulders. Tan overcoat, red leather waistcoat, spurred boots. He might have just dismounted from his horse having journeyed across the plains. He had an expectant air, his head tipped to one side. I realised he was waiting for my reply and I was about to explain I was deaf, when he leant towards me.

'"Ah, but when your eyes are on the lips," he said, "you are hearing every word."

'He smiled. A gold tooth glinted.

'"Runes," he said. "There was one particular photograph that seemed to capture you, am I right? Runes. An ancient alphabetic script. Northern Europe. In use from the first century until the Middle Ages, I believe. Norse culture not being my particular subject. Do you see, the circle is made up of interlocking symbols. Most intriguing. Yes, quite a talent."

'He settled beside Nyssa and me on the bench, laid his stick across his lap. The handle was carved into the shape of some strange beast's head, whose upturned eyes stared at me. I watched as he began to read aloud from the gallery catalogue, enunciating each word, it seemed, as if it were precious, fragile. As he turned a page of the catalogue, a slip of paper floated to the floor. He reached for it.

'"Erratum slip," he said. "Let's see. *A series of thirteen photographs by Viviane Goode – Telling Sories should read Telling Stories*. Of course. But a rather weak pun. Or is that what the artist is telling us, hmm? The redundancy of the word, the power of the image and so forth. But all this frothy blurb in the cata-logue. What I say is, let her images stand alone. And most power-fully compelling images they are too. A talent indeed. You are familiar with the artist?"

'"My sister."

'"Well, now. Happy fortune. And is she local?"

'"She's away," I said, "at the moment."

'"Perhaps you would be so kind as to give her this." He handed me a card. "When she returns. It would be in her interests. I am gathering material for a book, researching – on the hunt, as it were. *The Therapeutic Image*. But I must not bore you."

'He stood, walked over to Viviane's photographs, studied each one in turn closely, then he turned, smiled, leant forward on his stick, looking at me and Nyssa.

'"The white-haired young woman comforting the dark-haired child. I do believe I see a halo above you, fair lady. What an arresting picture you two make. Well, good day to you, Ms Goode. I do hope I hear from your sister soon."

'He made his way out, but at the door of the exhibition room he stopped, looked down, tapping the floor with his stick, then returned to where we were sitting.

'"The three monkeys," he said, "hear no evil, speak no evil, see no . . . But you do, don't you, my dear white-lady, you do see."

'I had slipped his card into my pocket, not looking at it until much later, sitting in Viviane's room, seeing the card on her desk.

'*Professor Prosefors, DPhil, RRMI, CRO*. A telephone number—

'*Professor*, I remember, that's what he liked us to call him. I was sitting on his knee one day, sucking a toffee. He was a doctor, Pappa had said.

'"Do you work in the hospital, then?" I asked him. "Do you have a surgery?"

'He was telling us a story, me and Vivvy. But never stories

from a book. All made up, out of his head. Pappa said he was a very clever man.

'"No, child," he said, "I'm not that kind of a doctor. And I'm not really a doctor at all, though this is a very special secret and you must promise never to tell anyone. You won't tell anyone, will you, not even your mumma and pappa?'

'We promise, Dr Reemie.

'He was trembling as he put his arms around us, the thick tongue struggling with the words. *Professor. Our special secret. Mustn't tell. Pro-feth-or Reemie*— I took Nyssa to the forest one day. As we entered the feathery fronds of autumn bracken parted to reveal a golden path of leaves. Bronzed beech, yellowed oak, ash. The forest was shining with dew from a heavy early mist. From every unshed leaf, a single tear about to drop. White, maze-like, dewy cobwebs. I could feel her. Viviane. Near. Somewhere. But she stopped going to the forest. *Why won't you come to the forest any more, Vivvy?*

'Tucked inside the shelter, Nyssa on my lap. Thermos of hot chocolate, pack of honey sandwiches. I felt Nyssa's small heartbeat. Like the stray cat that would not leave the forest. Its hind legs dragging, blood dripping from a paw, one of its claws torn. I carried it to the shelter, felt its wildly beating heart threatening its thin, fragile form. As if all I held was heart. Then its racing fear gradually slowing as I placed it in the box with blankets and straw. Later, smoothing its back, the soothing thrum of its purring through my palm—

'The forest was my place, my kingdom. The shelter my palace. Pappa dug out the side of a bank, lined it with thick plastic. He found a piece of corrugated iron for the roof. We covered it with branches, Vivvy and me, plugging the holes with leaves and moss. The whole of one summer holiday, we lived in the shelter, only returning to Castle Keep early evening for our supper. Sometimes Mumma would come down with a picnic at lunchtime.

'The first animal I took care of in the shelter was a young badger, one side of its face badly torn, its eye damaged, likely to go blind. The badger was suffering from shock more than the pain of the injury. After a time, it calmed down. I brought it food and water. After a week, when the skin had begun to knit, one day I found it had gone. I knew it would not return. But those first few days, it had lain curled beside me.

'One day, Vivvy didn't want to play in our shelter any more. I remember we were playing there and she'd seemed uneasy, looking up, white faced, anxious, as if aware of watching eyes, as if hearing the snap of twigs under approaching feet.

'The sky turned dark grey, as if night had come too soon, and though we were warm and dry in the shelter, long after the storm had passed over and we could see the blue between the high branches again, Vivvy stayed head bent, huddled against me. *What are you so afraid of, Vivvy?* But she kept looking over, to the dark centre of the forest, its heart of firs so close together they swallowed up the sky, where the leafy path turned to needles, where I felt the vacuum, less than silent, where even sound could not enter. One day, running down Hart's Hill, she stopped right at the forest's edge, would go no farther—

'Sitting in the shelter, Nyssa gathering moss, watching the sunlight weaving through the trees. After a while, I saw it. Between the branches, camouflaged. How long had I been looking at it, not seeing? Until my vision readjusted, and I realised they were not branches but antlers. A red deer. Majestic. A stag. I caught Nyssa's eyes, just as she was about to run with her bundle of moss and twigs. *Must keep still. Keep very quiet.* I felt the dark eyes of the hart upon me, its direct gaze meeting mine. As if this were no accident, as if it had sought me out.

'Sometimes, you can spot the swift bodies of fallow deer who dare to wander outside the safety of the trees up on the hill. But it was years since I had seen a red deer, had spotted the stag, up on the hillside, statue-like, between its antlers the sun, just before the sun dropped behind the forest, like a trophy it bore aloft. And the fawn, years ago, trapped in the back garden—

'The fawn. Something had woken me in the night. I looked out of the bedroom window to see the fawn running back and forth, in circles, panicking, slamming into the trunk of the Lightning Tree, racing the perimeter of the beech hedge in desperation to get free. I crept downstairs, out into the moonlight, moved slowly across the garden, aware that it was watching me from somewhere. Then I saw it, by the hedge, just to the side of me. It was panting, trembling. I reached out my hand. It did not move. I approached it and it edged backwards towards the house. I went up to the hedge at the far end of the garden, keeping my arm stretched out, my palm open. I opened the gate, went out on to the hill, looking back to see it standing now in the open gateway. I stopped. But it would move no farther. I continued, on down the hill, then, halfway down, I saw it pass by me, some distance away, its small form caught in the moonlight. Then it disappeared into the darkness of the forest at the bottom of the hill. I remember, walking back across the garden, I thought it was Mumma come back from her art class. The studio light was on. But it wasn't Mumma. It was him, Dr Reemie. He was looking at Mumma's paintings, at *The Mothers*. And I went upstairs to tell Vivvy, but she was asleep, the covers wrapped around her, her eyes tight shut. And I thought she must be cold, shivering in her sleep, her body trembling, like the fawn—

'I was looking for my Book of Words. After Viviane had gone. I couldn't find my Book of Words. The thesaurus Allie had given me. She'd covered it in gold paper. I had woken to see it on my pillow, like an ingot, the morning after she went away with Pappa.

   'Nyssa was standing on the blue chair in the bathroom while I ran her a bath one morning. She was making faces in the cupboard mirror. She lost her balance, reached for something to hold and the mirrored cupboard door swung open. After I'd comforted her and settled her in the bath, I saw my book. It was on the shelf, in the cupboard. I knew Viviane must have put it there. I saw the slip of paper sticking from the top, marking a page. As I reached for it, I saw the small flash of red. Flutter of wings. The robin. Flying at me.

'I dropped the book. The robin flew back, perched on the handle of the bathroom door. There. Between me and the robin. On the floor. My Book of Words. Beside it, the slip of paper, the page now lost.

'I reached and the robin flew at me again, this time I felt its claws on the back of my hand. I saw the bubble of blood. The robin flew on to the banisters, then away, downstairs—

'*Penknife, feather, book*. The book and the feather I'd found in the oubliette, the penknife with its lapis lazuli handle she'd left in the bathroom. Like a trail of crumbs but leading nowhere—

'One evening, after Nyssa had gone to bed, I went back into the Dark Room. Like a psychic visiting places frequented by the missing, I sat in the dark, her dark, for hours, just as she had done, trying to reach her, to feel she was still alive. I looked for something, anything that might tell me – photographs, a note. Had she intended to leave the door open? Then, in the stack of developing dishes, in the third tray down, I found a small black notebook.'

Phineas

'Last October, sitting on the bench, surrounded by the beech trees, about to open the package I had collected from the solicitors', reeling from what I, in all innocence, believed to be the generosity of my "dear old friend", Reemie. I remembered him once saying, *I have little to give, Phineas, but my time.* And I recalled then that he had been more than generous with both his time and knowledge, indulging my thirst for learning, reserving lecture seats even though I was not an official student of the university. And what had I ever given him? I wondered. Oh, but what, what had I given him?

'The package from Reemie. Like the weight of a small child on my lap. Thinking of Gwynne, climbing up – *for cuggle, Pappa.* Though Viviane showed affection in a different, more private way. I remember how she'd sidle up to my chair, stand beside me, her long fingers tugging gently at my hair. What different children they were. I used to think that was why—

'I had asked Mr Guild Junior to read the will twice over:

I, Jabz R. Reemie, bequeath the sum of thirty thousand pounds to Phineas Goode . . .

'Thirty thousand? I had no idea the old devil had such money. I thought of how frugally he lived. Not a Scrooge as such, but I recall the jam jar full of small change that stood on a bookshelf in his study and the jar full of sixpences that had stood on the mantelpiece since 1984, he ruefully told me, when they ceased to be legal tender. Why, I'd actually witnessed him picking coins from the pavement! His "cake fund", he called it. When the jar was full, he'd take it to the patisserie and buy cream cakes, half a dozen at a time, which he'd devour in one sitting, noisily licking his lips and fingertips, reluctantly giving me the plainest if I happened to visit at teatime. I wondered whether the money had come from having sold his precious books. He had a vast number, referring to them always as "the Second Collection". He had, I recall, some very special items, Spieler's *The Sorcerer's Apprentice*, Sven Tove Sisiliskosson's *Myths of Snow*, and Sorri Sturlsonsson's *Sons of Odin, Shamans of Ice*, all of which would have sat most comfortably on the shelves of the Reading Room, and these three alone would have fetched a healthy sum.

'He had mentioned once in passing that the first collection had been destroyed in a fire, waving away the memory, as if it was of no importance, but I gathered from the way the lips quickly twisted from the brief smile that it must still pain him. To think, at the time I sympathised. Though as I talk to you now, I am picturing a pyre, a flesh-and-blood Guy Fawkes strapped to a chair, begging for mercy.

'The parcel was securely wrapped in several layers of thick brown paper and bound with string and tape. It looked the perfect parcel, as if part of a shop-window display, as if whatever it contained had little significance. And what did the "mystery" package contain? Books perhaps? Those "lends", as he called them, I had let him have on loan from the rare books section of the Reading Room, which he had never returned.

'Taped to the outside was an envelope, with the instruction: *TO PHINEAS, READ FIRST*. Feeling rather like Alice with her Wonderland's tempting '*EAT ME, DRINK ME*' instructions, I opened the envelope. And I found this letter inside:

Inari, Finland
March 2003

Dear Phineas,

You will be surprised, I imagine, to hear from me after all this time. Can it really be almost four years? I hope the intervening years since we last met have treated you kindly and that you have found your peace at your retreat. I wonder if you have at last managed to still that restlessness you often spoke of. Your mind was ever 'on the move', Phineas, was it not, roaming the tomes of the great thinkers. Anchored as you appeared to Castle Keep, Phineas, it seemed to me that your heart was really that of the nomad, like the Sami reindeer herders of this unforgiving land, my dying place.

Finland? Already I hear your questions, Phineas. But a little patience is required. This letter will be brief, is merely by way of a prologue, if you like. It is in The Book that you shall find your answers, and to questions, Phineas, which would never even have crossed your mind. You will forgive me if I sound somewhat obtuse. Is it, I wonder, a fear of saying too much, or too little? And I fear I must tell you the whole story, the facts, the feelings. Ach, yes, the feelings.

But I do not wish this to be an explanation of myself, some kind of apologia. This letter is not intended to sway you, to colour your notion of what you will come to read in The Book. You must judge as you see fit. For my part, I have already judged, have stood as both accused and accuser. Though it is not absolution I seek, for – and I must impress this on you – absolution I shall never have.

By my estimation, many months will have passed before you receive this that I bequeath to you. (The financial gift, by the way, is of little consequence, is a mere gesture. I have no one else to leave it to. It is most certainly not to be regarded as 'payment'.) By the time you come to read this, I shall have long departed. And so, Phineas, I am dead. (Not then immortal – invincible?) However, I know that my death will not be an end. As you read now, my corporeal self will have been reduced to bones, it will 'feel' no more. Though my wretched soul will surely be condemned to suffer in the final agony of my dying. It will be an eternal death, then.

Today, I shall leave this simple dwelling for the last time. I can assure you, the final weeks of my life have been lived most austerely, all pleasures, all temptations, denied. I have existed on bread, water, a little dried fruit. I have provided myself *neither comfort nor warmth. I have walked through the snows without my coat, have felt the teeth of the bitter cold North, its hunger sucking the marrow from my bones. I have abandoned myself to this stark wilderness.*

When I have finished this letter and set down my pen, I shall step out into the dark of my last morning with my length of rope. I shall leave this 'last station of my cross' and make my way to my place of death. It is the only end I am worthy of, to die by my own hand. The tree I have chosen is not ideal, that is to say, is not 'Odin's oak'. But the manner of my death, I know, Phineas, after you have read The Book, *will be of no concern to you.* Mortui non mordent, *Phineas, dead men are no longer a danger.*

The timing is no arbitrary matter. In terms of the cancer, I have weeks, maybe a month or so, left to me yet. But I want to go before the thaw, to lie in the still-frozen ground of the long Arctic winter. It is all I deserve. Do I fear death? You would prefer an honest answer, Phineas. But what do I know of honesty? How could I even consider honesty?

And so, to the contents of the envelope, to The Book. *It is neither diary nor journal, nor even autobiography. It was neither conceived of, nor planned. Fifteen years ago, sitting up late one night working on a paper in my room at the university, I picked up my pen and began to write, while at that very same moment, my daughter Ingebiorg came back to me – into my mind, I saw her. I had a vision.*

Phineas, is it not the cancer that kills me, but the canker of my soul? Was it, maybe, a question of choice, of making the wrong choice? Consider Mrs-Do-As-You-Would-Be-Done-By, Phineas, and Mrs-Be-Done-By-As-You-Did. Yes, I noticed Kingsley's Water Babies *on one of your shelves.*

But there surely comes a point in every man's life when he asks: What am I, saint or sinner, angel or beast? But does one such as I (and there is only one such as I) have a choice? Malum in se, *Phineas, malum in se.*

You may recall the time we spoke of The Trial of Dr X. *Good and Evil, Phineas, the struggle within and all that. You were so terribly innocent. And I? I shall throw out a last couple of lines, riddle-me-rees, good essay titles, topics for discussion – remember those?: 'Loss of innocence should not mean one must automatically assume guilt', 'One can be guilty, yet not feel guilty – and vice versa', 'If God (ach!) by definition is Good – where does that leave the Devil?'*

Where, indeed?

The struggle, my young prince, the battle. The words and the stories. But the stories, the stories won in the end. And so, the cold wind doth blow and we shall have snow.

Stories, the myths. And what are myths but innocent containers of our deepest wishes, our darkest desires, our truths? Power. Power lies in the representation of truth. My story, Phineas, The Book. *Trust the words, the words. Trust the words . . .*

Now, in the last hour of this, my last morning on the earth, by the light of my oil lamp, I write the last word. My final say. In articulo mortis.

Mea culpa. I confess. I am sorry. Forgive me my sins.

Yours,

Jabz Robert Reemie

'Sorry? What, I wondered, could my dear old friend, as I thought of him then, be sorry for? It was a strange letter, somewhat cryptic, particularly towards the end, when I felt I should have known to what he was referring. (His handwriting was smaller than I'd remembered, feathery, as if executed with the barest pressure, as if he'd become frail.) I thought it might be another of his games, one of those intellectual puzzles he liked to set me. Like *The Trial of Dr X.*

'A few months into our relationship, when I was beginning to get used to – was actually enjoying – Reemie's mind-stretching exercises, he presented me with two sets of photocopied notes, extracts from *The Trial of Dr X*, a book about a notorious nine-teenth-century paedophile, and a biography of the celebrated criminal investigator who brought him to justice, Inspector Yarnforth. There was a connection, Reemie said, if I cared to look for it. The exercise, according to Reemie, was, he felt, relevant to my dilemma at the time. My *divided self phase,* as he referred to it, the nature of which I had tried to explain without giving too much away. It was a particularly difficult period for me. I was hearing two voices, each luring me in the opposite direction. I had met Allie by then. She had started coming regularly to Castle Keep to work with Gwynne. I realised I was in danger of falling in love with her. I knew it was wrong. I loved Maggie. But I could not deny my feelings.

'Reemie had invited me to his study one evening, having somehow persuaded me that it would serve me better than the film I had intended to go and see with Maggie. It was almost midnight when I left that evening. I could not believe four hours had passed. But I was always reluctant to leave Reemie's cosy study, its atmosphere of learning, work, serious application of the mind – all those books – reluctant to have to leave his company.

'"So, Phineas, young prince, what have you come up with?" Reemie wanted to know, after I had spent a couple of weeks of intellectual sleuthing.

'"You did say a pair, Reemie? Dr X and the inspector, X and Y, they were twins?"

'"Correct," he said, "identical in fact. Separated at birth."

'"But surely," I said, "if they were identical, when it came to the trial, when the public saw them together, their resemblance would have been remarked upon? And I'm not quite sure, anyway, what relevance—"

'"Ach, Phineas. Be not so ingenuous."

'I was aware I frustrated him at times, when I was slow to get the point. Quickly losing patience, he'd tap his stick – Mistletoe he called it – against the leg of his chair. On this occasion, as I recall, there was an unusual intensity about him. Indeed, he seemed almost boyishly excited by the whole thing.

'"Dr X dyed his hair, you remember. Jet black. Before any of the crimes were committed. You recall, Phineas, the paragraph when he describes how, after applying the dye, he was looking in the mirror and felt compelled to touch the glass? The Devil is not fair, Phineas, ha! You see, Dr X had to *see* himself as evil in order to do the evil he did."

'"But," I said, "he *was* evil, to do what he did."

'"Yes, Phineas. Of course. Yes. Must already have been . . ." He faltered. "Yes, I had not . . ." Reemie's eyes, their usual pale, often watery blue, blanched, as if dried to a winter-sky grey, appeared distant.

'But I still did not see the connection, I told him.

'"Reading the transcripts of the trial closely, Phineas, tells me that initially Dr X acknowledged his feelings regarding his crimes, the feelings which drove him to commit those terrible acts, as good. He felt good. He did not, to begin with, question. It was much later, when he appeared to have suddenly acquired a conscience, that, although he continued to commit evil, he immediately began to experience remorse, to finally acknowledge he was an evil man."

'"And the matter of X and Y being twins? It only came to light after they had both died?"

'"Yes. The point here is, Phineas, we have a do-gooder and a do-badder. Inspector Yarnforth was a fervent supporter of poor unfortunates. He was instrumental in establishing a number of charities for the sick and underprivileged, all for children. Surely you see it, Phineas? On the face of it, identical twins. But the cell had split . . . into a goodie and a baddie. Which brings us back to those two voices of yours, Phineas. Two sides, good and evil – the struggle. And if one side wins . . . think Jekyll and Hyde. If the good side loses . . . the evil . . . The cell split, the cell did not split. The undivided cell. What if . . . what if not a pair but only one?

A whole but in two halves . . . cleft within, a schism . . . the head and the heart, two opposing voices, thoughts and feelings, voice of the saint, voice of the sinner . . . wrong, then, to have feelings? And how to know which is which? What is right and what is wrong. Conscience. But what if there is no conscience, what if a conscience is denied? What if there is only one voice, only one side, no . . . choice?"

'He had spoken with quiet but mounting passion. As if I no longer existed, as if his words were directed inward. He was panting, his face reddening, as though he'd lost all control and was running in desperation to catch the words. Then, his voice low, weak, like the quiet protest of a timid child, he said,

'"Are not our feelings our truth? Are not our feelings more innocent than our thoughts?"

'And wasn't there a second's flicker? Did I not see it, not understand it at the time? That glint, fiendish.

'After reading the letter, I opened the padded envelope, thinking of all those similarly wrapped parcels I had received throughout my childhood containing the books sent to me by an anonymous donor. Inside was another padded envelope marked *The Book*. A timely treat, I thought, for the lack of reading material at the abbey had been my greatest deprivation. I had longed even to simply hold a book, to put my nose to the page, take in the deliciously sharp new-book smell or the familiar mustiness of an old favourite, had longed to hear the ever surprising crack of a new spine, feel the gentle current on my face as I thumbed through pages.

'Inside this last envelope – *The Book*, beautifully bound in cream leather, as you can see. Flicking through its vellum pages, I noticed that his handwriting appeared smaller than I remembered, extremely difficult to read, as though that of a prisoner who has to make the most of a finite supply of paper. I could see no dates or numbered sections, just blocks of neat uniform paragraphs interspersed with a line or two, sometimes just a phrase. Though I had an urge to devour it there and then, the temperature had plummeted. I decided to go back to the flat where I could read the book in warmth and comfort.

'After a nightmare journey owing to an Underground strike and horrendous queues at the supermarket, I finally arrived back at Nathan's, with just enough time for a quick dip into Reemie's book before meeting Nathan for lunch.

'In Nathan's parents' bedroom, in a home not my own, I was a boy again, receiving the next parcel from my mystery donor of books, holding my breath as I untied the string and unwrapped the crisp brown paper. I will never know who it was who sent me all those books, who must have worked hard to keep track as I was moved from orphanage to foster home, back to orphanage, another home. Often, I'd take my cue from the characters of all those stories I loved – my donor would appear as the tall, white-haired Earl of Dorincourt on the jacket of *Little Lord Fauntleroy*, his hand placed on the young boy's head, or he'd be the wise and compassionate Colonel Creighton, who recruits the hero into the secret service in Kipling's *Kim*, or I'd imagine him as the lama from the hills, in spirit alongside me.

'When did the books begin to arrive? As soon as I could read, I think. They were a thread through my otherwise dislocated childhood, a lifeline I clung to. I received the last on my sixteenth birthday, a signed first edition of Henry Gilbert's *Robin Hood*, published in 1912. When no more came, I felt adrift for a time, and I decided then I would one day own a bookshop, fuelled by a determination that I would never run out of books.

'I stretched out on the bed. Here I go, Reemie, I thought, whatever it is I am about to discover, this enigma you have set me, now my journey shall begin. It felt that way, an adventure, a plunge into the unknown. I was on top of the highest mountain, spreading my arms – my wings – toes at the edge. But I did not ever imagine how far I would fall. And then, I began to read . . .'

And so, I ask myself, what is this to be? That I have purchased such a luxurious, ridiculously expensive notebook, vellum paged (gilt edged?), bound in calf leather no less, must indicate a strong desire to . . . To do what exactly?

Vellum. The word suggests, inspires, a sense of ceremony, transports me back to an ancient world, to those first words written on bark, stone, hide − skin − the hide of a young sacrificial beast − a calf. Vellum. Linked to . . . derives from . . . what? Reemie, where are the words, man? Yes, vellum: borrowed from Middle French *velin*, from Old French *vel, veel*, as in calf, of course, and not to be confused with the noun 'velum', as in soft palate, or with the Latin *velum*, as in covering, as in veil, as in to hide, to conceal. Vellum velyn veallyum. Yum yum.

But this is not a good beginning. Already I have an urge to start over. I admit I am not accustomed to such spontaneity, to 'the flow'. For the art of the etymologist is to savour, to examine, to know each word inside out, pursue each word to its very conception, hound it to its truth. But I shall keep to the decision made today on my way back from the stationer's where I purchased this book: the immediate transposition of thought direct on to the page, 'as it comes' − as it were.

But why, then, for the first time in my sixty-four years, do I suddenly feel compelled − *cacoethes scribendi* − to 'lay bare my soul'? My *soul?* So that is what this is! My soul, in all its glory, naked upon these vellum sheets.

I feel a need to explain myself. To myself. To disclose. Two disclosures. The first: I fear I am losing my grip. The fear has been creeping up on me this last year or so. It began with the occasional slip-up, the odd misquotation or two, misspelling, malapropism, yet all fitting neatly under the wide forgiving umbrella of 'the absent-minded professor', my small errors having become something of a running joke among the students. Fortunately, I am no stranger to the often cruel humour of others. I learnt long ago to 'turn a deaf ear'. But the errors increase in both size and frequency. Yesterday, for example, the ticking-off by the Chancellor. If I am to be honest with myself, I have been aware, for some time now, of an increasing loss of control, of power. The words no longer working for me but struggling to break free. The second disclosure: *I am seeing her.* And I ask myself, why now, after all these years? What can it mean?

I have been seeing her for weeks – no, for months. In almost every face. Faces of strangers mutate into hers. During a lecture, a female will metamorphose before my very eyes. Then yesterday, in the cinema, *I smelled her.* My Ingebiorg. And I cannot help thinking there must be some connection, between these sightings of Ingebiorg and my struggle to keep hold of the words. The struggle. Then is she trying to help me? Why has she returned?

Yesterday, from Matyeus-Prinn, the Chancellor, a severe rap on the knuckles. For the first time since M-P has been head of this establishment, I was not offered a sherry. Though Matyeus-Prinn poured himself a large schoonerful which he placed strategically dead centre of his desk, as though it were the Holy Grail. It made a convenient focal point. I have never been able to look the man in the face. On account of his blind eye, the right, which I am sure has been turned on me more than once or twice. (Not literally 'blind' but an eyeless socket.) Did M-P pluck the eye by his own hand? I wonder. Was it, as in the case of Odin, a sacrifice? In exchange for wisdom. But Matyeus-Prinn, wise? I suspect he is not. I am well aware that Matyeus-Prinn suffers me, having inherited me from his predecessor, Charles Farley. Dear old Charlie, a lover of youth, of innocence. Charlie and I had an understanding. It was to my considerable advantage that I once caught him pecking the cheek of some blond while I was an undergraduate here. Caught him out, thus he felt obliged to take me into his confidence regarding his penchant. 'Hairier balls,' he once told me after a few too many gins in the university bar, 'yes, Reemie, the balls of the blonds are deliciously hirsute.' While there was a general suspicion regarding his philandering, I was the only one 'in the know'. I gather he paid the young men handsomely. I gave him my word – 'not so much as a whisper, Charlie,' I said. It would have been a terrible public disgrace, both for my dear old colleague and the university. And it gave me considerable bargaining power. My word, I said, but how much might it be worth? Not quite the chair, those glittering prizes, titles, the professorship. But a few papers published here and there maybe, invites to the highlights of the academic social calendar, my tenure at the university made secure, *guaranteed*. Good old Charlie acquiesced. Then Professor Farley got badly burned. One blond too many, I understand. Syphilis. So Matyeus-Prinn was elected. Charlie had promised he'd 'put a good word in'. M-P realised, I think, he would have to keep me sweet. Yes, I have been on a long rope. Which is why, not being offered a sherry, I felt I was being hauled in.

Matyeus-Prinn told me he had just received a complaint. From a certain American student. About a couple of lectures I gave last month. Yes, *The Language Gap* and *The Wordless Thought*. Somewhat suspect titles, I will now admit. I feigned innocence. Pulled on his tether a little. Did he have to spell it out for me? M-P said. Addressing the sherry schooner, I explained I had been unwell, that a dose of flu had prevented me from carrying out my usual rigorous research. It was the first and would be the very last time, I said. 'Sins, Dr Reemie,' said M-P. (I imagined him fixing me with the good eye.) 'Number one: thou shalt not steal another man's words. Begins with the letter P, Reemie, is an *ism*. Number two: thou shalt not make stuff up.' At this he stood, leant over his desk, flapped the wings of his black gown like some hovering vulture. I have tried my damnedest to warm to the man. He has always had it in for me. Sins? A couple of lectures. A lapse. A little 'borrow'. But I fear. The study of words, my life's work. *Master of the Words*. An overwhelming sense of impending impotence. And Odin? From where has Odin sprung? From whence crept in? Why Odin, now?

Yesterday evening, to take my mind off things, I took a stroll around town and ended up at the cinema. I am no film buff but my interest was engaged by the poster promising a story *. . . about beauty, love and death . . . the inability to communicate . . . about thoughts versus feelings*. The film was Godard's *Pierrot Le Fou*. That the heroine (the actress Anna Karina? Karenina?) is dark haired pleased me, was a relief, my aversion to blondes having increased over the years. The film was just at the part where the hero, Ferdinand, has driven the car into the sea and he's reading from his diary and asks Marianne why she looks so unhappy. *Because*, says Marianne, *you talk to me in words* (in or with? I cannot remember) *and I look at you with feelings*. And at that very moment, there she was, Ingebiorg, walking slowly up the aisle, carrying a tray of popcorn, staring ahead, as if she was in a trance. My Ingebiorg, in the clothes she was wearing the day she was taken from me: pale blue cashmere twinset, soft as her peachy skin, heather-purple skirt, string of pearls. As she approached, she looked right at me, her lips mouthing *Pappy, Pappy*, looking at me with such *feeling*, her mouth twisting, contorting, as though desperate to tell me . . . But she walked right past and as I turned to look – she was gone. It was, I realised, the usherette. I returned to my room at the university. I decided I liked the cinema, its darkness. And it was warm, almost hot. I stoked the fire but I could not settle. Ingebiorg, the usherette. But I could smell . . . Essence de Violets, the perfume I used to buy her. De Violets. Can still smell – de Violets. Vee-ol-lay. Violet. To violate. To transgress, to treat with dishonour, rape. Ach, the words, the feelings.

Was I ever the eminent etymologist, philologist, I aspired to be? A handful of passable papers, essays. But can I really say I have 'made my mark'? Hence the need for bargaining power I omitted to elaborate on earlier. Destined for greatness, she had told me. *My son, the renowned professor.* Mutti. She had me believe I had such power. But a dream unrealised, crushed, before it even blossomed. By who's hand, Mutti? Mother of mine, you gave, yes. But with the same hand, you took. And though you beat me only once, I tried but could never adequately explain to myself your cruelty.

Confess? The word is a wound on the page. A slip. So accustomed have I been to words carefully chosen. Is that what this is to be, then, a confession?

'. . . Confession? But how covered – words veiled, hidden by words.

'I keep seeing her face, even now, as I talk to you. Viviane's face, a moon in the window of the Reading Room. *Can't you help me?* It was the first, the only, time she had asked me. Believe me, I tried to help her. We all did. Me and Maggie and Gwynne – even Allie. But we didn't know how. We didn't know. We did not know.

'I had gone to a restaurant close to the flat, a Mexican eatery Nathan had recommended. Nathan was working at the market that day, said he would join me for lunch around noon if business was quiet.

'Unacquainted with Mexican food – Maggie was a good cook but not adventurous – I read through the bewildering menu of quesedillas and burritos, the fifty varieties of tequila, my stomach turning at the list of margaritas. Maggie and I had once got horribly drunk on a bottle of something devilishly potent called Ready Maid Margarita given to her one birthday. Sometimes, on a Saturday afternoon, we'd open a bottle of wine and go to bed, stay there for the rest of the day. Making the most of our freedom, before the girls came along, before we had responsibilities.

'I had taken Reemie's book to the restaurant. Waiting for my lunch, I mulled over the few pages I had read so far. I had to remind myself that the man was dead. As I read his words, he might have been there, whispering in my ear – that soft, seductive voice. As if I were sitting in his study again, listening enthralled. I pictured a familiar scene: Reemie with Viviane and Gwynne on that old seat in the garden at Castle Keep, telling them stories, when sometimes I'd linger in the background, mesmerised.

'He was like one of the family. A grandfather figure. By then, Maggie's father Jim had moved back up North. Jim was missed, particularly by the girls. His health wasn't too good. He wasn't up to travelling and we saw little of him, especially during those last couple of years before I left. I think the atmosphere in the house bothered him, the way things were – Viviane. Jim wanted to remember the happier times, of course, such as when he'd spend Christmas with us. On Christmas Eve, we'd all look out of the window for Santa Claus, watch him walk across the back garden in his red coat and hat, sack on his back, ho-ho-ing and waving. Even when Viviane realised it was her granddad she kept it to herself for another couple of years until her sister worked it out for herself. Viviane was good like that.

'Such wonderful Christmases we had. Except for one when everything that could go wrong did. The girls had measles, I had flu, the oven packed up halfway through cooking the turkey. We celebrated a week later instead, laughing our way through as we always did. We'd always cope somehow, in those early years. Even when Gwynne became deaf. Though that was hard for a time. There was tension between Maggie and me, the worry, the questioning. *Why us? Why our daughter?* Until one day Maggie threw a book at me, nearly taking my eye out. It broke the ice, pulled us together, fired our determination to do the best we could for Gwynne. Then, years later, Maggie for some reason started blaming herself, not just for our problems with Viviane but even for Gwynne's deafness.

'Like a grandfather to the girls. Reemie. I was truly fond of him, had thought of him always with affection, held him in the same regard as Wills the Whiff, as one or two of those foster fathers who had given me their time and affection as well as their home – in the same regard as my mystery donor.

'As I ate my Mexican lunch, I remembered his willingness to give of his time, to show his love of books, the way he had appeared to take my passion for study and learning as seriously as his own. Which was why, as I began to read *The Book*, I was surprised to learn about the "ticking-off" from the Chancellor. Reemie – a plagiarist? But surely not. Oh, I can picture Matyeus-Prinn now, his eye widening in delight, his self-satisfied smirk. He had a gangly, over-articulated look about him, like a puppet with too many strings, all arms and legs, a giant long-legged insect poised gleefully over Reemie, the smaller, plumper bug, one he could – that I would – now crush underfoot, grind out of existence.

'Reemie took a dim view of plagiarism. *No less than a sin, Phineas.* He'd once returned an essay of mine, a rushed affair and not, I admit, all my own work, the word **THEFT** written across every page in thick red letters. *Do you think I'm a fool, Phineas?* I'd felt similarly chastised when I forgot to return one of his books. Inviting me for a drink one evening, he sat sipping beer in silence before finally announcing, *Someone has stolen my copy of . . .* I could understand. He was a bibliophile, possessive of his library. I rather liked the way he "tended" his collection, running a finger along the row of spines as if over the strings of an instrument, smoothing the covers of the books, as if they might have been living, breathing, a collection of exotic species.

'He kept a list of every title, you know, every one of those damn books. He stuck a sign on one of his bookcases – ALL DAMAGES MUST BE PAID FOR – the sign pilfered from the Reading Room, I bet. And whenever I visited him in his rooms, he'd watch like a hawk as I packed away my study papers, eyeing every book I put into my rucksack. Yet, I could never quite bring myself to remind him to return the "lends", because I never stopped feeling uncomfortable about the unfortunate circumstances of our first meeting.

'I had seen him before, lurking in the depths of the Reading Room. A curious character, that heavy black coat, which I later discovered he would wear even in the mildest weather, almost until the summer, in fact, when it was exchanged for another equally dark coat, but lightweight, although he'd wear his hat all year round. It resembled an elongated fedora, but wider brimmed, with a feather, a small feather, reddish-brown, cream-tipped, stuck in its band. The wing feather of a partridge, he told me. *Perdix virginiana*, the Virginian partridge. A symbol of truth, I said, remembering the Messina painting. And immediately, I recalled the author Henry Gilbert's description of Robin Hood, his velvet cap, stuck with a short feather, pulled from the wing of a plover.

'Partridge, Reemie said, from Middle English *pertriche*, Latin *perdix*, which meant, he informed me, *the lost one*. He told me how a son of the goddess Perdix was thrown from Athene's temple by his uncle Daedalus. Athene turned his soul into a partridge.

'Until we met, I often used to watch him in the Reading Room. And I always had the feeling that somehow he knew. That slight angling of his head, the occasional sideways glance of those over-large eyes.

'He was lingering in the mythology section one day, running his finger along the rows of spines. I noticed his unusually delicate hands, rather beautiful, lily white. Then the index finger stopped, hooked out a volume which he began to browse through. My attention was then diverted by another customer, and when I looked back he, Reemie, still had the book in one hand, but the other hand was now lifting the flap of one of the outsize pockets of his coat and was slipping something inside. Such a smooth, slick, seemingly well-practised action. A flash of egg-yolk yellow, of the cover, surely, of one of my books! He then replaced the other book on the shelf and walked out, tipping his feathered hat. And I remember noticing too the peculiar gait. Or was it just my eyes? For he seemed to be gliding along the pavement. I was transfixed for a moment or two, then came to my senses. Although I did not relish a scene, I could not let the matter go. He was moving away down the street at such a speed, I had difficulty catching up.

'"Excuse me, sir, but—" I felt extremely awkward. It was the first time I'd had to apprehend a customer in this way.

'He turned, apparently bewildered.

'"Yes?"

'I was the owner of the bookshop, I said. I was sorry to have to ask, but did he perhaps have something in his pocket he had forgotten to pay for?

'"In my pocket? In my pocket?" He appeared confused, agitated. He mumbled something: *Mutt. Mutt he.* "Must he", was it?

'Just at that point, a young woman passed by, stopping briefly to ask whether she could rearrange the time of her lecture. *Dr Reemie? It* is *Dr Reemie, from the university, isn't it?* Dr Reemie? I felt dreadful, had evidently made a terrible mistake. Of course he had not stolen any book. And if he had, it was surely more a matter of the absent-minded professor. As though reading my thoughts, he put his hands in his pockets and pulled out the red satin linings which, naturally, were empty.

'And Dr Reemie went gliding away, waving a rather imperious goodbye, the long red linings still hanging from his pockets, like loose lolling tongues.

'Yet Dr Reemie was to return to the Reading Room. And it

was not too much longer, after I'd told him of my desire to extend my knowledge, that we began to meet regularly and our friendship began.

'What games he had played! What fun he must have had with his *terribly innocent young prince*. When he had returned one of my essays that time, when he said, *Your blood, Phineas, not Jung's*. He'd had more than blood. That accusatory *Someone has stolen my copy of . . .* his words cutting right through me. Wasn't there a flicker of a smile when he'd emptied those red-lined pockets, when he said, his voice soft, low, silvery: Nichts. Rien. *Nothing. You see?*

'Flickers, glints, signs, glimpses beneath the mask, which perhaps I did not wish to see at the time. Because I could see only good.

'Finishing my meal at Juan's Bistro, I ordered a coffee, opened *The Book* and began to read. *I saw her today . . .* Then something made me look up and I saw Nathan, outside on the pavement, looking through the window, his face pressed close to the glass, arms spread wide. And I thought of Viviane, that day she stood for almost an hour all those years ago outside the Reading Room.

'Nathan came into the restaurant, told me he was on his way to the market. *What's up with you, Funny-Arse?* he said. *Look as if you've seen a ghost.* But I had, in a way. After he went, I could not forget. Viviane. At the window. The pale moon of her face.

'She had looked worn out. Her pallor made whiter by her black hair. How thin she suddenly seemed.

'She was outside the bookshop, pressed to the window, for almost an hour. I kept going out to her, told her she was putting the customers off, that she was making a spectacle of herself. Eventually, when I said I'd have to call the police, she followed me into the stockroom. I made her some tea. She looked frozen. There was a bluish tinge to her lips, despite the coat. It looked like a man's coat, came right down to her ankles, swamping her. Her legs were bare. She wore a scruffy pair of trainers marked with strange black symbols. She seemed somehow empty, the coat just a shell. Yet there was a heaviness about her. She was staring at the floor, tight lipped, her eyes darting, as if searching, for words, for courage.

'"Why aren't you at school, Viviane?" I said. "Does your mother know you're here?"

'"What does she care? What do you care? What do you know?"

'"Of course we care, Viviane. But we don't know. Whatever it is that's—"

'I struggled for words. We were short staffed, I said. I had to get back to the customers. I made her a hot drink, told her to find a book, curl up in a corner. She could stay as long as she liked, I said. We'd have some lunch together later. I did not know what she wanted from me, what it was I was supposed to do. She shook her head slowly. She would not look at me.

'"Can't you help me?" she whispered. "Make it—"

'"What, Viviane?"

'"Make it stop," she said.

'She looked right at me, her eyes smarting with tears.

'"Make what stop, Viviane? Is it something I've done?"

'"No," she said. The word flew from her lips, like an accusation. Then she stood, staring blankly, as if something had suddenly switched off inside, her words sounding hollow, shells.

'"You haven't done anything," she said, "don't you see? Nothing."

'Then she unbuttoned her coat, letting it fall from her. Underneath, she was naked. I picked up the coat, pulled it around her.

'"Viviane, what are you doing? Why are you acting like this? What on earth's the matter with you!"

'I couldn't help myself. I snapped, shouted. She pulled away, walked out of the shop, head bent. She looked pathetic, broken. I ran after her, but it was too late, she had disappeared into the street.

'Sitting in the restaurant, after Nathan had left, I could not get it out of my mind, the sudden shocking image of her white naked body beneath the black coat. White wood beneath split bark. White root pulled from dark earth. I remember how helpless I felt.

'As soon as I got back to Castle Keep, I went to her room, to see whether we could talk. She was lying on the bed, facing the wall. She wouldn't look at me, wouldn't speak. *What's wrong, Viviane? Can't you tell us, tell Gwynne? We want to help you, Viviane.*

'Was she being bullied at school? Was she ill? Maggie had taken her to the doctor's several times. I'd contacted the doctor myself, thinking it could be something serious. I'd read how brain tumours could provoke irrational behaviour. There was a man who had climbed up on to the roof of a house. They thought it was because he'd been drinking. Maggie and I discussed seeing a neurologist. We'd already been in touch with a counselling service. We'd all but had to drag Viviane there. She wouldn't open her mouth . . . The counsellor said, *You know, if your daughter wishes not to speak, you cannot force her.*

'Of course we didn't want to force her. We came away feeling guilty.

'Coming to the Reading Room was her last stand, a plea, I realise now. After that, the crazy behaviour stopped. We thought she'd got back to her old self, you see. But she'd turned in on herself. Like that magician's trick, when they pull out reams of coloured handkerchiefs from their pockets. But the other way round, Viviane pulling it all back in.

'Desperate. Felt I'd lost her, that day in the bookshop. Naked. Stripped to her barest self. Yet lost to me, that day in the bookshop, lost my daughter.

'A strange and difficult experience, reading Reemie's words, about his daughter, as if I was revisiting my own sadness, my own loss . . .'

. . . I saw her. This evening. Ingebiorg. At the top of the stairs. A vision in white. The lace dress. The satin-slippered feet. Like a young bride. Walking up the stairs towards her reaching hand, as though I were walking back through the years to that day she was taken from me. But she looked so troubled. Pale face. Black hair. *Help me, Pappy. Please.*

Today, in the stationer's, I thought my mind was playing tricks again. I had gone to take my place in the queue when I saw the girl behind the counter serving customers. The shop was a-heave, heads blocking my vision, of the vision. She was the image of Ingebiorg. The girl who was serving. But her face had aged, as though she had suffered in the years since she had left me. Looking at the girl, dressed in blue, seeing my Inge. A cornflower among the weeds. And the serving girl was wearing that same ridiculous hairstyle Helnea would inflict upon our poor daughter, insisting it was *à la mode* — two coiled plaits, like earmuffs, grotesque black shells clamping the sides of her face, two umlauts above the sweetest softest vowel — *schöne schöne my beauty* — a style that gave her a general clumsy, top-heavy look, a yodelling *maidchen mit clogs* . . . *mit* . . . clogged. The girl had that same board-flat, ironed-thin look Ingebiorg had inherited from her mother. But my eyes, poor child. *My little froskr-frogge.* I could hear the girl: *Can I help you, madam, pleath?* That voice, that thick *th . . . th.* Thin, reedy, needy. Ingebiorg was always in need of help, to tie her shoelaces, to carry her books, brush her hair, do up her buttons — to bathe her. She had so little strength, her coordination hampered by a seemingly ever present anxiety I did my best to dispel. In the cinema, I had smelled her . . . *de Violets*, and now, so close that I could touch . . . Had she come back to me? I whispered her name, reached out . . . The girl swiftly withdrew her hand from mine. Gave me such a look. The serving girl. Not my Inge. I fled from the shop, away down the street, realising I had not paid for the pen. But I felt too ashamed, too disturbed to go back and return it. The poor girl must have thought me a madman. What was happening to me? Was I in danger of losing my grip on reality too? I walked around the town for a while, forcing myself to go to the library to prepare notes for my lecture. Though I sat for over an hour, the page remained empty, the words of the reference books on the table before me blurring into meaningless marks that danced and darted like scurrying insects. I decided to retire to the pub. The lecture would have to be 'ad lib', 'off the cuff'. I sat sipping beer, told myself I must be tired. I was overworked, in need of a holiday. Perhaps I should pack a bag, on the spur, just like Mother used to. Off we'd go. On a whim. Destination usually unknown. So many places. All a blur. Like the words.

It was late when I got back to the university. A good night's sleep, I thought, that should settle it. But as I turned the corner of the first flight of stairs that led to my rooms – there she was! On the landing. She had appeared. Flesh and blood materialised. Out of the air. Thin. She was always so thin. Ingebiorg, with her arms outstretched. The white lace dress. Skin so pale, hair so black. Oh, and her eyes. Those huge eyes wide with confusion and fear. *Pappy? Pappy?* Just as they were that day Helnea snatched her from me. Ripped out my heart. *Need help, Pappy. Please, help me . . .*

Helnea had taken my heart and soul. All those years ago. That day she made the bonfire in the garden. I was watching from the window, saw Helnea, carrying armfuls of those rare and precious tomes I had spent a lifetime collecting. She was feeding them to the flames, like titbits to a zoo animal – no, a beast. She knew I was watching. How cool and calculating she looked. Helnea was as cold as herring. A wonder the flames did not melt her. And what was that she had set atop the pyre like a cherry on a cake? Atop my beloved books? I did not try to stop her. To be hurt so deeply, the feelings die.

The books were just the tip. Helnea had told me, before she struck the match.

They were leaving, she said. She was taking Ingebiorg away. I was an evil man, she said. She told me they were leaving, that very day, as soon as she'd packed. *Mark my words, Jabz Reemie, you will never set eyes on your daughter again.* She was standing in the frame of the open doorway, a picture I titled: *The Ice Wife in Danger of Melting Herself.* She was suddenly aflame! I had never seen her like it. She threatened to go to the university. And tell them what exactly, Helnea? I said. And what right did she have to take my daughter away? How dare I talk about rights, she said. But I loved my daughter, I said, loved her with all my heart. How could I call it love? she said. She told me she'd pray that I rot in hell, that my soul suffer for eternity and never rest . . . *that your sins haunt you for the rest of your days and in the afterlife. You sordid slimy stinking slithering snake. You Satan.*

I had to hand it to her, coming out with such a stupendously scintillating twister. Communication had never been her forte. She refused to let me see Ingebiorg, had locked the poor child in her room until it was time to leave, denying me even the chance to say goodbye. My last memory, while Helnea was spitting curses, was seeing Ingebiorg, at the top of the stairs. *I don't want to go away. I don't want to leave you. Pappy, I'm sorry.* How frail she looked. Always such a rheumy child, prey to colds and viruses. It was the last time I saw her. Until tonight, at the top of the stairs. But as I walked slowly up towards Ingebiorg, she retreated, disappeared into the shadows. Why has she come back? Will she come back? What does she want?

After Helnea left, with Inge, the house seemed disembowelled, as if a vital organ had been snatched. A ghost house. From every room she had played in, I gathered her shed skins. Then it began. Two opposing forces preparing for battle within me. I tried not to feel. I tried not to think of Helnea's face, how she had looked at me. A luncheon engagement had been cancelled. She had come home unexpectedly early. She had come into the bathroom. *You, you . . .* she said, words failing her.

Days have passed. Days waiting, hoping. Until now. Yes, I can see her, here, in my study. I have been working on some long-overdue marking of papers, and just now I looked up to find her in the corner. She is still there. I dare not breathe. The strongest feeling she is drawing the words from me, that the pale, barely fleshed hand is pulling a thread of words from the skein that is my heart. There, in the corner shadows. A timid spectre, thinner and pale than ever I remember, a light-starved sapling from memory's dark wood. Ingebiorg, my Inge, I whisper. Inge. *I-nge*. But that *I* a pin, pricking the vision. For in a blink, she has gone.

I have waited until daybreak, a blanket around me, keeping my fire burning, my eyes conjuring shapes from the darkness, translating each and every shadow as her. As *she*.

Almost two weeks since I have had a sighting. I throw myself into work. Then I might glimpse a flick of dark hair passing by the window, or I catch that voice. And I put down my pen, rush out into the street, but find her nowhere. I am in turmoil. I cannot sleep. A sick note to Matyeus-Prinn. The agony after Helnea took her away returns. Why won't she come back? I have done nothing wrong. I did nothing wrong.

After Helnea left with Ingebiorg, when I had recovered from the shock, the anger surfaced. I wished all the evils I could muster upon the Ice Queen. To deprive a child of a father is an act of the purest cruelty. And I knew that Ingebiorg loved me with all her heart. Then, some months later, the most delicious grape was passed to me from Helnea's high-society vine. Helnea was suffering from a severe form of Raynaud's disease. A circulatory thing. Lost all her fingers and toes. I imagined them snapping off like icicles. Poor Helnea – no more manicures, then.

This pen. I did not intend to 'steal' it. Titanium nibbed. Guaranteed a lifetime. How much do I have to say? But a most attractive item, its body inlaid with lapis lazuli. Together with the penknife and toothpick – a matching set! Pen. From Old French *penne, pene, paine*; direct from the Latin *penna*, meaning feather; the word 'penknife' deriving from the fact that small pocket knives were originally used to sharpen quill pens. So, the words have not deserted me, not entirely, at least, not yet.

Did I read somewhere that 'a man's language is an unfailing index of his nature'? And this would explain, of course . . .

In my 'father confessor' role, I must interrupt again. For at this point Phineas stopped reading, just as he had done – and at the very same page apparently – while lunching at Juan's Bistro, disturbed now, as he told me he was then, by the memory of Viviane's pale moon-face in the window of the bookshop.

'An afflicted child,' Phineas said, 'Reemie's daughter. Just as Viviane had seemed, that day years ago, naked under her coat. Vulnerable, thin – a white root snatched from dark earth.'

Phineas then told me that after leaving the restaurant last October he had gone for a long walk to try to clear his mind of such troubling images from the past. He then returned to Nathan's flat, where, after supper and retiring early to bed, he tucked himself under the covers and read Reemie's story 'right to its bitter end'.

There was a long silence. Was it my fancy, or did this already shadowy room further darken? I waited for Phineas to speak. He closed *The Book*, and with an action so obviously conclusive, I feared Reemie's words would never be heard – and we'd barely begun! Then Phineas continued, *The Book* remaining closed on his lap while he spoke, an evident weight, as if pinning him there, the instrument of his pain.

'I'm sorry,' he said, 'but I cannot bear to read it again. The lies – no' – he shook his head – 'the way he hid the truth. I did not want to know what he was telling me . . . *what* he was telling me. Not what the book said, but what it did not say.'

Phineas stood, his face gaunt, drawn, as if suddenly aged. He walked slowly towards me, holding the book at arm's length, and placed it at my feet.

'Sorry? This is a confession? You tell me – can you – if this says sorry?'

And he left.

Poor Phineas.

So, it is up to me to continue the tale-telling, in other words to 'speak for Reemie'. I shall present his story in instalments, I think, as I believe its author intended, as all good stories should be told.

But before I begin the next – it was Allie's turn to tell. And somewhere along the line, as January passed to February, Viviane came back to see me. Because she'd suffered in silence too long, she said. Though hadn't she already told the family when she'd returned to Castle Keep last November?

The truth was out, yes, but not, I gather, the guilt.

Oh, light, light, I thought, let there be light—

Allie

'I wanted to tell you. Something the priest said, at the arboretum, on my way to visit my sister. *Know that others suffer in your silence.* It reminded me of something Reemie said.

'After I'd left St Bartolph's to start my sabbatical, I decided to visit Jo, stopped off first at the Arboretum of Life where Orelia was buried. That morning, the trees just visible through the low mist, it seemed the most beautiful place on earth, as I had thought of it the first time Phineas had taken me there, long before Orelia was born. He'd been reading some book, *Resting Places*, which included a piece on the arboretum, where, it said, a burial plot could be purchased and a tree planted to mark the grave. I thought it was a little morbid at the time. Then, when Phineas showed me . . . I had never seen anything like it, the trees, its serenity, those curious stone seats, each one formed from two semicircles of stone set back to back and scattered over the grounds, like those curly mathematical X's, kisses.

'One night, after the post-mortem, Phineas read a book to me, *The Magic of Trees*. He read the entire book through that long night, neither of us able to sleep. We decided on an ash, the World Tree, Phineas said, signifying new life, rebirth. We wanted a simple ceremony. Me, Phineas – and Jo was there too. Phineas spent hours at the arboretum. But I couldn't, not for months. Then one time I plucked up courage, and when I saw how her tree had grown it gave me strength to return. Every year, I have measured the ash, like a mother marking a child's height chart, taking a leaf to press between the pages of the baby book that recorded the first few, too few, years of her life.

'I was just reaching to touch the tree when I saw in the distance, in front of a group of elms, a woman dressed, incongruously for the time of year, I thought, in a white coat. She stood for a couple of minutes or so. She was looking in my direction, right at me, it seemed. Then she turned and disappeared into the group of trees.

'And I recalled, then, the scene from my childhood I'd always chosen to forget, my mother, standing in the garden, out on the lawn, the green of the lawn, her white suit. All dressed up ready to go to the presentation. Jo's prize-giving. Mother in her lily-white linen suit, blouse and shoes and hat. Pure white. Not a spot, not a stain. I felt as black as the tar-baby. The way Mother said, grave faced, *Are you quite sure you don't know where it is, Alethea?* Her voice deepening as she pronounced that *Al-e-the-a,* into what I could only hear as accusation. No, no, Mother, I said, no. There, on the lawn, staring at my mother's dazzling white suit, *tell her, tell her, Allie, tell the truth.* But I didn't. Each *no* was a turn of the key, locking the door upon myself.

'If I had just admitted, owned up. *Tell a lie and your child will die.* My child died because I lied. The longer you withhold the truth, the more you will be punished for it. I asked Phineas once, in those first few days after Orelia's death, did he ever think that one small wrong could affect your whole life, so that you must keep paying for it?

'*Stabat Mater dolorosa.* Hearing a voice, I turned, looked around but could see no one, then noticed, in the semicircular seat behind mine, the crown of a black hat. *Stabat Mater dolorosa – stood the mother, full of grief.* A soft, sibilant voice that was vaguely familiar. Then the man stood, a tall, six-foot figure. He was wearing a long black coat, with what appeared to be a cassock underneath and a large gold crucifix which hung from a heavy gold chain. He had shoulder-length white hair, a long white beard. The wide-brimmed hat, angled low, and the dark-tinted glasses obscured much of his face.

'"To see a mother at the graveside of her child," he said, "is the absolute translation of grief."

'He walked slowly around the stone seat, tapping a white stick.

'"Cold," he said, "even for this time of year, almost super-naturally cold. Hoar frost – Jack Frost – permafrost. Ah, those arctic winds doth bite. World's growing colder by the day, wouldn't you know. May I?"

'He sat next to me on the seat.

'"You are suffering, my dear," he said. "Is it grief you are full of? Something else?"

'He was staring ahead, into the distance.

'"Your child," he said, indicating the ash.

'"Yes, my daughter."

'I noticed then, above his collar, an ugly reddish-purple bruise, or scar, around his neck.

'"Ah, yes, I had a daughter, once."

'He shifted to make himself more comfortable, to reveal between the coat lapels, not a crucifix, but an eagle in flight.

'"Something on your mind," he said.

'Though his face was not turned to me, his head was tipped slightly, ready to listen.

'"An old secret," I said.

'"Ah, how easy to say 'best left kept'. *Veritas odium parit.* Truth begets hatred. But an unheard truth, my dear, is a canker of the soul."

'"It was such a small thing. Something I did. When I was young. Eleven years old."

'"Ah, but from an acorn, a mighty oak. And it has fed off you? The ravenous appetite of guilt, my dear. But please, continue."

'And I told him then, the strange priest beside me on the stone seat, the arms curving around us, what I had never told anyone. Clear, as though it were a scene being played out before me, there in the arboretum. Me, standing before my mother that summer's day, before we went to Jo's prize-giving, my eyes fixed on that lily-white linen. Each *no* a blot of black ink. My lips closing on that final *no* like the drawstring of the velvet pouch pulled tight.

'The minute we arrived back home after the prize-giving cere-mony, I rushed upstairs to my room, put my hand inside the pillow-slip to check it was still there. That night, I lay awake with my head pressed tight to the pillow, my fingers inside the slip, around the black velvet, already hating myself for what I had done. I kept it there for a few days. Then, fearing my mother would find it when she changed the bed, I found another hiding place. And I kept on finding new places – a drawer, behind a book on a shelf. But each new place worried at me, never seemed quite secret enough, always presenting some new risk I had not considered. So I kept moving it. And it followed me, a horrible black leitmotif that accompanied me through my adolescence. I could simply have thrown it away. But it had found its way inside me. Grit inside the shell. The black pearl. Or was I always waiting for that day when I had courage enough to return it, to own up?

'How easy it would have been to say, *Yes, Mother*. To loosen the strings of the velvet pouch. How different my life would have been. And it was my guilt, of course, which led me to study deafness. As if it could somehow make up for what I had done. I have often wondered what else, who else, I might have become.

'I can't remember what I told the priest exactly. It seemed as though I had been talking for hours. The mist had cleared and it was already growing dark. Then the priest turned to me, and I could see me, reflected in each of the tinted lenses, little, like a child. Me and my sister. Me and Jo – two peas, twins. Nothing between us, when we were little.

'"Such a small thing, you said, your crime," the priest said, "but you must remember, it is not so much the act, but the silence that follows it. Silence begets hatred, my dear."

'Then he got to his feet.

'"But I have not told you," I said.

'"The exact nature of your small crime? But it is not me you need to tell, my dear."

'And he leant forward, touched my forehead. "Know that others suffer in your silence."

'I watched him walk away, tapping with his white cane along the path, until he disappeared into the trees, and I looked up then to see above some bird of prey, its vast extended wings ridged and tapering like fingers. And close by, another bird, hovering. The larger bird was circling it, then closed in on the smaller one, which was flapping its wings hopelessly now, then it appeared to nosedive through the sky into a group of trees. I looked up again to see four arrows of migrating birds, perfect V's, one after the other, fleeing from the premature freeze. A sign I should be on my way. I should have left for Jo's hours ago, was delaying until the very last. But Jo had come to expect it. I sat a while, saying goodbye to Orelia's ash, switched on the Dictaphone, making notes for my book. *Which to choose? The bird that soars, or the bird that falls? The spirit of Orelia, risen, my angel, going upward from the tree? Or her body falling from the balcony? You see your dead child everywhere, always. A constant weave through your life. A thread of guilt.* I saw it open in my mind. The balcony door. I had fallen asleep. I was thinking of Phineas, that I had never told him the truth. Just as I had never told Jo. *Tell him, Allie, tell her, Allie.*

'As I drove to Jo's, I thought about what the priest had said. *Others suffer in your silence.* And I had not realised its full significance. For I had always been thinking selfishly of myself, how the consequences of what I had done had affected my life. Yes, it had come between me and myself, but it had also come between me and my twin sister. Ever since we were eleven years old. The black velvet purse. There, between us.

'It was an interminable journey, the fog thickening. I almost missed the turning into the lane, managed to catch, just in time, the sign of the hand, the finger pointing the way to Casajoca. Then, almost magically, the fog cleared and on either side of the road the flame-shaped lamps lit the track that led to the old farmhouse, its windows glowing with inside warmth. She was there, at the front door, Jo, as always a sixth sense alerting her to my arrival, and in the soft backlight of the hallway candles, her hair, a halo.

'I had sensed, in the silences, that she had something she needed to say, and I realised later how difficult it must have been for her to tell me. Not long after Orelia's death, in one of my bleakest moments, I felt as though there would never be another child, as though I did not deserve another child. *You feel as if a hand has come down, scooped your child from you, away – and all you see is that empty palm held out to you, returning, returning, empty . . .*

'After leaving Jo, at the abbey, when I met Gwynne . . . She had a little girl with her – Nyssa. I was so scared I would never be able to love a child, another child, again.

'Gwynne told me about Viviane's suicide attempt, that her sister had disappeared. She went back, to Castle Keep, to wait for Viviane, she said.

'Dr Reemie. I remember now, something he said. He'd come into my office once, at St Bartolph's, to borrow a book. I was busy preparing a tutorial, told him to look through the shelves. By then we were both regular visitors at Castle Keep, had been for some months. I noticed he'd picked out one of the old books from my university days, one I'd bought second hand, *Hearing and Deafness: A Layman's Guide*, published in the forties, out of date but one I was fond of. Its pages had a glossy, comfortingly substantial feel. Dr Reemie was thumbing through the pages, then he stopped at a double page of pictures, illustrating something called fenestration, an operation that created a new path of sound waves to the inner ear, a cure for what is called otosclerosis. Each illustration showed a deeper stage of entry into the ear, various flaps of skin and tissue clamped back, pulled open by instruments until you saw right through to the horizontal canal. The pictures were more than revelatory, almost nauseatingly invasive. Reemie was looking intently at them.

'"Genitalia," he said, "female. Of a child."

'And then he looked up, appeared not to know where he was, seemed confused, a little agitated. He snapped the book shut then walked over to the window, opened it, leant on the sill, breathing deeply.

'"She," he said, his voice low, "she. My mother. And how I suffered in my silence."

Thilenth. That lisp, somehow appealing. Just then I felt terribly sorry for him. My surprise, shock, at his curious comment about the pictures overtaken by how suddenly pathetic he looked, sounded.'

Phineas

'Since I gave the book to you it is as if I am released from its grip, from his words. *Master of the Words*, he called himself. Had us all playing into his hands. Sorry? I care nothing for his sorry. Cannot forgive. The words mean nothing, are untruths – almost worse than lies.

'When Viviane came back to Castle Keep last November, when she told us, only then did we know . . . I remember leading her into the kitchen. I suggested she have a rest. Maggie offered to run her a hot bath. Desperate to know, delaying the agony. Truth hurts. It hurts.

'At Nathan's flat, reading *The Book*, I felt I was looking into the very soul of the man – into the soul of a stranger. When I think now how I felt deeply sorry for him, to learn about how he'd suffered – his daughter, the cruel actions of his surely heartless wife, his childhood, his mother – how guilty he felt. As soon as I'd finished the book, I had an urge to go to a bookshop. There was precious little to read in Nathan's flat. And I think I needed to get Reemie's words out of my mind – the visions of his daughter, what he'd written about his mother.

'But I found myself paralysed by indecision in the shop, panicking before all those glossy covers set out on the tables. It was not what I would call, or what Reemie would have called, a "real" bookshop, but one of those high-street stationer's. And I was overwhelmed, I think, still getting accustomed to being among crowds. After half an hour or so, when the assistant asked again whether I needed help, I walked quickly down the aisles, grabbing books indiscriminately, as if I had won some "fill your trolley in sixty seconds" competition.

'And what had I come up with? Two piles on the bedside table. In one, a series of detective novels, a fictional autobiography, *Adventures of a Comic Book Hero*, a couple of blockbusters – doorstops – concerning drug cartels, espionage, set *in the cut-throat dark-double-treble-quadruple-dealing world of international finance*. And in the other pile, three memoirs: of a once famous comedian, of an opera singer turned carpenter, and the life of a nineteenth-century country lad, *How Narrow the Field, How Straight the Plough*, and the "book of the month" – *A Layman's Guide to Self-Analysis: Freud Slips on a Banana Skin*. Lastly, a celebrity cookbook I gave to Nathan. The two piles were organised into fiction and fact, either side of the bedside lamp. Like a set of balancing scales, the facts outweighing the fantasy. What was I telling myself? I wondered.

'It was late afternoon by the time I got back from my shopping trip, already dark. I glanced out of the window, spotted Nathan coming back from work, two bulging carrier bags in either hand. His gait was sprightly, light footed, and with those curious pointed-toed calf boots he wore with tight jeans gave him a distinctly elfin look, more suited to a woodland scene, I thought as I watched him coming along the street.

'I opened the door with a "Greetings, Robin Goodfellow", was then taken aback as he set down the bags, and stepped forward, sweeping one arm across his chest.

'"Thou speakest aright, I am that merry wanderer of the night."

'He laughed at my all too evident surprise.

'"Keep your hair on, mate. Did a couple of plays with this drama group. Used to do pantomime when I was a young kid too. To keep me occupied, my ma said. Bit of a troublemaker in my time. Nothing unlawful, practical jokes really, fooling around and stuff. Calmed down a bit now, though. Have a beer, Funny-Arse, steady your nerves."

'I sat in the kitchen, drinking my beer while Nathan prepared the meal, donning his apron, politely refusing my offer to help. I watched him chopping meat and vegetables, almost balletic as he moved about the kitchen, his movements quick and snappy. Like a professional chef, I said.

'"Don't know about that. Could do with some professional stuff, though, these knives are crap."

'He thanked me for the cookbook, flicked through it briefly, then set it aside. I said I'd been book-buying, told him he was welcome to borrow whatever he fancied.

'"Thanks all the same but I don't read much. My ma's the bookworm. You guessed, travel books. Got her this book for her birthday about this woman who gets lost in some African jungle, true story. Snakes, leeches, you name it, then she meets this scientist bloke. My dad says she should stick to women's stuff, sex and shopping stories. He don't read at all. Started going to these classes. But he couldn't keep it up 'cos he's away such a lot."

'"You don't mind, Nathan, being on your own so much?"

'"Mind don't come into it, mate. You just get on with it. It's the way it is. My dad's home for weeks sometimes. He's on the lorries. Long distance. Don't know how he gets about. Not being able to read, I mean. The road signs. Sniffs the air, I reckon, finger to the wind, you know, follow the stars."

'He turned then, looked at me, head on one side, the way he sometimes did, as if trying to figure me out. He asked whether I had children. I fetched the photograph from the rucksack. The four of us, sitting together on top of Hart's Hill, taken when Viviane had just got her camera. By whom? Allie? Reemie?

'"Knew you had to be a dad. Yesterday, when we met down the market for lunch. When that woman handed you the baby while she got her purse out for the bus. The way you were holding the little girl. Like it came natural. Like you'd done it before. And," he said, grinning, "the way you nag me to wrap up warm."

'I started to apologise.

'"No worries, mate." He turned away. "Actually, I kind of like it. It's good, you know, having you around and stuff. So, tell me, your kids."

'Where to begin?

'"Two daughters," I said, "my wife, Maggie. But I left them."

'Nathan, respecting my sudden silence, did not enquire further. But later, after dinner, a hearty meal of lamb stew, dumplings and a bread-and-butter pudding – a typical 'Goode' family supper – after I'd washed up the dishes, Nathan fetched a couple of beers and we settled in the armchairs and I told my young friend about Maggie and the girls. It was the warm, cosy atmosphere perhaps which loosened my tongue a little, which put me in mind of a similar evening, years ago, sitting, glass of malt in hand, in one of the deep pillowy armchairs beside the crackling ever-burning fire in Reemie's study. And I told Nathan just what I had spoken of with Reemie that evening. Though I had only known the man a short while, it had been long enough for me to feel at ease speaking about such personal issues, instead of the usual matters-of-the-intellect. By then, Reemie had met the family, although it was before he was to properly inveigle himself into Castle Keep. I remembered the conversation had been rather one-sided, Reemie seated opposite, listening intently as I explained how lucky I considered myself. I believe the subject had led from my attempt to explain the restlessness I occasionally experienced. Two lovely daughters, a loving wife, wonderful home – what more could a man wish for, Reemie, I said, asked, half hoping he'd come up with an answer.

'As I sat talking to Nathan, all those years later, I recalled Reemie's face, that quick shift of his features, his composure momentarily disturbed and resettling. *What more could a man want?* And it was only then that I wondered, having read about his childhood, his marriage, never having known a healthy family life, is that what Reemie had wanted too, is that why he'd appeared so eager to be, albeit in a small way, part of ours?

'I admitted to Nathan, just as I had to Reemie, how I'd always feared that it might all suddenly disappear one day, continually reminding myself never to take my good fortune for granted. Yes, Reemie was always aware of that fear, which I realise now he used to full advantage.

'I told Nathan of my dream since childhood, of the wife, the children, the home, the bookshop. I spoke of the early days, memories vividly returning of the Christmases and summer holidays, how, when the girls came along, after "our Eden", Maggie and I had to face the realities of having a family. Though we were like children ourselves, I said, thinking of the time Vivvy decided her bed was an aeroplane and we all had to board and Gwynne was the hostess. Maggie and I joined in the girls' make-believe, making it real for them. And Castle Keep was the perfect home for young children. All those rooms – a game of Hide and Seek could last hours. There was so much joy. And my occasional worries were surely those of almost every parent wanting to do right by their family. I questioned, often doubted, my abilities as a father. I remember Maggie, just before giving birth, how frightened she was. Wasn't it all fuelled by our desire to do our very best, to be good parents?

'Nathan opened more beers, said when his parents were back they all got on each other's nerves sometimes.

'"The times I've threatened to walk out, mate. And the times they've threatened to kick me out. But we all love each other really. From what you say, seems to me you did the best you could. You were a brill dad, I bet."

'Brill? Sometimes, maybe. Not perfect. But I had done everything I could, my best, and as I sat there with Nathan, I kept asking – then why had it gone so wrong? What had I not done right? The day Viviane had come to the shop, naked under that coat, her plea for help. And I lost my temper. There'd be no Goode family, I bellowed, the way she was carrying on. Words that now I deeply regret. And the night I left with Allie, Viviane in her nightie, in the rain.

'"But I left them, Nathan," I said. "There was another woman."

'"Not good, Funny-Arse," Nathan said. "Have to agree with you there. But it happens, mate. It's life. Shit happens. There's always a reason, though."

'And my reason? As I told you, an escape. I was running away.

And I asked myself again, sitting there with Nathan, what had ended it? What had turned all that good so utterly bad? What was the evil?

'In bed that night, my mind would not rest. I couldn't concentrate on my book, a murder mystery of all things, a case of mistaken identity according to the blurb. I kept missing vital clues, had to keep going back, rereading the same page until my eyes had sucked all sense from the words. I was looking at the mural, admiring Nathan's talent, thinking of what he'd told me about his mother's dream of living abroad. Yet, as he said, his ma kept coming back. I closed my eyes, had fleeting images from long ago, the girls as toddlers noisily playing in the garden, Castle Keep on the hill. And I kept hearing Nathan's words, *you did the best you could.*

'I had. We had, Maggie and I together. Hadn't we? I was glad that I'd talked to Nathan. I felt clearer, more settled. Like that day at the abbey, when I fell from the ladder on to the hard ground, winding myself, yet laughing aloud at my fall, a fall *into grace*. A eureka moment, I realise now. From the fantasy into reality. Into a clarity. Does it seem too strange, is it possible that in a single moment one can glimpse the entire truth of one's life? For in that moment, I saw that perhaps as a result of my childhood, falling so easily into those fictional worlds, I have always been as if one step removed from life, unable to fully engage – to believe that I could.

'I was staring at the mural, at Hermes who had now joined the two figures. I had not spotted the pair at first half hidden as they were, one behind each of the palm trees on either side of the painting. The smaller of the two, a child, perhaps, appeared to be reaching out. But what was it about Hermes that drew my attention?

'The previous evening, Nathan had been watching some holiday programme. On the screen, a young man, arms extended, preparing to dive into the water a hundred feet below. The camera drew back to show him on the edge of a cliff, poised, like a statue of Christ, a crucifixion. Then a close-up of his tight, muscle-packed torso, as he raised his arms, his hands meeting above his head. And then I noticed one of the postcards on the mantelpiece, not square but cut in the shape of a figure, a man. I reached to take a closer look. A card from Greece, Zakynthos. Nathan said I could keep it and I had stuck the figure at the centre of the mural's sun to begin with. It had the effect of giving the red ball a feline iris, transforming it into the evil eye of some watching creature. I decided instead to set him on the beach, on terra firma, at the water's edge. He gazed out to sea, his arms extending towards the horizon, Hermes, with his winged sandals and helmet, Messenger of the Gods. I realised why the figure of Hermes intrigued me. Given wings, yes, but how small they were, a mere detail. And then I thought of the arms of the diver, their beautiful strength, the taut muscles, and I remembered how I had been similarly struck by the statue of Hercules in the display cabinet when Nathan first brought me to the flat.

'A thin white root kept in dark earth. Protected. Up on Hart's Hill. In Castle Keep. In my dream. I thought we were so safe up there, in the wide freedom of the skies. Can one protect too much? Two images meet in my mind. Viviane, the shock of her thin pale naked body. And Viviane, a small baby, plump and compact, naked and innocent, falling through the air towards me. It was a summer's day, out on the hill. Her face was beaming. She was crying out, catching her breath, ecstatic with the sensation, the utter pleasure of free-falling. Maggie was calling over the beech hedge. *Careful, Phineas, you'll drop her!* I see it now, in slow motion, as I tossed her high, the sun raying from behind her black hair, and my arms, bronzed from the sun, muscles taut, reaching up and my hands gripping her small form. And always, always I caught her.

'Last October, in the comfort of Nathan's home, his warmth and companionship, as I lay there, it seemed my feathers were falling, like scales from my eyes. I held out my arms. Held them out, to Viviane, to Gwynne, and to Orelia. I had done my best to keep them safe. Had tried to keep them safe. Yes, had done my best, I thought . . . That night, I'd woken from a fitful sleep, words, phrases from the book in my head – as if I'd just woken from a dream. I was thinking about Reemie's love for his daughter Ingebiorg – *her name, a leitmotif, a soft pulse beating throughout these pages, the meditator's 'ohm' sounding through the delirium of my words, my beacon in the dark* . . . His words shadowed by an evidently long-harboured sadness. I remember how they'd touched me, for I knew the terrible pain of losing a child. And, at the time, I had felt honoured that he should reveal so much.

The Book

Ingebiorg. Today. In town. Outside the bookshop. Mid-January and she was without a coat, her skin as blue as the silk of her dress. So cold . . . but glittering, radiating light, life. As though I were temporarily blinded by such light. That ice-blue silk dress Helnea had once copied from some tittley-tattley society magazine. The child was nine years old, for Gottsakes! The way Helnea got her done up. It advanced yet reduced, somehow cheapened her, gave her the pathetic, uneasy look of a child prostitute. She came gliding towards me as if on ice and, as she neared, in that radiance, the dress appeared as white as . . . as snow. And those blue-green veins on her neck. And her breath condensing in the freezing air. Small clouds. Her breath? Then she lives, breathes? She is no vision, then, no hallucination, granted wish? Yes, living proof. I must admit, at first, I feared she had begun to appear to me the way loved ones are said to appear at the point of death, as if the departing spirit must bid a final adieu. Has she died? (I might imagine her in some far-off – Alpine? – sanctuary, consumptive, consumed, breathing her last.) It felt like a death. The day Helnea took her from me. And today, today I tried to reach her, weaving my frustrated path through sudden crowds conspiring against me, it seemed, there only to hinder. I was already undoing my buttons to wrap her freezing form in my thick coat. But again, as suddenly as she had appeared – she went!

The more I see her, the more I must. Those small puffballs. Her breath. Containing words of love? Like smoke signals. Of distress? Is she hurting, needing? Why has she come back to me? What is her need? This is hell. I yearn, ache. Can write no more.

A week passes, another. Then today – at last! In the lecture hall. Her arm. Like a white root – no, a stem, reaching to me. The lecture: *The Root of Evil*. (Old High German: *ubil*, Proto-Germanic: *ubilaz*, from Indo-European: *upilos*, root.) And a subject dear to my heart. But the lecture was proving one of my worst. I could see the students straining to hear through my numerous throat-clearings, the many pauses, stifling their yawns.

'Innocent,' I said, 'borrowed from Latin – *innocentem* – as in "not guilty". *In*, meaning not, plus *nocentem*, the present participle of . . . of . . . of . . . Now,' I said, 'which one of you can tell me?'

If any put up their hands, then I did not see. For again, glittering, radiating light, there was she. My Inge. Her white arm, reaching. Her mouth opening, about to utter the words she seemed so desperate to tell me.

'*Nocere*,' she said, 'it means "to harm".'

I was thrown. I stammered, gripped the lectern. I blinked and – yes – she was gone. Must have slipped out the door. And I found my eyes, now, alighting on *him*. In the back row. Dead centre. His good eye sending a laser beam to me. Matyeus-Prinn. A scraggy vulture watching his prey – me, the victim, Dr Reemie, dying a death. He looked so smug, catching me out like that. Oh, he knew.

Had it escaped my mind, he asked, after the students had gone. I was looking out of the window, feigning nonchalance. Yes, you self-righteous little man, I thought. Yes, I had forgotten – and well he knew it. It was a momentary lapse, I told him, a glitch. Surely he had experienced it himself, I said, the thoughts racing on, the words unable to catch up, the mind ahead of itself, of the less, that is, the slower, students— He cut me short. Stop blathering, man, he said. And he peered at me, bearing down upon me until I felt myself prostrate on the floor at his feet. I didn't fool him, he said. I've got your measure all right, he said. While he continued to chastise me, I looked out into the quad, at

Ingebiorg, outside, on the grass. White, graceful, still. I could not help myself, told him to take a look outside. A swan, he said, a statue of a swan. Because of the river, the River Swan that runs through the grounds of St Bartolph's, do we remember, Reemie? Oh, that patronising tone, that sneer, damn the man. But it was not a swan. Her. Ingebiorg. I can neither eat not sleep. Nothing else matters.

Nichts to report. Another cancelled tutorial. I told Matyeus-Prinn it was because I needed dentistry. Teeth a little too long, Reemie, he said, smirking. The man is a fiend, a devil. I am in despair. It is midnight. In my room, alone again. Can barely write, barely think, string two words . . . Even on the pages of this book, open on the desk before me, seeing the watermark of her face. This is grief. Then am I doomed *to neither escape this burning desire, nor extinguish its flame . . . aching with longing . . .* like Freyr, *Freyr aching for Gerd, fair maiden of the Underworld . . .* Freyr. Freyr?

I am in a better state of mind today. She will return. She needs me. Because I was the one who cared for her always. For I felt in part responsible. The tongue. Such a handicap. A grotesque fat serpent strangling – devouring – her every syllable. Poor child. How I could sympathise! The tongue took all her strength, was an incubus. She was five or six when I happened upon a tome: *The Book of Impedimentum*, medical facts, corrective surgical procedures and so forth. There was a section of exercises for daily practice. But it proved too much for my Inge. It was painful to observe her struggling as she repeated the lists: *thwitch, thtitch, thizzle, theventy-thix thlick thententheth, thpeak thad thithter thing thad thongth.* Half an hour left her exhausted, pleading, *Pappy, pleathe can we thtop, no more, Pappy, pleathe.* At nine, ten years old, she seemed to have used up all her resources. The migraines – caused by stress (because of her mother, I should think) – arrived with a vengeance. I worried how she'd ever get through the simple business of day-to-day living. She needed everything I could give her. All those hours I spent comforting her in her darkened bedroom while Helnea went off to her coffee mornings and lunches. Poor Inge, she could not bear me to even take her hand, to even lie beside her on the bed. She remained stiff as a corpse, until the pain had passed. Helnea's only contribution to alleviate her daughter's suffering was to refuse her chocolate. Heartless. There was only one occasion when Helnea gave the matter serious consideration. At dinner one evening,

'Jabz,' said Helnea, 'Ingebiorg, her speech, a therapist,' she said.

I told her there was no need.

'I am her therapist, Helnea,' I said, 'I can look after her. I have, after all, what might be called first-hand experience.'

The way Helnea looked at me! As if I were responsible for the myriad faults of mankind.

I dreamt of Inge, glittering, all in white. I woke aching like Freyr, felt I was a-shine. Freyr? Again? This Freyr keeps coming – is coming – back to me. Oh yes, I remember so clearly now. Freyr, one of the gods, with Odin and Thor. One of the principal deities. From the myths, the stories. *Skirnir's Journey.* Her stories. She told me. Mutti told me as I curled close to her warm body. Stories about Freyr, the God of Fertility. *Sitting on the High Seat, in Odin's great hall. And he had no right to be there. Then he saw the goddess Gerd, closing the doors of the hall, her arms glittering, so brightly, shining with such radiance. And Freyr knew that he wanted her, desired her with all his heart, his entire being. He could neither eat nor sleep. He had to possess this beautiful fair maiden. So he sent for Skirnir, his servant, to woo her for him. So, Skirnir set off on the horse Sleipnir.* Remembering, in spite of myself. Such passion. The way Mutti told it. Mutti. Me on her lap. Her arms about me. With Mutti, in her bed. Her soft warm body. Telling me the stories. Of the cold North. Her land. The stories I have fought against, have kept so long at bay. They must not come back. I must not remember. The words, Reemie, only the words! All those years, the words — my strength. But how to keep hold now, when it seems a thousand Sleipnirs are straining, chomping at the bit. *She agreed to meet Freyr in the forest. Tell your master, she said to Skirnir, tell him to meet me in the forest, but he must wait . . . oh, but Freyr could not wait. Even one night seemed to him an eternity, and two nights, three? How to live through another three? thought Freyr . . . I have lived through months that have seemed shorter than even half one such night aflame with this desire . . .*

I dreamt of Inge. So, she is to return only in my dreams? In the dream, her lips twisting, contorting. I thought of the grappling arms of an exhausted mountain climber, struggling to make that final haul up. Dreams of Inge traversing a barren land — stones, ice, the constant bitter wind. My Inge, do you remember? What secrets we had! You with your head on my chest while I told you the stories. We breathed in unison, did you know? As one. Your smell, that faint note of antiseptic. So far away, today, I could not hear. How you had to battle for every word. Struggling with the words, I am. Words escaping me, from me. Stories creeping back. Fenrir the Wolf, Garm — Hound of the Underworld, the wicked shape-changer Loki, who, some said, was the Devil. As evil as Odin was good. I remember when she told me the story of 'The Binding of Loki' I clung to her for dear life. And the tales of Sigurd the Volsung, slayer of the serpent dragon Fafnir. The scene, vivid, Sigurd, roasting the heart of Fafnir over the fire. Then he touched it to see whether it was cooked and the juice ran from the heart on to his finger, scalding him, so he put his finger in his mouth and when the blood touched his tongue he discovered he could understand the songs of birds. The myths, the sagas, the stories of my mother's motherland. Passed from mother to son. Oh, I am so afraid. The fear, the guilt. Oh, Mutti, you never heard me, Mutti, but I was, always, so terribly sorr—

Viviane

'How do I feel? Like my skin's all peeled off. Like there's nothing inside my skin. And I wonder sometimes, did it really happen? The way they look at me now, Phineas and Maggie and Gwynne. Did they believe me? When I left the squat, went back home, when I told them. Like someone had pressed a button, pulled a string. Like one of those talkie dolls. The kid had one. The kid, Nyssa, she'd brought to stay when I got out from hospital. All I needed, that kid being there. The doll. What did she have a talking doll for when the kid couldn't hear? *My name is Angel I love you kiss me I love you. Kiss me. Kiss. Kissy. Kith.* Give us a fucking kiss, bitch! Ventman, you know, the one who . . . Tight arse tight cunt tits like a kid's, Ventman said. Like a kid's, he said. And I was. When he'd stuck his cock in me. Like he'd pricked some bubble. All came rushing back. Dam-burst. What he did. *The man who lost his daughter.* Like a knife entering my flesh, gouging me out. Put his hand right inside me. Pulled out my organs – liver, kidneys, spleen, lungs, tongue. Pulled out my spine. Gutted, filleted, piece of flesh rubber-numb. No feeling. Just skin. A hiding hide. Oh, but my skin tingling. And shame-warm. A wail of shame. My tongue was a scold's bridle, a static metronome. Undressing in the dark, behind me – *a mountain of shed selves.* Now, inside, like rotten fruit. A walking wound. My flesh, sliced. No blood inside me. Blood let. Blood's water. Turned blood to water. The hairs in his nostrils, black grass I crawled into. Beguiled. Gilded. Guilty. *Like mad Miri-Anne who swallowed the key.* Washed my body. Lying on the cold floor. A crucifixion. Pen of feathers to write on my body. Secret knowledge, knowledge of secrets.

'Looking out the window at Gwynne and the kid. And through another window, through years ago, coming along the path to Castle Keep, black boots too small for a man. Where was Maggie? In the kitchen, setting out cakes on a tray, cream cakes. *Yum yum.* Phineas going out to his studies, rucksack on his back, a snail shell. *Tap-tap*, on the glass. Someone's knocking at the door. Maggie running from her studio, sketch pad open, drawing of the nude on the bed. *Who did this?* She knew I'd done it. It's a naked lady, Mother, I said, with a flower stuck in her cunt. She slapped me across the face. Then she was sorry. I didn't mean it, Vivvy, she said. She reached out. I pulled away. But I wanted her to stay. That's why I did it. Wanted Phineas to stay. Sticky toffees, so your mouth's all gummed up. Keeps you quiet. Going up the stairs, opening the white door, into the white room, lying on the floor, lino so cold it numbed, anaesthetised. Oh, but such a nice soft special feeling. Remember the stories, Gwynne, don't you? I said. *The Child and the Severed Tongue. The Ever-Bleeding Child. Once, there was a child so full of lies they flowed from her mouth one day as ruby-dark blood and she bled and she bled until she was leached to her bones, until all the people came to know how bad she was and they pulled her limbs from her body just like chicken bones and her trunk was split from top to bottom and when she looked down she saw the vultures stick in their beaks and peck out her organs.* Oh, but the special stories. The ones Gwynnie never heard. *Thpecial.*'

Gwynne

'The notebook. She must have left it there, in her Dark Room, had wanted me to read it. But it was only because of what Pappa had written about Mumma destroying her *Mother* paintings that my attention was focused elsewhere. I didn't realise what Viviane had done, what she'd left for me, like a sign.

'Signs, signals, clues. Did I see but not want to see? As soon as she told us, she burnt the notebook on a fire of forest sticks. I'd followed her down the hill, witnessed the ritual, how she tore out the pages and set them alight one by one, watching the black curls rising in the heat, her story disappearing into the air.

'On the front page, in her little-girl hand, she'd written, *Vivvy Goode aged ten and a half.* On the pages that followed, hieroglyphics that made no sense, words, pictures, scribbles, knives, scissors with handles drawn as huge eyes, tongues and feathers. And scattered throughout the book, a tiny bird, a cheeky-looking Christmas-card Robin. One page was patterned with the letter S, each letter a snake drawn with a forked tongue. One page was a mass of scrawl at the centre, like a spider in a chaotic web. Or the fly? A word, but tangled in black ink. In the middle of the book, a strange drawing, part man, part beast, *The Man Who Lost His Daughter, by Viviane Goode.* And on the last couple of pages, repeated over and over, symbols, the forked Y, and others. But these had been written in Viviane's adult hand.

'I remembered the professor in the gallery, when he'd told me about the runes in Viviane's photographs. I searched the books Pappa had left behind. I found *The Rune Book. The power of the runes . . . for the ancient Germanic people, they connected with learning and magic lore . . . The great Norse god Odin was renowned for the discovery or invention of the runic letters.*

Odin sacrificed himself by hanging himself from the World Tree in order to acquire secret knowledge. And then, reading on, I discovered what Viviane's runes meant:

ansuz:	Odin	ᚠ
naubiz:	need	ᚾ
gebo:	gift	ᚷ
mannaz:	man	ᛗ
opila:	home	ᛟ
algiz:	protection	ᛦ

'Protection. What did Viviane need protection from? The dark force that Pappa spoke of in his letter? That had cast its shadow over us all. The letter from Pappa had been slipped into the back of the notebook. It was dated August, two months ago. Why hadn't she shown me the letter? Why hadn't she even told me Pappa had written.

'In the letter he said . . .

'But here, you can read it. You can see what Viviane had done.

August, 2003

Dear Viviane and Gwynne,

I should not begin by asking forgiveness, for that would be asking too much. But this is written in the hope that you, my daughters, may still have room enough in your hearts to hear me. I am finding this difficult, and so it should be, having spent three years in a forced absence of words, they now elude me. But I wanted to write and tell you that my vow of silence is coming to an end.

I am sorry, deeply sorry, that I left our family, that I could not be the father I should have been, I so desperately wanted to be, that I violated your trust. My dear daughters, I have never had a chance to fully explain why I left. Perhaps, even now, it is not entirely clear to me. I felt that I had failed – as a father, as a husband. I saw our family breaking down. I did not know what to do, how to hold us all, keep us all together. Over those three years, it seemed as if some dark force had taken over our family, one that I was powerless to stop, a kind of – I can only call it – dark presence in Castle Keep that was poisoning the heart of our family. Or is it, and I have considered this often, is it that I am simply not facing up to the fact that whatever was wrong was within me? I struggled, honestly, I did what I thought was right. I kept hoping. But that day when your mother destroyed her paintings, in that terrible act of destruction, I saw it was a sign. It told me, 'However much you may want it, Phineas, it cannot be.' I could not understand at first – why had she done such a thing? As you know, your mother had spent over two, three years on The Mothers – all those hours of intense work.

Even now, after this distance of time, I still ask myself, 'What happened?' How to make sense of it? Even now, I must profess ignorance. One moment, the Goode family, happy, yes, I honestly believe we were. Then, by the end of those three years – we were the Goodes no more. I remember you two girls, playing so happily, how close you once were – we all were.

Viviane, I know you had your difficulties, but I should have, your mother and I should have, found some way to help you. And Gwynne, Gwynne, I feel I neglected you, though you were always such a wise, capable child.

My daughters, what am I saying? Nothing. Everything. Something was very wrong in Castle Keep. Was it its dark history that touched us?

You are older now, become young women, and perhaps might better understand if I admit that, after I left, I did not achieve happiness with Allie. And with respect to her, perhaps I was taking refuge in our relationship. You knew that Allie and I had a child, that our daughter was killed. It was her death which *led me to the decision to enter St Benedict's, to retreat. I was retreating from the world, from myself.*

But good fathers do not leave their families. And this is what I must live with every day.

In a few months' time, I shall be leaving the abbey. Now I have the words again, could we, I wonder, communicate? Though I shall understand if neither of you wishes to make contact again.

What else to say? That I love you both dearly, that I always have and will. And I am not asking for anything, that is, I do not expect, hope is all I have.
Your Pappa
  Phineas

'You see, you do see what Viviane had done?

'But I was only thinking of what Pappa had said about Mumma's paintings. *When your mother destroyed her paintings . . .* But it wasn't Mumma. It was Viviane. Vivvy did it. It was Vivvy who'd cut up Mumma's paintings. With the knife. She'd had the knife in her hand—'

Phineas

'Ignorance – bliss, Phineas, he'd say, he said, during one of our first conversations. *Blis-s-ss* – those long difficult S's.

'Previously we had met in a pub near the university, but on this occasion he had invited me to his room at St Bartolph's.

'The intense warmth hit me as soon as I walked in. Though it was early summer, Reemie was laying more coal on a well-established fire. I saw books – on shelves, in piles on the floor, on almost every surface – then on an old ring-stained table more books, papers, bottles of ink, a pot of fountain pens. The room was full of academic clutter, had an atmosphere of study, of intense concentration – a mind in itself, unravelling some intellectual knot. A room that drew me, that I longed to inhabit.

'"You say you want to learn, Phineas," he said, "but learn what exactly?" He had removed his boots, was warming his small feet before the flames.

'"To find out—" I began.

'"What?"

'His eyes shone in the firelight. He leant forward, licked his lips. Something delicious before him. Like one of those cream cakes. Something to relish – a mind to guide, to direct.

'I told him I was not entirely uninformed. I had read, I said, and I liked to consider myself a thinking man.

'"I think about life a good deal," I said.

'"A little too much perhaps, Phineas?"

'I needed to refine my thinking, I said. A path to follow, a clear way through.

'He suggested we begin with a little philosophy, not that it was his subject, he said, but he would pick the brains of a colleague. Shortly after our conversation, he presented me with a reading list – Joachim's *The Nature of Truth*, if I remember, Nietzsche's *The Twilight of the Gods*, Brentano's *Our*

Knowledge of Right and Wrong. He gave me a sheet of questions, points to consider while reading. Then we touched upon the philosophy of religion – *Does God exist?, Do you have a soul?, Why is there suffering and evil in the world?* Then we moved on, literature, *English, Phineas, medieval, back to basics* . . . Then language, philology, etymology – *we shall languish in the English language* – his passion.

'I often felt out of my depth, inadequate, ignorant. All those essays he set: *The Saussurian Paradox, Chomskian Syntax, Skinner's Theory of Language Acquisition by Imitation and Reinforcement.* The workload increased. Sometimes I'd study through the night, finding myself nodding off the next day at the bookshop. But I was desperate to learn, wanting to repay him for his interest. Got you wrapped around his little finger, Phineas, Maggie would say. It irritated her, my "devotion" to him. *Reemie this, Reemie that. He's not God, Phineas.*

'I believed my industry gave him a certain pleasure. He had come to the library at St Bartolph's one evening. I was deep in work, had glanced up to see him watching me from the corner. He did not respond to my acknowledgement, leaning forward, the dainty hands folded over the cone handle of his walking stick. But I had seen the intense focusing of those protruding eyes which, at the time, I had interpreted as the gaze of a master appreciating the diligence of his pupil, noting the absolute power of that gaze. Sometimes, during one of our discussions, or while he was giving a lecture, I would be lulled into a trance, merely by the sound of his voice.

'There was that time in the university bar. A student approached us, female, blonde, disarmingly attractive. She had a slight accent, German, I think. She did not like to have to point it out, Dr Reemie, she said, but there appeared to be an error in one of the lecture handouts. The quote he had attributed to the linguist Edward Sapir, from his book *Language*, was surely from George Lockoff's *Women, Fire and Dangerous Things*. It was obviously a typing error, she said. She was shaking, poor girl.

'I thought Reemie's eyes would pop from their sockets. He was staring at her, his thick lips twitching, his hand tapping the tabletop in a quick light movement, more, I thought, through nerves than impatience.

'"A little test," he said, his smile brief, more of a wince, not enough to mask his annoyance, or discomfort, at being caught out, perhaps. "Yes, a test, my dear. Which of my students are on the ball. Full marks to you. And may I ask your name?"

'"Sigrid," she said.

'All colour drained from Reemie's face then, as he stood there, his jaw dropping, it seemed, in utter disbelief.

'"Thi . . . thi . . . Sigrid?" He could barely speak. "Thi . . . thith . . . this is some cruel joke?"

'"Joke? Forgive me. No, no, Dr Reemie." The poor girl, evidently as confused as I was by his strange reaction, backed away, dropping her books and papers.

'Reemie looked down at her as she scrabbled about at his feet, his composure now returned, a look of disdain hardening his features as the girl retreated, apologising. And his eyes, as if his gaze were a physical force, repelling, pushing her away.

'I bumped into the girl, Sigrid, later, assured her she'd done the right thing, that Dr Reemie would rather have been told of his error. I told her he really wasn't such an ogre. But his eyes, that power, I remember so very clearly. Never shall I forget.

'To think – how I used to wish Reemie had been an earlier influence in my life. I had always been grateful for the interest and loyalty of my mystery donor. Those fictional worlds I had discovered as a child were more real and reliable than my own. They were worlds I could enter, places of refuge, of more certainty than my constantly changing existence, worlds from which I would not be suddenly uprooted but within which I could linger, roam, remain long after the story was over. And there were always happy endings. My escape began with Blyton's *Castle of Adventure*, *Boy's Own Stories*, then *Happy Days at Cheverill*, *Barney of Buffin*, *The Fifth Form Detective*.

I was there on Coral Island with Ralph and Peterkin and Jack, with Dickon and Mary in the secret garden. Will Scarlett and Friar Tuck and Robin, all of them were friends, siblings, mothers and fathers accompanying me on my difficult route through childhood. But while the flow of books had stretched my love of literature, they left me hungry for more than escapism and companionship. I remember Reemie's look of disgust when I'd mentioned the books I'd read as a child. I wondered what he'd have to say about the books I was reading while staying with Nathan.

'But I could not have coped with anything serious, heavy. I went to the bargain bookstores, chose titles at random, could hear Reemie's comments about "such low and indiscriminate reading". I had almost finished *Fall from Grace*, about the rise (and fall!) of a Hollywood actress who, at the height of her fame, endured public humiliation after revelations of her father's shady past. Her real name was, would you believe, Grace Falls, though prior to her rise to stardom she had changed it to Madeleine Xenia-Davis. There was a photograph of her reaching out to her adoring fans. She was something of an icon, a saint, could do no wrong, her name heading countless charities. Yet she proved herself to be a nasty piece of work as it turned out. Even darker than her father. Though the picture had been taken before her downfall, when she was the "good Grace", her duplicity showed itself in her wide, open-mouthed smile, which expressed her gratitude and love for those who revered her yet also, in the curl of her lips and the show of teeth, avarice, self-adulation, something wicked, the self her talents as an actress could not hide.

'But Reemie had the superior gift.

'Was I really so innocent? Wasn't he really so very evil?

'Tell me, is there a God, could there be? When I first entered the abbey, before taking my vow of silence, Abbot Lenten told me that belief in His existence was not requisite, that first I should find the true voice of my soul. And I believe I did when, in that pure silence, I looked up at the stained-glass face in the chapel and I heard another voice. And I still cannot say "yes, I believe". But if I have not heard the voice of God, what I can say, with all conviction, is that I have heard the voice of the Devil.'

The Book

Can't, Pappy, she said. This morning. Crouched in a corner of my room. Though I had barely opened my eyes, no shadow, no dream. And singing to me . . .

> *Oh, you theven thweet thithterth*
> *with innothent eyeth*
> *thing thongth of the thummer*
> *and tell me no lieth.*

   Can't, Pappy, she had said. Because they laugh at me, Pappy. Poor child. She had come home from school, her eyes red and swollen. I decided then and there. I would take her out. Nothing but a charm school turning out featherbrains. Ingebiorg was really quite a bright child in many ways. Though, admittedly, sing she could not. And she had so longed to be in the choir with the other girlies. I told her, she could be in her pappy's choir. The principal soloist, I said. And I told Helnea straight, Ingebiorg had to get out of that school. I would tutor her, I said. Helnea had no interest in the child's education anyway. She had other plans. Those silly girlie books she bought for Inge, debutantes whizzing all over Europe, falling madly in love: *Mademoiselles from Monte Carlo, Debs in Peril, The Blue-Blooded Bachelor, The Million Dollar Dowry*. Helnea treated Inge as eight going on eighteen, encouraged her from the start to dress up in the style of the debutantes who tittered through the pages of her high-society magazines. Because Helnea wanted – nay, needed – to be the mother of a debutante. We lived a comfortable life but 'our lack of social standing', as Helnea called it, was not up to the luxury Helnea had been bred to expect. Helnea would return from one of her all-day lunches with some ridiculous gift for her darling – a necklace of seed pearls, a solid gold mirrored compact, a mini crocodile-skin evening bag. Once, a mink cape costing a fortune that rendered Inge more animal than princess. Those eyes, peering from the fur! Helnea, I said, you cannot make a pig's ear— But she never listened. The name of a leading plastic surgeon began to pepper our brief post-prandial 'chats'. I had caught her on several occasions, lifting the child's chin, perusing that unfortunate face with— What? Certainly with neither sadness nor empathy. Ingebiorg was beautiful. To me she was.

Some days I sit here in my study, this book open, pen in hand. And I write nothing. I look out of the window, to the quad below, expect to see her running across the . . . no. No, she never ran. She was a delicate, tiptoeing child. Undernourished, I feared. I worried Helnea was not feeding her properly. I worried she never dressed her warmly enough. Deathly pale, always. A transparency of skin. On her neck, two veins running from just under her chin to her collar-bone. She called them her 'strings'. *My thtringth, Pappy.* Of a puppet. One vein running from her hip-bone to her sweet little *mons veneris*. Always so cold. Even those places on the body which are ever warm. I stoke up the fire in my room. I don't want her to be cold.

After lunch today. Hellish. Matyeus-Prinn had me sherry-less before him. 'You know, Reemie,' he said (the 'Doctor' has now been dispensed with for good, it would appear), 'the Greek, Reemie, Mr Saspa — whatever his name is, the father of the student. He donates substantially, Reemie.' Helps to fill the university coffers, M-P meant. 'You are aware, Reemie,' he said, 'that Mr Saspa's daughter has only recently joined us, that as far as her father goes, we are still "under review". And like her father, Reemie, she does not suffer fools. It will not do, Reemie, to upset any more students.' The blind eye winked. He told me – snarling – I was making an idiot of myself. It was a matter – apparently – of pulling up socks, a smartening up of ideas all round. He had the audacity to suggest I begin by getting a new hat. An idiot, then, am I, a fool? The devil I am, I thought. Was he aware, I said, that 'foolscap' comes from 'fools' and 'cap' because the size of paper was watermarked originally with the cap of a court jester? M-P was a-rant and a-rave, red faced, spluttering, told me I could stop looking so pleased with myself, this was a serious matter. I was about to tell him, Proof, your Right Honourable Lord Almighty Chancellor, proof! The words – I am still the Master. The words are still in my bones, my dear Matyeus-Prinn-My-Highness. But he did not give me a chance. He ordered me to apologise to the student – *toot sweet, Reemie!*

Sissy, she had said. The Greek girl. A set-up. Had to be. The tutorial. Before lunch, today:
– Lisp, she said.
– What? I said.
– The answer, Dr Reemie.
– What answer?
– To the question.
– What question?
– That you have just arshed me.
(I was beginning to smell a rat. *Arshed*. The accent, thick. The metal teeth-brace.)
– I did?
– The root of lisp, Dr Reemie. The root is *wlyspian*.
– Dear girl, I meant lipsh – I mean lips, I said.

I walked out at that point. Abandoned the tutorial. Someone was having a laugh at my expense. I was finding it hard to concentrate anyway. Thinking of Ingebiorg, early morning, in the corner, singing. The student had wanted me to read her essay (title: *Rasmus Ras: Sight and Sound*). 'Ah, a new girl,' I said, 'and your name is . . . ?' 'Sissy,' she said, 'Sissy Sasparisius.'

Thith-ee. A hoax, a silly cruel student prank. Thithee Thathparithiuth. Rathmuth . . . The tongue will not, is leaden . . . I am supposed to be drafting a paper. Right now. For the university journal. *The Language Tapestry: Tongue as Needle, Word as Weave.* Word as . . . stones, sticks. *Sissy. Sissy-boy. Mummy's boy.* Sticks. Stones. Silly schoolboys, she said, feathers for brains. Not like my Rob-err, she said. Mutti.

Earlier this evening, I must have dozed off in front of what should have been the first page of my paper. A dream. I was seated at a vast banquet table in Gladsheim, within the golden walls, beneath the golden roof of the greatest of the palaces of the Norse gods. Beside me, in his cloak of dark blue, his helmet decorated with an eagle, sat Odin, the Great One. He was throwing bones to the hounds at his feet. Odin and I were chatting – like old friends! And there was Mutti, with her tarot and schnapps, making a show of herself, letting me down, the drink, as usual, causing her to become increasingly morose, her cards predicting more and more doom. *You will look after me, won't you, Roberr, when I am old? Oh, but look, Roberr, the cards, they tell me you are leaving. Oh, don't leave, don't desert your poor Mutti, Roberr!* Dess-air, she pronounced it dess-air. Could she never get the words right? You're the one, Mutti, who wants me to go to university. No, stay, Rob-err, she pleaded, stay with me. And she clung on, even as I walked away, out through the great door of Gladsheim, dragging her as I shuffled along, her arms wrapped tight around my calf. Not a dream. A memory. Among many others. Mutti. At the front door, in her oyster silk dressing gown, waving me off to school. Mutti, at the door, still in her oyster silk, waving me home from school. Never once so much as let me kick a ball around with the other boys. *Sissy-boy, Mutti's boy. Rob-err, Rob-err, Mutti wants, Mutti needs* . . . I was never allowed to play. I had little time. I had to look after her. She was always so, so demanding.

I loved my Mutti. Very much. To love is to please. *Lieber. Lee-ber-ater*. To love is to free. It was never freedom. Her white-frosted talons — like teeth! The female mouth. The horror. Could not move, breathe. *S-mothered*. Her cold fingers — like ice.

I discouraged Ingebiorg from playing with other children. She shied from their company anyway, from their cruelty. She was ripe fodder. Their robustness overwhelmed her. There were, I recall, a couple of young males — twins — who lived across the way. The father was something high in banking, extensively well connected, according to Helnea. Helnea invited the boys to lunch with Ingebiorg on several occasions, leaving them to their own devices while she gadded about town with her ladies. Leaving them to me. But I had important work to do, Helnea, I said, papers to mark, papers to write, surely she could not expect me to, to . . . One time, the noise below was intolerable. I came down from my study to find them charging about the rooms, whooping like savages, chasing poor Inge, who was looking dangerously high coloured. How old are you boys? Eight years, sir, they said, in unison. Just the right age, then, I said. Now, see that cellar door? There's a troll behind it, sharpening his knives, waiting. And do you know, boys, what he's waiting for? I put my hand to my trousers, to my flies, stuck out a finger, waggled it. They knew, all right! Their faces! They fled. Last we saw of the little maggots. I had to protect her.

You have to protect me, Roberr, she'd say. From what, Mutti? I never knew. She never told. I was born with the rope already around my neck. Her cord, like steel, steel. Clever, my son is very clever, Mutti would say, to everyone, anyone. In the bank, in the butcher's buying sausages. Always got his nose in a book, she'd tell them. *My zohn, the professor*. She'd rehearse it, in the mirror, slurring and wobbling with the schnapps. *My shon, extraordinarily clever. My zhon, the profeshor. Eth, Mutti, eth.* I tried to tell her, to get her to pronounce those S's. It was the blind leading the blind. Just like my Inge, I practised and practised. *What'z zat? What'z zeez, Rob-err?* I suspected she was doing it on purpose. I spent hours writing them instead. After school, after what I'd had to endure in the playground. That indescribable pleasure – after tea (Mutti was a lamentable cook, it was eggs and fish mainly) I would take out my softest pencil and cover the white space with those beautiful curls, forming the letter with its double twist, over and over. It gave me, I see now, a release. As I drew each letter, I forgave myself, though I had never been able to articulate precisely what it was I had done wrong. I drew those letters with such intense concentration that sometimes she would catch me drooling on to the table. *Close that filthy little mouth of yours, Rob-err.* And Mutti would box my ears. She was like that, one minute soft as wild goose down, the next . . . Ach, I see her holding aloft that huge pair of dressmaker's scissors. Though Mutti never made a dress in her life. Sharp scissors, and cold against my skin. *I shall cut that tongue off, Rob-err, if you don't close that mouth. Cut it right off – and zumzink else too!* And her eyes would flash and, though she'd never say it, I knew what she was silently threatening to do.

I have been invited to a party. In honour of Gordon McGourd, newly elected professor of the English Language. Ha – huh – ach. Cannot attend. Sick. So sorry.

To profess. (First recorded, so it is said, in English in Palgrave's *Lesclarcissement.*) Amongst other things it means: to claim openly to have feelings. To profess – lay claim to, allege, pretend to. I profess. I had feelings. Feelings awakened. When Ingebiorg was born. Between a father and daughter, a most special love. Between a mother and son . . . ?

Where is she? She comes now only in my dreams. And even then is somehow less a presence than an impression. Glittering, radiating light that day I saw her in town, by the bookshop. But as if that were her zenith and she is a falling star I shall never catch, a moon on the wane, a sun going down – she who was once my whole world. Reaching but not touching me, mouth opened but no words, and I fear I shall never hear what she was . . . How to bear losing her again?

Summoned to the Godfather again. Back to the real world. I am bedevilled. The paper I submitted for *QUID* contains errors. Errors that ranged, in M-P's words, 'from the simple typo to the grossest faux-pas'. And I had misquoted, twice. He wanted to know what I meant by (quote) 'all this nonsense and rubbish about feelings, about proposing a world without language'. M-P stood then and read from my paper, as though announcing a verdict in court – *thought is feeling bowdlerised by words . . . a Utopia of silence and actions*. He asked me what it meant – he asked me what I thought it meant – he asked me what I thought I was thinking of. By then I was confused. According to M-P, my paper fell far below the standards of the *Quarterly University Digest*. He asked whether I was a hundred per cent. Was it stress, age, perhaps? I wanted to vanquish His Most High Executioner Prynn then and there. I had nothing to say. As I turned to close the door of his study, I raised Mistletoe high, as if in a gesture of farewell. Who does M-P think he is – God?

Allie

'Jo had given birth to a baby without eyes, ears or mouth. The baby was struggling, as though trying to find a way out of itself, and though Jo was trying to comfort it, the baby was more and more distressed. Then she handed it to me but it was slippery with blood and the pathetic little body dropped from my hands, falling on to the concrete floor which had turned into a slow-flowing stream of blood. I could see its tiny hands reaching out, heard the thin exhausted wailing, as though the baby had been suffering long and terrible distress. And all the while, it was drifting farther away and I was reaching for it. My arm growing, extending, but never quite far enough. Then the stream turned into rapids, into a waterfall, and at the edge, just before the baby went over, it raised its head, and I saw the fair curls, saw it was her face, heard her voice calling, *Mummy, Mummy*.

'In Jo's house, the next morning, I woke, just before dawn, with her name on my lips, *Orelia . . . Orelia*. My arms still reaching, the nightmare still vivid. Through the half-closed curtains, the metal-grey sky turned to black as I switched on the bedside light. I thought of the night before, in the Womb Room with Jo, when she'd told me her news.

'The way she had greeted me at the front door, I sensed there was something on her mind. The long, intense enveloping, then patting my back to comfort rather than in welcome. As she held me, I briefly pictured us, as one, the cell complete, unsplit, in our mother's womb. As we drew apart, I felt an acute sense of separation. And I saw that small smile playing over her lips, when she'd looked away, into a private place, her arms loosely wrapped about her, nursing a secret.

'Welcome to the Womb Room, she'd said, leading me to what had been called the den, tucked at the back of the house, now painted a deep pink, all the furniture replaced by giant red velvet cushions scattered over the floor, two speakers angled in such a way as to send the music pulsing through the bare floorboards. Someone had told her it was like a womb, she said, and she laughed awkwardly, eyelids lowered as though in embarrassment.

'She looked beautiful that evening, particularly so. She wore a long dress, pink with gold stripes, which folded softly about her. Sitting cross-legged, her head back against a cushion, she reminded me of an illustration of a goddess in a book I had read on ancient civilisations, both regal and primitive, an earth mother.

'She poured red wine, though none for herself, told me the latest news about the boys' progress at school, how Mikey was jealous because Jake was going to be fitted for a brace, that Bart was away on some self-development course. He had to climb a forty-foot pole, she said, with a harness.

'"But you know what Bart's like with heights," she said.

'Then she coloured slightly, remembering perhaps that I had once told her that anything could be a trigger. For that slow-motion imagined scene, Orelia, falling through the air. As though it were a memory.

'We were sitting directly opposite one another, not quite a mirror image. When we were very young, people couldn't tell us apart, our only physical difference that Jo was deaf, obviously not immediately apparent. I remembered the frustration, why Jo often seemed to ignore me. When I was old enough to understand, I saw how her deafness, rather than being a lack, made her special, exceptional, was something I did not have, that I was merely, only, normal. Her hair always seemed shinier than mine. She was prettier. Because she smiled more.

'A mirror image, at first. But something came between us, disturbed the symmetry. We were no longer two separate beings. It was as though Jo was the real flesh-and-blood person and I was just a weak reflected version. The first time I felt it was at the prize-giving, when I saw her upon the stage receiving the young journalist's prize. Since that day, because of what I had done, because of the guilt, there was a boundary between us.

'Sitting with Jo, that night, in her red room, I realised I was the one who had drawn the boundary. And thinking of the words of the priest, I felt our separation more acutely than ever. I wanted to confess. I had no idea we both had a confession to make.

'I used to worry that Jo might read my thoughts, would hear the voice of conscience. There were times I wished she could, if only to be relieved of having to tell her myself what I was about to tell her, in that long silence, when she was changing the music. An African drumbeat. She sat with her arms out, her palms flat on the wooden floor, feeling the music. Looking at her, thinking, in her pink-and-gold robe, she appeared like some exotic butterfly stretching its wings. Pink and gold.

'She was wearing pink too that day, so many years ago. A new outfit. We'd all had new clothes especially for the occasion. Mother in her lily-white linen. Jo, up on the stage. "In the pink," mother said. She was. Up on that stage, she was shining.

'I was steeling myself to tell her when the African drumbeat ended, gradually ceasing like a weakening heartbeat. She looked at me.

'"Allie, I'm pregnant."

'I swallowed. My smile pushed against my cheeks.

'"Not quite three months," she said. She laughed. "It wasn't on this year's shopping list. I'm blaming Bart."

'In the brief silence – the words she couldn't say:

'*Sorry, Allie, sorry I'm having a baby, another baby, and you've lost your only child.*

'I thought I'd got over it, that darkest despair that had made a witch of me. I grew warts, a hooked nose, carried a child-catcher's net, played the Pied Piper's tune. For weeks after, I'd go to the swing park. I cast spells on every innocent cherub, on all those pregnant women who seemed to cross my path with the perverse insistence of single magpies. I walked through a park one day, came across a hillside of newly planted saplings, each one supported by a small white cross. Graveyard of a hundred children.

'A girl. A girl, Jo, so happy for you, truly. I was. But I knew it would be a girl.

'I did not sleep easy, looked at the clock, watched the second hand shuddering into place, each second an effort. I thought of the child growing inside her, laid my hands on my stomach, palms flat against its surface. A surface, nothing inside. I heard the creak of floorboards as the twins made their way along the landing to my room. They peeped around the door, shuffled in, holding hands. Jake and Mikey. Little between them except Mikey's slightly smaller and Jake has his father's dimple on his chin. Aunty Allie? they whispered, Jake's hand fluttering a sign, *Hi, Auntie*. I thought of Jo's joy as she'd answered my silent question when they were born. Perfect, Allie, she'd said, eyes, mouth, nose, fingers, toes, ears, she said, ears, perfect. They can hear me, Allie. But she'd taught them to sign. To think, she has never heard their voices. And I hear Orelia's, every day.

'Before returning to their beds, they climbed beside me for a hug. When I held them, I recalled that intimacy of holding a child fresh from their bed, as if the memory comes fresh, is that palpable, before the full realisation hits, as it still does, that I've lost her.

'The mother-protector, Jo, at the wheel the next day, driving us back from the outing, through blustery wind, at the helm of a storm-tossed ship. She has always had a solid anchoring presence. She had a sheen, already wore that "bloom". She caught me looking, smiled apologetically. I felt grey, used up by the night, a shrunken version of my sister. The sky was also grey, darkening in places, collecting into heavy clouds, the wind gusting. Jo's always loved wind. Breath of the world, she says, voice of the earth. Since childhood, she's always had special words for wind – *crazy, hysterical, naughty, seductive, demonic*. When people say the wind dances, Jo says it's doing the can-can, the foxtrot, a dreamy pas-de-deux. Wind for Jo is seen, is more than simply felt. *The summer rain speckling your skin, the fingertips of falling snow.* I used to believe the world Jo inhabited was enhanced by her missing sense, that I was the one lacking.

'After we'd had our sandwiches and tea in the car, we walked, watching the boys running on ahead, arms raised, half jumping, half lifted by the strong gusts. What's the wind like, Jo? Dangerous, she said. I heard the gutsy laugh, saw the mock-evil look in her eyes, the lunging-forward movement she does sometimes, like a low, dipping tango step, her arms high, those theatrical exaggerated movements of hers, that ease and freedom to which I could never abandon myself, that I envied.

'As she drove us back, I looked out of the window at the countryside – field hedgerow field. A somehow satisfying repetition, Phineas once told me. Satisfying? Free and enclosed, he said, free and enclosed, neither too much of one nor the other. I could see how it appealed to him.

'Phineas never liked to be too enclosed, never felt at ease in the confines of the flat – his love of the sky. But I sensed also that he was afraid. He'd asked me, once, if I fancied renouncing the world of academia to be a farmer's wife. He harboured a pipe dream, he told me, of acquiring a small-holding. It was the word "wife" which had snagged, somehow seeming far more preposterous than the image of myself tending goats, collecting eggs. I realised I had never imagined, never so much as considered, our future, not even when I was pregnant with Orelia, and after she was born her presence only kept us, me, somehow more fixed in the present.

'Hedgerow field hedgerow. The silences between my sister and me, the brown-earthed, crop-bare fields. We were at the farthest edges of that which had always separated us, of all that was unspoken. You will come and see us? Jo had said earlier that day. I knew she meant "after the baby's born". I thought again of her baby inside, connected and warm, plumping into life. Within me, the memory of a child, a small cloud.

'In one of the fields, there was a scarecrow. He wore a stovepipe hat, a black frock-coat, one sleeve held out as if he were waving. As we went past he seemed to follow us, his head turning. A scarecrow, I said, look, boys. Just then the car swerved, the force throwing us forward, as Jo took the bend too sharply, the car crashing into the bank on the opposite side, Jo crying out as she was thrown against the steering wheel.

'We all sat in shock, white faced. Mikey whispered *Mummy?*, patting her shoulder. Jo gasped, reached out, head down, palms pressed against the dashboard, panting heavily, like a woman in labour. Black ice, she said. Then she went quiet. Then she began to moan. I drove us back. When Jo got out of the car, I saw the blood staining her jeans. Jo saw it too and just then rain fell, icy, fat, heavy drops. Ink blots, ink blots, she kept saying, her voice thin, pathetic. She was holding out her palms, screwing up her eyes as she looked at the sky, as if she'd forgotten the bloodstain blooming between her thighs and growing down one inside leg like a reaching arm. She stood, as if paralysed, back bent, legs apart, looking down now, like a comedian exaggerating surprise. Ink blots, she whispered. Then her face crumpled as she clutched her belly.

Page 213, draft, A Parent's Guide to Bereavement.

Many parents fall prey to the same magical thinking that stops you stepping on pavement cracks in case you'll be poisoned. This, of course, is about setting boundaries in the uncharted territory of imagination, of fear of the unknown, in order to provide oneself with comforting limits and struc-ture. It is also a way of controlling one's own punishment, rather like a patient allowed to administer and regulate post-op medication. Pain control. We need a reason for the death of a child. We need to feel guilty to survive.

A mother has an argument with her teenage daughter before the daughter goes out with friends. The daughter is killed on the way by a drunk-driver. Yet the mother will find

*a way to blame herself. If she had not upset her by shouting,
her daughter would have paid more attention crossing the
road, and so on. Magical thinking takes over, can be used to
explain the rest of one's life long after the death of the child,
even extending, sometimes, back to the period before the
child was born. In fact, one's entire life can be reinterpreted,
so that one small, bad but relatively insignificant act in one's
childhood is the seed for everything bad that has happened
in one's life – a false star, wrong-guiding. Life becomes a chain
of negative connections, consequences, the death of the child
merely another, and so the chain may continue . . .*

'A nurse took Jake and Mikey off to get something to eat. I
found myself in the hospital chapel, making notes for my book
to take my mind off what I was sure they'd have to tell me
about Jo's condition. A small and claustrophobic room, inten-
tionally, perhaps, in order that you would not linger too long,
that your grief might be temporarily contained to be unleashed
elsewhere later. The air was thick with the pain of loss, loss
concentrated, compacted, concertinaed, which would unfold
into an eternal threnody. White walls, pale blue carpet, on one
wall a small blue stained-glass arched window, an eye. But on
the facing wall a large plain wooden cross, rough hewn and
with large iron nails, appeared overwhelmingly life-size and
disturbing, its surface bereft, as if the Christ had just slipped
from it and walked away. I imagined him lying in one of the
hospital beds, a nurse tending his wounds.

'Jo was sleeping when I went in to see her. She looked pale,
her hands on the sheet protecting her belly.

'"I'm sorry, Jo," I whispered.

'She opened her eyes, her smile quick but, I knew, sincere.

'"It's OK, Allie." And she reached to pat my hand.

'Bart came to take me and the boys home. Jo had to stay in
hospital overnight, to make sure there were no further complications. Before he went to bed, Jake gave me a present. I opened

the handkerchief to find a tiny plastic lamb inside. There was a mark on its back in red felt pen. *It's got a hurt, Auntie Allie, like Mummy.* I closed my fingers around it. Bones inside flesh. Stone inside soft fruit. Such a small thing. Such a bad thing to do. Took my innocence away.

'Stolen, wasn't it – her innocence. And Viviane can never have it back.'

Marguerite

'*Mea culpa Mea culpa*. Whispered over and over, in that silvery voice, like a mantra . . . that had me believe . . . *Mea culpa*.

'"A bad mother, Markeet?" said Max. "You tell me about your wild-child Viviane. But not so much of your other daughter, Gwynne."

'"Gwynne is deaf, Dr Kenning."

'Perhaps it was the way I said it.

'"And you blame yourself for that too, Markeet?"

'I showed Max the two paintings in the madonna book that reminded me of Gwynne. The Cassatt, *Baby Reaching for an Apple*. Look now, how your eye is drawn to the child's hands, that pouchy flesh, just like Gwynne's. Then the Batoni, *Mother and Child*, the infant Jesus with his hand upon Mary's face. And I felt, as I feel it now, her small hand on my cheek the day she lost her hearing.

'*Your fault, Markeet? Something you did or did not do?*

'She was four and a half years old. We were having a picnic by the weir. Phineas was telling me some awful joke. What was it? Something about "*le monocle de mon oncle*". That awful French accent! Phineas couldn't tell a joke to save his life, and so corny I'd always laugh. Gwynne came running to me, a puzzled look in her eyes. *Mumma, where's your laughing gone?*

'*Your fault, Markeet?*

'*Your fault, Maggie.*

'*Your fault, Mrs Goode . . .*

'We didn't know, realise, until later. After the picnic, when we got back to Castle Keep, Gwynne went out on to the hill, to be with the animals, she said. When she came home, she still had that puzzled look. *The animals won't talk to me, Mumma*, she said.

'The doctors asked whether she'd recently had mumps.

Scarlet fever? Any serious infection? But neither of the girls had suffered so much as a cold. Healthy, always. You must be doing something right, Maggie, Phineas used to say. There were countless tests, consultations. Severe sensori-neural deafness. Nothing they could do.

'"Severe sensori-neural deafness, Markeet? Then nothing you did, or did not do," Max said.

'And it was then, at the hospital, talking to Max, that I remembered how hard Phineas and I had worked to give Gwynne as much stimulation as we could. We learnt sign language, found a good deaf school. Phineas must have read every book on the subject. With my artist's eye, I showed Gwynne a world she couldn't hear but could still see, still feel, smell. We did our best to give Viviane equal attention and love. And it was Viviane who accepted her sister's deafness more readily than anyone. That bond they had was strengthened by it. Gwynnie hears with her eyes, she'd say proudly.

'Talking to Max, memories . . . *traces of the original . . .* reappeared. *Love and memories.* Like Gilda said.

'One day, in Gilda's room, she was making a cup of tea and I was telling her about the girls, how, when they were little, they'd take their toy animals and dolls for a picnic in the garden.

'"They had these plastic tea-sets, Gilda, and I'd give them chocolate fingers and grapes and jam sandwiches cut into postage-stamp squares."

'Gilda was standing beside me, pouring the tea, and she reached out, placed her hand on my head, stroked my hair.

'"Love and memories, Maggie Goode," she said, "that's what children give you."

'And I thought of a scene, an everyday moment I'd witnessed as a child. I was on my way to school one morning when, passing by a window, I saw a mother giving breakfast to her daughter. The girl was chattering away, the mother pouring a glass of milk, listening, stroking her daughter's hair, in such a familiar, absent-minded way, which somehow made it seem more intimate, more enviable. Sitting with Gilda, I saw myself with the girls, having tea after school in the summer when I'd put a little table in the garden and they'd tell me their news about school. I saw myself, pouring glasses of the home-made lemonade they loved, then leaning to kiss them, my hand smoothing their backs, brushing hair from their eyes, small spontaneous acts of affection. Memories returning, memories that had been buried beneath darker scenes, hidden, like Viviane hid.

'A scene: Viviane, perched on the back of an armchair, huddled, the hood of her black jacket pulled up. Her face looks sallow and through the window its surface appears like craquelure. I wave but she does not respond, though she seems to be looking right at me. She's staring, her dark-ringed eyes seeing something I cannot. I don't want to leave her this evening. *Are you all right, Viviane? Will you be OK?* All through the art class, I am picturing her face. I hurry back home but she is asleep. He's in the studio. Reemie.

'"Was everything all right this evening, Dr Reemie?" I say. "Only I was a bit worried about leaving Viviane."

'"What? Oh, yes, everything has been fine, Mrs Goode, just fine and dandy."

'"I know she's in safe hands, Dr Reemie. But she's been quiet lately, you know, wrapped up in herself. I don't know if you've noticed—"

'"Nothing," he says, "nothing at all. Worrying over nothing, Mrs Goode. She's been delightful," he says, "absolutely delightful. An angel, in fact. Mothers and daughters, Mrs Goode. I can imagine how difficult it must be sometimes."

'He was looking at a postcard I'd stuck to the wall. A greenish-grey lichen-covered gravestone, with its bleak epitaph. I'd found it among some of my sketches, had no idea where it had come from. Reemie was muttering to himself . . . *Mea culpa, mea culpa.* As if he was putting the words into my mind.

'But they were there already, since that day I went up Mount

Repentance with my father, since that sun set like the eye of the devil on my back.

'And I think he knew that. The guilt I had lived with ever since. I think Reemie knew. And that's how he did it – isn't it?

'Early this morning before the family was up I went to my studio. *Family* – seems such a fragile word. We are getting stronger. It's hard, but I feel our growing strength. Together, yet inhabiting our own spaces. Though Gwynne and Viviane are never far from one another . . . seeing Viviane brushing Gwynne's hair, the way she used to . . .

'I go to my studio most mornings. I love the light in the early mornings, the light now returning to Castle Keep . . . The dawn sky was clear, the sun coming up and the moon still bright. And I could hear it – *Mea culpa* . . . becoming fainter and fading into silence, and within me, a measure of peace.'

Viviane

'Don't you tell. Don't tell a soul. Don't you dare. Down in the oubliette. To forget. With the dust of the bones of her family. *Mad mad Miri-Anne Dupree. Pray, do you pray for me?* For three years I kept the secret of Castle Keep. Did it protect us? Sweet Jesus, no. Because Gwynnie was asleep and Maggie was at her art class and Phineas was out with his books and Allie Finlay. I was praying. *Please, please, Gwynnie, find me.* In the bathroom. Behind the white door. Open the door. No, don't, Gwynnie! Don't come in. No, please don't do that, you mustn't do that. Watching Maggie painting in her studio, following the tip of her brush on the canvas. She was painting a body. Her brush caressing the canvas. It felt like that. The tip of the feather over my skin. Our secret. Safe in Castle Keep. Not a word. Not a dicky-bird. The Goddess of Silence, I was, I was Sige. A finger over my lips. Tell not a soul. The story of the broken-hearted man who lost his daughter. I was holding the broken heart in one hand and in the other a feather. Maat's plume. I read it in Mumma's Bible, the one she never read. *Daniel, chapter five, verse twenty-two: Thou art weighed in the balance and art found wanting.* And I was found wanting. Playing the feather over my skin. Feeling the hairs raising goose bumps over my skin. Feeling in spite of myself, hating myself for feeling. The feather. The fear's in *fea-the-r*. Not the pheasant plucker but the pleasant fucker's son. *Yankee Doodle riding on a pony, stuck a feather in his hat, he stuck a feather in his hat now she's his one and own-lee.* To love like no one else has ever been. With Ventman, like with all the bastards. Not a pleasant fucker but a dirty bitch. Lay there so cool, like a shop-window dummy. Like rigor mortis had set in. My cunt was a hole they fell into. And I let them. Do whatever they wanted. Hit me, slap me, beat me. Because I was just a dirty whore. And all the while they were fucking me, I was fucking the life out of him. I'd think, one day I'm gonna clamp my itsy-bitsy little-girl teeth down so hard and bite it off that Little Hans. *Little Hans, see him, weeny Little Hans.* Little Hands. *Little Hans.*

Down in the oubliette and I could hear them above me, Gwynne and the child. Gwynne was calling, *Nyssa, have you seen Viviane?* I couldn't bear the kid being around. Her face. *So-o-o-o innocent, sweet child.* That's why I went. Had to get out of Castle Keep. Couldn't stand it. Gwynne and the kid. And drowning, suffocating in the flood of memories returned. Was like an animal searching for a dying place.'

Gwynne

'Waking that night when Mumma's paintings were destroyed, anguished cries cutting through me, the shudder of doors slammed. Something happening downstairs—

'I got out of bed, crept along the landing. I could see downstairs that the light was on in Mumma's studio. And there was Vivvy, coming up the stairs towards me. And she frightens me, the way she looks, like a dark angel, slowly ascending. Staring, in a dream, a trance. *Vivvy? Vivvy? What's happened, Vivvy?* I can see the thin dark line of her lips pressed tight, see, as she passes by at the top of the stairs, that she's shivering, trembling. Then I see the carving knife in her hand. I call after her again but she goes straight to her room. So I creep downstairs, to Mumma's studio. *Oh, Vivvy! What a mess! What have you done, Vivvy?* All Mumma's painting things, her brushes, her beautiful paints and canvases, all over the floor. And the paintings – *The Mothers* – torn up, in shreds. The canvases look like tongues, like the lolling tongues of dead animals. *Why have you done this, Vivvy?* Then Mumma comes running in. Her hair wild, sticking out. She looks like a madwoman. And she's all covered in paint, her hands, her face, her clothes. And she's talking so fast I can't work out the words. Viv, she's saying, Viv! *Viv! Viv! Viv!* Saying her name, over and over, hands clutching her head as she runs round the studio. And then she goes out. Oh, she's going to kill you, Vivvy, for what you've done to her paintings. Then I run upstairs to look for Vivvy. I'm angry, so angry because of what she's done. When I look back, I see Mumma, outside her studio, down on the floor. And Pappa's beside her, his hand smoothing the hair away from her face. And I turn away to go back upstairs. And what do I see? In the bathroom, the carving knife spearing the seat of the blue chair—

'By the next morning, the mess in the studio had been cleaned up. The torn paintings had been removed. No one spoke of it. Vivvy kept out of everyone's way.

'"Vivvy," I said, "Mumma's paintings. Why, Vivvy?"

'"Who cares?" she said. "Who cares?"

'Never mentioned. It might never have happened. But I could not forget Pappa's face as he crouched beside Mumma, his face smoothed by, settled into, resignation, a relinquishment. And I see her now, Vivvy, standing there, her cry of anguish caught in her eyes.

'Sometimes, after that night, Vivvy would still come to my room, slip into my bed for comfort. But I wouldn't put my arm around her. Not any more. Not after what she'd done to Mumma's paintings.

'Early one morning, I woke to find her sitting at the end of my bed, hugging her knees. She looked cold, her eyes hard, determined.

'"Gwynnie," she said, "promise you won't tell—"

'"Go away, Vivvy."

'"But I want to tell you, Gwynnie. I've got something to tell you. It's a secret."

'I told her to go back to her room. I didn't want to know her secret, I said. I wouldn't listen, I said. And I pulled the covers over my head. Vivvy pulled them back. She was standing over me, her fists clenched, her whole body tight with anger.

"I don't care," she said, "I'm telling you anyway. I will," she said, "now."

'She was looking down, away, her lips quivering. She was fighting back the tears.

'Just as once I had been desperate to know whatever it was she would not tell me, I think she was desperate then – but she couldn't, she could not tell.

'One night, after Viviane had left Castle Keep, one bitter-cold October night, I looked up to find one star shining through a space in the clouds. I remembered a book Pappa had read to us. An important book, Pappa said. *The grown-ups stop seeing . . . that which is most important cannot be seen . . .* Saint-Exupéry's *The Little Prince*. I thought of the last page, the little prince about to fall back to his star. *Everyone finds their way back to their own star.* And I thought of Viviane out there, somewhere.

'I looked out, over the beech hedge, aware, even as my eyes travelled across the field, of him standing there, on the hill, as if his presence had drawn me, held me, as though I had momentarily stepped out of the garden, of everything that lay behind me, of Castle Keep, of my fears for Viviane, of all that was turning over and over within me, as if all that existed in that moment was me and the stag, the branching antlers, like arms supporting me, like the sign for peace. *Quiet*, he seemed to be saying. *Be still, listen, see.* The stag bowed his head, as if to bid farewell, before turning away, moving slowly down the hill, proudly, like the king he was, and disappearing into the forest.

'Earlier that evening, Nyssa was in the bath. She'd wanted me to play, she wanted us to sing. But all I could think of was Pappa's letter, and Viviane. *Quiet, Nyssa, please.* I made the sign: thumb and forefinger making circles, eyes, fingers curling. Like a face, a mask. Nyssa copied, looked through the eyes, laughing, wanted to see herself in the mirror. The mirror was misted. I wiped the glass, saw the white reflected door. Star, scar, white door. Signs in Viviane's notebook, signs collecting—

'There was a stag, years ago, I sometimes caught fleeting glimpses of him through the trees, down in the forest. Sometimes, if I'd woken in the night, I'd look out through my bedroom window and see him up on the hill, watching, watching over me, I liked to think. Sometimes he came right to the beech hedge. But one night, somehow, he had got right into the garden. Perhaps the gate had been left open, or he'd found a gap in the hedge, but there he was, looking up, beautifully majestic in the moonlight. I wanted Vivvy to see. I wanted to tell Vivvy about the stag. But

I couldn't tell, Vivvy. Why couldn't I tell? Because of the story. Because of what he'd told me. *Keep your mouth closed, child. Mustn't listen.* But I wasn't, Professor Reemie, I said, I can't.

'Little hands. He had dainty little hands. Hands you could imagine making lace. For intricate work. Unravelling spider's webs. Teasing. Entwining. Small white fingers weaving Vivvy's raven hair. I'd imagine his voice, soft, snow soft, cotton-wool soft, cloud soft. Hissy, Vivvy said. Like a nest of snakes. And sticky, she said, sticky-thick. As sticky toffee. *Thticky toffeeth—*

'*I bet they wouldn't let you girls have so many toffees.*
   '*Oh, Mumma and Pappa wouldn't mind.*
   '*I rather think they would. But I shan't tell. Not if you girls don't. Go on, have another one.*

'Vivvy was sitting on the arm of the Story Seat, legs swinging. She was singing. She was always singing, rhymes, things she made up . . .

> *I go by the name of a man, a man*
> *Yet as little I am as a mouse*
> *When winter-time comes, I so love to be*
> *In my red undershirt near the house, the house . . .*

'Vivvy, her cheeks bulging with toffees. Two at a time. He always gave Vivvy more than me. I counted. Because she was older, probably.

   '"Five years, three months and six days," I told him, the first time he came to the house.

   '"And Vivvy's eight," I said, "which is only three years more than me."

   '"Ach, eight," he said, "what a good age."

   '"Read us a story," Vivvy said. "Pappa reads us stories. We've got tons of books, heaps, me and Gwynne. But Pappa's got the most. Come and see."

'And she took his hand and I followed as she led him to the library.

'"Hundreds," she said, "look, hundreds and hundreds. Pappa keeps them all in order. He gets cross if you put them back in the wrong place."

'She was skipping, twirling about the room, clapping her hands.

'"What a lot of books, indeed. And which one to choose?"

'I found him one of Pappa's favourites. From the Hans Christian Andersen, *The Wild Swans*. And we all sat together, that first evening he came. And he read the story about the eleven princes bewitched by their stepmother. But not like Pappa read it. Pappa knew the story off by heart. Sometimes, Pappa would even close his eyes, especially when he got to the part where the swans, who are really eleven princes bewitched by their stepmother, fly over the sea, when they see the mountains in the sky, their ice-clad summits shining. *And right at the heart, the most beautiful castle, towered and turreted, surrounded by flowers and palm trees* . . . The look on Pappa's face, as if he were right there, flying with them.

'After Professor Reemie had finished reading, we wanted another story, and another.

'"Ah, but Grimms' tales are so much better," he said. "You know, some of Grimms' tales are true, but they only turned them into stories so children wouldn't be afraid."

'"I'm not afraid," Vivvy said. And she went and fetched Pappa's copy of the Grimm tales.

'"Which one shall we have, girls? 'The Maiden without Hands', 'The Boy Who Went Forth to Learn What Fear Was?,' 'Clever Hans, Lucky Hans, Iron Hans'?"

'"Little hands," I said.

'"But there is no such story, child," he said. And his face went red, deep red, deeper than the scarlet of his waistcoat, than even the crimson lining of his coat. Like he was going to burst. Like he was very very angry.

'"No, Professor Reemie," I said, "I mean you've got little hands."

'I liked it when Dr Reemie started looking after us. *Pro-fess-or*. He told us there was going to be a big ceremony for all the new professors at the university. But we mustn't tell anyone. Not even Pappa. Because he wasn't quite a professor yet, he said. A big secret, he said.

'"What does it mean, then, if you're a professor?"

'"It means you are very clever, child. That no one can trick you."

'"If you're so clever, then you must know lots of stories. Pappa tells us made-up stories. He calls them head stories. But his are always about flying."

'"No, child," he said, "real stories are always from the heart."

'"Then tell us a heart story, Professor Reemie."

'And he did, when the summer had passed, when it was too cold to sit out in the garden. Pappa made a fire in the living room and Mumma made a hot whisky drink for Dr Reemie before she went out teaching.

'And we all got cosy on the big sofa in front of the fire.

'"Are you two girlies sitting comfortably? Good. A heart story, then. *Once upon a time in a distant land of ice and snow, in a place called Nifleheim, there lived gods and giants and dwarves. And the great and noble ruler Odin, descendant of the first frost giant, Ymir. . . .*

'He told us about Odin and his eight-legged steed, Sleipnir, Odin who paid the price for drinking from the Well of Wisdom by plucking out his own eye, about when he hung from the World Tree for nine days and nine nights stuck with his own spear. Dr Reemie's eyes went sad. He stared into the fire with a faraway look. Like me and Vivvy weren't there. Like when Pappa told us the story of the wild swans.

'"Go on, Professor Reemie," Vivvy said, "don't stop."

'"Ach, child, but I cannot."

'Then Vivvy got naughty. If he didn't tell us, she said, she'd take his stick. And she did. Danced around the room with it like a majorette. His walking stick he called Mistletoe. She'd put it on the fire, she said.

'"Give me the stick back, child, there's a good girl."

'"Only if you tell us an Odin story, a heart story. You promised you would."

'"It's not a real stick, anyway," he said, "it's a snake. Look!"

'The stick dropped from Vivvy's hand.

'"I thought you said you weren't afraid of anything," Professor Reemie said.

'"I'm not," Vivvy said.

'"Aren't you, Vivvy? Ah, but everyone's afraid of something. Now, let's have another toffee and I'll tell you a heart story, a different one."

'I never knew when he was going to do it. Pinch my fingers as I reached into the bag. And I loved those creamy toffees. Pinched so hard sometimes. Sudden. Like the beak of a vicious bird. It frightened me a bit. And some of those stories he told us, they frightened me too. And I didn't like it that he liked Vivvy more than me. And I didn't like it when I had to go up to my bed first—

'It was after Viviane left, when I found the notebook, that it began to trickle back. The child lost in the forest following the stream back home. To safety? To answers? For they were there, in Pappa's letter, two words she'd copied over in pencil, like a forger practising another's hand, so that they stood out from the rest, words that I did not notice until much later. Only by then I already knew. Her secret. But one, perhaps, I had always known, had always feared.

> *Pitter-patter, well-a day,*
> *Little Robin flew away;*
> *Where could little Robin be?*
> *Hop-hopped into the Lightning Tree. . . .*

'Always singing, Vivvy. Then she stopped.'

Marguerite

'Old snow grey, the colour of the clouds first thing this morning. But later, on my way here, the February sun was just breaking through. It's been so long a winter, I wondered if there'd ever be a spring.

'It was hard, December was hard, thinking how "new" the year ahead would be. It didn't seem right to be too happy. We celebrated simply, quietly. I bought a present for the family, a journal, leather bound in summer sunshine yellow. You may not understand its significance. A book of truth – for good thoughts, a record of good times, memories, hopes. The book helps us to focus, to look forward, is connecting us. Viviane has taken a photograph of each of us. In our eyes – she's captured it – hope, strength, truth.

'Old snow grey, you know, how snow acquires that grimy film after a few days. *Why don't you paint your old Gilda a picture, Maggie Goode? All those pretty colours.* But I stopped painting. After *The Mothers*. For ten years I did not pick up a brush.

'*The Mothers* – vast ten-by-ten foot canvases ranged around the studio walls like a growing rank of avatars ready to swoop. There was no initial grand vision, you understand, no conscious design, but something inspired perhaps by a dream recurring over years.

'In the dream I am holding a pen and set before me, not paper, but a sheet of mirrored glass. I have been instructed to draw her face, my mother's face. I know that if I do not draw her face I shall be annihilated. I hold the pen raised above the glass. I long to draw, can almost see it. Her face. But each time I put the pen to the glass, I freeze, am paralysed. I look down into the mirror until my eyes ache, until my eyes feel as if they are popping from their sockets. But I see nothing in the mirror, neither my mother's face, nor my own.

'Phineas was so happy at first, to see me so engaged. I picture him now, standing in the doorway of my studio. He was leaning against the door frame, as he sometimes did, one leg bent behind him. Like a bird, a crane. It could have been a casual pose, nonchalant, his hands in his pockets, head back, watching me. But Phineas would grip the wood of the frame, his hands behind him, as though he were on a high mountain ledge.

'"No more sunsets, then, Maggie? I envy you, Maggie," he said. "Your creativity. It is as if you have a root down into the soul of the world."

'I had imagined there would be three paintings, a triptych. I completed twelve in all. Towards the end, I was driven by an uncontrollable force. I was like a mad musician, the music turned up full volume, filling my studio, my brush, my instrument. Each painting followed the same process. First, I'd sketch in the figures, just basic shapes, then I'd paint in the background, blues, browns, lilacs, soft muted colours. And then I'd go over the background again, working on areas, tones, the shadows, the suggestions of shapes I could never quite realise. The background completed, I'd then set to work on the figures. Sometimes they were close, the mother with her arms around her child, the pair huddled together. Or sometimes I would draw them apart, looking for or turning away from each other. But however hard I laboured, they remained featureless, indistinct, each face a cloud that would not pass over what it covered, blank ovals I could not humanise. And each time, though I experienced a mounting tension, I could not resist, I had to continue. With each painting, there was what I can only describe as a disengagement within as I stared at those empty faces, my eyes deep in the canvas, as though I were buried in a snowdrift, going farther in, down.

'And, simultaneously, an awareness, a shadow on my back, his eyes on me. As though he were there, behind me, Father. *Look to thine own heart, you sinners, look for the source of your sins*, cried out my father the preacher, loud, deep, booming. Then that low, soft, almost sweet sibilant silky whisper . . . *Guilt, Mrs Goode, every mother's burden. Ach! the sorrows of hell, the sorrows of hell.*

'I began work on the paintings just before Allie Finlay started coming to Castle Keep, worked on them for almost three years until a few weeks before Phineas left us. At first, I believed that was the reason he'd left, because I was painting by then with such fierce and overriding passion, obsession, to the exclusion of everything. I thought I had driven Phineas away, into the arms of Allie Finlay.

'That blue of her dress. The first time she came to Castle Keep. The first time I saw her. She was wearing a blue dress, cobalt, the exact blue I was using in *The Mothers*.

'When I was a child, before I learnt the proper names for colours, I made up my own – pollen yellow, petunia pink, summer grass green, conker brown. But red was always naphthol crimson. And blue, blue was the colour of my mother's eyes, manganese blue hue.

'I used to paint at Miss Connova's house. She was my favourite teacher. Once a week, when my father had to work late at the office, Miss Connova would take me home with her after school. She'd give me tea, fish paste and cucumber sandwiches and vanilla cake with lemon icing, a mug of warmed honeyed milk. She'd sit in her armchair doing her marking on a small card table. I'd look over at Miss Connova, imagine this was what it must be like, how it was for the other girls at school, to have a mother. I'd look at her, whisper to myself, *Mother-mother-mother*, feeling the soft shape of the word, which I'd whisper aloud in bed, the dark silence replying, *Not here-not here*. When I'd finished my tea, she'd cover the table with a turquoise-and-green paisley plastic cloth.

'Then Miss Connova would fetch the box of paints and paper. We'd talk about school for a while and then she'd fall silent, engrossed in her work. I loved being there among the brightly coloured pottery and paintings the children had made for her at school. My pictures took pride of place in her mini-gallery. I loved the quick sound of her red pen making ticks down the page, *swish-swish-swish*, like the gentle regular ticking of a grandfather clock, constant, dependable, while I covered the large squares of paper Miss Connova bought in bulk. Butcher's paper, to wrap the meat for customers. Smooth and shiny on one side, dull on the other, which was better for painting. My pictures were neat and predictable at first, houses with four curtained windows, smoke curling from the chimney, rose bushes in the fenced garden. Try to see things as they really are, Maggie, Miss Connova said one day, not how you think they're supposed to be. She said I should try to find the truth of what I saw. And my drawings began to come to life on the page, as if the colours had an energy of their own. Miss Connova told me I had talent, a gift I'd been born with. I must never give up, she said.

'Miss Connova gave each of the class a new pack of crayons. Our homework was to draw a picture, a special holiday memory. I knew what I was going to do. But next morning, I had nothing to show Miss Connova. *No picture, Maggie? But you must have done something special over the holidays.* We had, my father and I. A fortnight at the seaside in the guest house with the kind landlady, like we did every summer. And every summer there was a fair, and after we'd had our tea with the other guests, when it was getting dark and the fairground was lit like fairyland, my father would take me on all the rides, the waltzers and the swing-boats, and best of all I loved the Ferris wheel, my father holding me close. And that was special.

'But even more special was my birthday present that year. My birthday fell a week after we'd come back from the seaside. A pink quilted dressing gown and matching nightie. I looked like a proper young lady, my father said. A special memory. Me, in my new pink dressing gown, fitting at my father's feet while he plaited my long hair before bed, his fingers gentle, patient, though it must have been hard to do those plaits, which must have reminded him of my mother. But I couldn't tell Miss Connova why I hadn't done my picture.

'The evening before, after we'd had tea, I settled down to do my homework. Which crayon to use? Pale pink like dog-rose petals or the bright pink like bubblegum? I can't decide. So I draw the outlines of my picture first, the kitchen, the cooker, me and my father. But I want it to be my mother, my mother plaiting my hair before bed. My father's drying the dishes, listening to the radio, so I ask again, *How did my mummy die?* And he stands there for what seems like ages, rubbing the cloth over the plate, over and over. So I ask again. And then he stops drying the plate and he comes over, and there's such an odd look on his face. Like he's going to cry. Like he's crosser than I've ever seen him. And he picks up my crayons and he breaks them in half – *snap-snap-snap*. And then he stops, and blinks quickly, and looks down at my crayons in bits, shaking his head like he can't believe what he's just done. And I don't know either why he's broken all my colours. And my father opens his mouth, like he's just about to speak, to say he's sorry, I'm hoping. But he doesn't say sorry. He just goes away, upstairs. And now I can't do my picture – even if I had more crayons I couldn't.

'I've often wondered whether Miss Connova had spoken to my father. Because I came home from school one day to find a wooden box on the kitchen table, an artist's box of supplies, full of paints, crayons, pens and drawing paper. He never actually said sorry, but I knew he was, realise now how difficult it must have been for him. And some time around then, on the way home from school one day, out of the blue, he told me my mother liked to paint. Not professional, he said, like Miss Connova said I'd be one day. Like a hobby, he said. He told me that was how I got my name, after Marguerite Gerard, an artist my mother loved. Years later, I discovered her work, her paintings of domestic life, mothers and daughters, recognised the fading framed print that had always hung in the kitchen at home – *The Drawing Lesson*. My father fetched a box from the attic that evening. That was when he showed me the painting. Up until then, I remember only an old battered photograph that my father kept in his wallet, of him and my mother, taken before they were married. The two of them on a tandem. The photograph out of focus.

'The painting was wrapped in thin beige cloth, the cloth stained, like bruised skin. A head-and-shoulders portrait. I saw the ornate M in the bottom right-hand corner. M for Marie. My father hung it on my bedroom wall. But I didn't take it with me when I left home.

'Once, Phineas brought me some art books from the Reading Room. I came across a portrait, *Head of a Woman*, by John Currie. A dark-haired woman with an earthy-gypsy look. Solid, strong, the forehead square. She wore her hair in plaits. Phineas said the woman reminded him of me. The long dark plaits, the background glowing scarlet crimson, vivid red orange. Just like my mother's self-portrait. Only my mother's eyes were blue. Manganese blue hue.

'There was a tube of paint in the box. Naphthol crimson. My father said I could have it. I liked untwisting the cap, looking at the gleaming red paint. But I didn't use it. I kept it on the table beside my bed. It made her seem real to me.

'*Her eyes, you've your mother's eyes, lass.* Even at eight years old, I knew, from the painting that looked down at me from my bedroom wall, that I would become the image of my mother. I was already beginning to understand, from the way my father looked at me, I was a continuous reminder of what he had lost. I was born and she had died. But I still did not know how she had died.

'I remember visiting her grave, the way my father carefully pulled the weeds from the headstone, as though their roots might be curled around her bones which in my mind I fleshed so she became a sleeping princess, the way he set the daffodils one by one in the vase, his lips moving in silent prayer. The way he'd wipe over the gravestone, over the letters of her name, the way he'd brush and plait my hair.

'But as I got older, I became more aware – among the tenderness, those black moods, the voice of the preacher like the voice of another speaking through him. The voice of the accuser. Because I was alive and my mother was dead. Watching my father, shirtsleeves rolled up, oiling Old Balthazar, polishing the blocks of letters, making them shine, his movements slow, considered, like a surgeon, or someone taking care of a sick person. When I was a teenager, I told him once he cared more for that damn press than he did for me.

'Did his moods get worse as I got older, did I just imagine what was in his eyes, his voice? What was it Miss Connova once said? *You know, Maggie, it's an awful job sometimes, trying to understand other people. But if we love them, we must keep trying.* And I knew she meant my father. And I did love him. Even when he held that chair high as if about to strike.

'Did he know I was there, in the kitchen, one night, late? I was on the floor, under the table, collecting up the crayons that had spilled. My father came in. He was muttering. I heard his fist banging on the table. I was frightened then. I don't know why he'd gone into such a rage. I could see his slippered feet pacing about the kitchen. He was growling. *Please don't hurt me, Father.* I looked from under the table. He was shaking, spluttering, almost choking on the words. *You, you! Why did she have to die? Why couldn't she live? Why couldn't she live, live, live!* And I shut my eyes tight, heard the chair come down hard on the kitchen tiles, heard the wood splintering like the shrieks of a living thing. Then there was a strange muffled sound. And when I opened my eyes and crawled out a little from under the table, there was my father. He was leaning over the sink, his face buried in a tea towel, crying. Yes, I loved him, but I couldn't understand him. *You, you* . . . I was so sure he meant me.

'And I loved Viviane. But I could not understand why she . . . what was . . .

'Gwynne was never much interested in painting. Gwynne preferred her forest, the animals. But Viviane used to love to draw. She'd come into my studio sometimes while I was working, take paper and charcoal and stretch out on the floor. She'd do these odd Lowry-type stick people, or mazes, intricate labyrinths begun at the edge of the paper, working in towards the centre, her face close to the paper, the tip of her tongue poking from the corner of her mouth, her body appearing somehow retracted, as though clutched up, as though she were drawing the lines of charcoal around herself, as though that was where she wanted to be, at the centre of the maze. Or was she at the centre and trying to find a way out?

'One day, she must have crept into the studio without me noticing, the music too loud, perhaps. When I turned to reach for more paint, I saw her sitting at the table, a stick of charcoal in her fingers, the paper still blank. She was staring at me. I set down my brush, turned the music down, went over and sat at the table beside her. And her eyes seemed suddenly to find me, as though I had just come into focus, and she put down the charcoal and slipped off the stool and stood close by me. She put her hand in my lap. She was just nine years old. *I belong to you and no one else, don't I?* Then she climbed up on to my lap, curled herself up tight, small, fetus-like, like she was looking for protection, was trying to crawl back inside me.

'Just over a year later, when Viviane seemed to have passed through that wild stage, there was a moment when . . . We were making a birthday cake for Phineas, a lemon frosted layer cake – his favourite. I was surprised – delighted – that Viviane had joined me and Gwynne in the kitchen, had asked to crack the eggs. I noticed how careful she was, breaking the shells cleanly against the edge of the bowl, her face brightening briefly at a job well done. She appeared settled, somehow resolved – yes, resolved within herself. A couple of the sponge layers had risen unevenly. The girls were disappointed. It would be covered with the icing, I said, no one would notice. And Viviane· had sidled up to me then, leant against me, put her hand over mine. A gesture, it seemed, of reassurance, unity. Just in that moment I thought, I've got her back, my little girl.

'Old snow grey, dog-rose petal pink. The colours are coming back to life, becoming richer, deeper. And I've started a painting. Just a sketch. But in my mind I see the finished picture.'

Viviane

'Hands, my hands, over my skin, my scars. Jack Frost patterns of ice on windows. Forgotten. But memories returning, appearing. White scars turning red, opening. Slits. Mouths. I was in my own Dark Room. But my skin began to speak. My pictures developing. And oh, it was so cold. Oh, sweet Jesus, so cold lying on the bathroom lino. *Lie-no-lie-yes.* A way with words. He had a way with words. Tied me in knots. Tongue-tied. *Silence, child, is the key to all secrets. And I have the secrets of the world,* he said. Do away with the words. *Dou waye, Robin, the child will weepe.* Silence is a mask that innocence must wear.

'I had been in the squat, two days. Crept out of Castle Keep one night, last October. Didn't tell, couldn't tell Gwynne. Had to get away from Gwynne and the kid. Away from that room. From the white door. From my dark. I ran down Hart's Hill. Took the midnight bus into town. Running. Didn't know where to. The bus was full of kids. One of them called out, you going to the party, love? Give us a kiss, love. No party, no kiss. Someone had his tongue down a girl's throat. Someone got my tongue. When the bus reached the terminus, I got off. Drank coffee all night in the transport café. In the morning I left. I was walking back home. But I couldn't go back. Could see Castle Keep up on the hill. I walked to the forest fence. Followed the fence to the housing estate. They'd razed half the forest to build houses. Houses safer than the forest. I stopped going to the forest a long time ago. I walked through the streets of the housing estate. Outside the community centre, there was a pile of wood ready for Guy Fawkes night. Crates, boxes, wood and on the top a cart, its back wheels in the air. Like the carcass of a dead animal. I walked down an alleyway to a row of houses, no curtains,

217

windows and doors boarded up. On one of the doors there was a padlock hanging open in a devil-may-care grin. I pushed open the door. I unrolled my sleeping bag, slept. Must have slept through the day, through the night. When I woke, I opened my eyes to see a boarded-up window, a bare room, one chair, weeks of papers and junk mail over the floor. I looked up at the ceiling. I was looking down to see the body that was me, curled in the green sleeping bag, tight as a chrysalis, in the corner. I imagined I'd emerge a moth, dusty winged, creature of the dark, looking for light. Touch moth and she'll die. Then tap-tap-tap on the window. *Tap-tap-tap*. There was a fly buzzing at the glass, trying to get out. *Tap-tap-tap*. I wanted to die, could already see the black-frocked priest coming my way, making a bee-line, crossing the road, coming down the alleyway, crossing himself before he knocked. *His small fingers, his small hands*. The girl's possessed, Father. Who possessed her, my child? Pressure inside, building, scars splitting, felt I was going to explode. Wanted to tell, couldn't tell. Not anyone. Lying on the floor of the squat, could see someone, there was someone in the corner. Please don't hurt me. *Please don't hurt me. Tap-tap-tap, on the window. Let me in, sweet child. Go away, please. Leave the child alone. Go away go away go away go away. How old are you, child?* Nine. Nine, I said. Tap-tap-tap, on the window.

'On the window, at Castle Keep. I was nine years old. I was trapped in the outhouse, the door to the garden in front of me, the door to the kitchen behind, and I couldn't get to one and I couldn't get to the other. When I moved, it hopped, fluttered its wings, fixing me with its black beady eyes. I called out for Phineas. Where was Phineas? Where was Maggie? I called for Gwynnie but Gwynnie couldn't hear me. It puffed up its red belly. *Don't hurt me, please, don't hurt me*. Then hop-hop-hop, it flew at me, wings beating. Like my heart was in two halves. My breast bleeding. *Go away, Robin, go away*. I was crying. I didn't dare move. I was crouched in the corner of the outhouse.

It flew at me again and then Gwynne came in through the garden door. She saw the robin, shooed it out. Why are you crying, Vivvy?

'"Why are you crying?" he said.

'I looked up, pulling the sleeping bag around me. In the corner, a creature slipped through the membrane between dream and consciousness. The creature was sitting on the floor, spider arms and legs. He got to his feet and walked over to the window, peered through a crack between the boards. Wings grew from his shoulder blades. He lifted his arms, ran his fingers through the spiky black hair. He had big hands. As he turned to look at me, the wings shook, fluttered ribbons of black leather. A motorbike jacket opened to show the dark red waistcoat – like he'd opened his heart to me. On the floor, a pair of black leather gloves caressed a motorbike helmet.

'"I'm Rob," he said. "Hi." And he held out his hand, a big safe hand.'

The Book

Too long, too pointed, as though filed, not neatly spaced, as though jostling for position. The teeth were stubborn. The dentist had to pull — and pull. For greater resistance, they decided to strap Helnea to the chair. (An image flashed of the devilish Loki, bound.) Her eyes nearly popped from their sockets. Blood all over the dentist's white coat. Blood everywhere.

From the moment I saw her, I knew ours would be a special love. I shaped Ingebiorg. She was all mine. Eve from Adam's rib.

Not quite. The day she was born, when I saw the neat shape — minus protrusion — I knew, in that moment, that had she emerged male I would have become a Herod, would have drowned it in a river like a kitten in a sack of stones. Where is she? Weeks, now.

According to the midwife, who marvelled at Helnea's super-human resistance to pain, she had given birth in complete silence. It had not been the swiftest entry into the world. Helnea should have been screaming blue murder. As I had predicted, she showed no desire to nurse her newborn. When eventually she took the pathetic bundle into her arms, reaching for the babe with such arch stiffness, she looked down upon Ingebiorg, eyebrows raised, leaning away, half fearful, half with disgust. Those huge just-opened eyes. Yes. A child afflicted from birth. If not before. I am in part responsible. As soon as she came into the world, it was clear she had inherited my tongue's blighted gene. Her birth cries were feeble croaks compared to the usual unbridled bellows of the newborn.

The moment she opened her mouth – all you saw was its size, thickness. An ox tongue. I had made Ingebiorg mine. Had willed it. Helnea had gone up for one of her usual afternoon naps. She had fallen into a deep sleep. She was five or six months 'with child'. ('Pregnant' is too warm, too fleshy a word for Helnea.) I went into the bedroom, kneeled beside the bed – as though about to say my prayers! – and I slid my hand under the covers, under Helnea's gown. The feel of that drum-tight skin. And I pressed my palm against the swollen mound. I felt her. Inge. *Mine,* I whispered, *you, to love as no one else will love you.*

Could the conception have been immaculate it would have been. It was not love we made. How many times? Once, twice, thrice? We never kissed. I wish to have a child, I said. Helnea's legs parted, slightly. I closed my eyes. I thought I was dying. And what – who – did I see? *Her.* Mutti. And what was I doing? Riding Sleipnir. I was Odin, God of Gods, jumping the torrents beside Valhalla, springing over the wide river that glinted like a thousand spears, Odin riding ever onward to Jotunheim. Odin, the God of Poetry, of Inspiration, aka God of the Dead, *the Arch Deceiver.* I imagined it was a spear, my stick Mistletoe – Mistillteinn, the sword, I imagined I was wounding her. What did I see in Helnea? A means to an end. Because had it not been for Helena, there would have been no Ingebiorg. Such an icy maiden, incapable of warmth, of love. How did we meet? Was I lost in some snowstorm? Having trouble getting my skates on? *Helena.* Strange that I should write it now. For I rechristened her long ago in my head and ever since she has remained. I toyed with 'Hildr', one of the Valkyries, a battle maiden. Better to have named her after a frost giantess. But Helnea, had a better ring, sounded more true. Inge. A child of my loins, a little girl. And Helnea was moneyed, of course. Family money. Money I required. How many times did I meet Helnea's family? Six, seven, in almost as many years. I must not be ungrateful – after all, it was their money that had financed my indulgence. Another bribe. Helnea's daddy, a banker, had got a little greedy, it seemed. On a rare visit to the palatial home of my in-laws, I came across a letter, slipped inside the pages of a book I happened to pull at random from the library shelves. The letter referred to evidence of 'haute cuisine' in the double-dealing kitchens. Helena, I said, half your father's monthly cheque paid into my account and I shall forget I ever read it. She acquiesced immediately. I had the devil's own job not to burst out laughing, at how *easy* it was.

Bribery. Second nature. In the genes. A Mutti trick. Goes like this: comply and nothing bad will happen to you, refuse and something bad most certainly will. Either way – fear, guilt.

I am guilty   I am sorry
I am sorry   I am guilty
guilty, sorry
words, barriers
to keep out
the stories she told me.
Beguiled, seduced, by the stories, bribed – a trick! In the beginning was the word. No, was the gaping mouth of silence. And I see her mouth, Mutti's mouth, open wide. Those pearly-whites. Sometimes, I used to imagine myself growing small, so small I slipped inside, fell all the way down the red lane.

Prelapsarian. The word will not leave me, has teeth. I begin to fear my days here at the university are numbered. Matyeus-Prinn is a hawk. Caught him looking through my file. Am waiting for him to point the finger – at the door. Jabz R. Reemie: charlatan, mountebank, filibuster. All my academic life. Old Charlie Farley knew. I remember I found him, eyes glued to the binoculars. *All those beautifully hung blonds out there on the rugger field, Reemie.* And still with his peepers on the game, he told me, *We are becoming a mite slapdash, Reemie, skating on thin ice, Reemie, very thin.* Slapdash, it was true. But the ennui had set in long ago. Inadequate preparation for lectures. Daydreaming during tutorials. There was the matter of my thesis. Based on the work of an obscure Scandinavian academic. Aidan Kielissonsson: *Reinterpreting Kielissonsson — The Myth Man — Words as Truth, Words as Mere Belief.* Exposing the man as a charlatan. Yes. Of course, I knew Charlie had his suspicions.

The thesis. A fiction. The whole thing. She, Mutti, had wanted it for me. *My son, ze brilliant Professor.*

Nota bene: Should it come to it, should I be put out to grass — shall research. Subject? How about *The Language Kaleidoscope — Words as Patterns of Increasing Intricacy (???).* *How this smacks of desperation* was the tutor's wounding comment on one of my first undergraduate essays. Over forty-five years and still I smart with shame. The struggle, even then.

I have done words to death. (Shall say it myself before they do — and they will, oh, they will.) Have sucked language dry. Listen — *words, once ripe juicy fruits, are now husks. I am the aged world-weary ape atop a rock in a barren landscape, the dried skins of mango and papaya lie scattered about me like the dugs of hags, the brittle brown crisps of the world's last leaf-fall banked about me* — how does that sound? How easy it is, non-sense from sense/ the slaughter of language/ the laughter of slanguage. That I should have studied chemistry, mathematics — the safe precision of symbols, numbers, that stand-alone purity, essence, *unadulterated by thought.* The words, the thoughts. The stories, the feelings. Florio's *World of Words.* Where is book? Cannot find. Need.

Yesterday. Fears confirmed. Retirement, said Matyeus-Prinn.

Working on The Dictionary. Before I met Helnea. After graduation. Perhaps the one time, apart from those years with
Ingebiorg, that I honestly felt happy. To do with the camaraderie as much as the work. Four of us in that musty dusty
old room. Cobwebbed windows to boot! Smythe, Selwyn,
Simpson and Stimm. All brain, no brawn, in-sec-ty, bespecta-
cled, angularly huddled. And myself. Ah, the delicious silence
of those long hours, a comfortable comforting silence patterned
only with the faint leafing of pages, the mouse-paw scratch of
pen-nibs. I recall the first words I was given when I went to
work on The Dictionary. Surely it was by chance, an honest
mistake, coincidence? The Giver Out of Words gave me the
slip. What had I to research?

   SPECIAL SOLIPSIS STUCK (define locate source)

Paragraph? I could have written a book. But I stuck to the
rules, applied myself with verve and gusto. My first assign-
ment was lauded. My four peers were green. I was asked
whether I would like to work on the reference. No, thank
you. The words. Only. Purest form. I was on a mission,
hunting, trapping. A tireless pursuit to original source, to the
point where meaning no longer means, to the point when
the mouth opens, the word not even begun to sound. But you
know where all this is leading, Reemie. I see her, kneeling
before me, her lips already parting, mouth opening. Mutti.

The camaraderie – yes, almost as much as the work. Never
any playmates. She never let me play.

I was not expecting her. At the graduation ceremony. Mutti.
Turned up steeped in schnapps, teetering on gold kid heels,
tripping on the hem of one of her Schiaparelli evening gowns,
for Guntersaaks! Shocking pink. Or was it blue? A caped
affair, a sun raying hugely in gold embroidery over her back.
Hair upswept and piled in front in tight curls, giving her a

back-to-front look. No hat! Could she not have gone for a more appropriate 'Mrs Simpson' look, at least tried for a little tailored elegance. Was the intention to show me up? The males she bee-lined were hopelessly embarrassed. On the cusp of WW2, the university had become preponderantly full of 'shes'; the males were scarce and those who remained were either medically unfit (plus the odd objector, one or two barely pubescent bum-fluffed youths) or, like myself, *EXEMPT. Ox-furred, Ox-furred*, she slurred, *my dream since he was in lederhosen* . . . short pants, something like that she said. I put her on the first train home. I even pictured a wayward test bomb. I felt – so ashamed. I wished – for a hole in the ground – to be saved.

And so, leaving Mutti, as though we both knew it was finally over. By then, of course, we had permanently left 'Europe'. In the late thirties, not a good place to be. She'd found a flat – or someone had – the first of many increasingly small and dingy abodes – Maida Vale, Chiswick, Crouch End, I think. I went back to wherever home was occasionally during the holidays, but our relationship suffered an irrevocable change. After I left, she shopped, drank – schnapps, and akvavit (something akin to that Scandinavian potato-based spirit she got from some murky source). I cared nothing. As if that first train journey to my student life were the true severing of the umbilical cord. I almost heard the *snap.* I was relieved, faintly surprised, by the lack of contact on her part. I had envisaged regular boxes of goodies, long tearful phone calls, tear-soaked letters. But she even stopped asking whether I was coming home for Christmas after the first year. I did not go to the funeral. I think it was the guilt that consumed her. Which leaves her, sadly, 'unavailable for comment' – for confirmation.

These pages, this paper, sucking the ink from this pen, this nib. Pen beak mouth – the link? *Nibbe? Nabbe? Schnabel?* A link.

What? Old English? Old High/New High/Highbrow German/Danish/Dutch — double. I forge . . . forget. *I imagined I was nothing inside. A gourd, a husk. I imagined she was starving, that I was nourishing her. I imagined it was a poison, that I was killing her.* This pen I have stolen. And what else? On my desk, the small paperweight, glass. An eye. Imagining Matyeus-Prinn popping out the dead one. Pinkish, with a small red bubble inside. I look at it. It looks at me. Like the eye of a hostage victim. Defiant and accusatory. I shall put it in a drawer. Out of sight. I took it when he turned to reach for the sherry. Slipped it into my coat pocket. When someone takes something from you . . . M-P raised his glass. Before I knew it, I was toasting my retirement. Retirement? M-P was gloating, sugaring the pill. As he explained it, it was not retirement exactly — 'semi', reduced workload, responsibilities diminished — taken away, is what he meant. Painting a merry picture, he told me to consider the advantages — the freedom, the time, to research, write books. There would be the odd lecture, he said, 'to keep your hand in, old boy'. Old boy, already. I was looking at the grille covering the radiator. What did it remind me of? How *impotent* I felt. Increasing impotence.

Everything is being taken from me. The words deserting me. She. My Inge — gone again. Now, my work. Career practically over. Being withdrawn. Over forty-five years. And forty-five years ago, seeing Mutti waving goodbye from the platform as the train pulled away, taking me to university. Got herself all done up in honour. Another of her Schiaparelli's. (Where did they come from? We had no money.) A white evening dress with a musical notation design in red and black. A ridiculous schoolgirlish 'plate'-type hat with navy ribbons. A dull October morning and dressed for a summer evening do. She was always so inappropriate. Mock stoic. And who now, in hindsight, does she remind me of? The question: *whatever did I see in Helnea?* uncomfortably answered. University. Not a good time. War on the horizon. I ended up with a second. I told her it was a first. A starred first, I said.

On that train, eager to get away, leave her. I recall that thrill, that *propulsion* from my mother to those hallowed halls of learning. Escape. I tried not to worry about coping with the work. A struggle, I knew. I remember the university drama society asking whether I might consider playing the role of Claudius in *I, Claudius*. Was not one impediment enough! Imagine – all that stammering and lisping – a joke, surely, at my expense. I declined. As expected, I was to be ridiculed at university just as I had been in the playground, even by some of the teachers. The struggle to survive a cruel world was to continue. But later, another more desperate struggle – the battle of thoughts versus feelings. Powerless, against the feelings. To survive, I applied myself with ferocious determination to the work. I laboured harder than anyone. To keep my mind on the work, shut out the . . . But I needed to work. She'd had me believe I could achieve anything. But I did not match the dream, Mutti. Could only struggle . . . Just as I had done at school. Just about kept my head – above water. The School of English Language and Literature. I joined forces with the former, of course. Tucked myself under the wing of a certain Professor Chew, an eminent 'word-man' who, I recall, had once made some comment about those philologists who turned a blind eye to the stories. What was it? Some comparison about doing an anatomical study in an autopsy and not considering who the dead person might have been, not even knowing their name. And the word heroes kept me going: Humboldt, Jakobson, Chomsky, Saussure. For here was all that I craved, was structure and system. Words as elements, the place of each defined by its relation to others.

Rousseau's idea of an original language so exact that it catches the 'itness' of everything, so immediate, of the moment, that emotion is directly expressed, that is so transparent one cannot evade or deceive . . . Do I quote, or are these my words? I vividly recall the first time I read about Rousseau's idea of *la langue primitive*, his words setting my body a-quiver. It was only after I had left her, was freed, that I realised just how she had deceived me. Mutti. The stories. Her trick. My trust. How she had *abused* it. And it was only then that I allowed myself to hate her, pity her.

Mistletoe . . . Mistletoe . . . She had her own stick — birch, was it? — which she had "lifted" from a Swedish masseuse. I'd picture her in the snow, naked, imagine the suppressed groans of the flagellant.

A question. Before I answer another. Was I ever innocent? I mean, when I was a babe, in the cradle, her arms. I remember. Standing in that freezing bathroom. Toes and fingers, blue. Naked. She never felt it, Mutti, the cold. Skimpily dressed almost always. Those silk robes she wore about the house/flat/bedsit. And the rooms unheated, even in the depths of the most chill winters. Hailing from the North, she must have been hardened to it. And the schnapps. Yet she *felt* cold, her skin, hands. But her mouth, a small glowing cave, which warmed my blood, heated me until the fire blazed within me. Hellfire. And a warmth I did not understand, which I came to fear, which set my cheeks burning, shamed me.

My question: why remain here at St Bartolph's? But where else to go? Is it that if I left she might not find me, and I might never see my Inge again? Will I?

For weeks I have not written. This book sits open on my desk, the sunlight yellowing its pages. Face up to it, my Inge is never coming back. Have renounced all hope.

Phineas

'I did not know the man – not a man, less than human, a beast, devil.

'At Nathan's flat, last October, I was by turns confused, disturbed, appalled at what I had read in Reemie's book, at what he had kept from me. In all that time, never any hint, clue . . . Then I recalled one particular occasion when we had met for a drink at the university bar, when I noted a certain look in his eyes that, at the time, I could not fathom.

'We had been talking about names.

'"*Phineas*," he said, "a rather unusual moniker, is it not?"

'But I had no explanation for why my parents had christened me with such a name.

'"Phineas," he went on, "Greek hero, King of Thrace and a prophet, I believe, although my knowledge of the Greek myths is somewhat scant. Too good at his job was old Phineas, revealed too much of the truth of the gods to mortals – so Zeus blinded him."

'"Phineas Herminius to be exact," I said, "the second a name given to me after my parents died. Herminius, a hero who saved Rome, so I was told. *Phineas saved*."

'"Phineas saved. To save," he said, "or to *be* saved."

'And I commented then that the name Jabz was also uncommon.

'"Sorrow," he said, "it means sorrow."

'I recalled that he'd looked away, that he was silent for quite a time, and when he turned back his large eyes seemed darkened, as if he had briefly visited some ugly place and returned changed by it. At the time, I remember feeling momentarily close to him, believed something connected us on a deep level, buried sorrow, loss. I found myself telling him how my parents had died, about how, sometimes, when I was young, I'd picture

229

myself a Greek god, observing the human spectacle, my hand reaching down and tipping the Cessna out of kilter, that it was my fault. For it was easier to imagine I was the instigator of their death. Did it seem strange, I asked Reemie, to say that imagining I was responsible for their death was strangely liberating, for it meant I was not then responsible for saving them?

'"Yes," he had said, "better to believe one has had a hand in one's own fate. Or is it?" he said. And something else he said, I remember now . . . about . . . *fate taking the place of conscience.* Conscience? Did the man have no conscience? Is that what he believed? Was that his excuse – that it was somehow his fate?

'But, last October, I was more concerned with questions concerning my own fate. Recalling that conversation with Reemie, I began to think, *Saved*, or *was saved*. Had I only ever heard it one way?

'I was delighted to discover, in the second-hand bookshop one day during my daily sorties around Nathan's neighbourhood, Lindbergh's account of his transatlantic flight in 1927. The copy was pristine, intact, as if rarely opened. I remembered my own copy, still somewhere on a shelf at home and bound by a rubber band, its pages loose from continual readings as a boy. *Home* . . . Did I still think of Castle Keep as home?

'When I was a boy, I had shied from reading it at first, from that disturbingly fragile-looking plane on the front cover, from the illustration of Lindbergh, his face appearing as leathery as his flying helmet, which rendered him, for me at least, less human, less real, more like one of my comic-book heroes. I kept the book turned over, preferring the black-and-white photograph on the back cover, the long, lean frame, the feet planted firmly, yet as if he is about to spring into action, as if he cannot wait to climb into the cockpit of the plane, a monstrous, or rather fabulous, winged beast behind him. Lindbergh has an arm tucked behind him, appears to have a grip on one of the propeller blades, as if he has momentarily stilled its spinning, has the machine under control, is master of the beast.

'The photograph of this strong, handsome hero was immensely comforting to me as a boy. And, plucking up courage, I read Lindbergh's story of his 3,500-mile flight from New York to Paris, paying particular attention (as he did!) to details of safety, glossing over the excerpts from press reports of other doomed attempts, the crashes which had fortunately been set out in newspaper-column style and thus were easy to avoid.

'In my mind, I was Lindbergh flying through the night, the dusk, the dawn, and by the time he describes his final descent in Paris, touches down on solid ground, I was the pilot of the Cessna that had taken my parents "on the ride of a lifetime", the plane taxiing to a halt, and as I switched off the engine I turned round to see my mother and father safe.

'*You are so sure, Funny-Arse, that you could have caught, would have saved me?* I could not get it out of my mind, on my return from my book-buying, seeing Nathan up on the balcony, leaning dangerously over the edge. I pictured him toppling over the balcony rail, falling head over heels through the air like an acrobat. That night, as I lay in bed, I felt as if my arms were still reaching, a real physical ache. I thought of keeping the Lindbergh to read to Nathan, who appeared increasingly curious about my books. A "book for bedtime" maybe, for he sometimes seemed unsettled in the evenings and there were many nights when I was aware of him up until the small hours, working on something in his bedroom, perhaps, for there was often a distinct smell of glue and paint.

'When I saw Nathan leaning over the balcony, I shouted, "Nathan, don't!" I'd stood with my arms outspread.

'I was picturing Orelia, each excruciating detail, her tiny hand reaching for the handle, opening the unlocked door, stepping out, climbing up the rails, that determination, her three-year-old face tight with intent, the way she'd look trying to climb trees in the park, her eyes fierce with it. And all of it leaving her the moment she slipped over the side. And I am standing behind her, pulling her down, prising her white-knuckled fingers from the rail, feel her kicking against me in protest as I bring her inside to safety.

'Then Nathan pulled away from the balcony, out of view. I looked like I'd seen a ghost, he said.

'"You didn't think I was going to jump? Anyhow, you wouldn't have caught me. Never would have saved me, mate. Think of the force. From the sixth floor, mate. Would have slammed right into you. Crushed you more like. And you had your eyes shut. Never been out there, have you, mate?"

'There was a mark on his face when I got back. A smudge of green paint. Viridian, Maggie would have called it. She's always been precise with colours, pronouncing the names as if she could taste them. I remembered, the first time we met, a spot of red on her cheek. Cadmium red, she said.

'I had advertised for local artists to exhibit in the Reading Room. Maggie brought along a series of six sunsets. Vivid, bold, impasto, breathtaking, nightmarish, full of passion, and fear. Those first years before the girls were born, she was the colour in my life. I tried to tell her but I knew I made it sound like something from a bad romantic novel or film, mawkish, inadequate. I felt grey beside her.

'Once, we ran through the rain holding hands like silly teenagers. She was wearing turquoise, pink, purple, her clothes clinging to her strong solid body.

'I remembered the first time I watched her painting. She had mentioned she was looking for somewhere to work. There was a room she could have, I said, at the back of the shop, small but well lit with large windows and a skylight. It had its own entrance separate from the shop. She could come and go as she pleased. I gave her the key. I'd got to the Reading Room early one morning to sort out deliveries of stock from the previous evening. I saw her through the window, the way she attacked the canvas, a fierce intensity, an almost savage passion, the canvas bleeding vivid reds and oranges. I was in awe, in envy. Maggie lived at the very heart of life. Would you understand if I said at that point where life meets death?

'And I had never been there, had never even come close. I used to wonder, later, what had made her lose that passion. Years later, when things were bad – I found Maggie sitting by the fire one day. The fire had gone out. She was wrapped in some old blanket. Just staring at the coals, those blue eyes soulless.

'Just came to me – I was telling Reemie, one day, how delighted I was that Maggie had begun to paint again. And this time with even more passion. A series of paintings she called *The Mothers*. I asked whether Maggie had shown him her paintings. He did not answer. He was stoking the fire in his study, ramming the poker into the coals with a fury. Mothers, he was muttering, mothers. He kept a fire blazing night and day. A plump figure, insulated enough, you'd think, against the cold, and that huge coat, yet he had the fire going all year round.

'I had been at Nathan's flat just a matter of weeks when I sensed an inner clarity, a resolution of that which perhaps I had never fully articulated even to myself. I knew I was approaching the end of my stay with Nathan. *If you love them, Funny-Arse, why don't you go back home to them?* Those last nights I lay awake, the question continually circling my mind.

'And one night, in the early hours, Reemie's voice, waking me from a dream. A dream about Orelia, running to the balcony, climbing, up, over the rail, the determination slipping away as she fell. Her small hand reaching. Her eyes. Her face, stricken. No. Not Orelia. Viviane. Vivvy. Ten years old.

'*Phineas saved . . . Phineas did not save . . .* I heard his voice, as I can hear it now, whispering from the shadows . . . *did not save her.*'

Viviane

'In the squat, crying with the cold one night. Coldest October for sixty years. Rob said. He came to see me almost every day, brought me blankets, a hot-water bottle, water, bread, soup. One morning I woke to find beside my sleeping bag a towel, soap, a toothbrush, a box of tissues. I cried in my sleep, he said. He came one evening and opened a bottle of red wine, warmed up tomato soup on a Primus stove. Red, red. Like a warm transfusion.

'"Why are you being so kind?" I said.

'"You're not used to people being kind?"

'Rob was standing by the window, his back to me while I sipped the soup, reaching up, his arms stretching wide, his leather jacket rising above his jeans, exposing a tattoo at the base of his spine, an angel with spread wings. He was lifting the boards from the window.

'"It's what I do," he said, "helping out people in trouble, you know, drug addicts, alcoholics, people who've lost their way. It's this organisation. Call ourselves the Angels. Original, eh?'

'I wasn't taking drugs, I said, I wasn't an alcoholic.

'"In some kind of trouble?"

'I didn't answer.

'"It's OK, Viv, no more questions."

'I didn't answer because as he removed the last board from the top of the window, I saw the moon. The moon, sweet Jesus. *Like an eye on me. Nobody could see except the moon. Lying on the bathroom floor, I was looking up, away, beyond, at the mirror, the door, the window, at the moon. No other eyes but that white round growing rounder, wider, watching us.*

'All coming back, sweet Jesus. Remembering.

'We were sitting on the Story Seat, me and Gwynnie. She was straining to catch every word that slipped over his thick

234

wet lips. I didn't want to sit that way. Me then him then Gwynnie. I wanted it to be Gwynnie then me then him. I wanted to be in between her and him. I said, I'm going to sit by my sister. I wanted to put my arms around her because she was my sister and I wanted to keep her safe.

'We're fine as we are, don't you think, he said. I didn't know, I couldn't be sure she was safe. Then, somehow, I just knew. That it wasn't Gwynnie he liked, not Gwynnie he wanted. And she couldn't hear his voice anyway, his words. *Words are magic, are hidden pockets, sweet child, are the hands of the magic man, are the sleight of tongue.*

'Sweet Jesus, coming back, coming back, his words.

'One day, Rob brought me a coat, a long thick coat with a crimson lining that brushed the ground as I walked. Clasping the front together, six pairs of small silver hands, their fingers entwining. I looked like a Russian princess, Rob said. You'll need it, he said, when you go out.

'One night, I put on the coat and I went out, walked through the housing estate. The moon was grey, as if filmed with a cataract of ice, old man's eye, seen enough. A night so strangely still I thought the world had ceased spinning. Beneath the street lights, the ground glistened, crunched beneath my boots. I walked to the community centre. The stacked bonfire reached ever higher. I climbed up, pulled down the upturned cart. I pushed it along the streets to the other side of the estate, to the edge of the forest, to the pile of stones. The cart took two, three stones at most. I pushed the cart laden with stones back to the squat. The cold inside me. And a voice. A voice with the power to stop the beating of my heart.

'"What are you doing with the stones, Viv?" Rob said.

'A stone. Like a stone. Hard-tight. Then no one will know. So they don't ask. Fine and dandy. And so you don't have to tell them.'

Gwynne

'Your hands. Like those of a great pianist having sounded the last note of the performance of a lifetime. They speak of huge accomplishment. They speak of grace. Each time I come here, you greet me with the three-fingered blessing of a Christian clergyman. And I feel you are full of goodness, are godlike.

'Yesterday, Viviane asked me to come with her to the forest. She was frightened, you could see. It was something she had to do, she said. Strange, to think she had been just the other side, in the squat. But somehow I had known she was near. She told me about Rob as we walked down the hill. Her guardian angel, she said.

'She was shaking as she climbed over the fence, but as we weaved through the trees she seemed to relax a little. And she told me about the nightmares, the butchered children hanging from the branches. We had almost reached the middle of the forest. She leant against a tree, looked at me.

'"It'll always be there, Gwynne," she said, "what happened, it will never go away."

'"Remember, Viviane," I said, "how we used to play down here. Spillikins – you always won, remember?"

'She nodded, smiled briefly. And she looked up at the small patch of sky between the tree tops.

'"We had such fun, didn't we, you and me?"

'Then we made our way back home. At the top of the hill, Viviane turned and opened her mouth wide. And I felt it, from the depths of her soul, a cry of long-buried hurt and pain and anger.

'Then she sank to the ground and sobbed for a time, then she reached out to me and I held her hand.

'And I thought of her hand on the hospital sheet last October, after they'd given her the transfusion, white, lifeless, a renunciation. And I remembered the same hand, years ago, like a flower, growing through a gap in the beech hedge.

'*Something to tell you, Gwynnie.*

'*Don't want to hear, Vivvy, don't want to be your friend any more—*

'Mumma says to go and find Vivvy. Vivvy's been missing the whole day since before breakfast. Didn't even come in for her lunch, which was her favourite, beans on toast with melted cheese. *Go and find your sister, Gwynne, she must be starving by now.*

'But I don't care. Right now, I don't care two pennies whether Vivvy's starving to death, right now I don't. I don't care much about Vivvy any more. Not after what she'd done to Mumma's paintings. And the way Mumma's crying, like she just can't stop the tears and not even bothering to wipe them away, so I go and get her a tissue. And Pappa looks like an old man, he looks so tired. I feel sorry for them because they don't deserve what Vivvy's done. Because we thought she'd stopped doing all those bad things and worrying us. But you can tell they're still worried, Mumma and Pappa. Because it's like Vivvy's not one of us any more, not part of our family. The way she is now, it's almost worse than the crazy Vivvy. I've tried to be nice even when I don't feel like it. But I really, really don't care, not for all the money in the world. *You can starve to death, Vivvy Goode.* But Mumma wants me to look for her, so I'm going round the house, into every room, but I'm not really looking, *my heart's not in it*, like Pappa says after he's had a bad day at work. Because I don't want to find her. But if I found the Vivvy like she used to be, who used to be my friend, then I would. Don't want to find her. But I know where she is. Out on the hill. By the beech hedge. Can just make out her shape between the leaves. The closest she can get to being outside. So I sit on the other side of the hedge and I say dinner's nearly ready and Mumma wants her to come in. And she turns round a little bit. But she doesn't speak.

'Come and eat your dinner, Vivvy, then we can go down to the forest.

'Don't want to. A girl went in there once and got her tongue cut out. He told me. He said. Professor Reemie.

'But that's just a story, Vivvy.

'And she looked right at me then. *I hate you*, she said. *I hate you*. And she's never said that, never ever not ever once. *I hate you*. And I felt the tears coming in my eyes just like Mumma's, and I told her I was going in for my dinner and she'd die without food and I couldn't care. *Don't care about you, Vivvy, and I hate you too*. But I didn't like saying that. I hated myself for saying that. And I looked back and I saw she'd pushed her hand through the hedge. But I didn't take it. When she reached out to me.

'I think I understand how sometimes she must have hated me. Just a child who could not protect herself. But she could protect me. And that is a terrible thing for a little girl to have to do.

'After I found the notebook in her Dark Room, read the letter from Pappa, I decided I would go to the abbey. Perhaps it was her way of telling me where she'd gone. And I had nothing else to go on. I decided to take Nyssa with me, explained to her mother that I had to visit my father but I was happy if Nyssa wanted to come with me. I told Nyssa we were going on a little holiday. We were singing on the coach. *A sailor went to sea, sea, sea*. Nyssa was laughing, delighting in the wordplay, wanting to sing it over and over. *To see what he could see, see, see*. Her hands deliberately confusing the signs . . . *sea* . . . *see*. Her eyes alight as she realised how the lips can hide meaning. My hands are better at talking, she said.

'I was looking at the reflection of our faces in the coach window. I kept thinking of the mirror in the bathroom at Castle Keep. Seeing . . . what? And looking at Nyssa's hands as the coach drove into the evening, and the light was going. Looking at Nyssa's hand on her doll, the fingers curling open, like a whispered goodnight, a relinquishment to sleep.

'I was travelling farther and farther away from Castle Keep, but gradually things were clearer, coming into focus.

'Almost worse than knowing. That it happened to my sister. Because it did not happen to me. Because I was safe. No, because she'd tried to keep me safe. Tell me, how do I bear that?'

Marguerite

'*Eine Kleine Nachtmusik*, by the artist Dorothea Tanning. Of two girls, one fair, one dark – oh, you know the painting. That pale yellow petal fallen from the giant sunflower. Like a glove, a gloved hand, its fingers crawling up the stairs towards the dark-haired girl. His hand, pale and delicate, raised as if to wave to me. Yet strangely lifeless.

'He was standing at the front door when I left for the art class that evening, just as Viviane was, later, when I returned. That terrible night, towards the end. Why did I start teaching? I still don't know. It was hardly a question of needing the money. But I was out of the house. Got me out of the way. Had I been at home, it would never have happened.

'They were sitting on the sofa when I left. The three of them. He was telling them a story. I told the girls I'd come in to kiss them goodnight when I got back. Viviane, looking at me with that hard-faced defiance. I think of one of those sepia Victorian family photographs, the chin-up stiff stance. Yet, in the children, an exaggerated pride belying reluctance. I did not see how afraid she was. But I was growing ever more concerned about leaving her, and as I looked back, I saw Reemie in the doorway.

'And that's where I found Viviane, at the front door, as if the dark bulk of his shape had shrivelled, in her nightie, shivering, her face deathly white. It was late, after eleven. Did her father know she was still up? The motorbike was there, so I knew Phineas was back and Reemie had probably left. *Why aren't you in bed, Viviane?* But she wouldn't answer me and slipped away inside the house.

'I followed, saw that the light was on in my studio. The door was wide open.

'She was in there, Viviane, pacing the room like someone possessed – wild. Not again, I thought, please don't say it's all happening again. Like a caged animal, desperate, panting, moaning, her hands clutching at her hair, her face. *What's wrong, Viviane? Tell me. Why are you behaving like this?* I tried to hold her but she pulled away, and then I grabbed her, tight, went down on my knees. *Talk to me, Viviane. Tell me, what's the matter?* She reached for a chair, held it high. Where did she get the strength? I thought she was going to bring it down on me. I fell away, covered my head, cowering. She let the chair fall to one side, yelping as it caught her foot. Then she ran out.

'And that's when I did it. I closed my eyes, saw again the picture of Viviane holding the chair high over me, her face tight with fury, the picture transmuting into the memory of my father, standing just like that, over thirty years ago.

'The first, the only, time I was to witness his rage, as I ran to the corner of the kitchen after he'd reached for one of the chairs and swung it high. Hearing his words. *Live, live, why couldn't she live!*

'I was on the floor, in the studio, my father's words, his voice, booming in my head, seeing Viviane with the chair, thinking what we had come to – our family falling apart – Phineas and I like strangers – and all of it my fault – and the way my mother had died – all my fault – bad wife bad mother bad daughter – Kali Ma – I was Kali Ma – Mother Creator and Mother Destroyer. And I saw the knife, the carving knife from the kitchen, and I did not stop to think who had put it there. And I reached and I grabbed the handle and I lunged at the painting on the easel. And I stabbed and stabbed and kept on stabbing, then pulled the blade through the canvas. Again and again and again, ripping the canvas apart, again, again, again. Then I started on the others, stabbing and tearing until I had destroyed every one of those paintings I had laboured so hard to create.

'All I remember afterwards, on the floor, outside the studio, Phineas doing his best to calm me.

'Because I killed my mother, because I killed my mother. *Kali Ma, Mother Destroyer.*

'*How did your mother die, Markeet?*

'*Father, how did my mother die?*

'How old was I when he told me? Nine, was I? Old enough to ask, young enough to forget.

'Towards the end of my time at St Bernard's, I was able to tell Max . . . a memory . . . My father, see my father now, poised over Old Balthazar, oil-rag in one hand. As if captured in a long-ago moment, like a figure in a museum tableau of past times, as if the words I had just asked him had cast a spell.

'*Daddy, how did my mummy die?*

'"Father?" I whispered again.

'And then he was back with me, in the kitchen, rubbing the rag over the bones of the old press. But still he would not answer and I continued with my homework. Then, after a time, he took a long, deep breath and I looked up. He was smoothing the cloth over the machine, smoothing over and over the same spot, his eyes fixed on the movement of his hand. He spoke slowly, faltering, his voice low and unsteady, as though accustoming himself to its tone, to the words.

'"Your mother . . . She . . . Just after you were born, she started to bleed. She seemed so well after the birth, although exhausted. Ah, but those blue eyes shining, lass. I was at the bedside. They'd taken you away to clean you up, to check you were . . . that everything was all right. You were a large, healthy, bonny baby. I was holding your mother's hand. And then I felt her grip, sudden, tight, and I could see her colour, her face suddenly draining of colour. And the way she looked at me, I'll never forget that. Something's wrong, something's wrong, Jim, she was saying. And I looked down, at the bed, at the white sheets, saw the blood. So much, too much, blood. She had haemorrhaged. They couldn't save her, you see. She was dying And I could hear you, somewhere, hear you crying, your lungs fit to burst. And your mother was dead."

'My father hung his head. I had asked and he had answered. And he never spoke of it again. I looked the word up in the

dictionary: *Escape of blood from a ruptured blood vessel,
especially when profuse, an evidence of damaging loss.*
Damaging loss. The words would not go away, coloured the
facts. Like my mother's blood coloured my world. I saw my
father and me drifting on a raft upon a sea of red and my
mother, hovering above us, an image in a cloud, of ice, a
shadow, a trick of the light. I took up my brush and painted
my skies red. I painted my father's eyes black with blame. And
the eyes of my child . . .

'*But sunsets are not always blood red, Markeet.* No, Max,
and I see them now apricot, cadmium orange, light magenta,
portrait pink.

'*A good force once, our family* . . . When I finally read the
letter from Phineas, I asked Max what I should do.

'"Be reunited with your family, Markeet? But that is surely
your decision," he said. And his hands, held together as if in
prayer, moved slowly apart, as if granting me permission to
decide, and I was looking at that wide space between his hands,
thinking that is what the Goode family had become. Like a
space in a painting, like the empty faces of the mothers I could
not find, a space that I was daring to hope we might fill.

'It was time, Max said, to start thinking about moving to
the rehabilitation centre, to Halfway House. But before I could
leave, there was still some work to do.

'Shortly before I was to make contact with my father, Max
hypnotised me. "Soon, you will be ready to leave here, Markeet,
but somehow we have to get you to walk out of the door, to
find the source of your agoraphobia."

'He counted me down to a time not long after I had learned
the facts about my mother's death, counting me back through
the years, eighteen, fifteen, twelve, eleven.

'Ten. Ten years old. One Saturday evening, going up Mount
Repentance with Father, with that big old black pram. My pram.
For years I had this recurring dream. I'm going up the hill,
pushing the pram, slow as a funeral march. The pram's an open

coffin and I look down and see myself lying there, a baby, my blue-white face haloed by a black organza bonnet.

'Ten years old and as we begin the walk up the hill I run to the street sign.

'"But it's not Mount Repentance, Father, look."

'And I spell out the letters: M-o-u-n-t P-l-e-a-s-a-n-t.

'But my father's shaking his head, and on we go, stopping at each house to push the pamphlets through the doors. Up and up Mount Repentance, the muscles in my legs burning, my chest and arms aching. My father behind me, booming, *Behold they sin, stare it in the face, know it.* And as we reach the top, it gets easier, because the pram's not so full now, and I know, soon, we'll reach the grassy mound where sometimes we sit and rest.

'"It's getting late, lass," Father says, "sun's going down."

'All the way up, ever since Father told me, I've been thinking of nothing else but how my mother died, and each time I picture it more vividly, and now I'm seeing it in brilliant, almost blinding colour and I'm thinking I was the reason for all that blood. As we walk up, I notice then the light is changing, the blue of the sky is tinged with salmony pink and darkening. I'm aware of the sun behind me, the dying sun, and I think of my mother dying, the blood flowing from her, just as the sun is bleeding into the sky, its red flowing into and darkening everything around me, and though I don't look up, I imagine the whole sky coloured with its red and I dare not look because I imagine she is up there, that it's not the sun but my mother, and my heart's thumping and I can hardly breathe. I want to get away, run away, am beginning to feel swamped, engulfed, as we go over to the mound. But this time I cannot look out at the view as we always do, but only down into my lap, and I shut my eyes tight because everything, the whole world, is red now, this red which is no longer light but liquid flowing, blood, and I fear I am drowning and I sit beside my father who is aware of none of this, who's pointing out landmarks in the town below us, and I wait, wait for the sun to finally drop below the horizon, for my father to say, as he always does, "Time to be on our way, lass."

'Something he said, Reemie, about mothers and blame. Before I'd left to go to the class, I was in the studio. He was staring out of the window. I couldn't hear him at first. What was he saying? *They are responsible for so much, Mrs Goode, aren't they, our mothers.*

'Something else he said, the first time he came to the house. He was telling me how lovely the girls were. *I see you've done a good job, Mrs Goode.* Almost as if he knew that was what I needed to hear. Winning, wooing me.

'"Maggie," he said once, "Margaret. It's meaning is *pearl*, is it not? Ach, *must bereavement new until death be mine?*'

'Whispering those words, he seemed so terribly sad. I could not but feel sorry for him.

'That morning when Viviane came home, it was bitterly cold. She was sitting at the kitchen table, lost in this thick black coat. I thought a bath would warm her up. I wanted to look after her, comfort her, wanted to do something for her. She gestured with her hand, waving away my offer to make her a drink.

'And it came back to me just then, with such terrible significance, Reemie's hand, pale and delicate as he waved me off, standing at the front door of Castle Keep, looking oddly proprietorial. That wave, an almost careless gesture, contrived and terribly conclusive. The way a murderer might wave to his intended victim. And I realised he was always there, in the background, a figure sketched in, like someone in a dream you cannot recognise, a presence hovering at the back of my mind.

'I was in Max's room waiting for one of our weekly sessions. Max was late. He'd stuck a print of *The Laughing Cavalier* to his chair. He'd drawn in a speech bubble. Some awful joke, "How many psychiatrists does it take to change a light bulb?" And I remembered then another painting by Hals. The young man. He's holding a skull in one hand and the other is reaching out. The skin is mottled. It looks like an old man's hand which

245

seems to be reaching right out of the painting, inviting you to take it. He's wearing a red beret, the feather stuck in it is thick, luxurious, bushy, like the tail of a fox, and pinkish. But it was the eyes of the young man I kept seeing. Something about those protruding eyes. And for the life of me, I couldn't think at the time who those eyes reminded me of.

'But I remember, now I remember. Am beginning to see, now, *traces of the original* . . . that flicker in my . . . Like a hand pulling me from that dark. Oh, I understand now, why I was so desperate to see clearly that childhood memory, why I was so ready to blame myself, why I felt so guilty, why I could not see *with innocence*. You see, that story I told myself, another had joined in the telling, whispered false words, helped paint my false picture with a thick brush. *Like the tail of a fox.*

'He was there one evening. In the garden of Castle Keep. The sun was going down, the sky changing. Had he noticed, perhaps, how I had turned away? Had he caught that look of . . . *Fearful indeed, Mrs Goode. One could say, more hell than heaven.*'

Allie

'*Innocence can be taken from you only once.* Did I read that somewhere, something someone said? Was it Phineas? Or . . .

'The last time I came here, I said her innocence had been taken. And she'll never get that back. She'll never be who she was, will she? Yet I suppose we are all continually being shaped, altered by experience, by what happens to us. But what she went through – that should never have . . . I am sorry. I seem to be less and less articulate. There are things almost too hard to say. I'm trying to—

'You see, for most of my life I have longed to be able to return to that moment before, to that state of being before that moment when I took . . . when I stole . . . Such a small thing, to take, to do. Yet I was forever altered by it.

'I needed to tell her.

'While Bart went to fetch Jo from hospital, I helped Jake and Mikey make a "welcome home" banner. I was watching from the window as the car drew up outside. Jo seemed unsteady as she walked to the front door, each step slow and careful, as though she were carrying something heavy, something precious in her arms, her body at an awkward angle, tilting to one side. Yet she appeared oddly insubstantial, a shadow, even as she reached with both hands to the door frame for support, as she hauled herself in. Then, as soon as she saw the brightly coloured banner hanging across the hallway – *Welcome Home Mummy and Baby* – her face opened in a wide warm smile. After she'd kissed the boys, we hugged. Was she OK? *Fine*, she said, *tired, but we're just fine.* Then she went upstairs to rest and Bart told me that the baby's heartbeat was steady, stable, but Jo needed plenty of bed-rest, because of the trauma and the bleeding, that she'd be monitored carefully. I offered to stay to help with the boys, help look after the house and so on, but Bart said he'd arranged a few weeks off work. He had time owing anyway, he said, and if necessary he'd work from home. His mother lived fairly close by and she'd step in if he had to go in to the office. But if I wanted to stay, he said, I was more than welcome.

'Later, after lunch, Jo came down and we watched an old black-and-white movie. Jo fell asleep before the end. Bart and the boys were in the garden, collecting leaves, making a bonfire. It was still burning when they came in for tea.

'Just leaves. The words I had written. I fetched the manuscript, the unedited version of my book, *Beyond Hearing*. And I burnt all those words I'd hidden behind.

> *Let us now consider the following case history. A set of twins, identical save for the fact that one twin was born with severe hearing loss. They had just celebrated their twelfth birthday. The parents had just acquired a sophisticated, costly hearing aid which enabled the deaf twin to have a level of hearing she had never experienced. Shortly before they were to attend a prize-giving ceremony during which the deaf twin was to receive a national prize for journalism, the hearing aid went missing. The parents were unable to replace it for some time because of the expense. The original was never found.*

'Watching the flames eat up the words was somehow freeing. Such a tiny thing. A needle in a haystack, mother had said. They gave up looking after a while, Mother, Father and Jo. Such a small thing. But it grew huge inside me, filled my heart, grew into my bones, was the very marrow of my bones.

'I went up to bed early, left the family together, with Jo in the bedroom, Bart reading the boys a bedtime story. I had made him promise he'd call if he needed me. But I sensed the family wanted to be together, on their own.

'After breakfast the following morning, while Bart and the boys set off to the local shops, I went to see Jo. She was lying on the bed, on her side, her back to me, half curled on the blue bed cover. She was wearing a pale pink nightgown. I thought of a shell, a beautiful shell on the sand of the shallows. Then she turned.

'"Yesterday," she said, "when I thought I was losing the baby, I was thinking, maybe it was God's way of telling me, you know, that's enough, that maybe I was asking for too much. Because I've got two already," she said, "two healthy boys."'

'Because I had lost my child, she meant.

'She mustn't think like that, I said.

'"You know that's not how it works, Jo. You and the baby, you and Bart and the boys, you'll all be fine."

'"It makes me realise, Allie, just how easily you can lose them – I'm sorry, I didn't mean—'

'"Please, don't be sorry, Jo. It's OK. Jo, there's something I need to tell you."

'And then I did.

'I had lunch with Bart and the boys and I left. I was on my way to St Benedict's, to see Phineas. He had always believed it was his fault, you see – Orelia. I had decided, for better or worse, that he had to know. Driven to confess, I pushed the car to ninety, ninety-five, a hundred. I remember thinking, was that how it had felt, for Orelia, as she was falling? Once, and I know this must sound stupid, but some time after her death I'd watched some programme about unusual wedding ceremonies. There was a couple who'd said the last of their vows while bungee-jumping. I saw them dive from the scaffold, hands held, arms spread, then that jolting rebound, like a reprimand for flouting the laws of gravity. After too many glasses of wine, heartlessly, I think now, I suggested to Phineas that we might try a jump. I wanted to know what it was like. I had been haunted by that need to know, to feel, to get the closest I could, trying to imagine . . . If I could have been there, beside her, the two of us falling through the air, with her.

'Phineas had always been convinced it was his fault. Because he had been out on the balcony that morning. Because he had not shut the door securely. He had been up early, reading on the balcony, and I'd heard him call out, asking for the time because he couldn't find his watch, and he came rushing into the living room and gathered his books because he was late for some one-day course at the university.

'I clearly remembered shutting the door after he'd left.

'It had been a beautiful day until then, but suddenly it clouded over, turned cold. I remember telling Orelia we had to keep the door closed to keep that old cold out. And she'd repeated, *old cold, oldie, coldie*, and started to sing 'Old King Cole'. *And he called for his finnerless free*, she'd sing.

'I was resentful of Phineas leaving us on such a lovely day. I have never admitted, perhaps because of Orelia's death, that things were not exactly right between us. He was spending so much time with Reemie, reading, writing essays, going to lectures, courses. I asked him whether he'd thought about doing it seriously, enrolling on a degree course, seeing he was spending so much time studying – at least he'd have a qualification, something to show for it. Apparently Dr Reemie had advised otherwise. To tell the truth, I was beginning to resent how much time Phineas was spending with Reemie. He was in thrall to the man – in his eyes, at the time, Reemie could do no wrong.

'Spring. It was early spring. Bright, a warm morning that turned cold. April the sixth. She ran. Orelia ran everywhere. It should have been a ground-floor flat. She should have had a garden. I had taken her to the swing park. I see her clearly, watching the older children climbing the frame, then she followed them, tagging behind. We stayed out until early afternoon. I had taken a small picnic. I couldn't get her to sit still, not even to eat. By the time we got back to the flat, she was exhausted, was fast asleep, so I left her in the pushchair in the hall. I went to the bedroom, lay on the bed, intending to have a quick nap. The next thing I was aware of was a wailing siren. I ran to the living room, saw the balcony door wide open.

'I did not have to go out, to look. I already knew.

'I went to the hallway. The pushchair was empty. I remember vividly, how *vacated* it looked. Like, yes, a shell.

'And then, only then, did I go to the balcony. I looked down. I saw them crouched over her. I saw her arm, its almost jaunty position, the angle of the bones, the splayed palm, the way she'd waved, as if she were waving to me. I wasn't expecting Phineas back until the evening. But he had forgotten to take some books or something and he'd left the course early.

'He blamed himself, for not being careful about locking the balcony door. I tried, I started to tell him. But he would not listen.

'I kept going over it, over and over. I was the one who had shut the balcony door. I had gone out there after Phineas. I had fallen asleep. I had left the door unlocked. My fault. *Grief and guilt are inextricably bound. You feel the horns sprouting from your scalp, hear the swish of your tail as you walk.*

'But I never did get the chance to tell Phineas about Orelia, about the balcony door. Confession. It's good for the soul, isn't it? But what a selfish act it is. You feel better. You feel good again, don't you?

'When I told Jo it was me who stole her hearing aid all those years ago she said, *I know, Allie, I've always known.*

'I can't imagine how they must be feeling, how they are coping, if they are – I keep thinking, there must have been something I could have, that I should have—'

Viviane

'Went out at night to fetch the stones. Safest at night. Didn't want to be seen. Didn't want them to find me. Imagined Gwynne, up on Hart's Hill, looking down on the town, searching. In my dreams she was an eagle soaring above Hart's Hill, scouring prey. Gwynne, Castle Keep, the hill beyond the trees.

'I pushed the cart right to the edge of the forest, to where the piles of stones lay, and the sheets of corrugated iron. A shelter long forgotten, perhaps. Like the one that Phineas built for Gwynne. Gwynnie's forest. Not mine. *Beware the forest, said the Bird of Truth, for there inside you shall find unimaginable terrors, unspeakable horrors.*

'I piled the stones around the sleeping bag.

'"What are you doing with the stones, Viv?" Rob said. "Looks like a burial mound."

'Piling the stones, one by one, the wall growing higher around me. But one night, I dreamt of the Lightning Tree, that one of its branches began to grow and grow, over the garden at Castle Keep, over the beech hedge, down the hill, through the forest, like a root, like an arm reaching through the streets, to the houses, to the squat, curling about me and lifting me high and back, back to the trees and setting me down in the heart of the forest where the trees grow thickest, where from the branches hang the tongues and severed limbs of all those children who had dared to tell. And I heard the knife come singing through the air, saw it flying through the air at me.

'"What knife, Viv?"

'I woke then, to find Rob kneeling beside the sleeping bag.

'The knife. *See, sweet child, its handle of lapis lazuli, see, feel, its oh-so-sharp blade.* In the story. The knife. In his hand. Whose hand? The tip of the knife. The tip of the feather. From the Truth Bird. In the story. What story? Tip of the feather tickling my skin.

'*Tickles,* I said.

'*Tickleth, he said. Is it soft? Is it nice?*

'*Soft, yes.*

'I was lying on the cold lino, those huge eyes popping, mesmerising, memorising every inch. Drawing the signs with the tip of the feather, over my body – to protect me.

'"Has someone hurt you, Viv?"

'I could feel the weight of Rob's hand on the sleeping bag. And on my face, the soft beating of an angel's wings.

'"If someone has hurt you, Viv, and you don't tell and you keep it a secret, they're still hurting you. Keep silent and they keep their power."

'"Come with me, Rob. Will you come with me to get the stones?"

'Rob piled up the cart with all I needed, carried the sheets of corrugated iron. And when the last stone was set in place and the sheets of iron placed on top for a roof, I crawled inside.

'"Viv, tell me, why are you crying?" Rob said.

'"Because of the story. About the man who lost his daughter."

'"Tell me the story."

'"I'll tell you the truth."

'I climbed through the opening in the stones. I reached and took Rob's big, safe hand. I opened my mouth, began. Once, long ago . . .

'*Once, long ago, in a world very much like ours, there was a wise, kind, gentle man who, some said, was a descendant of . . .*

'Not to Gwynnie, not to anyone else. Only told me. Bit by bit, gaining my trust, keeping me hooked. And I liked the story, at first I did. I wanted it to have a happy ending. But it didn't. And it scared me. And I wanted to tell. *But I couldn't.* I wanted to tell Mumma and Pappa, about when they went out, about

253

those evenings when they left us. Sometimes, I'd have my mouth so full of the words I couldn't speak. I tried to tell them. *But I didn't dare.* Because of what might happen. Because of what had happened to the raven-haired girl, to the spirit of his daughter who told about the secret symbols and, because she told, the black tree plucked her from her bed and an eagle carried her off to the forest, where her tongue was cut out and she suffered eternal torture.

'In the beginning, it was OK. Three of us together.

'On the Story Seat, on the settee. Toffees. The stories. "The Wild Swans", "The Real Princess", "The Little Mermaid", "The Castle of Murder", "Bluebeard", "The Hand with the Knife"'. Leading us further into the dark, into fear. And then "The Man Who Lost His Daughter". After a while, he'd say Gwynnie had to go up to bed before me. Because she was younger, he said. I wanted to tell her. Gwynnie, eyes glued to his lips. He kissed me, just on the cheek. *Just one little kissy before bed.* Thick, wet lips. Slimy. Like slugs. One night, after Gwynnie had gone up, he said,

'"I've got something very special to show you."

'"Why is it special?"

'"Because it belonged to my mother. Look."

'And he reached into his pocket and opened his hand. A penknife. Pretty. Like jewellery.

'"Lapis lazuli. Semi-precious. But precious enough. See," he said, "it matches my toothpick."

'And then he opened the blade and held it close to my face.

'"You can hold it, if you like," he said, "but best take care, for it is extraordinarily sharp. Dangerously sharp."

'And he placed the penknife in my hand. I looked at it, felt the cold steel on my palm.

'"Time for bed, now. A little kiss, if you please. Just one. There. That was so nice. Thank you."

'We went upstairs. He tucked me into bed. Another kiss. Close. And closer.

'One night, he said I should have a wash before going to bed. I took off my nightie. In the bathroom.

'I stopped dreading the evenings Mumma and Pappa went out. Going up the stairs. Gwynnie asleep. Gwynnie safe. Counting the stairs. My hand in his. My heart beating wildly. *Up we go, no reason to be afraid.* Into the bathroom. Pure white. Praying for Gwynnie to wake, for Mumma and Pappa to come home. The flesh beneath the clothes. The black hair. The breathing. The tongue, lips, the quickening of his heart. The penknife and the stick on the floor beside me. *Here, a knife to stick in your heart. Here, a stick to beat you.*

'*Why are you locking the door? said the raven-haired girl.*

'*To keep us safe, child.*

'If you concentrate very hard, you can slow the beating of your heart to almost stillness, you can stop the flowing of your blood, you can feel the gradual ceasing of your body and what is in your head flies away. There is a stage of numbness that must be the closest you can ever get to death.'

Marguerite

'Like that shift in perspective, you know, when you slowly move back from a painting, when those areas of colour, those daubs and lines that up close appear meaningless, suddenly fall into place, and you can see how they relate, and the picture is seen entire, is understood.

'When Phineas came back to St Bernard's to take me home . . . On the train, looking out of the window at the wide, cloud-free sky, I felt strong, ready to face the world again. Phineas was holding my hand. He was quiet, pensive. Getting used to us being together again, I thought. Like the lovely awkwardness of new lovers, I thought – hoped. But too quiet, grave faced. I was wondering whether we'd ever escape the shadows. When we got back to Castle Keep, Gwynne left us together, on our own. She knew Phineas needed to talk to me. He held me close, tight, and told me about Reemie's book, about what he had suspected, was almost certain had happened to Viviane years ago . . . That shift – agony – then – crystal clear.

'On my way to bed last night, passing by Viviane's room, I saw the girls sitting together on the bed. They seem to need to be near each other. Like they used to, years ago. Gwynne's face was turned to her sister and Viviane looked up at me, her grey-blue eyes fresh, that look of accusation fallen away.

'She's started having some kind of counselling. Someone she can talk to, she said, someone outside. Someone like you, I suppose.

'This morning, I remembered, after Phineas had left one evening during that last year, before I had left to go to my art class, he had come into the studio. I'd been working feverishly all day, Gwynne bringing me food, like I was one of her creatures in the forest. I'd turned the music up loud, thought it was Viviane who'd switched it off, the way she did sometimes to get my attention. But when I turned away from the canvas, I saw it was Reemie.

'"I have come to remind you, Mrs Goode, the time. Getting a little late. Your art class. Shouldn't you be on your way?"

'He was staring at the paintings, pursing those thick lips, tapping that stick of his, muttering to himself. He walked around the studio, studying one painting after another, then he stood before the one depicting a mother on her knees before a seated child.

'"Like a courtier before a queen, Mrs Goode," he said. "The word 'beholden' springs to mind." His eyes bulged, he was staring hard. "They are responsible, are they not, Mrs Goode, for so many of our burdens – our mothers, I mean?"

'When I got home after teaching, Reemie couldn't get out of Castle Keep quickly enough. He'd left his stick behind and I had to run after him. His face was ashen. I thought he must be ill. I was worried, offered to call a taxi. He didn't even say goodbye. I watched him disappear over the hill. I never saw him again.

'You feel you should have protected them. How to accept that you couldn't. *However hard I tried, lass, I knew I couldn't protect you from everything.* Something my father said on the tape he sent to the hospital. Thinking about what he said and wanting to put my arms permanently around Viviane. If only I could have protected her always. I keep listening to the tape, to my father's words, in those low moments when I can feel myself slipping back. *So proud of the way you mothered those two . . . The fairground, Maggie, you remember, how you'd plague me to take you up on the big wheel.* Feeling my father's arm, stronger, safer than the metal bar, around my waist. Towards the end of my time at the hospital, as part of the healing process, Max suggested I make contact with my father. So I wrote him a brief but heartfelt letter, to tell him I was "healed", that I hoped to return to Castle Keep, that Phineas and I both wanted to get back together. I told him that I was sorry I had pushed him away, that I hoped we too could pick

257

up where we'd left off. Shortly after, I received a package, a cassette tape. His voice had mellowed, was softer than I remembered.

All coming out a-jumble, Maggie, but a voice from my heart . . . too much to say on the telephone and my handwriting's never been up to much. What I want to say, Maggie, I have always loved you, even those times when it might have seemed otherwise . . . somehow it was easier to love you more freely when you were a tiny baby, so innocent . . . children do not ask to be born, now, do they? . . . though I never stopped loving you, lass, but when I started to see . . . but it seemed like it happened overnight. One day, I turned around and there you were and there she was, in miniature, my Marie. Not just in your face, your eyes, she was in you, your mother, had given you a gift, your painting. You know, I used to take those pictures you did to work, put them up on the wall behind my desk. But I know I did not always show you that love, not even when I wanted to. Sometimes, how can I explain, it seemed like there were two of me, the man who loved his daughter with all his heart, and the man who'd lost his dear wife. You had been given to me. You were what I had been given and what had been taken from me and maybe it's wrong of me to tell you all this, Maggie, but I want to be honest with you. What a blind fool I must have been, seeing only what I had lost. And I can't forgive myself for that, not ever. It was hard when you went off to your art college. I was so proud of my girl, yes, but it felt like a loss. And I know how much you loved that painting of your mother. The one she'd done, on your bedroom wall, you remember. And I knew why you'd left it behind. Knew that you'd left it for me. When you were born, I remember looking down at you, so perfect, your lovely dark hair, and I knew right then that I would never hurt you, that if anyone ever laid so much as a finger, just like I told that husband of yours, but I could see you'd got yourself a gentle man . . . I did my best to be both father and mother and I know sometimes I failed . . . Something you said, Maggie, when it was all going wrong for you and Phineas, all that trouble with Viviane, I never had a mother, Dad, you said, so what the hell made me think I could ever be one? And you'd asked me then, that last time I came to visit you all, what's gone wrong, Dad? Tell me. But I couldn't tell you. All I know is I was proud of the way you mothered those two beautiful granddaughters of mine. I'd watch you with the girls, saw how happy you all were. Even when my lovely Gwynne went deaf, you all got to grips. I remember Vivvy showing her old granddad how to sign the words. I missed them, you know, wondered if I'd done anything . . . The fairground, Maggie, you remember, how you'd plague me to take you up on the big wheel. You wanted to go on again and again. Loved it best right at the top. Because it's nearer heaven, you said, and I knew you meant your mother. Reaching up with your little hands, touching heaven, you said. I had never been much of a religious man but I turned to the God they all said would help me after your mother's death. But look what the good God had done, taken the woman I had loved. So I found my own god and I found my own demons . . .

'I kept playing the tape over and over at the hospital. *Proud of the way you mothered those two.* But if I was so good as a mother, what then had gone so wrong with Viviane?

'One of her teachers asked to see us. Felt like the third degree.

'"Viviane's a naturally bright child, Mr and Mrs Goode, but the standard of her work is slipping. She seems to have lost interest, become withdrawn – suddenly so. Noticeably so – particularly for a nine-year-old."

'The teacher looked at me then, leaning forward.

'"I was wondering, Mrs Goode, is there anything wrong, at home?"

'Wrong? What could be wrong? I became defensive, wanted to scream at the woman – *Nothing's wrong, no one's . . . It's Vivvy, Vivvy, that's what's wrong!*

'A stick. A black walking stick. Can hear it now. Tap-tap-tapping along the path to Castle Keep. Viviane inside, silent. I could not bear those silences. Worse than her anger, than the wild-child rebellion, the temper, the shouting.

'The day before I left the hospital I went for a walk with Gilda around the hospital gardens. It was the first time I was able to step outside without looking at the ground, the first time I was able to look up at the sky. Gilda pushing her empty pushchair, me beside her, crunching through the brown leaves. It was a wonderfully clear, crisp October day, everything shone, had a resonance, a newness, as if I were seeing for the first time. I once read of an artist who had survived a near-fatal car crash. During his recovery, he took up photography. His subjects were simple, the ordinary, the everyday – frosted branches, a leaf, blades of grass growing through pavement cracks. His work was described as brilliant, fresh, innocent. He spoke of how, after the accident, he felt he was seeing the world for the first time. And it seemed I was, that crisp autumn day.

'But questions were still unanswered. And then Phineas came to St Bernard's to take me home.

'The awful irony was that at the hospital with Max I was doing so well. After almost three years with Max, I was almost healed, ready to leave, had come to accept my – and I still find this hard to say – my innocence.

'You remember, I told you about that time we were making the birthday cake for Phineas, and I said Viviane had appeared resolved. Not resolved, I know now, but relinquished.

'The blood, her eyes. Signs. How could I have missed the signs? Because I would never have imagined . . . Because I was so sure it was my fault . . . *responsible for so many of our burdens, our mothers*. But I should have known. That last year, before Phineas left, when we thought our troubles with Viviane were over – the relief. But she was so withdrawn, I still felt . . . But feeling something is wrong is not the same as knowing.

'One day, after Phineas had left with Allie Finlay, I was sitting by the fire, trying to get myself together to go and teach the art class. I was teaching a couple of times a week, trying to keep myself busy, from dwelling. But I dreaded having to go out, even to the shops. If it hadn't been for Gwynne . . . I was doing my best to keep things going. I didn't mind that it was getting late and Reemie still hadn't arrived. I was praying he'd telephone to say he couldn't look after the girls. Viviane came in, stood beside me. I looked up to see that her face was smeared with red. But it wasn't paint. I could smell it. And I'll never forget her eyes shining through the mask of menstrual blood. She looked . . . victorious.

'Last night, for the first time in years, Viviane put her arms around me – light, hesitant. And beneath the thin cotton of her T-shirt, she felt so thin and brittle. But as I touched her face she smiled and her cheek plumped and, just for a moment, she was my little girl again, that happy, innocent child. And I sensed, although that child had left her long ago, Viviane had, for a moment, found her, found strength from her.

'I have a gallery of paintings in my mind. The first is almost finished. The background is now complete. I've used subtle yellows, greens, a touch of summer blue. All four figures have been drawn and positioned at the centre of the painting, close together. Closer than they've ever been. There's a feeling of intimacy, of solidity, as if they will remain all four together for a very long time.'

So, Maggie/Marguerite/Mrs Goode departed, those eyes of blue brightened by her mind's 'picture of togetherness'. And to put *us* in the picture: at the end of last October, Gwynne was on her way with Nyssa to St Benedict's, remember, hoping Phineas had not yet left. On the train she kept turning the pages of Viviane's notebook, read again the letter from Phineas that

Viviane had kept from her, read again the words her sister had highlighted. That which she was already beginning to fear like an elusive word dancing on the tip of . . . the fly just out of reach of the frog's flicking tongue. And the north winds they blew. And the world was freezing to a standstill. And all Gwynne could think of was Viviane.

Arriving at St Benedict's, Gwynne was taken to Abbot Lenten, who told her that, yes, unfortunately, her father had left the abbey at the beginning of October, that she was, in fact, the second person to come looking for him. After the initial shock, for the two had not seen each other for more than ten years, Gwynne explained to Ms Finlay that Viviane had disappeared, that she was desperately worried, for only weeks ago her sister had attempted to take her own life.

Allie

'I have let go, finally, of her spirit. As if I was meant to meet Gwynne at the abbey, with the child.

'Gwynne and I had been talking for some time. It was late afternoon, already dusk. The little girl, Nyssa, looked tired. She asked me for a cuddle, had climbed up on to my lap. She took off my glasses. I had pretty brown eyes just like her mummy, she said. I was frightened, of putting my arms around her, of how it would make me feel. When she leant back against me, I could smell her hair and, for a moment, it took my breath away. I couldn't breathe, my chest was tight, I felt . . . locked up.

'Then yesterday, thinking over what I needed to tell you today, I was looking through the window, and I saw her, Orelia, running away. And then she stopped, turned and waved to me. She was smiling. She was shining. Like an angel, I thought. And then she was gone. But I had no sense of loss, no sadness. I knew it was her spirit, realised I had harboured her spirit for so long it had become a burden, that I had now let her slip away and I was free to love another child again – and in my heart, hope, light . . .

'Last October, with Gwynne, at St Benedict's, I told her how it had always played on my mind, that night I came to collect Phineas from Castle Keep in the storm, the night her father left, seeing Viviane barefoot, in her nightie, drenched and shivering, crying out as I drove away.

'"I hated myself for destroying your family, Gwynne, but I was determined I wasn't going to lose him, let her stop him leaving. I feel so ashamed. And you probably hate me for it too."

'"He had a choice," Gwynne said, "and he chose to go. And I knew they weren't happy, Mumma and Pappa."

'Phineas must have told her, I said, that we were later to lose our daughter.

'"So you believed that because of what you had done you did not deserve a child, did not deserve to be happy?"

'And Gwynne looked at me then, reached out her hand to touch mine, and I felt, in that small gesture, forgiveness.

'We were sitting in the room where Phineas had stayed. The abbot had told me I could remain at the abbey for a while as the room would be empty for the time being. Gwynne and I talked for a while about the past, watching Nyssa through the window playing in the garden.

'"Did she really resent me that much, Gwynne? Was that why she was so difficult?"

'"It wasn't you, Allie," she said. "Something was wrong, very wrong, with Viviane. Perhaps I didn't want to see it, didn't want to know. But it's coming back to me now."

'Nyssa was playing with her doll, throwing her up in the air, catching her, laughing. Then she turned, saw us watching her and ran over and pressed her lips to the window in a kiss. Then she signed and waved, raising her doll's hand to wave too. And Gwynne turned to me then, her face suddenly blanched but her eyes wide as if in alarm, as if in sudden awareness. "Her hand," she said, "in the mirror."

'I had no idea what she meant. She couldn't explain, she said. She told me she would take Nyssa back. Her mother had a friend Nyssa could stay with until her own mother was out of hospital. Then Gwynne was going home, to Castle Keep. She was sure Viviane would come back.

'"I need to see, Allie," she said, "be certain it was what I saw."

'Before she left I made her promise.

'"If . . . when she comes home, you will tell her, won't you? You will tell Viviane I am sorry."

'Something on my mind I need to tell you. A small detail and perhaps of little benefit now. Something that dawned on me when I received the letter from Gwynne after the family were reunited at Castle Keep. The haunting picture of Viviane, crying out through the wind and the rain the night Phineas left.

'She was calling to us, not "don't make him go away" but "don't. Make him go away". I was lip-reading through the rain, you see, and I was all mixed up, angry and confused and . . . I saw the words but I couldn't hear – the sense, I mean. I misunderstood. *Make him go away.* After I'd read Gwynne's letter, I realised. She meant Reemie.

'I remember, not long before Phineas and I met, seeing Reemie, at the door of the lecture hall, waiting to begin his lecture just as I was concluding mine. Up until then, we'd barely exchanged two words. A strange little man, I used to think, eccentric, harmless. A bit of a joke among some of the students. He'd given a little bow as I came out. "Your style is most enviable, Ms Finlay. I have been listening attentively. One is never too old to learn, as the saying goes." He went on about how well my students were doing, how I was born to the work and so on. I had felt really rather flattered.

'It was Reemie who'd brought us together – Phineas and I. Reemie was gushing . . . *One of our finest young minds at St Bartolph's . . . expertise unmatched . . . a breath of fresh air . . . greatly loved by all her students . . .* The look on his face when he'd introduced us – glee, delight, something akin to entrapment.'

Gwynne

'The stag, standing beneath the Lightning Tree, its eyes glinting in the moonlight, its antlers, fingers. *Go, Gwynnie, go look—*

'Pappa had already left St Benedict's and part of me had known, even as I got on the coach, that I wouldn't find Viviane there. But the last person I had expected to meet at the abbey was Allie. Over nine years since we'd last seen each other. We spent a few hours talking, about Pappa, about Viviane, and I suppose we could have gone on talking but . . . like a misted mirror becoming clear I knew I had to get back to Castle Keep.

'She wasn't there when I got home. But I waited. Because I knew she would be coming back. Of course, I couldn't sleep so I stood at the window of my bedroom, looking out. And I remembered the stag, the night it came into the garden, its antlers, like fingers pointing . . . *Go, Gwynnie, go see . . .* And just as I had done that night years ago, I turned away from the window and went to the bathroom. But this time the door was open, this time I went in. I sat on the blue chair, where Viviane would later tell me he would sit—

'Seven, I was seven years old and Vivvy was ten. I'd had some bad dream, I think, and I got up and went to look for the moon as I always did when I couldn't get to sleep. Sometimes, on the hill, on the other side of the beech hedge, I'd see the antlers, the gentle bowing of its heavy head, as if it knew I was watching. But I couldn't see it anywhere that night. And it's so cold out tonight, my breath's misted up the window and I wipe the glass with the sleeve of my nightie and I look out, I'm looking out and I see it now, right there, in the middle of the garden, by Vivvy's tree, and I'm thinking Vivvy must have forgotten to shut the fence again because she's always forgetting things now, like all the time her mind is somewhere else, like most of the time she's not inside herself at all. It's like a statue but no, it's not, because I can see it blinking now, slowly, the way my dolls blink, and I can see it's breathing and it's looking right at me, I know it is. And it stays there for hours, it seems, and I've forgotten all about my bad dream, but then it turns and walks away into the shadows. And I turn too then and I see, across the landing, the light under the door of the bathroom, and I'm wondering why the door is shut because Vivvy never shuts the door, like she's afraid of being in there, even when the light is on, and Mumma's always telling her we don't want to see you on the toilet, Viviane, thank you very much. And it's the strangest thing but it's like the stag is right there behind me, leading me to the bathroom, but it can't be, of course, because how could it have got into the house. And I call softly, Vivvy, and I turn the door handle and open the door but just then Professor Reemie is there and he pushes the door back a little. I can see something in the mirror and Professor Reemie's face is peering round the door, like he's just a face and no body, and he's panting like he's just been running and his face is all red and he looks very cross.

'"It's late, Gwynne, you should be asleep by now. Go back to your bed."

'So I go right back to my bed but I can't get back to sleep, I don't know why. I'm feeling there's something wrong.

'Then, after a little while, Professor Reemie comes to my bedroom and he sits on the bed and switches on my bedside light and he looks at me. And I see his fingers curling over the handle of his walking stick and that black ring of his is just like an eye, a nasty dead eye, like a fish's. And I see his thick lips moving slowly.

'"You seem to be having difficulty getting to sleep tonight," he says, "so I think I shall tell you a story. A special story. I haven't told you yet, have I, the story of the curious child. About what happened to her."

'And now he's telling me this story I don't like at all, about a strange and nasty creature called Puki. And Puki's got this big pair of scissors with sharp blades. And he tells me about the child who was always listening at doors and hearing things she shouldn't be hearing and one day Puki comes along and while she's sleeping in her bed he slices off her ears and plunges the blades right into each ear-hole so she can't hear any more.

'"So it's not a good idea, Gwynnie, to listen at doors, is it? Just in case Puki comes along."

'And I'm just about to tell him I wasn't listening at the door because I'm deaf. But he's pointing that stick of his at me now and I shut my eyes tight and pretend I'm going straight to sleep—

'Sitting in the bathroom, on the blue chair. Feeling it creaking. Vivvy used to kick it, hard. Creak-creak. Old man's bones. I sat in the dark. I looked at the mirror. And it all came back. I knew then why he'd been so eager to put a new lock on the bathroom door. I remembered what I saw that night. A sound forgotten, suddenly recalled, all other sounds falling away and one note striking out of the silence. *His hand*. Reemie's hand reflected in the mirror. And what was missing?

'I remembered how he'd look at her, the way he touched her, his hands caressing the nape of her neck, her hair. Such a strange look in his eyes, not love, but a fearful passion. The way he'd say, *Come, sit on my lap, Vivvy*. And she did at first. Because she liked him at first. But after a while, she didn't want to sit on his lap any more. But she'd sit next to him anyway. And I remember his hand patting the sofa. And she'd go to him, as if he were reeling her in. That hand, the ring. The black onyx ring. The hand in the mirror. Small, delicate. Like a child's hand. But there wasn't a ring. It wasn't his hand. In the mirror. It was her hand. Hers. She was in there with him.

'When she told us. Must have been like a flaying, a self-flaying.

She was raw, opening herself up, pulling it out. A disembowelling. Every word – vinegar on wounds.

'I'll tell you a story . . .

'Once upon a time, a magical time, when summers were always warm and snow fell thick every winter, there lived two sisters. The sisters loved to spend their days playing on the high hill which was their paradise. In winter, they liked to lie on the hillside and wave their arms up and down, which made the shape of angel wings in the snow, and they'd imagine themselves to be real angels flying up to the stars. In the summertime, they would stretch out on the grass and make daisy chains, dreaming about what they were going to be when they grew up. One sister said she was going to look after all the sick and injured animals that lived down in the forest and build a huge house where they could get better but there'd always be room for her sister. And the other sister said she was going to be a famous photographer and take pictures of all the things people don't usually get to see, like a falling star, or a chick hatching from its shell, or the moment a flower opens its petals, and she was going to travel all over the world but she said she'd always come back to see her sister. And both sisters agreed that whatever happened they'd never forget each other. One day, they took a sharp knife to the high hill and they each made a tiny cut in their finger and squeezed a little drop of blood and pressed their fingers together . . . through thick and thin, sisters we've been, come what may, sisters we'll stay . . . and they promised they'd always be together, no matter what happened.'

Phineas

'I have never found leaving easy, am not good at saying goodbye. Nathan sensed it. One evening, in the kitchen, he was preparing our meal. Out of the blue he said, "It'll be all right, mate, honest. I'll just have to remember to buy the milk."

'It saddened me even to think of leaving. And I saw it in Nathan's eyes too, when he showed me the puppets one evening. I was reading *The Spirit of St Louis* to him one evening after tea. I'd begun it a couple of nights earlier when there was, Nathan said, "nothing on telly." How about a story, then, he said. We had reached the point where Lindbergh had begun his transatlantic crossing.

'"Don't stop, Funny-Arse."

'"Glue," I said, "it's putting me off. What on earth is it, Nathan?"

'"Promise you won't tell. If I show you."

'I followed him into his bedroom. On the bed, a roll of wire meshing, a small black wig, limbs, a torso, a hand. Nathan opened the wardrobe. There were three, sitting on the floor. Their faces grotesque and beautiful, the clothes exquisite. A Teddy boy with greased quiff, drainpipes and blue suede creepers, then a Marilyn Monroe figure in a white diamante-studded gown, and a cassocked priest, this last a double-headed puppet that, turned upside down, became a horned, tailed devil. Nathan took the crossbars that attached the strings to the devil, began to manipulate it, making it dance.

'"I sell them down at the market," he said. "There's a woman on one of the stalls helps with the clothes. My dad says I'm a wuss messing around with dolls. I just like making them, you know?"

'In a corner of the wardrobe, four smaller bodies in a heap, entwined, unclothed, hopelessly clutching each other, heads hung, like victims expiring under the threat of discovery.

'"I'll have them finished soon," he said. He reached for something on the bed. "Another postcard. From my ma. I'll get them every few days now she's thinking about coming home. Three weeks," he said. He looked away, fiddling with the puppet strings. "How long you staying, then, Funny-Arse?'

'I'd be well on my way, I said, before his mother got back.

'"I wasn't saying that you had to . . . you know. I just—"

'"I know, Nathan. It's OK. But it's time I was leaving anyhow."

'Later, he asked me, "What will you do? Where will you go?"

'To find my plough? My field? I could see it, stretching before me. And could I see her too – Maggie?

'I thought of Nathan and his family. All back together again. Reunited. *We just pick up right where we left off*, he said. *Couple of days and it's all back to normal*. I was envious. Could picture the three of them. And was it too much to ask, I thought – Castle Keep, the four of us? A dream. But I had done enough dreaming. Hope. *I have renounced all hope*. Indeed, you may have, Reemie, I thought. But somehow, in spite of all that had happened, I had not.

'Six floors up. The ground far below. Carrying the heavy pots of earth out on to the balcony. Their weight giving me courage, anchoring. I knew nothing about planting bulbs. October, a little late in the year for putting in crocus and daffodil perhaps. And it was so cold. But the pots would be sheltered in the corner. A spur-of-the-moment buy. For the spring. Satisfying, to plunge my hands into the rich compost. I stood for a while, out on the balcony. I wanted to close my eyes, see the flat, Allie, Orelia.

'But I looked out, at the view, towards the horizon, was aware of a kind of inner readjustment. When I turned to go back in, there was Nathan, just inside the doorway, and as I approached he reached, put his arms around me. And I felt . . . safe, yes. I knew he was saying goodbye.

'But I knew I had to get back, to the real world, to life. And I was feeling lighter, ready. Increasingly, I thought of Maggie

271

and the girls. No dream, I thought, a real possibility. I believed I had lost that innocence, you see. But how wrong I was. The Goode family, up in Castle Keep, a dream to be shattered once again, a mere illusion. The mirage of the parched traveller.

'Tell me, is that what life is, a series of shattered dreams, shimmering promises forever just out of reach?

'When I left to come here today, Maggie was in her studio. She's started to paint again, a sign that her passion is returning. But the strain has clearly marked her. The skin seems to stretch tight over the contours of her face, has reduced her. Even her paintbrush seemed heavy in her hand. Gwynne and Viviane were in the kitchen, together – yet not . . . Viviane was staring out of the window. How brittle she looked, as if she had stood too long in that shaft of sunlight, her eyes scrunched and blinking, against the intensity of light, with an inner struggle. In the warmth of the sun, she appeared horribly cold and I wanted to put my arms around her. But I am still uncomfortable about touching her. Even words feel somehow too intrusive, too intimate.'

I (that is, as Confessor) was waiting for her, for Viviane. And on cue, she came. She would not sit, was a penitent, in the corner, head hung.

'Scared – that I was going mad,' she said, 'like mad Miri-Anne. Split in two. There was the me he did that to. Then the other me, silent child, hiding in the Dark Room. So sure they could see – that I was stained with it. Like my drying developing photographs, showing the truth of me.

'The story,' she said, '"The Man Who Lost His Daughter". That's how he did it,' she said, 'got to me. One night, after Gwynne had gone to bed, he told me.'

I was not looking forward to what I knew was going to come, to that which I had been powerless to prevent, the reminder of my impotence, that I was not powerful enough to overcome the bad, the evil in him.

Viviane left without telling me the story. Perhaps she had somehow sensed that I knew it already, sensed who I was. The Man Who Lost His Daughter. The story. It's here, in Reemie's book. Listen.

This is the story of the man who lost his daughter, one that, if you listen carefully to what lies between the lines . . . Ah, but you listen already. And so, I must begin.

Let us travel now, to once long ago, to a faraway world where lived a kind, gentle, good man, who, it was said, was descended from the great Norse god Odin.

Now, unknown to this kind, gentle, good man, his wife had a heart of ice. She had tricked the good man into marrying her solely for an heir, a son who would inherit her great wealth. But the Ice Wife gave birth to a daughter, and when this heartless woman looked upon the face of her poor newborn only to see the face of a frog, she cried out, 'Take this ugly bundle of bones, go drown it in the river!'

But from the first, the good man saw only beauty in his daughter, and his large warm heart beat only with love for her, though she was a sickly child, skin as pale and thin as the membrane of an egg, hair as black as a raven, her huge eyes ever filled with fear.

The Ice Wife was jealous of the love between father and child and while the good man was nursing his daughter one day, the Ice Wife, her steel-grey eyes now shining like emeralds, now red as hot coals, told him they were leaving, and she snapped her thin fingers and a carriage carved from Arctic ice pulled by six white bears appeared, and there inside, shivering with fear and cold, was his daughter.

'Cruel, heartless wife!' cried the good man. 'You cannot take her away. I love my daughter.'

'Love?' spat the wife. 'You call it love!' And then, the words freezing in the air as she spoke, she told the good man he would never set eyes on his daughter again. And with that, she climbed up into the carriage and, with a crack of a whip, they were gone.

Now, the world might as well have ended for the good man. He sat in the house, hearing only the singing, laughing echoes of his beloved daughter. And sometimes, in the long lonely nights, he thought he saw her, in the shadows.

One day, he heard a 'tap-tap-tap' and looked to see a bird with a crimson breast perched on the window sill.

'I am the Bird of Truth,' said the bird. 'Tonight you shall dream. Pay heed.'

That night the good man dreamt of a castle with walls of dazzling white, atop a high mountain. The next morning, the bird appeared again and told the good man that there in the Castle upon High Mountain would he find the spirit of his lost daughter.

'But I know of it!' cried the good man. 'For I have read of the castle in stories, though I know only that it is far away.'

That very same day, the good man set out on the long journey to High Mountain. After many weeks of travelling, he found himself in a wilderness where he wandered in vain, tired, hungry and thirsty, until he came upon a well. And just as he looked down into the well, only to find it was dry, a feather floated down to him.

He looked up to see the Bird of Truth hovering above him.

'Take the feather,' said the bird.

And as the man reached for the feather, it turned into a knife with a handle of lapis lazuli.

'All is well and all in the well will nourish you,' said the bird.

Now the good man was by then desperate for water. He noticed some vines hanging from a tree near by and with the knife he cut one of the vines for a rope and then he took off his hat for a bucket and he lowered the hat into the well. But when he drew it up, he found not water, but a stone upon

274

which was written WATER, and the moment he took it in his hands, his thirst was quenched as if he had drunk from the freshest mountain spring. Then he lowered the hat again and drew it up and this time the word on the stone was BREAD and he instantly felt as full as if he had dined on the feast of a king. But the third time the man drew up that hat, the word was LOVE, though he had to look closely for it had worn, as if it had been held by many before him, all seeking the same. And when he held it, the good man felt only cold stone.

'Why do I feel nothing?' he asked.

'Because you know not its true meaning,' said the bird. 'Tell me, good man, what are you, innocent or guilty?'

The good man looked at the bird, unable to answer.

'Good man, are you so innocent you forget what it means to be guilty?' said the bird. 'Or are you so guilty you forget what it means to be innocent?'

'You talk in riddles,' said the good man.

'Not I,' said the bird, 'it is how the words assemble themselves. And you have forgotten their meaning. So listen most carefully as I tell you now where to find your daughter.'

And the bird told the good, kind man that he must journey towards the north until he came to a dense, dark forest of firs. And there he would witness the terrible fate of all those children who could not keep secrets. But his desire to find the spirit of his daughter would drive him on to the other side. And there he would see, rising up into the clouds, a steep-sided mountain with a brilliant white castle upon its summit. And there he would find that which he was seeking.

Then the bird told the good man that he must look on the path that led from the forest to the mountain. For there would he find protection. But he must think carefully about the choice he made.

Now, the good man, desperate to find the spirit of his daughter, entered the forest and, as he made his way farther in, the sunshine was left far behind and there was an eerie twilight. Little by little, his eyes adjusted and he saw, hanging from the branches of the trees, like strange and terrible fruit, the tongues and limbs and still-bleeding hearts of all those children who had not been able to keep secrets. And he heard the echoes of their wailing and screaming resounding through the trees. And steel blades flashed and danced about him like the eyes of beasts. But the good man continued onward, driven by his love for his daughter, until finally he reached the other side.

There, in the distance, rising majestically to the heavens, was High Mountain, its steep sides glinting like glass in the sunshine, and on the summit the gleaming white castle.

The good man followed the path before him and before long he came upon a small black drawstring pouch. When the good man opened it, he found small black stones inscribed with strange symbols.

Just then, the Bird of Truth hopped on to the branch of a nearby tree.

'These stones belonged to your forefather, the great god Odin. They bear the runes of magic and wisdom which you may use as protection.'

The lapis lazuli knife fell from the good man's pocket and just before it hit the ground it turned into a feather. Then the bird said,

'Take this cup of blood I have squeezed from my red breast and take the feather, for one is ink and one is pen. Now, good man, learn by heart these symbols, for the stones must remain for others who find themselves on the path.'

Then the bird sang,

> 'Wisdom magic feather blood
> make the good choice that you should
> paint on thine own skin or hers
> the decision is only yours.'

But there surely is no choice to make, thought the good man, for I am in no need of protection.

After many hours of climbing, the good man finally reached the summit of High Mountain, and there before him was the vast white-walled castle, and just as he sat upon a grassy mound to recover from his arduous ascent, he saw, through a window, the King and Queen seated around a dining table with two princesses, one fair and the other raven haired, who reminded him so much of his daughter that his heart bled. Then the raven-haired girl looked up and saw him and smiled most tenderly. And his heart was filled with joy.

The good man knocked on the castle door, which was opened by a footman who led him to the servants' quarters, where he was given a hearty meal and a bed. Wanting to thank someone for the hospitality, the good man wandered until, sitting by an open window, singing, he saw the raven-haired girl, who introduced herself as Princess Mariane.

'Forgive me, I am sorry,' said the good man, 'I did not mean to scare you.'

The girl said she welcomed his company because she was very lonely. The King and Queen were always involved in Far More Important Matters of State and loved her fair sister more because she was their true child.

Now, the castle was vast and, just as the girl had said, the King and Queen were so busy that they did not notice the good man, who remained in the servants' quarters and soon became the secret companion of the Princess Mariane.

One day, the good man said he had a secret to tell the princess. But before he could tell her what it was, she had to promise never to tell a soul. And the princess crossed her heart and said she hoped to die.

And so, the good man told her all about how his daughter was taken from him by the Ice Wife and that he was the saddest being on earth until a little bird told him that his daughter's spirit was still alive.

'Alive in you,' said the good man, 'for your heart is warm and large and open enough for her to live inside. And so you are very special. But I cannot risk losing even the spirit of my daughter again, for then my world should end.'

Then the good man told the girl about the symbols and showed her the blood and the feather and said they would protect her. And Mariane took the good man to a room high up in the castle at the top of a winding staircase where nobody went, and she did as the good man instructed. She took off her robes and then she was cleansed and lay down on the floor while the good man painted the symbols upon her soft white skin.

And the good man reminded Mariane that if she breathed one word about their secret she would suffer the fate of all those children in the forest.

But Mariane's sister was a suspicious girl. She knew just by looking that her dark-haired sister harboured a secret and asked Mariane a hundred times a day to tell. But when Mariane, despite the warnings of the good man, eventually told her, the fair-haired sister almost laughed her head off.

And from that moment, Mariane felt her heart begin to shrink a little and she grew very afraid.

And well she might, for that night, while she was shivering in her bed, fearing the worst, the worst happened. The black tree in the garden below her window reached up into her window with one of its long branches and plucked her from her bed and dropped her into the thick forest below the mountain. There she was chased by a thousand dancing knives and there was nowhere to hide and there was no way out, and she saw the hearts and tongues and legs and arms of the children hanging from the trees, and as she opened her mouth to scream, one of the knives neatly sliced off her tongue, which wriggled away from her. Then another knife sliced off her arms and legs and then, just when she thought she could stand no more pain, a knife pierced her chest and dug out her heart and there she lay, or what was left of her, the blades slicing her torso into tiny pieces to be devoured by the forest beasts.

And the heart of the raven-haired girl hung from a branch and bled, her cries joining the terrible blood-curdling chorus of agony of all the other children who could not keep secrets.

A nasty warning tale, indeed. And the fate of the good man matters little. Perhaps I have coloured the tale a little, added an element of moral dilemma. In so doing, what I wanted to impress, and what, of course, in his telling of the tale, Reemie did not, was that he had a choice, but like poor Miri-Anne he made the wrong one.

Or did he?

An hour or so passed before Viviane came back. I imagine she must have been pacing the streets, the way she paced around the shadows of this small (intimate) room. Crouching in a corner, she said,

'With a pine cone. A fucking pine cone.'

Pine? Yes. It is referred to somewhere in *The Book*. And I quote:

Bacchus Liber/Liber Pater – possessor of a phallic sceptre tipped with a pine cone. I found myself looking up the etymology of 'pine', I know not why:

Pine 1: evergreen tree, developed from Old English/Latin/ French etc. etc.

Pine 2: to yearn. From *pinen*, to crucify, to torment, to punish.

Ach, and she did, Mutti, how she punished me.

Viviane went and a few days later her father paid me a visit. He sat here for almost an hour, saying nothing, his body shuddering occasionally with silent sobbing, his arms hanging limp at his sides, slumped back in the chair, like an exhausted torture victim.

At this point, I have to say, I sensed a darkening, that 'darkening of the sun' before Ragnarok, the Twilight of the Gods. But there were to be no battles. And I must confess to feeling slightly bowed myself. As anyone surely would. By the weight of their burdens, by the effort and frustration of having to hear their unfolding stories without being tempted to say: 'Yes, I know, I know'. How hard it is to appear – and yet not be – innocent of the truth. Every good priest must first find the ear of his god, for one cannot keep within each and every sin one hears. And thus are the sins of mankind returned to the Maker?

But who am I to speak of such things? For I am most certainly not a holy man. (Though I dared not tell them who I was. And it would have made little difference. A sin is a sin whoever the sinner. Yes, better they did not know.)

Phineas

'*The Difficulty of the Hill* . . . The ascension. Almost impossible. As if I still carry *The Book*, its weight, in me. Like Christian in Bunyan's *Pilgrim's Progress,* climbing up the difficult side of the Hill. Progress?

'Almost four months now since we've been reunited in Castle Keep. At first it was as if we were all on separate paths, disoriented, strangers in our own home, to each other. But beginning now to come to terms, each in our own way, with the knowledge of what happened, beginning to connect. And, every now and then, the familiar briefly returns . . .

'The other day, Maggie was taking a tray of tea up to the girls. She stumbled going up the stairs. The plate of biscuits fell to the floor. We stooped together, reached for the same biscuit, one of those 'dammy jodgers', as Viviane used to call them, with the cut-out smiley faces. Maggie and I laughed as we bumped heads and I knew she was remembering, as I was, Viviane's funny baby-talk, but the memory disappeared as quickly as it had come, as our smiles simultaneously faded and we saw in each other's eyes that which we each felt, an awareness of something found, of the possibility of a new way of being.

'Viviane. About what happened to Viviane. I'm not sure I can, know how to, tell you. How it happened. But now I know, how he did it, how he got to us. You see, we'd had another of those fireside chats, Reemie and I, though it was not so cosy, when I'd poured out my troubles, about Viviane mostly. By then, I had convinced myself of my failure. And I left his study that evening neither reassured nor with hope but with the conviction that I had failed, a conviction I held throughout that last year with my family, which remained through my time with Allie, which I only began to let go of during those years of silence at the abbey, which finally left me in the last weeks with Nathan. It was some time in that

last year at Castle Keep when I told him I had never felt so inse-
cure, that it was all my fault. *We cannot all be angels, Phineas.*
Parenthood is not for everyone. I understood his words as those
of a true and wise friend. Words I trusted, found myself believing.

'Coming here, sitting and talking in this small, safe place –
am I baring my soul, or am I still hiding? Oh, but this is no
pilgrimage. I thought I had climbed my hill, that day, leaving
St Benedict's, surveying my road ahead, that day I stood on the
balcony at Nathan's thinking of Orelia falling.

'Watching poor Icarus melting away that last night at
Nathan's, as the two flames at the tip of each high-extended
wing burned to eventually merge at the figure's head, I became
aware of an inner stilling, as if the flames were consuming
the last breathy whispers of the voice of judgement, which, as the
flame was extinguished in the pool of wax, was finally silenced.

'Nathan and I had been subdued all evening, wary perhaps of
the conversation turning to my departure in the morning. I would
miss him, had come to regard him with brotherly affection.

'He'd prepared us a feast, forbidding me to go into the kitchen
until it was ready. Pasta and fish, the exact meal he'd cooked that
night at the hostel when we'd played table tennis. I was touched
by the evident care he'd taken with the table setting. There were
candles, napkins and he'd even bought new wineglasses from
which we drank the very decent claret I'd contributed to mark
the occasion. I noticed he'd had a wash and brush-up, was dressed
'to the nines', in apple-green shirt, tan suede waistcoat, with a
red handkerchief at his neck, and new boots, the toes tipped with
metal, a clinking mock spur at each outer ankle, giving him the
curious appearance of sprite and cowboy. His hair was gelled
and spectacularly spiked and I even detected a whiff of after-
shave, of pine.

'That he had made such an occasion of it was heart warming,
restorative, for throughout my itinerant childhood there had been
a distinct lack of ceremony regarding my toing and froing from
one home to another, which may have been arranged thus with

the good intention of giving me a smooth passage but had in fact the opposite effect, so that I would dwell on my situation.

'We spoke a little about his plans. He was going to finish his job at the hostel soon, he said, get the catering business up and running. And what about me, he said, was I going back to 'that castle of mine'? But all that we could have said, about our friendship, how good the last weeks had been, it seemed we had no need to say.

'We cleared away the dishes then watched a seventies film about a DJ pursued by a psychotic female, the scene where she repeatedly and viciously stabs and rips a portrait to pieces, making me think briefly of Maggie's paintings.

'I could not sleep that night, my thoughts turning to the world outside, to Maggie and the girls. I thought of my brief time at Nathan's as some necessary rite of passage. I could only have slept a couple of hours, but I remember the strange dream. That I was standing at the foot of a tower looking up, my eyes blinded by the sun but aware that something was falling towards me that I could not see until it landed heavily in my arms, making me stagger and almost lose my footing on what I realised only then with horror was a tightrope, and when I looked at the creature in my arms I knew it was Nathan, but a horned, fanged, hairy, grotesque Nathan with a long, lolling tongue. I woke, my eyes opening on the mural's sunset, knew that it was both end and beginning. It seemed I had learnt far more in those few weeks with Nathan than I had learnt in my life so far.

'In the morning, I stayed in bed, until I heard Nathan leave. When I went into the kitchen, I found them hanging over the backs of the chairs, the four puppets in Nathan's wardrobe, now finished, dressed and painted, a king, queen and two princesses, one fair and one dark. Me, Maggie, Gwynne and Viviane. I realised Nathan must have copied from the photograph. On top of my rucksack, which I had packed ready the night before, was a card, a picture of a farmhouse at the heart of a valley. Inside he'd written in childish scrawl, "Remember, you can't save everyone, Funny-Arse." I folded the puppets carefully into a bag. And then I set my own gifts on the table, an artist's set of pencils, paints and charcoal and a block of 'state of the art' kitchen knives. As a last-minute thought, I went out and bought eggs, bread and milk.

'When I picked up my rucksack, I bent under the weight, discovering that Nathan had filled it with large bricks and a note at the bottom telling me where he had hidden my things. Unable to think of anything funny, I piled the stones in a mound on the table. And I left.

'I walked into a freezing November morning and headed towards the town. It was the kind of day Maggie would have liked, the sky a blanket of heavy dark grey cloud. Wishing I'd had a thicker coat, I bought myself a hat and gloves from a charity shop. I couldn't remember whether I had reminded Nathan to bring in the tubs from the balcony until the cold spell had passed, to remember to water the bulbs in the spring.

'I walked, but had no idea where I was heading. Should I look for a job? It was approaching the Christmas season, there were plenty of vacancies for temporary work. Should I look for somewhere to stay? But there'd be little point without a job to my name. Should I find a bed and breakfast, then? One thing I knew, I would not be going back to the hostel. But my thinking was half hearted. What I really wanted was to go home, to return to Castle Keep, and to see Maggie. And would Maggie want to see me? I found a phone box and, gathering my courage, I rang the hospital. A nurse told me Maggie was coming to the end of her treatment and was due to leave St Bernard's within the next few weeks. If I wanted more information, she suggested I call back the next day when I could talk to Dr Kenning. Then I telephoned Castle Keep, heard Gwynne's answerphone message to e-mail or text.

'Increasingly unsure, I went for a coffee. I would give myself an hour to make up my mind. I shared a table with an old man peering short-sightedly at a newspaper who had merely grunted as I sat down. The smell of frying bacon was too tempting. I ordered a full breakfast and waited for my food, the old man grunting again as he got up to leave. My head was spinning, my thoughts running in circles. I was thinking too much, perhaps. I took Reemie's book from my rucksack. Leafing through the pages, I read again about his wife taking his daughter from him, her cruel words, *not fit to be near a child, any child* . . . You see, I thought the reason he'd wanted me to have the book was to unburden his conscience, about his pilfering from the Reading Room. And the business about the photograph, thinking she was the spirit of his daughter. I thought he must have become delusional. I was sorry for him. The waitress brought my order and I began to eat. I noticed that the man had left his newspaper. I glanced at the front page, saw a photograph of a benign-looking man next to another of a child, a young boy. Then I read the caption: *Would you let this man near your child?* And I heard the words of Reemie's wife as if she were there now, before me – *not fit to be near a child* . . .

'And then it hit me. Like a physical force that took my breath away. Like something hard rammed into my guts. I grabbed my rucksack, made for the toilets, falling back against the cubicle door behind me, my hands pressed to the walls for support. And then I was sick, with the pain in my body and the pain in my heart, gasping in horror, disbelief, as I retched over the bowl. I splashed my face with cold water, recovered enough to leave.

'My first thought was to go to Maggie. But how could I tell her? What would it do to her?

'I had set my burdens down, only to pick up what felt then like the weight of the world. And I walked, and I kept walking. As though a hand had taken mine, I found I was making my way to the coach station. Within fifteen minutes I was on a coach, on my way to Castle Keep. I had no idea what I would do, what I would say to Viviane. All I knew was I had to get back, that we would need each other now more than ever. We needed to be home, together.

'It was hard, that homecoming walk up Hart's Hill. I had forgotten how steep it was. I sat on the doorstep, unable to find my key. It was only then that I realised why he had had given me the book, what it really said, between the lines. Hell's Bible. How *deceived* I was.

'Half an hour later, I saw Gwynne, coming down the path. She ran to me. We hugged. We were both too frightened, I think, to speak. Then,

'"Pappa," Gwynne said, "about Viviane—"

'"I know," I said, "I think I know, what he did."

'A week later, I brought Maggie back. I had spoken to Dr Kenning, explained, without saying too much, that we had a family problem, that Maggie would have to be told, that I was concerned about whether she would cope.

'Then Viviane returned.

'A gale had been howling all through the night, was still raging. We all sat around the kitchen table. Viviane looked so cold, so consumed. I told her we didn't need to know where she had been, what she'd been doing. We were just thankful, I said, that she was back home. "In one piece," I said, "safe." And she looked up at me then and I could see in her eyes – not in one piece, not safe, they said.

'Knowing was harder than anything we had endured. I have often since, in weak moments, longed for innocence. But it, he, did not destroy us.

'I wanted to tell you, before I go now, leave you for the last time, about yesterday evening, after we'd all sat down to supper.

'What a supper! One of Maggie's roasts, smoked salmon to start, fruit crumble, wine. I'd caught them all in the kitchen earlier, the girls helping Maggie. Someone had put on music. Viviane was humming to herself. There was an air of quiet cele-bration. We sat at the table, about to eat. Then Maggie reached out to Gwynne next to her and Gwynne took her hand, then Gwynne to Viviane, Viviane to me, as I then reached to Maggie. And we all looked at each other, one to another. It was a kind of grace, not for our food, but our survival. And I felt a strength passing from one to another around our circle of four, a force that I knew would pull us through.'

The Book

My eyes deceiving me, surely? In the lecture hall this morning
. . . Too jittery to sleep, to write. Three thirty a.m. What to
do? This young fellow. That photograph. The Next Move?

Matyeus-Prinn, on the prowl. How he'd love to bring me down!
I care nothing, now, for she is back. La Bella. *Meine.* It was an
almost supernatural turn of events. Because it was not the
lecture I should have attended. How could anyone in their
right mind confuse *Man's Strange Being: Existentialism from
Kierkegaard to Camus* with *Phonological Analysis in Panini's Astadhayahi
(circa 5th Century BC)*?!!!! But I did. Onset of blindness, of old
age? Or loss of passion, for the words. And so, one title translates into another before my very eyes. Then, quite suddenly,
another passion returns . . . This morning, the lecture. The
hall was jam packed, a tin of sardines. And there she was,
swum from the sea of my dreams. I was about to tap the
shoulder of the fellow seated in front of me but the lecture
had begun. We all stood, applauded the great scholar who was
taking the podium. I had never clapped so loud nor so long.
Could it really have been coincidence, that I should have
attended a lecture on man's strangeness, on philosophy instead
of philology, that I should have been sitting behind *him*? When
the lecture was over, after interminable ovations, the sardine
tin was finally opened and we all filed out. I kept a beady eye
on the fellow. It proved not too difficult. He was an unusual-
looking sort of chap, striking. It was the longish greying hair.
I could imagine him dressed in brown habit, sandals, a soldier
of Christ seated in a monk's calefactory, or in a hand-woven
tunic, with scythe, out in some medieval field. I just managed
to keep him in sight, lost him, then found him again, in the
university common room. Was he a mature student, perhaps?

He was engrossed in a book. *A Question of Existence*. I sat myself down at a nearby table, occasionally casting an eye. When he left I followed him through the city centre to a bookshop, the Reading Room. He unlocked its door, turned the sign over to *Open*. So, he was the proprietor, then. I was desperate to see the photograph again. The one in his wallet which he'd opened while sitting in front of me in the lecture hall. A flash of her face, of that raven hair, that pale . . . I am too charged with emotion to write more. Oh, the uselessness – the *yoothlethneth* – of words. Come clean, Reemie. I will: the wallet had slipped from his jacket or back pocket as he sat down. I picked it up off the floor and handed it to him. Cleaner still: at that same moment, the lecture handouts slipped from my hands and I inadvertently picked up the wallet with the lecture sheets. Pristine: on the pretext of picking up the lecture sheets I had (accidentally on purpose) dropped, I gathered up the wallet but just at that moment the fellow turned round. Excuse me, I said, but I rather think this is yours.

Yes. I do feel better. Cleansed. NB. A calefactory? Not in my Ref. Dict. The words, the words . . .

With Matyeus-Prinn, late this afternoon. In his study. He told me his glass paperweight had gone missing. It had been a present, apparently, from his . . . wife, I think he was going to say, the word swallowed mid-pronouncement. Did he love his wife, I wondered, or was he bidden, fearful? I know from experience how those dissatisfied at home often give vent on acquaintances, strangers. He asked whether I had seen it, the paperweight.

I was looking again at the radiator grille, at the latticed front of the drinks cabinet behind which lurked the sherry decanter. I was thinking of the one and only occasion on which I have entered a confessional. Mutti was more pagan than/if anything. Her dabblings with the tarot, for example. A lapsed Catholic, I always suspected. I once found a black lace veil and a rosary at the bottom of her knicker drawer. (What was I doing in there?) God forbid – had she been a believer, Mutti would have been Hail Mary-ing 'twenty-four-seven', as is, I believe, the phrase of the moment. The Church – indeed, religion in general – did not figure in our lives. In fact, she'd give them a wide berth, all those monumental erections, testaments of faith, in the countless towns and cities we sight-seed – (???) – visited. Though I yearned always to go inside. I remember, in Strasbourg, the cathedral of red sandstone, that spire – enormous! – pointing heavenward. I wanted to go inside – really I did, I wanted to see . . . the wonderful stained glass, the rose window. And Verdun's twin-towered cathedral rising high above the Meuse. But Mutti would always grab my arm, pull me away. It was always what she wanted to do, always. Selfish. Where were we that day I dared to step over one of those apparently forbidden thresholds? Mutti had gone to have her hair done or something – *Mutti wants a bit of frou-frou, Roberr*. Mutti spent hours titillating in her boudoir. She had left me in some Kaffeehaus or hotel tearoom. Vienna, was it? For I remember eating Sachertorte. Swallowing the last mouthful, I had a sudden fear she would not be coming back. Because of me. Earlier that day, I'd overheard her telling some shopkeeper, *When one is on one's own – children – you know how it is, so difficult* . . . So, I was an encumbrance, then. There was a church opposite the Kaffeehaus/hotel. A blue-robed lady hung over the door. I wanted to go in. I wanted to see – no! – I had to go in. *The Church of Our Lady.* I needed to tell . . . But I dared not leave the café. Then, two catalysts: a squirrel on the road, on its back, dead, hind legs spread, blood seeping from between – and a woman, bending over a drinking fountain across the street, her head bobbing as she tried to catch the water – the bobbing head. The blood. I asked a waiter, should my mother return, to kindly tell her that I had gone to the bookshop down the street, and I ran over to the church. And I went inside. I did. I dared. And I saw, in a far dark corner, the box-like confessional. A small red glow of a lamp inside, like a heart, drawing me in.

– Oh father (capital F?), I have sinned.

– Tell me, my son.

– I hurt my mother very badly, I said. I thought I'd killed her, I said.

(I heard the sharp intake of breath. Had I taken the Father Confessor by surprise?)

– There was much blood, I said.

NB. *vate*, Titi – *vate*, I meant.

PS. Confession – a kind of exorcism?

Two catalysts. For two memories. One later and one from a dark and distant (aren't they always?) past. (Helpless, now, against the clichés – sorry.) Some people repress, bury. But I never could. Though I have always done my level best to forget. The later memory: she was on her knees. (I was, I think, sixteen.) Whether you love or hate or care neither way for your mother, it is not good to see one's own in the act of supplication. Such a shameful sight casts a shadow, is shaming. Mutti, with the professor from England. He had travelled to the flat in Paris. The one on Quai Kock? No, it was Lyons. An apartment block built into the rock face on the banks of the Rhone – the Saone? Quai Pierre-something. Come all the way just to talk with Mutti about my place at the university. She was lauding the 'haloed halls', as she called them – and me. *My zohn will be an azzett. Azz-ette*, she said. *A breeze, Rob-err*, she had told me, *you'll sail it – walking blindfold!* He was vile-looking, this professor – liver-spotted pate, lashless watery eyes. Afterwards, I'd think about what she had put herself through for me. And then I'd think – but look what she put herself through! Either way, guilt. I thought she was looking for something, on the floor, by his feet, a dropped earring perhaps, she was forever losing those. Her head was bobbing up and down. Mutti, what are you doing? I said. The scrabble and confusion. Their crimson faces. Half an hour later, after my 'interview' with the professor, when my place at the university was then assured, after the professor had 'legged it', shame faced, Mutti said, 'Well, Rob-err, we must celebrate. You have passed the oral.' (A code, was it? *Oral*. For, in that one word, my entire childhood kept its silence.) I was almost seventeen. A man. Strangely, of my mother I had less fear. A mystery to me that I also later passed the written entrance. Just how many times had she gone on her knees for me? Why degrade herself so? Because she knew the truth. I simply did not have what it took, the brains — I could not 'cut the mustard'. Was it was her way of giving back? Because of what she'd done to me, what she had taken? The nightmares, continuous, of being swallowed alive.

Her face. In the photograph. On the floor of the lecture hall. Ingebiorg. Looking at me. The passion. Suspense is killing me. Shall bide my time. Just a couple more days. The surface cracking. The feeling threatening to spill. She has come back to me. Sweet, gentle child. Do anything for her Pappy. What did Helnea know? *You disgust me, Jabz Reemie*, she said. She did not understand love. Shall bide my time. Two more days and then I shall visit the Reading Room. Semi-retirement. I feel no different, as I kept telling Matyeus-Prinn. (He keeps asking.) Looking for any excuse to oust me. *How does it feel to be a man of leisure, Reemie?* He lurks, he hovers outside my study, eavesdropping on tutorials. I feel no guilt. Do I? Semi. Part-time. Time on my hands, then, to pursue.

I have been, today, to the Reading Room, to see Mr Goode. And a coincidence, coming across the book as I browsed the mythology shelves. Flicking through its pages, I experienced a powerful reaction. Practically Pavlovian. An ejaculation, *un petit* but *puissant* all the same. I repeat — there are things over which I am powerless. This Phineas Goode followed me into the street. I could see he was embarrassed to have to ask me. *Dr Reemie* . . . Saved by a passing student. How 'lyghtlie it trippeth off my tongue'. I told a little story. Won him with words. A gift. A Mutti trick. It gave me great pleasure to acquire the copy of *Tales of the Nordic Gods* – a glorious eggy-coloured cover. And by this method I have accumulated much of what Helnea destroyed in the Great Fire. Not simply the pleasure of acquisition which led me to pocket the book. (Awkward phrase, yes, but so is the sentiment behind it.) Not only pleasure – shame. Or rather – how inextricably the two are bound within me. I mean, while Mutti told me the tales of those powerful Norse Gods, I experienced both shame and pleasure. The feelings, in my body. The irony makes me weep. You see, she made me feel 'impotent'. The book was sticking out from the shelf. Offering itself to me. When something is taken from you . . . I want to remember none of this. But I got away with my pilfer. I always have.

I went to the Reading Room today. Interest is engaged. This Phineas fellow and I, we connect. The phrase 'eternal student' comes to mind. After a brief but intense conversation, I suggested he might care, to begin with, to skim through Nietzsche's *Beyond Good and Evil*. And, yes, he said, he'd be 'honoured' to attend my lecture. I must bone up. Put on a tip-top show. In need of a mentor, then, was he? (And might I be in need of a research assistant, I thought, a doer of the dirty work?) Love to study, he said, but what with the book-shop and the family, Dr Reemie. Oh, you have children, I said. A daughter? Two? How wonderful. Oh, yes, yes please, I would love to see a photograph. Five and eight years old. One fair, one dark – raven. She. The body may grow old but the love does not. Her spirit – my Ingebiorg.

So much in such a short time. Too fast almost. I had imagined it would be tricky, if not impossible. But events unfold swiftly and with ease – proof that what is, should be. I have received an invite – RSVP'd in the affirmative. Yes, I would love to come to tea. There will be cream cakes, I hope. I think he likes me, this Phineas fellow. And the more study I throw his way, the more he hungers. The light in his eyes when I call him 'young prince'. A week's time, then.

This p.m. 'You're looking bright eyed and bushy, Reemie,' M-P said. Too bright, he meant.

> *From a crystal sea the lucent rays*
> *And beams in splendour lift their light.*
> *A child abode there . . .*

From 'The Pearl'. *Circa* 1400. Author unknown. An elegy on the death of a child. Apparently. But so much more. Christ, God, the Lamb, Apocalypse.

It is her. My Inge. A most curious abode. Castle Keep on Hart's Hill. The climb left me puffed. I am not used to such ascents. Inside the house, blinding colour. The wife, Mrs Goode, was painting when I arrived, in her studio, 'The Ride of the Valkyries' blaring, deafening. Typical artist, daubed and dreamy eyed at the front door, greeting me with a were-we-expecting-you? look. Dr Reemie? Oh, please, so sorry, please, do come in. And in I went. They were out in the back garden, playing. The girls. When I saw her, I could have wept. Mrs Goode had evidently been informed of my sweet tooth. We all have our vices, I said, and one I happily admit to. Warm 'milk-cream' strudel *mit* vanilla sauce! And something akin to Linzertorte. And dishes of whipped cream. The girls were charming, delightful. A credit to you, Phineas and Mrs Goode, I said. Oh, Maggie, please, she said. One of the family, then.

The eager student and I meet regularly for a beer, for a philosophical/theological/book discussion. He has taken to attending my now few-and-far-between lectures. I threw out a line – perhaps he might care to put together an essay or two, to help clarify his thinking – his passion for philology runs deep, his is a soul in search. So I feed him titles: *No Man Is An*

Island — Discuss; Evil Begets Evil? — Discuss; essays, recommended reading. *Chicken and Egg/Innocent and Guilty — Discuss with ref. to Milton's* Areopagitica: *the knowledge of good and evil, two twins cleaving leapt forth into the world.* This Phineas is ravenous. I suggested the university library might be ideal for his studies — no family distractions, reference books galore; evenings best, I said, after his work at the shop, when the students are tempted to the pub. The other day, while on our way to St Bartolph's main library, I noticed she caught his eye — Ms Finlay. Now Ms Finlay is what one might call a *Blaustrumpf* — a seriously academic lady, but 'a looker', as I overhead a male student remark. Oh, how Phineas looked. I made a mental note. Could be of advantage. A little later, I put it his way — with regard to your daughter Gwynne's deafness, I said, Ms Finlay is something of an expert, it is her forte, you know, Deafness and Communication. Yes. The bookshop, the essays, now Ms Finlay — Phineas will be occupied. And the wife? I happened upon a leaflet in the common room. The local adult education centre is advertising for an art teacher — evening classes. I shall wait a while, then slip it her way. But — oh my — with the parents so otherwise engaged, who will look after the girls — the encumbrances?

What a perfect family — the Goodes. I was rather envious. As if nothing could penetrate their paradise. Yet — little cracks? I sense Mrs Goode is not entirely confident in her abilities as a mother. I had the devil's own job to convince her that young Vivvy was the model of good behaviour — at least, with me. And Phineas, I smell fear in his need to keep/protect his family. Heaven forbid anything should spoil it. They would look to their own hearts first, these two, I think. I have work to do. Such are the soft spots, the Achilles' heels, the cracks in the souls. How easy to turn a man's heart against himself.

An encumbrance. What kind of life must it have been for a single mother? I have often wondered. What a waste. For Mutti was an attractive woman. And full of passion. And mystery. In another life, a countess – a goddess. Other women paled beside her, in my view, were mere sackcloth, calico. But Mutti was a cloak of midnight-blue velvet. Did she never long to be wined and dined by some handsome escort? Did she willingly sacrifice such pleasures to be with me? She never left me, with anyone. For fear of what I might tell? About the way she loved me? Hers was the allure of the foreigner, of the accent (which lured because it gave her a helpless quality, i.e. of helplessness. I think of a baby learning to talk.) She was a bottle blonde (schnapps and peroxide). *My roots! My roots, Rob-err!* she'd exclaim, pulling me to regard her hair in the mirror, as if I were responsible for the dark line of her centre parting. Truth was, she had no roots, or none that I knew of. Her English was peppered with German, French, Finnish. Her accent a 'smorgasbord'. (She referred to herself sometimes as Ci-Ci, though Sigurd was the name on the parcels that were sent from Europe. Though sometimes she'd refer to herself as Gerd or Ran or Roskva, Sif, Volva, Freyja, Frigg. I see her waltzing through one of our German (was it?) apartments, flinging open the windows, face upturned as if to the sun, though it was snowing outside. *Roskva needs to breathe, Rob-err!* And she would describe to me then sleigh rides through the land of the midnight sun and seal-hunting expeditions and battles between the great gods of the North . . . As if she had lived and breathed them. I never knew 'from whence she came'. *Out of the mists of far away, Rob-err . . . From the frosty breath of a snow giantess.* Or she would stand in the middle of the room, head held high, proud and defiant, as if before a judge: *I am of Scandinavian extraction.* She'd speak of her birthplace in the plural. Sometimes it would be Helsinki, sometimes Copenhagen, or Trondheim, Uppsala, or dead centre of the mountain plateau of Finnmarksvidda, or Hammerfest at the junction of Storvannsvein and Strandgata. Either inexact or over-precise, the effect created a haze over her origins. And it left me rootless too. But I knew she loved me. A special love, she said. I was all she had. The matter of 'the father' was mentioned only once. I was nine or ten years old when she showed me the photograph. I glimpsed a fine figure of a man in uniform. She had waved it in front of my eyes. To be kind, cruel, who knows? *Theez iz vat I do to zat man!* And she tore the photograph into pieces and threw them out of the window. *Through the night air they fell like flakes of snow.* Cruel. For some long time after, it unsettled me. Her habit of confusing tenses: *Theess ist vat I do . . .* I imagined her ripping his body to bits and throwing them on to the street. I remember, she had held the picture between clawed hands, caught like prey between two rows of pearly-whites. Her teeth, yes. An image ever in my mind: the white tombstones of a grinning comic-book baddie. She was forever picking at them with the silver toothpick. When she gave it to me before I went away to university, I intended never to use it, thought of her gouging out the slivers of rotting meat from her cavities and gaps – though somehow I picked up the habit. Those ever-white varnished nails. F R O S T E D W H I T E, it said on the bottle which stood on the bathroom shelf. I came to know each letter, each space between, intimately. Cool, white, blonde, semi-transparent, pellucid. Yet hers was not the luminescence of a film star. Her transparency suggested lack rather than lustre. She liked to wear her hair in what she called a *Dietrich*, or was it a *Harlow*? But I remember it tumbling and soft – its feel. I remember the dark triangle, the blood. Hard to believe blood flowed in her. Oh, but it did. *Blod bluot bloth.* It bloomed. NB: *blowan*, relates to Old English – root *blowan*, meaning 'to flower'. A crimson rose between her thighs. Her thighs . . . Once she told me she had been a dancer with the Russian Ballet – *the stage was strewn with red rose bouquets, Roberr, they loved – adorred me.* Another time she told me the long-ago love of her life had run off with a prima ballerina and this was the source of her sorrow. *A ballerina? Ha! Should have seen her thighs, Roberr, trunks of a tree . . .* stories, the stories. I tried. I so much wanted to trust.

Viviane

Just a voice, Viviane said, speaking through the mouth of her stone mound, telling Rob what she was eventually to tell her family. Rob told her to go back home, where she found Gwynne waiting for her in Castle Keep. But she had not been able to tell them everything. So you must hear it, she said, in order for me to be truly free of it. She knew somehow she had to learn how to forgive him, she said, although she still did not know whether that was possible. It had happened, she said, over the course of three years. It had started when she was eight. She told me how, little by little, he got closer and closer. Rather like Gwynne's robin, I should imagine. It was all mixed up in her head, she said, and the only way she could unburden herself of it was to tell it as if it had happened but once.

'I am afraid you will judge me,' she said.

'Like there was two of me, the Vivvy he did those things to, and the other me who pretended he didn't.

'After Gwynnie had gone to bed. We are sitting on the sofa. Him and me. I know it will be time for me to go up to bed soon and I'm tired now but Professor Reemie says he has a special story for me.

'"Are you sitting comfortably, Vivvy?"

'"Yes, Professor Reemie."

'"Then I'll begin."

'I can feel his fingers playing in my hair as he tells me the story of the Man Who Lost His Daughter. I can feel his fingers playing at the back of my neck. I quite like this tickly feeling. Though he does not say it in so many words, I know somehow that the girl in the white castle is me, that I am the spirit of the good man's daughter.

'"Time for bed, now," he says. He takes my hand and we go up the stairs together, and in my head we are climbing the spiral staircase up to the hidden room in the tower where no one will find us.

'"Now we must be very quiet because we don't want to disturb your sister, do we?"

'"But my sister can't hear," I say.

'"Then that's all fine and dandy, isn't it?" he says.

'He closes the bathroom door and locks it.

'"Just to keep us safe," he says.

'I know that I am very special. I know that this is our secret and no one else must know, not even Gwynnie. I am thinking of the story and remember what happened in the forest to the girl. I have decided I shall not go down to the forest ever again.

'I do exactly as he tells me. I know I must. I hear it in his voice, a kind of shaking, like he's a little bit scared too, and in the way he's breathing, slow, heavy. He sits on the blue chair. He unties the belt of my dressing gown and undoes the buttons and takes it off. Then he reaches for the hem of my nightie and lifts it up over my head. I can see his thick tongue licking over his lips the way it does when he's eating those cream cakes.

'I do just as he says.

'Now I lie down on the bathroom floor. It's very cold. Like ice.

'He runs water into the washbasin, warm water, which is good. Then he takes a flannel and dips it in the water and squeezes it out. And then he washes me.

'He washes my face, my neck, my arms, my chest, my tummy, my legs. And a little bit in between my legs, which I don't like very much because . . . Because I wouldn't go sticking my finger into any old hole because of spiders and things, because . . . Because it's a private place.

'Now he dries me in exactly the same order.

'I think I have stopped feeling cold. Or I am not feeling. Like my skin is made of rubber. But then he reaches into his pocket for the feather. And I see it's the one from his hat. Just like the feather in the story.

'He gets a glass from the shelf, the toothbrush glass, and dips the feather in it. The glass contains the blood the robin squeezed from his red breast. Then he draws the special signs over me, on my body. From my head to my toes. And I laugh a little bit and go all squirmy like when Pappa tickles my feet. Because this really tickles and this I can feel.

'And I quite like it. But I don't think I should be laughing. I mustn't laugh too loudly, he says, in case Gwynnie wakes up. But Gwynnie can't hear, I tell him.

'When this is all done, he leans to kiss me. He kisses me because he loves me, because I am the spirit of his daughter.

'Now, suddenly, I am older. I am not eight years old any more. My body has changed. It is still changing. Sometimes, I look in the mirror naked and I think, is this body really mine? I have small breasts now. And down there, in between my legs, the shape is different, looks more hidden. But I still want to cover myself up when I'm lying on the bathroom floor. Because I feel ashamed and dirty. It's like something has been taken from me. After he has kissed my face, he moves slowly down me, kissing my body. His lips are cold and wet. But my skin does not belong to me. Now he is whispering, *Inge, my Inge, I won't hurt you.* But he hasn't hurt me. Until what he does next. He gets to his feet, which takes a little while. Because his belly's so fat, I suppose. Then he looks around for his stick and I'm wondering why he's brought that old stick up to the bathroom. Mistletoe. The stick with that funny old handle. Like one of the pine cones down in the forest. I can see the knife with the blue handle on the floor next to me. That is always there. I must close my eyes now, he says. And I do. Don't open your eyes, he says, this won't hurt, I'm not going to hurt you. His voice is funny, thick and low. Like someone's got their hands around his neck and squeezing tight. Like he's got a toffee in his mouth. Then something hard between my legs. This hurts. This is not nice at all, I do not like this. Please, please don't, I am saying, very quietly, because I really don't want to wake Gwynnie up now, I'm thinking, even though I know she won't hear. And he doesn't hear me. He never hears me when I ask him not to, when I see that thing sticking out between his legs and . . . it's like the taste of salt, like swallowing a gulp of sea water.

'I was eight and then I was nine and then I was ten. And then it didn't happen any more.

'I was never frightened of blood, ever. That's why I cut. To see the blood. To know I was real. To feel. It stopped when my periods started. A bit early, Maggie said, but I must follow her because she started early too, she said.

'One day, up in the bathroom, I told him.

'"I'm bleeding, Professor Reemie, look, there's blood."

'And then he went. Away. Away he fled.'

They did not come to me again. The six stories were told. Six? Ah, not quite, for Reemie's book is yet to be finished, and I suppose he must have his say. Although he shall not have the last word. But the 'how' has been answered – guile, tricks, words. (Though they will always question how they never knew.) And I wonder, did Reemie help things along a little? For example, I refer now to the story of St Anthony in the wilderness, who was tempted by the Devil (who changed into a beautiful seductive woman). Ms Finlay was a temptation, wasn't she? And Maggie/Marguerite put heart and soul into those art classes, though she could never quite understand why she was teaching at all – that advertisement for a teacher, how fortuitously it came her way, fell into her lap, so to speak.

The Book, then. I see its pages are not gilt edged, as one might expect, but well thumbed, as if by one repeatedly searching for – what? Absolution?

Oh, by the way, look what turned up – Viviane's drawing. Black and white except for . . . If I may say so myself, an excellent likeness, indeed – those tiny feet, hands, the bulging eyes. And that fox-tail of a feather sweeping down from the hat. Yet the figure has a bird-like quality, the nose a beak, the fat belly feathered, and coloured red, red as . . .

One small point – the blood. Was that the reason Reemie stopped going to Castle Keep? But why?

Mutti. She wore a cross, a tiny black-enamelled cross that hung from a silver chain and sat at her throat. Like a neat scar, post-operative. Had someone gone in and replaced the voice of an angel with that of a— Sometimes, it seemed she was not my mother, as if she spoke with the voice of another.

The blood, yes. Between her thighs. Those open thighs — Helnea's . . . Why does Helnea have to appear now? Yet vividly I see her, burning my books, what she set atop the blazing pile. She was neurotic about dirt, about cleanliness. Much disgusted her. Whenever Ingebiorg was ill, as so often she was, the migraines invariably triggering a stomach upset, it was I, not her mother, who was left to clean up. Helnea used to change her nappies with rubber gloves. Though, I have to admit, certain things disgust me. The female students, at 'those times of the month', smell to high heaven. Wasn't it the Persians who believed it to be a curse, banishing their women to caves and distant places? (As a 'by-the-way', another Persian belief: God and the Devil were twin brothers.) And rightly so. It is a form of corruption, of decay, of loss. On certain days, in a crowded lecture hall, I heave. Thankfully, most of the schools I attended were 'all male'. So many schools in so many places. Why? Always on the move. Running away from? Or towards? What was the story? I never knew. She, Mutti, had so many.

Helnea burned them, every month, her soiled sanitary towels. She had set the bloodied pads on top of the burning books that day she took Ingebiorg away. Stoking the fire and looking up at me with pure hatred. As if she knew.

It was Mutti's stories which got me into the schools. She chose always only highly academic establishments of the greatest repute. She'd show the head the portfolio of diplomas and certificates, the glowing reports from previous schools. How she had manufactured them I could only imagine. A winning way, a disarming smile, a show of leg, or breast even — the gift of the gab. They all fell. I was accepted every time. But I never remained more than a few terms. I would have trouble keeping up, they said. Though I do remember once I won a cup. What for? — English probably. I recall distinctly and with a shudder that when I took it home, Mutti was ecstatic, held it out then kissed it and danced around the room holding its tiny silver arms as if with her beau. She filled it – it was a tiny cup – with Riesling and sipped, her lips, I remember, so lovingly curled over the rim.

Matyeus-Prinn, today, wanting to know whether I was having trouble keeping abreast of things. I had just mentioned to His Lord High Executioner that I was considering engaging the services of a research assistant, a certain Phineas Goode, I said. I told M-P I had a book in mind, a big project. I mentioned that it is often the case that such assistants continue the work where their masters leave off. I meant when they die, I said. Smirking, M-P then asked whether I was not long for this world. He told me he felt he should mention – 'just between ourselves' – that the coffers were emptying more quickly than they could fill. In a word, cutbacks – an overall reduction in staff, he said. I looked away. Let them reduce, I thought, I have enough anyway to fill my mind. She. Inge.

I am thinking it might be useful to find a way to meet more frequently. I must give it some thought. See what can be done.

As if beginning this book summoned her into existence, to Castle Keep. And now that I have found her, I do not feel the need to write another word, cannot.

March 2003. Thirteen years have passed since I last wrote. I am in a different place, Lapland – more precisely, Inari. I have, as they say nowadays, 'a different mindset'. Thirteen years later, and in answer to Matyeus-Prinn's long-ago question: No, I am not long for this world. Hours away, in fact. Oral cancer. Which is why, perhaps, I do not sound like myself, why you may have noticed a change in tone. It was never my intention to continue these pages, but here I am, on this last morning

303

of my life. I cannot die until it is done. And the answer to my original question may be no clearer. For if I know not what this is, I know for whom it was written.

It is well before dawn. I am experiencing a more profound darkness than I have ever encountered and it is so very cold.

A couple of years ago, I retired myself from St Bartolph's. The last eight or so years after Matyeus-Prinn suggested semi-retirement were a sham. My work, such as it was, dwindled to a once-in-a-blue-moon lecture. I began and abandoned numerous research projects. For the most part, M-P ignored me, breathed a deep sigh of relief when I told him 'I am going'. And I went. And did not look back. Since my departure, I have been travelling around Europe for a year or so, visiting my childhood haunts, all those museums, galleries, theatres and churches – all those wonders denied me as a child. The Church of Our Lady still stands, the confessional little changed, even the voice that whispered to me through the grille may have been the same.

Ah, but how hard it is to write about one's life in one's last hours. Suddenly, there is so – too – much. I feel perhaps like a man on death row now summoned to the execution room, a sense of relinquishing life, that 'one was what one was'. The struggle, you see, Phineas. The battle, it is won. I am what I am. There is no time left to be anything other, to prove otherwise, to make amends. Death: *tod daudhi dauthuz*. Hard to believe I am going to . . .

Her life, her stories, her fiction. Mutti had a gift. A silken tongue. Beguiled me. Without even closing my eyes, I lived in those worlds, was there with Gerda and Kay in that blinding snow white. I was Kay, the glass shard in my eye, in my heart, a shard of the Magic Mirror that made beauty ugly and ugliness beautiful. She was the Snow Queen, tall and slender and in her cloak of snow, dazzlingly white. Sometimes, she spoke in the strangely distant soulless voice of the Snow Queen, and though I was in her arms, I would see her throned within a vast edifice, a cathedral of ice, would see the sharp features, the sculptured folds of her cloak, and hear the faint crack and tinkle when she moved and, outside, the howling of tethered dogs.

Had she lulled me with the stories even before I was born (somehow, I see her as a careless gravid, sipping schnapps, eating little), whispering through the thin walls of her belly? Hans Christian Andersen, the Brothers Grimm, and when I was a little older those stories she'd heard from her mother, the gods of the North, Freyr and Balder, son of Odin, Bragi, God of Poetry, Mimir the wise, the wicked Loki. I was terrified by the tale of 'The Binding of Loki', when Mutti told how he was captured by the gods and taken to a cavern where he was bound to the rocks. The giant Skali found a serpent with deadly venom and hung it over Loki's head, the drops of venom falling upon Loki, who was left in torture, screaming in agony, twisting in his bonds. I was there, bound, feeling his pain . . . But I was Odin. She told me. *Roberr, my own little Odin*. Mutti had me believe I was invincible. She did not tell me about Ragnarok, the Twilight of the Gods, the end of their reign when all those gods perished.

Now it is my twilight and I am going to die.

I believed I had hurt her, that I regularly wounded her. Exactly how and when, I had no idea. When the revelation eventually came, via a library copy of *The Female Body*, when I read that the monthly bleed was a fact of life, the relief was overwhelming. Then, anger. Because of her, what she did. Because I felt so guilty.

I remember her body in the bath. She liked me to keep her company while she washed. *Roberr, come and talk to me, Roberr, Mutti's lonely*. I'd sit on the lid of the toilet seat, trying not to look but always catching a glimpse of her breasts, the nipples just below the surface of the water like the eyes of some watchful beast. Then, a suddenly gracefully extended leg which she'd linger over soaping, glancing my way now and then with brows nonchalantly raised, chin flirtatiously tipped. *The towel, Roberr, vite-vite!* And quick-quick, I'd hand her the towel, for already she'd be rising from the water. Venus out of the waves. Though I do not recall her body with any exactitude. The memories vary, range from fleshy curves, a Rubinesque female corpulence, to the spiny, angular near-skeleton of an anorexic.

Perhaps I do not want to remember. When it began. Or how often. Since that time, perhaps, whence memories are never recovered, that time of true innocence, when there is only the pain of hunger and the cessation of pain, by which we learn love. It was her way of loving me. Many times. Countless times. But compressed into one. Once is easier to forget, to tuck into the cache of memory, to forgive.

In her arms, warm. Her smell – powder, perfume, musk, edged with alcohol. Her soft, smooth silk robe. Her skin. Her fingers caressing my brow as she told me the stories while her fingers travelled along my body. *Odin, Odin, Odin. How powerful he was, Roberr. Just like you, Roberr.* She kissed my head, my face, my hands. *What little hands!* Her kisses reaching further, her lips soft and moist. I always sensed her quiet passion. And warm, warm her lips on me. Her mouth, warm and wet. Her tongue. I was part of her, connected, rooted.

The threats came when she had tried to drown those seem-ingly ever present sorrows. *You do love your Mutti, don't you, Roberr. Don't you! You know, if you ever did anything to hurt me, if you ever dared go against your Mutti, if you ever even once dared to think about it – I'd know! Mutti would know! And you know what I'd do? Like this, Rob-err!* And too inebriated to find her dressmaker's scissors, she'd make a scissors with her fingers and I knew what she meant. I dared not tell. My tongue grew thick and swollen, to stop the words slipping out. Little Hans, she called it,

My Roberr's little sword. I was terrified I had harmed her. When I saw the blood.

She was in the bathroom washing herself, standing at the sink, wiping between her legs with a flannel. The white flannel was bloodied. When she turned to see me, the fear in my eyes, she dried herself with the towel then took me by the hand and led me to the bedroom and laid me beside her on the bed. She told me the story of Thor, how he got to the magic land of everlasting life after bathing in a river filled with the blood of the powerful giantesses. She told me how Odin became the supreme power by drinking the blood from the womb of Mother Earth. She told me about the runes, how Odin received their magic and knowledge by hanging from a tree . . . *And Odin spoke to Vidar his silent son, O Silent One, only you could know why I, Odin All-Father, hung from the World Tree for nine long days and nights, when on the ninth night, the Runes of Wisdom suddenly appeared, shining in the darkness, like eyes, like stars, and I cut myself from the tree and took the runes into myself* . . . She told me how those Norse heroes followed his sacrifice by cutting the runes into their breast and bleeding to death.

And did she? Did she then, with her finger upon my child-breast, draw a cross with her blood? Did she? For it seems I have worn the stain all my life. Turning the pages of my life by the light of the oil lamp, scenes flitting before my eyes. A swarm of butterflies, of cabbage whites.

She had a robe of the same green-tinged shade as the butterflies that flitted out either side like sea-spray that day she walked through the garden. I was ten, eleven years old, watching her from an upstairs window, and suddenly — her robe opened in the summer morning breeze and I remember thinking how lovely she looked. She was beautiful, my mother. Look beyond the careworn lines, the used-up face, and you could see she was. And it was in that moment, or maybe there were other such moments, when I saw past the tantrums, the lies, the stories, what she did to me, when I thought of those times she had held me close and wept, because she was so alone, because I was all she had, because, I think, she realised that what she did to me was wrong and she wanted my forgiveness, because she loved me. And so, always, because I wanted her love, I did forgive her, always I did.

Mine — a story amidst stories.

It was because of Inge, you understand. I needed that love again. But she wasn't my daughter. Yours. Was that why Inge had come back to me? *Pappy, pleathe, no . . .* Those visions — was she trying to warn me, to stop me?

When I saw the blood — we were in the bathroom, in Castle Keep — you see, the guilt returned, that I had hurt her — Mutti's blood, between her legs, when I was a boy. I had done wrong. I knew I had done wrong.

The struggle, to keep the feelings at bay. I shall die no hero's death. There is nothing left to say. And so,

I shall set out soon to walk through the dark and snow to my tree.

I shall lie alone, though shall not rest quietly,

And when you think of the soul condemned to wander eternally

Know that my death shall not be the end of me —

And for all that I have done, I will say, 'I am truly sorry'.

In my capacity as 'Father Confessor' I must refrain from judgement and verdict. As I said, I am neither orator nor scribe, have merely listened, presented the stories as I heard them, although not entirely word for word, and with one or two slight embellishments, perhaps. But they have spoken. Through me, I have let them speak. I have drawn them to me. And now I have let them go.

I must admit a couple of the names have been changed to preserve anonymity. (Thus it has been necessary to edit a little

Reemie's book.) For example, Phineas is Phineas but not 'Goode', while Ms Finlay was not Alethea. And while Castle Keep is 'real as real can be', it does not stand upon Hart's Hill. (As for the child Nyssa – did she ever exist? Was she perhaps too heavy a symbol – of hope, of light?) But rest assured, what I have told is the truth. And a most dark tale it is.

And what else to tell you? But you do not need to know or are aware already that robin's eggs are powder blue, that rowan is believed to ward off evil spirits, that Odin, Herne, Puck and Robin are all connected in mythology, that guilt is both yoke and shield. You do not need to know, or have guessed already, what was missing from Reemie's hat, or those two words Viviane marked in her sister's book.

By the way, Gwynne asked me whether I could imagine what it must have cost her sister, having to keep her safe all those years . . . *the silence of my sister was a circle of protection she kept around me*. But of course, her greatest protection was to be 'so fair of face', the very opposite in colouring to her sister Viviane, who was, I know, as dark haired and pale skinned as Reemie's daughter.

With regard to Viviane, must I be accountable for the fact that her words were so few, that her truth was so lost amidst the stories? But that is how it came, notes slipped between the pages of a tome, and that is how the truth so often hides.

But now, to come to the sting. Re. me – have I anything to confess? If I had, I might say that I came in many guises: the professor in the gallery, the priest in the arboretum, Dr Y, Gwynne's stag, the 'gate-crashing' robin – or the Reemie of that unrecoverable time of true innocence he spoke of, the babe in the cradle, the good Reemie who never 'was' – well, maybe not. With reference to Gwynne's reason for coming, having heard, am I no longer innocent? Or, having told, am I less so? More? Or both? Angels and devils reside within us all.

Now, the family are united, but in a different way, and for good. I see them standing in the hall of Castle Keep, within the protection of the mandala circle, holding hands. Now, it is spring, and I picture bulbs in flower on some balcony, and tiny green shoots sprouting from the branches of the Lightning Tree.

And so, I am alone, in this room, which has, as Reemie might have said, the 'claustrophobic intimacy of the confessional'. And what a relief to get things off one's chest, to 'wipe one's breast clean'. I feel I have ascended a great height, that I am looking down from the summit of Mount Olympus, perhaps, from the rooftop of the great hall of Gladsheim, or from some other celestial vantage point. And if I looked long enough, I might see Phineas tending his vegetable plot, and Maggie adding the final brushstroke to a large canvas. I might see Gwynne reading a letter offering her a position at a research institute for the deaf. Oh, and the Goodes' *Book of Truth*, shining within their stronghold, like the sun at the centre of their universe – how nice.

And Viviane? In the near future, her pictures in the critically acclaimed study *The Therapeutic Image* will be widely lauded and she will become a famous photographer.

Oh yes, it has been a long day, and will be an equally long night, of course. There is something ultimately satisfying about an equinox – the light and the dark in exact measure, equal forces in perfect opposition.

All gone – and nothing here but me and a verse in a broken frame, an empty velvet purse, and the drawings of a child. As for *The Book*, it shall remain closed.

Imagine me, then, like Messina's St Jerome in his study, rising from my desk and leaving my carrel as I move now towards that window with the far-reaching view, where I stretch my arms wide and – hop-hop-hop – on to the window sill I would go. But I put on my hat and heavy black coat and now I'm opening the door, breathing in the fresh spring air as I step over the threshold into the everyday bustle of the high street and rapidly make my way towards those so-called Realms of Light, my feet barely touching the ground.

Acknowledgments

My thanks to the following:

Dr Matthew Woodcock, and the Storytellers – Roger Hurn and Tina Bilbe – for being so generous with their time and knowledge; Carole Welch at Sceptre for editorial expertise; Gillian Stern for helping me 're-see'; Vivienne Schuster at Curtis Brown for 'being there'; Barbara James and Carol Cornish for invaluable research; and, as ever, deepest gratitude to Carol Cornish for her belief in 'the work' and understanding of 'the tightrope walk'.